THE PRICE OF LIFE

THE PRICE OF LIFE

A Sci-Fi Novel for Engineers

Andrew J. McNabb

Copyright © 2022 Andrew J. McNabb

All rights reserved.

TABLE OF CONTENTS

Preface · ix
Prologue · xiii

The Alpha One · 1
CHAPTER 1   Home World · 5
CHAPTER 2   The Tour · 13
CHAPTER 3   Emergency Launch · · · · · · · · · · · · · · · · · · · 23
CHAPTER 4   Battlefield Strategic Command · · · · · · · · · · · · · · 32
CHAPTER 5   Communications · 37
CHAPTER 6   The Thulien Bomb · 41
CHAPTER 7   Illusions and Delusions · · · · · · · · · · · · · · · · · · 47
CHAPTER 8   The Hound and the Hare · · · · · · · · · · · · · · · · · 55
CHAPTER 9   Attack from Within · 68
CHAPTER 10   Cost Versus Value · 87
CHAPTER 11   The Book of Hager · 93
CHAPTER 12   Learning from the Past · · · · · · · · · · · · · · · · · 100
CHAPTER 13   Death with Honor · 107
CHAPTER 14   The Net ·115
CHAPTER 15   Plugaria ·135
CHAPTER 16   The Road to Armageddon · · · · · · · · · · · · · · · ·145
CHAPTER 17   The Attack ·158
CHAPTER 18   The Armageddon Defense · · · · · · · · · · · · · · · ·165
CHAPTER 19   The End of the World · · · · · · · · · · · · · · · · · · ·168

Secrets of The Universe · **175**
CHAPTER 1   Evolution ·177
CHAPTER 2   The Manna Project · · · · · · · · · · · · · · · ·186
CHAPTER 3   The Chupacabra · · · · · · · · · · · · · · · · · · ·196
CHAPTER 4   The Pearly Gates · · · · · · · · · · · · · · · · · · 200
CHAPTER 5   Control Center for the World · · · · · · · · · · · · · · · 203
CHAPTER 6   The Travel Bureau ·213
CHAPTER 7   Biology Heaven · · · · · · · · · · · · · · · · · · ·217
CHAPTER 8   The Design Workshop · · · · · · · · · · · · · · ·224
CHAPTER 9   Meeting with God · · · · · · · · · · · · · · · · · 235
CHAPTER 10 The First Question for God · · · · · · · · · · · · · 239
CHAPTER 11 The Second Question for God · · · · · · · · · · ·245
CHAPTER 12 The Third Question for God · · · · · · · · · · · · 250
CHAPTER 13 The Fourth Question for God · · · · · · · · · · · · · 253
CHAPTER 14 The Fifth Question for God · · · · · · · · · · · · · · · 256
CHAPTER 15 The Sixth Question for God · · · · · · · · · · · · · · · 263
CHAPTER 16 The Seventh Question for God –
            The Price of Life · 270

In The Shadow of The Obelisk · **281**
CHAPTER 1   THE HUNTER · 283
            1.1 The Pragmatic Hunter · · · · · · · · · · · · · · · 283
            1.2 The Conquest at San Jacinto · · · · · · · · · · · 288
            1.3 The Hunt ·291
            1.4 Progress · 296
CHAPTER 2   THE MISSION OF THE MERPS · · · · · · · · · · 305
            2.1 Launch Preparations · · · · · · · · · · · · · · · · 305
            2.2 The Launch · 308
            2.3 The Merps ·312
            2.4 Finding Eternal Life · · · · · · · · · · · · · · · · · ·316
            2.5 The Doorway to Eternal Life · · · · · · · · · · · ·318
            2.6 Shutdown ·321
            2.7 Life in Eternal Life · · · · · · · · · · · · · · · · · 323
            2.8 The Formula for Life · · · · · · · · · · · · · · · · 327

CHAPTER 3	The Genius	330
	3.1 The Handicap	330
	3.2 The Analytical Director	333
	3.3 Graveyard Shift	336
	3.4 The Factory of Life	339
	3.5 The Storm	342
	3.6 Riches Beyond Belief	344
	3.7 The Fortress	346
	3.8 Making a Better World	348
	3.9 Armageddon	351
	3.10 The Aftermath of Armageddon	354
CHAPTER 4	The Creative Engineer	355
CHAPTER 5	When Do You Plan To Die, Sir?	360
CHAPTER 6	The Rabbit That Saved The Universe	365

Showdowns With Death · **379**

CHAPTER 1	The Forbidden Zone	381
CHAPTER 2	The Cosmic Cannon	388
CHAPTER 3	When Life Goes Down the Drain	393
CHAPTER 4	Transition	396
CHAPTER 5	The Other Side	402
CHAPTER 6	The Most Important Question in the Universe	413
CHAPTER 7	The Old Man's Advice	417
CHAPTER 8	The Real World	420
CHAPTER 9	The Impossible Quest	423
CHAPTER 10	Dragnet	430
CHAPTER 11	Contact	437
CHAPTER 12	Battle Preparations	442
CHAPTER 13	The Battle of San Jacinto	452
CHAPTER 14	Faces of Death	467
CHAPTER 15	Ground Control	470
CHAPTER 16	The Lemurs	472
CHAPTER 17	Paradise	474
CHAPTER 18	All Dogs Go to Heaven	477

CHAPTER 19 Passengers for Eternity ·479
CHAPTER 20 The World of the Living · · · · · · · · · · · · · · · · · · 486

Epilogue · 489
About the Author ·491

PREFACE

This book takes the reader on a journey, and in the great science fiction tradition, boldly goes where no one has gone before. The avid science fiction fan has no doubt been on many journeys, so what makes this book so unique?

For starters, one of the main characters is an engineer, more specifically a chemical engineer. In literature one seldom, if ever, has a chemical engineer as a main character. There is a good reason for this – engineers, especially chemical engineers, are usually not very exciting and are often labeled as being boring and somewhat nerdy. As a chemical engineer myself, I have worked with these people for over forty years and I kind of have to agree – generally they are not the most colorful characters.

Secondly, this book is unique in that many scenes take place at the San Jacinto Monument located on the outskirts of Houston, Texas. Science fiction books often take place on faraway planets with futuristic technology and great starship battles. Rest assured sci-fi fans, those settings are definitely part of this book, but many scenes also take place in modern times in the greater Houston area. There are very few books that I know of that have the San Jacinto Monument as a backdrop.

Finally, this book is unique in how it examines life, or more specifically the price of life. Philosophers have been writing about life probably since the beginning of time, but engineers have seldom tackled the subject. In the course of this book, life is put under a microscope and analyzed from many, often very unusual, perspectives.

ANDREW J. MCNABB

I would like to thank Dwaine Benson and Jennifer Strachan for their creative and organizational ideas. I would also like to thank Sean Strachan for his formatting expertise.

I hope you enjoy this book – it is an incredible journey!

Andrew J. McNabb
April 21, 2022

For engineers…everywhere

PROLOGUE

The elderly engineering professor stood in the front of the classroom on the first day of the new semester and surveyed the students. His welcoming stare was met with glazed looks. Who knew how much sleep the students had the night before? They were young, they were free, and they would live forever...or so they thought. Probably none of them wanted to be there. In their lives there were spirits to consume, virtual worlds to conquer, and sexual encounters waiting.

He thought back on his life and his...ahem, adventures. His engineering career and been long and illustrious. After he retired, he decided to give back to the profession and had become an Honorary Professor. If he could motivate just one student, he told himself as he spent long hours preparing materials for the course curriculum. Fortunately, he had special access to The Archives, which had proven to be invaluable.

He addressed the students, "Someday, if you survive the debauchery at this fine institution of higher learning, you will become an engineer. Does anyone know what engineers do?"

His question was met with stone silence. The students stared at the walls, ceiling, and their books – anywhere to avoid his gaze.

"Engineers are the creators of the world. They utilize the forces of nature to produce things that make the world a better place. Engineers see the problems of the world as opportunities for improvement. As the saying goes, imperfection is perfection and chaos is an engineer's paradise."

He looked around the classroom and again faced lifeless faces. That certainly seemed appropriate for his next question, "Okay, does anyone know what is life?"

No hands were raised, no one looked toward him.

"Over the centuries, questions about life were relegated to the philosophers. Approximately two hundred years ago biologists became involved in the discussion. In more recent times, the medical community and even the damn lawyers have put in their two cents." He was pleased to see some of the students take interest after his profanity and he wondered how many of the students had lawyer parents that he had just offended. "What about the engineers? What do they have to say about life? Can life be put under a microscope? Can life be analyzed? Is there a formula for life?"

He paused briefly allowing time for the concepts to sink in before continuing. "The official title of this course is Engineering in Literature 1004. This is a hybrid course offered by joint agreement between the Engineering Department and the English Department. This may sound like just another course, but it is much more, so much more." He despised the course's sanitized name and description, but compromises had been made since, even with his unique abilities and special connections, it had not been easy convincing the university to allow him to teach this class. "The unofficial title of this course, and the title that will be used henceforth in this classroom, is The Price of Life." He picked up a sheet of paper. "You will see from your syllabus that the course literature is referred to as a sci-fi novel for engineers." Really? His life, and all that he and the others had been through, was going to be called a work of fiction - of course it wasn't like he had not been forewarned.

"The first textbook that we will study, and note the term in this classroom is textbook not novel, is titled The Alpha One." The university higher-ups would not allow the books in this course to be referred to as 'engineering textbooks' because he did not have a PHD degree and the books were not 'engineering'. That was a bunch of crap –

there was a hell of a lot more practical engineering knowledge in these books than in any of the typical engineering textbooks filled with their Greek letters and mathematical symbols. "The first textbook is about the greatest military spaceship ever created and, in my humble opinion, should be required reading for all aspiring engineers. It certainly is a lot easier to read and is a hell of a lot more practical than those boring required engineering ethics and social responsibility textbooks." There was no reaction from the students – they probably had not yet taken their ethics and social responsibility classes.

"The second textbook," he slowly and carefully enunciated the word textbook, "is called Secrets of the Universe. In this book you will receive a behind-the-scenes look at how the universe really operates." He knew the lawyers would prefer that he use words like 'hypothetically' or 'possibly', but it is what it is.

"The third textbook is named In the Shadow of the Obelisk. This book examines life from some very unusual perspectives." That certainly is an understatement he thought.

"The fourth and final textbook is titled Showdowns with Death. This book ties together and is an extension of the first three books and provides a more in-depth look at life and, of course, the price of life. Upon completion of this course, you will have a much better understanding of life and the universe." As he looked around the room, he thought he saw sparks of interest in the eyes of some of his students, but they may have been thinking about their after-class plans. They all looked so innocent he thought, and they were…up till now.

"In conclusion, I hope you find this course mentally stimulating and that it enriches your life. Welcome to the world of The Price of Life."

THE ALPHA ONE

The Alpha One is the greatest military spaceship ever built...it was created in the minds of the engineers...it was constructed by skilled craftsmen employed by the finest defense contractors in accordance with the engineering and construction standards of the day...it underwent rigorous testing during its multi-day commissioning trials...at the end of the sixth day the Chief Inspector proclaimed, "It is good".

CHAPTER 1

HOME WORLD

The junior Arminius Percival read the decoded message for the fourth time in the privacy of the Alpha One commander's quarters. He ran the decoder calibration twice and each time the results were the same.

> "REPORT TO HOME WORLD BASE #1 IN FORTY-EIGHT HOURS FOR SPECIAL ASSIGNMENT."

Alarm bells, deep within his mind, were clanging loudly. He trusted his instincts, and they were telling him something was wrong.

▲ ▲ ▲

Capital City on Home World was awash with rumors. The chancellor had unexpectedly died two days earlier. In accordance with the succession by-laws, the vice chancellor was now the leader of the Home World Empire and the position of vice chancellor needed to be filled. After much behind-the-scenes maneuvering, it had been determined that the current secretary of defense, Arminius Percival Sr., would fill the position. The new chancellor summoned the senior Percival to his office to notify him of the decision.

The private shuttle carrying the Secretary of Defense was plush and filled with the trappings of power. Like all shuttles, it was driverless. Being a government shuttle, it was designed to withstand attack from Plugarian terrorists, even though internal factions posed a much greater threat.

In his mid-fifties, the senior Arminius Percival was tall, trim and had dark hair with distinguished touches of gray. He was blessed with dashing good looks and could have been a movie star if he had not pursued a career in politics. As he stared out the shuttle's large view window, he could not help but notice that the skywriters had been busy with their colorful and creative artwork. Skywriting was a spin-off from laser weapon research and it was a hot button political topic. During the early days of laser weapon research, it was discovered that certain types of lasers left a glow in the sky. This led to years of government-funded studies. The effects of various types of laser beams on a wide assortment of dust, pollen, moisture, etc. had been studied ad infinitum. This spawned a revolutionary breakthrough in the field of advertising. Suddenly the skies were filled with multicolor advertisements for a wide assortment of products and causes. Environmentalists opposed skywriting and, for a while, it was banned. The commerce leaders then became involved and instigated legal actions. The highest courts ruled that if skywriting was 'artistic expression' it could not be banned. The skies were now filled with artistic expressions, which just happened to promote products and causes.

The shuttle circled the Obelisk prior to landing. It was early in the evening and thousands of points of light from nearby pulsating lasers shimmered on the grand structure giving it an even more spectacular appearance. The Obelisk stood over two thousand feet tall and was the center of power for the empire. It contained the executive offices and was the official home of the chancellor. An enormous bronze star – the symbol of Home World, topped the Obelisk. The star was designed so that it appeared the same when viewed from any direction.

The Binary Star System had two stars – Astar and Bstar. The now setting Bstar was the dominant star for Home World. Astar, the home of the dreaded Plugarians, was not yet visible this evening. The three Home World moons were rising and provided an enchanting view –

the larger Luna 1 and the slightly smaller Luna 2 each contained sizeable colonies that lived below ground. The desolate Luna 3, a craggily former asteroid only five hundred miles in diameter, was uninhabited. It contained a large array of electronic equipment that was used to boost the communication signals that were sent to the far reaches of the Binary Star system. All three moons were full this evening, an event that happened infrequently. In ancient times this was taken as a premonition that something very, very good or very, very bad was eminent.

The senior Percival waited for over an hour in Chancellor Simeon Thager's outer office. While waiting, he reflected on what he knew about Chancellor Thager. The new leader of the Home World Empire was medium built, in his mid-sixties, and had short gray hair. He was well known for his quick temper and aggressive style. Like himself, the man was extremely ambitious - the only way to the top in any profession is to walk over others. Behind every super ambitious person there is always a wake of broken people and shattered dreams. Percival knew the Chancellor was a very shrewd politician and that early in his career he had adopted the campaign slogan, 'Think Hager vote Thager.' Hager was a legendary leader from long ago that was held in high esteem for both religious and historical contributions. He was well known for his 'Firm and Fair' doctrine. There were those that believed that religion would not have existed, if it were not for Hager. The 'Firm and Fair' doctrine had been incorporated into Thager's campaign rhetoric, but Percival thought, isn't 'Firm and Fair' what people have always wanted from their leaders? Does it really matter what type of government one has as long as the leaders are firm and fair?

The lavish double doors to the chancellor's office opened and the Secretary of Defense was hurriedly summoned inside. As he glanced around the opulent office, he could not help but notice the large ornamentally framed portrait and nearby granite bust that topped a rich marble pedestal. Golden plaques beneath each proclaimed 'Simeon Thager – Firm and Fair.' The elegant desk, credenza, and back bar displayed a collection of expensive gifts from various parts of the empire, each engraved with the 'Firm and Fair' mantra.

There was no offer to sit, have a drink, or socialize. Chancellor Thager got straight to the point and hastily blurted, "Percival, I would like to offer you the position of vice chancellor."

The senior Percival paused. It would have been nice if the new chancellor had praised him for the excellent job he had done as secretary of defense. It had now been over sixty years since the Great War with the Plugarians. Under his watch, defense spending had increased thirty percent and many new powerful weapons had been developed, including the Alpha One - the greatest military spaceship ever created. The senior Percival always took full credit for the Alpha One. The fact that it had been designed by some of the brightest engineers in the empire and had been built by highly skilled nameless craftsmen did not matter. It was *his* ship and, in case anyone had doubts, it was his son that was its first commander.

The Secretary of Defense was also wise enough to know that unseen forces behind the scenes had contributed to his accomplishments. Great fears had been instilled into the minds of the residents of the Home World Empire that made them believe that horrific attacks from the Plugarians were imminent. Higher defense spending was needed for their protection, so the citizens overcame their fears by paying higher taxes and accepting reduced benefits from social programs. The same unseen behind-the-scenes forces had now, no doubt, influenced Chancellor Thager in his selection of the next vice chancellor.

"It would be a great honor sir to serve as your vice chancellor," beamed the soon to be former Secretary of Defense.

"Good," replied Chancellor Thager. "There is one other matter that needs to be addressed." He paused and then slowly spoke, "The Alpha One has just completed its commissioning trials." He paused again.

"Has there been a problem, sir?" He had seen the reports and knew the Alpha One had performed flawlessly.

"Oh no, no, no," assured the Chancellor. "It has done very well, as is expected with *my* best ship."

The senior Percival remained stoic. His best ship – really? The new chancellor was trying to steal the credit for *his* ship?

"The matter is that *my* best ship cannot be commanded by the son of the number two person in my administration. The ship is being recalled for a change in command. You will take care of this as your final act as the secretary of defense. That is all."

"Of course, sir," agreed the soon-to-be Vice Chancellor as he left the room that he had entered less than two minutes earlier.

▲ ▲ ▲

The junior Arminius Percival had inherited his father's good looks and ambitious personality. He was tall, in his late twenties, had dark hair, and was in top physical condition from years of military training. After completing the commander's rounds on the Alpha One he retreated to his private quarters. They were now twelve hours away from Home World Base #1 and the crescendo of the alarm bells inside his head was deafening. The return to Home World just did not make sense. The commissioning tests had been flawless. There was no reason to return home for any repairs. They had enough fuel to operate for ten years at high speeds. The synthetic food makers could generate food and drinks for at least that long and, even if they failed, there was a year's worth of food and beverages in storage. It was possible that there was a top-secret message - perhaps a surprise attack on the Plugarians? That certainly would not startle him as he expected Home World to launch an attack now that it possessed such a technologically superior weapon. He was looking forward to that scenario – he would go down in history as the leader of the first Plugarian assault mission in over sixty years. But there was no reason to have a face-to-face meeting. The ship's communication system had the latest encryption technology, so why meet in person?

The only other thing he could think of was that there was going to be a personnel change. But who would be leaving? His crew was the best-of-the-best. If a crewmember was to be replaced, the standard procedure would be for him to be notified and to rendezvous with a ship carrying the replacement. Unless, unless he was the one to be replaced. But why replace him? He too, was the best-of-the-best.

There was talk that Arminius had been given command of the Alpha One because his father was the secretary of defense. Arminius knew better. He had excelled in athletics, academics, officer training school, and his previous military assignments. He was always at the top of his class and he had done so without even the slightest recognition of his accomplishments from his father, who was always away at important 'business' functions. The only thing important to his father was his political career. No matter how hard Arminius tried, no matter what awards he received, his father was never there for him. Not once could he recall his father ever giving him any praise. He totally despised his father, and yet, because of his attempts to please his father, he had become the best at whatever he put his mind to – he was the greatest.

As they approached Home World, Arminius scanned the headlines. The biggest news was that the chancellor had died and the vice chancellor was now the new chancellor. The cause of death was listed as heart failure. There was no mention of whether the heart stopped on its own or if it had received external assistance. With the controlled media, questions were seldom asked. Instead, the media was speculating on who was going to be the new vice chancellor. There was a top ten list of favorites and Arminius was not surprised to see his father's name included.

Arminius paused, what if his father was going to be the new vice chancellor? How would that look? If the son of the vice chancellor commanded the most powerful spaceship in the Home World Empire, there were all kinds of coup possibilities. Yes, he could see how those in power might want him replaced. Could it be that in twelve hours he would lose the position that he had worked so hard to obtain because of his despised father's political career? What could he do?

"Chirality."

"Yes, Commander." The synthesized female voice of the ship's computer control system immediately answered.

"Call my father's private line. Security code number 297."

Arminius was startled when he heard, "Yes, Junior," and his father's face appeared on the large three-dimensional view screen in his quarters. This never happened - his father was always too busy for him. He was usually either put on hold for a long period of time or told that his call would be returned later, more often than not – much later.

Arminius quickly recovered, "Sir, let me first offer you my congratulations for making the top ten list for vice chancellor candidates."

"Thank you Junior, but as you know that is just a lot of political gossip."

"So, any hints on who will be the new vice chancellor?" Arminius knew that his father could not answer the question, at least not with a 297-security code, but he wanted to see his father's reaction.

His father's eyes looked straight into the camera. A little too straight thought Arminius as his father replied, "I am sure the new chancellor will choose wisely at the appropriate time."

Yes, thought Arminius, he is definitely hiding something. "Father," he continued, "What is going to be discussed in tomorrow's meeting?" Another question that he knew his father could not answer with the current communication security level, but he wanted to see his father's reaction.

Once again, his father's eyes looked directly into the camera, no doubt from years of training, as he calmly stated, "I am very proud of you son and am looking forward to our discussions in private tomorrow."

"Me too. Thank you, Father. Until then."

The three-dimensional view screen went blank. If others had been listening, which of course they were, the conversation would have appeared perfectly normal. Arminius, however, knew his father all too well. I am very proud of you son – really? Where the hell did that come from? He has never told me that before. As far as the vice chancellor position, his father was definitely hiding something. His father was a deceitful, lying, power-hungry, son-of-a-bitch that never cared about anyone but himself as he ruthlessly rose to the highest ranks of the empire.

The apple had not fallen far from the tree.

CHAPTER 2

THE TOUR

The engineering design concept for the Alpha One, the greatest military spaceship ever built, was really quite simple – create a ship that is the fastest military ship in the Binary Star System and arm it with the most powerful laser weapon ever placed on board a spaceship. The Alpha One consisted of two long tubes, each twelve hundred feet in length and one hundred feet in diameter. One tube held the powerful laser canon and the other held the enormous engine. The tubes were bound together with two large circular collars, A-Collar and B-Collar. The collars had an outer diameter of two hundred and fifty feet and an inner diameter of two hundred feet. The Engine Tube and Laser Tube extended two hundred feet past the collars at each end of the ship. A-Collar, in the front of the ship, contained the primary Bridge and living quarters. B-Collar, at the back of the ship, consisted of identical facilities and currently was not occupied. If needed, A-Collar could be shut down and the ship could be operated out of B-Collar. The Alpha One was designed for missions that could last up to ten years in areas that had no bases for repairs or resupply, so spare equipment and back-up systems were essential.

The ship's one weapon, a gigantic pulsating laser, was seen by many as an engineering marvel, but it was really just a logical extension of technology. By scaling-up existing designs, the engineers were able to equip the Alpha One with a laser that had a range of five hundred miles. This was much greater than the four-hundred-mile range of the laser-equipped ships in both the Home World and Plugarian fleets and gave the Alpha One the ability to destroy hostile ships before they were close enough to attack. The Alpha One laser was always fired from the front of the ship. A computer-controlled laser distribution system directed the blasts at various angles. This enabled the laser to attack targets that were above, below, at the sides, or even behind the Alpha One. The intensity of the laser beam and its dispersion radius were adjustable, so a very narrow beam could be focused on one specific area or a less intense 'shotgun' setting could attack a larger area. The pulsating laser was considered superior technology because it allowed the target to cool slightly before the next laser burst. The thermal changes supposedly weakened the target, resulting in greater destruction. The defense contractors charged considerably more for the pulsating technology and there were those that thought it was just a marketing gimmick.

As powerful as the Alpha One laser was, it was no match for the land-based laser cannons installed on Home World and Plugaria, which on a clear day, had a range of two thousand miles.

The engine on the Alpha One was the largest ever installed on a military ship. It was a modified version of the Benson-Clements engines that powered the gigantic freighters that hauled the massive cargo containers at high speeds between the planets. The engines on the freighters were powerful enough to pull a train of up to one hundred freight cars at the tremendous speeds needed to meet the demands of interstellar commerce. For those trips, freight cars that were twelve hundred feet long and one hundred feet in diameter were launched into orbit by a tug ship. While in orbit, the freight cars were tethered and attached to the giant freighter. The distance between the engine and the 'caboose' depended upon the tether lengths, but was often over five hundred miles. When the freight train arrived at the destination planet, the freight cars were placed in orbit until the tugs from the planet could bring them down, one at a time, from orbit to the planet's surface.

The living quarters on the Alpha One were very small compared to the size of the Laser Tube and the Engine Tube. The Alpha One was fully automated and ran with a full crew of only twelve people – the commander, laser canon subject matter expert, engine subject matter expert, ship's doctor, and two shifts of four senior technicians that monitored the ship's performance and maintained the daily operating systems. Most of the military ships in the fleet carried crews of one hundred or more people. Since the Alpha One operated with fewer crewmembers, a much smaller life-support system was needed.

The fifty-foot-wide collars at each end of the ship, A-Collar and B-Collar, were bisected with ten-foot-wide central hallways. There were individual rooms for crew members on both sides of the hallway as well as rooms filled with equipment for carbon dioxide removal/oxygen purification, water reclamation and purification, climate control, and synthetic food preparation. Two long corridors connected A-Collar and B-Collar and provided access to both the Engine Tube and the Laser Tube. One could also travel from A-Collar to B-Collar by walking through the Engine Tube or the Laser Tube.

The individual rooms in the crew quarters were equipped with beds, showers, closets, and a desk. Built into the walls were floor-to-ceiling video screens equipped with endless programmable possibilities for changing the room décor. The designers recognized that transformations are needed to make life interesting.

The medical facilities were similar to those found in the large Home World hospitals. Laboratory analysis was fully automated and, if needed, robotic arms controlled by the ship's computer could perform surgical operations. The pharmaceutical cabinets were stocked with lifetime supplies of various medications. The adjoining laboratory contained bottles and vials of a very large number of chemicals as well as pharmaceutical manufacturing equipment that could produce virtually any medication.

The kitchens were fully automated and cooked synthetic food. The look, texture, smell, and taste of the foods was so similar to animal-based foods that most people could not tell the difference. The killing of animals for food was becoming a rare event on Home World because the development of synthetic food machines made the raising of animals for food uneconomical. The ship also contained stores of rations that could be used in case the synthetic food makers failed. This was unlikely since there were two full kitchens in the living areas of both A-Collar and B-Collar with an abundant supply of spare parts.

The dining room was adjacent to the main kitchen. It contained a large rectangular table with twelve chairs that also doubled as the ship's conference room. The table was made from a translucent material that could be programmed for various displays. The walls in the room were three-dimensional video screens that could be used for entertainment programs, technical presentations, or for room décor. On extended voyages, the ship's designers recognized the need to provide variation in the living environment.

The Bridge was located in the collar above the gap between the Engine Tube and the Laser Tube. The front wall was rounded, matching the curvature of the ship. The walls were lined with large video screens. There were screens dedicated to monitoring various aspects of the ship's performance as well as camera views of critical areas both inside and outside of the ship. There were two separate communication stations – one was a three-dimensional video screen and the other was a state-of-the-art holographic projection station. The holographic images were so realistic that it appeared that one was talking to a real person. There were four workstations located six feet away from the curved walls. Behind the workstations, in the center of the Bridge, was the captain's chair. All of the chairs on the Bridge were equipped with hideaway harnesses for use during launches, landings, and when the ship was conducting evasive maneuvers.

The guidance system was controlled from the Bridge and was a technological marvel. Even though the Alpha One had an enormous engine, it could still perform intricate maneuvers that far surpassed the capabilities of any ships in the fleet.

The Alpha One was designed to be a very fast attack ship. In order to increase speed and save costs, it was constructed with no defensive shielding. The design philosophy was that the shielding was not needed since the Alpha One could attack from a safe distance with its superior laser capability and could outrun and out maneuver any opponent due to its superior speed and agility. Not said, but well understood, was that since there were only twelve people on board the ship, loss of life would be minimal. Also not said, but well understood, was that replacement of a destroyed ship would mean large profits for the defense contractors.

The ship's design engineers provided lifeboats for the crew. There were four 'Cubs' in both A-Collar and B-Collar. Each was twenty feet wide and eighty feet long and was equipped with sufficient supplies for twelve people to survive for two weeks. Whether or not a rescue ship could arrive in time, was always a subject for debate. If all eight lifeboats were available, the crew could theoretically hold out for sixteen weeks, which greatly improved chances for rescue. In addition to their role as life rafts, the Cubs were also designed to serve as tenders for shuttling people and supplies between the Alpha One and the surface of planets they visited, since not all worlds had spaceports capable of handling large ships. The Cubs each had a small laser weapon with a range of one mile that was designed primarily to blast any small space debris in its flight path.

The Alpha One also contained eight two-man 'Buggies'. Each was eight feet in diameter and sixty feet long. They were designed primarily for shuttling between ships and for inspecting the exterior of the Alpha One, but they could also be used to travel to the surface of a nearby planet. The Cubs and Buggies were stored in the Launch Bays located in A-Collar and B-Collar.

▲ ▲ ▲

After his three-dimensional view screen went blank, the senior Percival wondered why his son had called. He was suspicious because many times he himself had made calls to 'read' what was going on with powerful people. Junior, however, would not be doing this because he was not that kind of person. The suspicious feelings faded as he thought about the next day's formal announcement ceremony. He, Arminius Percival, was to officially become the second most powerful person in an empire that encompassed multiple worlds and billions of people. After a few years, those behind the scenes would tire of Chancellor Thager and it would then be his turn to be chancellor. And if they did not come through, it was never too early to start thinking about how to depose the new chancellor and pin the rap on his enemies.

▲ ▲ ▲

When they were one hour away from Home World Base #1, Commander Arminius called an all-ship meeting. Everyone sat around the table in the dining/conference room. Images on the video screen walls created the impression that they were in a rich corporate conference room atop a skyscraper in Capital City. The tabletop displayed a computer-generated image of the Alpha One flying with a large trailing message banner saying, 'Mission Accomplished! Commissioning Success! We are the Best!!!' Arminius explained to everyone that soon after they docked, he would be attending a special briefing. A fumigation team was going to spray the living quarters and they would all need to be off ship for at least twenty-four hours. He congratulated them for the excellent job they had done during the commissioning trials and he encouraged them to have a fun time on Home World since it might be a long time before their next shore leave. Arminius then returned to his quarters where he accessed the ship's computer.

Upon landing, a small military-grade shuttle was waiting to fly Arminius to the meeting with his father. He arrived at the headquarters building on Base #1 and was quickly escorted to its historic conference room. At one end of the spacious room was a large rustic conference table with twenty stout hand-crafted wooden dining chairs. A floor-to-ceiling stone fireplace and three antique-looking sofas were located at the other end of the room. One of the sofas faced the fireplace and the other two faced each other, forming a three-piece setting. A large hand-woven rug separated the sofas. Arminius's father and another officer were seated on the sofas facing each other. They both rose when Arminius entered the room and his father greeted him professionally, "Thank you for coming so soon, Commander."

As if I had a choice thought Arminius.

"I believe you have met Captain McDonald." He looked over at the tall, thin blonde-haired officer with rugged good looks standing at attention in his military dress uniform.

"Yes." Commander Arminius nodded at the captain. "We were in training school together for the Alpha One."

His father motioned for them to sit. Arminius sat beside Captain McDonald. "In approximately two hours, Chancellor Thager is going to announce that I have been selected to be the new vice chancellor. He did not want Arminius to have command of the Alpha One while I am the vice chancellor. I am not sure why," he smoothly lied. "Anyway, effective immediately, Commander Percival is the new commander of the military base on Silzold Two. Captain McDonald is to assume command of the Alpha One. I believe these are great career opportunities for both of you. Do you have any questions?"

Commander Percival and Captain McDonald shook their heads.

"Very well then, dismissed."

As they rose and started to leave, the senior Percival addressed his son, "Junior, your flight out does not leave until tomorrow afternoon. Tonight, I will be attending a great celebration dinner, but would you be available to have breakfast with me in the morning before you leave?"

"Sure, Father. With your permission, I would like to return to the ship to remove my personnel belongings."

"That will not be necessary. Captain McDonald can arrange to have them shipped."

"Sir, there are a few nuances on the Alpha One that are not mentioned in the commissioning reports. With your permission, I would like to show them to Captain McDonald and give him a tour of the ship."

"Very well," agreed the Secretary of Defense, "but I insist on sending bodyguards with you. Both of you are very valuable and I do not want to take any chances, especially with the recent Plugarian terrorist attacks."

As they left, the senior Percival reflected on how things had gone surprisingly well. He had expected Junior to put up a fight and show resistance, but he was docile and spineless, nothing at all like his father. Just in case, sending bodyguards to prevent Junior from thinking about any trickery was a good idea. With that behind him, the important thing now was to become vice chancellor. He sent a message to Chancellor Thager, "Last act as secretary of defense complete - the Alpha One has a new commander."

▲ ▲ ▲

A mid-sized military-grade shuttle flew Arminius, Captain McDonald, and four armed bodyguards to the Alpha One. They entered the ship and encountered a beehive of activity with people scurrying everywhere. A harried programmer approached.

"Commander Percival, we are trying to reset the codes for the new commander, but there seems to be a glitch in the system."

"No glitch," replied Arminius, "there is a failsafe that I need to unlock. It is designed to prevent anyone from hacking into the system and taking command control of the ship. After I give Captain McDonald a tour of the ship, I will show him how to change the code."

"Thank you, sir," sighed the greatly relieved programmer.

Arminius began the tour on the Bridge and then proceeded to show the living quarters and the kitchens. When they arrived in the dining/conference room, the wall settings still gave the impression that they were in a corporate boardroom high above Capital City and the tabletop still showed the Alpha One with a trailing message banner saying, 'Mission Accomplished! Commissioning Success! We are the Best!!!' Arminius addressed the bodyguards, "Gentlemen, if you like, you may stay here while Captain McDonald and I tour the Laser Tube."

The stocky squad leader declined, "Sir, our orders are to be your bodyguards." He, like the other bodyguards, was dressed in full body armor.

This is going to be a problem Arminius thought. Even if I could get the drop on them, the laser pistols in the ship's armory are not going to penetrate their body armor. He had to find a way to ditch the bodyguards. "I do not think we need to be concerned with Plugarian terrorists while on this ship. This is the most advanced military ship in the Home World Empire. Only people with the highest security clearances are allowed on board." He pushed buttons on a console and the corporate boardroom scene on the walls was instantly replaced with a sports channel. "Why not stay here and relax? We have state-of-the-art food and beverage generators. I understand an important news item is imminent."

"No thank you sir," the rough-looking squad leader firmly replied. "We are elite forces and have been assigned as your bodyguards. We *will* accompany you."

So much for that idea Arminius thought. He had doubted it would work, but figured it was worth a try. Now it was time for Plan B. "Very well, let's all go down to the Laser Tube."

They walked down the long corridor that paralleled the Laser Tube and connected A-Collar with B-Collar. When they came to a door that provided entry into the Laser Tube, Arminius entered a six-digit code on the keypad. Instantly the door rose vertically and they crossed the threshold into a cavernous room filled with the largest and most powerful weapon in the Home World fleet.

"Six digits?" questioned Captain McDonald as they walked out on a platform overlooking the gigantic laser. "That seems cumbersome. Only a four-digit code is required."

He is sharp, thought Arminius, but does not know that the extra two digits just initiated my emergency protocol program. He quickly changed the subject, "the Alpha One has some really neat technology features, watch this…Chirality."

"Yes Commander," the female voice of the ship's computer echoed across the enormous room.

"How many Type One lifeforms are on this ship?"

"Forty-six, sir." That is forty-five more than are needed, thought Arminius. "Was that forty-six or sixty-four?"

"Forty-six, sir. Do I need to recalibrate my thermal scanners?"

"Yes," ordered Arminius, "Begin recalibration sequence…one…two….one…Alpha…now." Arminius looked over at Captain McDonald, "Isn't that amazing? The computer can track everyone on this ship."

"It definitely is," replied Captain McDonald calmly, while trying to contain his inner excitement. Very soon he would be commanding the most powerful military vessel in the entire Home World fleet. "But is the recalibration really necessary? Surely it was recently completed."

"I," boasted Arminius, "keep all things on *my* ship in top working order."

One hundred and twenty-one seconds later, alarms all over the ship blared incessantly and mayhem ensued.

CHAPTER 3

EMERGENCY LAUNCH

The tranquil conditions aboard the Alpha One were suddenly disrupted by the shrieking sounds of alarms and thundering prerecorded warning messages.

"EMERGENCY!...TOXIC GAS!...EVACUATE IMMEDIATELY!...EMERGENCY!...TOXIC GAS!...EVACUATE IMMEDIATELY!"

The computer repeated the warning continuously as hazard lights flashed throughout the ship. Clouds of white vapors suddenly began streaming out of vents.

"Shit!" shouted Arminius. "One of the workers must have broken something. We have got to get out of here fast! Follow me!"

Captain McDonald and the four bodyguards followed Arminius as he ran through the Laser Tube. Finally, they came to a keypad at the entrance to A-Collar. Arminius entered a four-digit code and the vertical door instantly ascended. They ran down the A-Collar hallway to the Launch Bay Control Room. Arminius quickly entered a six-digit code and the vertical door rose. They entered and the door automatically closed behind them and locked. The Launch Bay Control Room was eighty feet long and twenty feet wide. From the large view window, one could see the four Cubs and four Buggies that were stored in A-Collar. On the far side of the Launch Bay Control Room, an airlock provided access to the Launch Bay. The door between the airlock and control room was open, but the door between the airlock and the Launch Bay was closed. Arminius ran into the airlock and pushed six buttons on the keypad. Captain McDonald and the bodyguards were close behind. Black smoke started flowing into the airlock. Arminius coughed deeply and screamed, "NO! GO THE OTHER WAY!" He motioned for them to run the opposite direction back to the door they had used to enter the Launch Bay Control Room. Arminius followed them for a few steps and then reversed course and returned to the airlock, which was completely filled with billowing black smoke that was now flowing out into the Launch Bay Control Room. Suddenly the door between the airlock and the control room slammed shut and the lights in the control room and the Launch Bay went dark.

▲ ▲ ▲

A few seconds later, the door between the airlock and Launch Bay opened. It was pitch dark. Arminius felt his way along the wall until he came to the airlock that accessed the Launch Bay Storage Room and entered a four-digit code on the door's keypad. The airlock door opened, Arminius stepped inside, the door closed behind him, and the door to the storage room in front of him opened.

"Let there be light," proclaimed Arminius as he exited the air lock. The storage room instantly came to life.

The room had rows and rows of floor-to-ceiling shelves packed with neatly stacked storage containers filled with an immense quantity of spare parts. There was a sign on the wall, 'Next Service Station One Billion Miles.'

The alarms continued to repeat and were very annoying.

"EMERGENCY!...TOXIC GAS!...EVACUATE IMMEDIATELY!... EMERGENCY!...TOXIC GAS!...EVACUATE IMMEDIATELY!"

"Chirality."

"Yes, Commander."

"Shut off the alarms in the A-Collar Launch Bay Storage Room." The alarms immediately went silent. "Set security locks on all doors to the A-Collar Launch Bay Control Room and kill all power to that area except for the alarms. How many Type One lifeforms other than myself are currently on the ship?"

"Five, sir."

"Are they all in the A-Collar Launch Bay Control Room?"

"Yes, Commander."

"Notify me immediately if any Type One lifeforms leave the room. Seal all external doors on the ship and initiate emergency prelaunch sequence."

Arminius exited the storage room and entered the A-Collar hallway. He was greeted with flashing hazard lights and blaring warning messages.

"EMERGENCY!...TOXIC GAS!...EVACUATE IMMEDIATELY!...EMERGENCY!...TOXIC GAS!...EVACUATE IMMEDIATELY!"

Arminius quickly hurried to the Bridge. As he passed the Dining/Conference Room the video display showed the chancellor's news conference. Chancellor Thager was speaking and his father was standing nearby, "I am very proud to announce that the new vice chancellor is Arminius Percival."

"Chirality."

"Yes, Commander."

"Silence the alarms in all areas of the ship except the A-Collar Launch Bay Control Room." Instantly the alarms ceased.

"How long before we can emergency launch?"

"Sixty seconds, sir."

"Begin prelaunch sequence."

"Receiving a high priority communication from the control tower, sir."

"Display with one-way only communication."

The three-dimensional video screen in the Bridge came to life. From the control tower a controller frantically shouted, "What the hell are you doing?"

"Chirality, send recorded message number 104," replied Arminius calmly.

"Control tower, this is Commander Arminius Percival. We have had an explosion in our Laser Tube. A chain reaction has started that we cannot stop. We need to be as far away as possible when the ship explodes. Request clearance for immediate emergency launch."

The supervisor in the control tower had been watching and quickly took charge. "Clear all air space immediately and patch me through to the Secretary of Defense." He then joined the frantic controller, "Alpha One, we are in the process of clearing air space. Please hold your position."

"Chirality, send recorded message number 105."

"Control tower, this is Commander Arminius Percival. Your message was garbled. Repeat. We have had an explosion in our Laser Tube. A chain reaction has started that we cannot stop. We need to be as far away as possible when the ship explodes. Request clearance for immediate emergency launch."

"The Secretary of Defense is unavailable," one of the controllers informed the supervisor.

"Patch me through to his designated back-up," ordered the supervisor tersely.

"There are three incoming freighters in the launch window," reported another controller.

"Sir," announced Chirality, "Emergency prelaunch sequence completed. Ready for emergency launch. Three incoming freighters detected at 522.8 miles, 1068.6 miles, and 2117.4 miles altitude."

The control tower supervisor appeared on screen, "Alpha One, No go on immediate launch. There are three incoming freighters. Repeat, no go on immediate launch."

"Chirality, send recorded message number 106."

"Control tower, this is Commander Arminius Percival. Repeat, your message is garbled. A second explosion has occurred in our Laser Tube. We need to be as far away as possible when the ship explodes and are leaving now."

As soon as the message ended, Arminius calmly issued the command, "Chirality, emergency launch now!"

▲ ▲ ▲

As the Alpha One lifted off, the control tower supervisor weighed his options:

1. He could issue an order for the Alpha One to be immediately shot down. He was authorized to use the Quadrant 100 laser to destroy anything threatening the base as well as any defective launches that endangered the immediate area. The Alpha One was not attacking and the launch, so far, was going smoothly. There was no procedure to cover this situation, so he would be personally held responsible for destroying one of the most expensive military ships ever created. Many would perish from falling debris. Many? It would be a huge number. The ship was enormous and who knows what type of weaponry and advanced technology was onboard? Currently, the launched ship was not posing any danger to the base or the surrounding area.
2. He could scramble military ships to pursue the Alpha One. But, if the Alpha One was going to explode, he would be sending the pilots to their death.
3. He could pass the decision up the chain-of-command - this situation was way beyond his paygrade. The supervisor notified the Home World Command Center and informed the incoming freighters of the emergency launch.

▲ ▲ ▲

"Chirality."

"Yes, Commander."

"What is our current altitude?"

"94.5 miles, sir."

"What is the status of incoming and outgoing ships?"

"Incoming at 487.2 miles, 984.3 miles, and 1920.8 miles. There are no outgoing ships other than the Alpha One."

That's good, thought Arminius. They haven't scrambled. Maybe they will buy the ruse of the explosion in the Laser Tube for a while longer.

"Chirality, activate battlefield hologram showing land-based laser kill zones based on current weather."

▲ ▲ ▲

Home World was protected by an extensive land-based laser system. The first lasers had been installed over one hundred years ago to protect the planet from errant meteors. Then came the Great War with the Plugarians. The Plugarians never actually attacked Home World, but the fear of an attack was enough to justify the construction of an elaborate protection system that was built at great expense with huge defense contractor profits. The planet was now protected by fifty powerful land-based lasers with twenty-four in the northern hemisphere in quadrants 100 to 2400, twenty-four in the southern hemisphere in quadrants 2500 to 4800 and one at each pole – 4900 and 5000. The lasers had a maximum kill range of two thousand miles which was considerably more than the four-hundred-mile range of the ML class battleships and the five-hundred-mile range of the Alpha One. The lasers were capable of penetrating storms, but there was a reduction in effectiveness. A severe storm could lower the range by up to eighty percent, which would reduce the laser kill zone to four hundred miles. The storm would also reduce the range of the attacking ship's laser, so there was no danger of the laser base being hit by the attacker. The worst-case scenario was a storm above the laser base and clear skies over a nearby urban area. Even in this scenario, the reduced land-based laser range was four hundred miles, which matched the range of the attacking ship. However, the Alpha One laser, with its five-hundred-mile range, would be capable of inflicting serious damage.

▲ ▲ ▲

The Command Center on Home World was located in Capital City deep below the Obelisk. The front wall of the Command Center contained an immense holographic battlefield stage - three hundred feet long and five stories high that showed the locations of all ships and nearby celestial objects. There were five smaller holographic screens located on the first level in front of the main battlefield screen. These screens, sixty feet long and one story high, could be used to show close-ups of various sectors in case multiple battles were fought simultaneously. A giant three-dimensional video screen, one hundred feet wide and thirty feet high, was installed above the main holographic battlefield stage. The walls of the Command Center were lined with multipurpose video screens. The first level contained hundreds of workers and their workstations. The Battlefield Strategic Commander's station was located in the middle of the second level. On the third level, behind the Battlefield Strategic Commander's station was the VIP Conference Room. Theater seats on the second and third levels could hold up to one thousand observers.

An hour earlier, the Command Center was silent as the Home World Empire paused to watch the new chancellor's speech. The news of Alpha One's unexpected launch spread quickly and the Command Center was now alive with flashing video screens and hundreds of scurrying people. Chancellor Thager arrived and, with the aura of a god, assumed the position of power at the front of the glass-enclosed VIP Conference Room. From this vantage point he could see the entire auditorium and the many displays below. The new vice chancellor arrived and sat in a position of lesser power in the back of the VIP Conference Room. General Thomas Hayden, a seasoned military commander with over thirty years of service was standing in the conference room in full military dress uniform. His gray hair with short buzz cut, square jaw, and muscular upper body on a medium frame projected a persona that he was a no-nonsense leader that one had better not cross.

Chancellor Thager sternly addressed General Hayden, "Briefing report, now!"

"The Base #1 commander is on screen, sir," responded the general respectfully.

The glass walls in the conference room darkened and a three-dimensional image of the Base #1 commander appeared. He appeared to be in his mid-forties with receding dark hair and wire rim glasses. He was visibly shaken as he read his notes.

"Two hours and seventeen minutes ago the Alpha One landed at Home World Base #1. The landing was routine and there were no signs of any problems. The twelve-member crew departed the ship. A forty-person maintenance and service crew, all with the highest security clearances, boarded the Alpha One. Commander Percival left for a meeting with the new vice chancellor. Fifty-eight minutes ago, Commander Percival, Captain McDonald, and four bodyguards, all with the highest security clearances entered the ship. Thirty-six minutes ago, an emergency evacuation alarm on the Alpha One was activated. In accordance with procedures, the forty-person maintenance and service crew exited the ship. There is no record of Commander Arminius, Captain McDonald, or the four bodyguards leaving the ship and they are presumed to still be on board. Twenty-seven minutes ago, the engines of the Alpha One were activated and Commander Arminius requested immediate clearance for an emergency launch. He reported that there had been a detonation in the ship's Laser Tube and the ship was in danger of exploding, which would cause great damage to the surrounding area. The request was denied due to incoming freighter traffic. Commander Percival repeated the request two additional times and stated that he was having a difficult time receiving transmissions. During his last transmission he said a second detonation in the Laser Tube had occurred. Shortly thereafter, the Alpha One lifted off and you and the new vice chancellor were notified."

"Is there any indication of damage?" asked Chancellor Thager.

"No, sir," replied the Base #1 Commander. "No one at Base #1 has reported seeing or hearing anything unusual. There has been no seismic activity other than the launch, which was flawless."

"Have any military ships been scrambled?"

"No sir." The concern is that if an explosion is imminent, the area in proximity of the ship should be clear."

"Am I the Supreme Leader of a bunch of idiots?" screamed the chancellor. "There is no damage! The bastard stole *my* ship!"

"Should we shoot it down?" asked the Base #1 Commander meekly.

"Shoot it down? Hell no! What a complete bunch of imbeciles! This is the most advanced military spaceship ever created. We do not want it destroyed! We want the ship back and we want its good-for-nothing commander strung up!"

CHAPTER 4

BATTLEFIELD STRATEGIC COMMAND

The chancellor's orders were quickly relayed from General Hayden to Major Tom, the Battlefield Strategic Commander. Located in the middle of the Command Center, in front of and one level below the VIP Conference Room, Major Tom could not help but think people were always looking over his shoulder. In his mid-thirties, the tall, slim, dark-haired man looked sharp in his deep blue military uniform, but he certainly did not project an aura of power. The number of people in his direct command actually was quite small - he had a staff of only a dozen or so, most of whom he never saw face-to-face. They were all in remote locations and had their own support staff and facilities. But as the Battlefield Strategic Commander, and through the power of matrix management, he issued orders that were instantly obeyed by forces all over Home World, as well as Luna 1, Luna 2, and the outer planets. In the age of fast-paced intergalactic battles, decisions had to be made quickly and decisively. There was no time to second-guess. The generals handled day-to-day activities on bases throughout the empire, but when it came to battle, there was only one Strategic Commander.

Major Tom and his staff had practiced countless war game scenarios, but nothing like this. In training exercises, they usually simultaneously battled large numbers of Plugarian military ships at multiple strategic locations throughout the Binary Star System. This time, however, there was only a single ship and it was not even attacking - it was running away. He had no knowledge of the Alpha One's capabilities – that information was 'need to know' and thus far there had been no need, but it was only a single ship so it should not be very challenging. His orders were to capture the ship, not destroy it, and to spare no expense. Capturing was slightly more difficult than destroying, but even that should not be difficult. The tough part was going to be the 'spare no expense' - that was political doubletalk. Afterwards there were always nit-picking auditors that questioned every expense. His ability to win the mission simulation exercises at minimal costs was a key factor in his rapid ascent to the top of Battlefield Strategic Command.

Major Tom's staff was linked by a state-of-the-art communications system equipped with the highest possible security features. All team members had access to all communications. During battlefield scenarios, there was no time for updates and complete knowledge of all factors that could impact decisions was essential. Major Tom activated his horizontal command console, which was the size of a large desk, and was greeted by headshots of each of his team members. The headshots bordered the perimeter of a large, currently blank, center screen. When Major Tom wanted to address an individual team member, he touched their headshot and they instantly appeared in the center screen. There was also an advanced holograph station adjacent to the console. The holographic images were so realistic that it was difficult to distinguish between an image and a living person. For security reasons, the names of each staff member and their locations were highly classified. The Strategic Command staff referred to each other by a single letter that corresponded with their job function. A number, indicating their rank in that job function, followed the letter.

"B" was Battlefield Strategic Command. Major Tom was B1, although often the 'one' for the leader was dropped. Major Tom worked closely with B2, his next-in-command. Major Tom knew of only ten people in the "B" chain-of-command. He suspected that, with the computer facilities required to conduct the various simulations, thousands of support personnel must be employed.

"M" was the Military Director. As per the treaty with the Plugarians, both sides were allowed five hundred and twelve battleships. M was responsible for positioning ships in accordance with the Battlefield Strategic Commander's orders.

"L" was the Laser Director and was responsible for directing lasers in accordance with the Battlefield Strategic Commander's orders. There were fifty land-based lasers on Home World, eight on the Luna 1 moon, and six on the Luna 2 moon. Each had on-site operation and maintenance crews. The smaller Luna 3 was uninhabited, but had a single remote activated laser to protect the communications array located on the side of the moon that always faced Home World.

"C" was the Communications Director. A vast communication network connected the Battlefield Strategic Command Center with all of the military bases, battleships, and planets in the Home World Empire. Communications were always coded. This group also intercepted and deciphered enemy communications.

"N" was the leader of News Control. The right spin was needed for all military activities, especially when deaths occurred.

"S" was the Spy network liaison. Since the Great War, an immense spy network had developed across the Binary Star system.

"R" was the Research Leader. This team quickly retrieved information on a cornucopia of topics.

"P" was the Psyche Ops Leader. This was the most recent addition to the staff and the one that received the least respect from other members.

Major Tom stood by his console and addressed his online staff. "Okay team," he began, "our mission today is to capture the Alpha One – the most advanced military spaceship ever built. It made an emergency unauthorized launch and is currently about one hundred miles above the planet."

With the introductory remarks complete, he issued orders:

"R," the research leader, a bookworm-looking balding man in his mid-fifties, appeared in the center of his console. "We need to know the capabilities of the Alpha One. How powerful is it? What are its vulnerabilities? Link up with the designers and find everything you can."

S, the spy network liaison was next. A bearded man in his sixties with a checkered hat smoking a pipe filled the center screen. "S, the Alpha One just completed its initial commissioning run. There have got to be reports on how it performed. See what you can find from the intelligence files."

"M, scramble six birds immediately from Quadrant 100." The military leader was a man in his mid-forties with short salt-and-pepper hair. "Laser ships, ML class. Notify the bases on the far side of the world and on Luna A and Luna B that they may be asked to scramble at any minute."

"C." The communications leader was now in the center screen of the command console. She was a cute female in her young thirties with long blonde hair. A lot of the guys thought she was 'hot', but Major Tom was not one of them. Oh, she had the looks and she certainly had a great body, but there was something about her that turned him off. She had to have been very ambitious to become a leader at such a young age and she was always a top performer in their training exercises. Perhaps she was too good, too perfect for him...maybe he desired a girl with at least some flaws, some imperfections. "Contact the Alpha One. The ruse is that there have been detonations on board and the entire ship may explode at any minute. Go along with the ruse. Tell the Alpha One we are scrambling rescue ships. Encourage them to enter life boats for pick-up."

"L." The laser leader appeared in the center screen. He appeared to be in his forties, had thinning dark hair, and black plastic glasses, a white buttoned-down shirt, and a thin blue tie. "Notify the laser cannon stations that are currently in range as well as those that will be in range in the next hour to prepare to warm up their guns, but wait for my command. We do not want to spook the Alpha One."

"B2, set up the battlefield hologram." A slender dark-haired computer geek appeared on the center screen. He could pass as my younger brother thought Major Tom. "Range is sea level to ten thousand miles. Program laser coverage with current weather conditions."

Last and least was the psyche ops leader. She was a dark-haired shapely woman in her late thirties. She was absolutely gorgeous and her beauty stunned Major Tom every time he saw her - except for her eyes. She always had a strange crazed look, but oh the things he would like to do with her – if only she had different eyes. He usually conversed with her in 'holographic mode' and briefly thought about switching his view from 'console' to 'holograph' so that he could admire her body, but then had second thoughts. Others around him, including those in the VIP box, might wonder why she was the only one on his team that he was conversing with in holographic mode. "P, pull the medical files and testing reports on Commander Arminius. If you need any help, get with S or R. We need to know who we are dealing with."

After issuing the commands, Major Tom took a deep breath and sat down in the Battlefield Strategic Commander's chair. Momentarily he fantasized about P and how good she would be in bed. He made a note to himself that, because of her crazed eyes, he would definitely need to turn out the lights when they were in bed together. That part excited him, but at some point, they would have to go out in public. What could be done? Could he get her to wear dark glasses every time they went out?

Major Tom's mind snapped back into professional mode. He was really good at what he did. He was the best and that was why he was the Battlefield Strategic Commander. He had successfully won countless war games that were far more complicated. Today's job was a breeze. He had control of fifty Home World lasers that could lock on to the Alpha One and blast it out of the sky in ten, maybe fifteen seconds tops. He could immediately scramble over five hundred battleships. He was used to fighting simulation games with invading armadas. Today all he had to deal with was a single rogue ship that was trying to escape, not attack Home World. How hard could it be?

Unfortunately for Major Tom, he vastly underestimated his prey.

CHAPTER 5

COMMUNICATIONS

"Chirality."
"Yes, Commander."
"What is our current altitude?"
"124.6 miles, sir."
"Have there been any recent launches from Home World?"
"None in the last five minutes. Communications scans indicate that six ML class ships are preparing to launch from Quadrant 100."
Have the Home World lasers been activated?
"No, Commander."
Arminius knew that he was in an extremely vulnerable position and had to act quickly since on a clear day the Home World lasers could take him out at two thousand miles. On a cloudy day, that range could be reduced to four hundred miles, but currently the skies above Quadrant 100 were clear. He had the advantage of surprise, but that would not last long. The Home World Command Center would surely be activated by now. It would take only a few minutes to warm up the lasers and scramble more ships. He had to buy some time.
"Chirality, plot alternate paths from five hundred to two-thousand-mile elevation that minimize Home World laser kill zones."
"Completed sir. All paths go through kill zones, paths with minimal time in kill zones are shown."
Commander Arminius studied the battlefield hologram showing the alternative flight paths. This was not going to be easy.

▲ ▲ ▲

C, the Communications Leader, was operating out of the high security wing of the Base #1 Control Tower. She was an expert at hostage and terrorist negotiations and could have easily been the top control tower operator. She was very attractive, but often sacrificed her appearance in order to better perform her job. For this call, she wore the standard control tower uniform, tucked her long blonde hair into a ball cap inscribed with 'Traffic Control', and slipped on a pair of wire rim glasses in order to give the appearance that she was young, nerdy, and inexperienced.

"Commander Percival, this is First Petty Officer Gates from the Home World Base #1 control tower." C was using her cover name and did not want to alarm the Alpha One by saying that she was really a senior member of the Strategic Battlefield Command team. "We understand that you needed to make an emergency launch. How are you and your ship doing?"

"Thank you for calling, Officer Gates," replied Arminius. "Those of us on the ship are doing fine. We have an unstable situation on board. We need to get to a clear area in order to minimize potential collateral damage."

"Copy that Commander, I've got you a clear space in Sector 450-117, this will put you four hundred and fifty miles up and away from all traffic. Suggest you and your crew board a Cub. We are scrambling rescue craft."

"Copy that, Officer Gates. We will deploy."

From his command console, Major Tom observed C's communication with Commander Arminius. Once again little Miss Perfect had done a good job. He tapped M's face on the perimeter of the console and the military leader appeared on the center screen. "Scramble three birds from Quadrant 200 for rendezvous with Alpha One Cubs." All was going well. He would soon be getting his ship and the run-away commander without a fight and with minimal cost.

▲ ▲ ▲

"Chirality."

"Yes, Commander."

"What is our current altitude?"

"409.4 miles, sir."

"Have there been any recent launches from Home World?"

"Nine ships total. Six from Quadrant 100 and three from Quadrant 200 that launched thirty seconds ago."

Have the Home World lasers been activated?"

"No, Commander."

"Call my father's private line. Security code 297."

"Yes, Junior," came the almost immediate response. Commander Arminius's three-dimensional viewer was blank. His father must be in a classified area, perhaps in the Command Center under the Obelisk. "What the hell are you doing? Was there an explosion? Why did you launch?"

"No explosion, Father. Thank you for your concern about my well-being. Are you aware of project C41889B6, also known as the Thulien project?"

The senior Percival paused and carefully chose his response. Chancellor Thager and General Hayden were in the room and listening to the conversation. The call had come through with a high security code, 297, but it was not the highest security code and there was a good possibility that others were also listening to their conversation. "The Thulien project was rumored to have taken place over sixty years ago during the Great War. It was supposed to be the development of a planet destroying bomb." This was common knowledge, which he had heard all of his life. As secretary of defense, he had known of countless Thulien projects that had nothing to do with bombs, but had been used as slush funds for politicians and their pet projects.

"Father, the Thulien project is real. It was brought on board this ship. I think Captain McDonald is planning to use it against the Plugarians."

"Junior, you were relieved of the Alpha One command today. You must return the ship immediately."

"Father," pleaded Arminius while trembling, "something happened today after we returned to the ship. We received a warning message that the Thulien bomb brought on board had somehow become armed and was unstable. I had to get the bomb far away from Home World quickly. Do you know the range of the bomb? How far out do we need to go to protect Home World?"

"Junior," replied the senior Percival, "let me get back to you."

▲   ▲   ▲

The Psyche Ops leader, P, was on the center screen with Arminius's medical files and testing reports. Wow, she is so beautiful, thought Major Tom as he admired her long, wavy black hair, except for her eyes. Her eyes are downright scary.

P summarized the findings. "Commander Arminius's physical and mental test scores are extremely high, but then that is to be expected of someone selected to command the military's top battleship. He has an extraordinarily high ego, but this is fairly common among battleship commanders. During training exercises, Arminius stood out for his ability to be calm under great pressures. He also received high marks and was known for unconventional warfare tactics."

Major Tom found that last part interesting, but it did not really apply in this case. Arminius had taken a military ship for an unauthorized trip. He was now quietly giving up. Maybe the Laser Tube explosions were a ruse for his future court martial defense. Arminius is talented, thought Major Tom, but he no doubt got his command because of his father's position.

Major Tom was interrupted by a call from C. "Major, we intercepted a call a few minutes ago from Arminius to his father that I think you are going to want to hear. Sending the recording now."

Major Tom listened to the recording. This is starting to get more challenging, he thought.

CHAPTER 6

THE THULIEN BOMB

Chancellor Thager was going through the roof. Everything was falling apart and he was surrounded by a bunch of incompetents. Here it was, only his third day of being chancellor, and **his** prized battleship had been stolen. Now, to make matters worse, there was the possibility that the ship contained a live bomb that could blow up all of Home World! His thoughts were interrupted by a steaming vice chancellor.

"Did you authorize placing a Thulien bomb on board the Alpha One?"

"Of course not," the Chancellor angrily roared back. "Did you?"

"Hell no!" yelled the Vice Chancellor.

"Hayden, get me General Lokai, now!" screamed the Chancellor.

▲ ▲ ▲

Major Tom was contemplating the latest information. A classic war game strategy was to be the first to develop and deploy a new super weapon. If a Thulien bomb existed, and if it was placed on the fastest and most powerful military ship ever created, then it could be used to destroy Plugaria. That would make Home World the indisputable ruler of the Binary Star system.

So, what would be the range for such a weapon? The Plugarian laser system technology was similar to that on Home World. That would mean that the bomb would need to be able to destroy the world from outside the land-based laser range of two thousand miles. Maybe less, if the ship could get closer due to bad weather or if it could find a weak point in the laser defense system. Plugarian military ships would be used to stop the attack. An attacking fleet would be easily detected, but it might be possible for a single ship, like the Alpha One, to elude detection. And what if it was detected? What if the engineers had created a ship so fast that it could evade the Plugarian defenders? The ship could deliver the bomb, annihilate the planet, kill billions of Plugarians, and escape. It was a superb strategy!

Major Tom tapped on the face of the bearded man wearing the checkered hat while smoking a pipe. The spymaster instantly appeared in the center of the command console screen. "S, run a search on project C41889B6."

▲ ▲ ▲

When the Alpha One reached four hundred and fifty miles, Arminius called C in the Base #1 Control Tower.

"Officer Gates, there has been a complication. I am not sure if four hundred and fifty miles is a safe elevation to protect Home World. I have requested information from the former secretary of defense. Until I hear from him, I will be going to a higher elevation."

"Commander Percival," replied C, "Negative. Four hundred and fifty miles is a safe elevation, you are to remain there until further instructed."

"Officer Gates, we have a highly classified situation that I cannot discuss on this channel. Please contact the vice chancellor. Until then, I *will* be going to a higher elevation...Out."

▲ ▲ ▲

Major Tom had been watching the exchange between Commander Arminius and C. If the Alpha One had a Thulien bomb, it needed to be taken as far away as possible. However, Arminius may also be bluffing his way past the land-based lasers. Major Tom checked the holograph showing the laser ranges. Skies were clear over the Quadrant 100 laser cannon, so its range should be the full two thousand miles. It could be warmed up and fully functional in just a few minutes. Alpha One's elevation could increase, at most, three hundred miles in that time. That would put the ship at about eight hundred miles elevation - an easy target for the powerful weapon. There was no reason to alarm the Alpha One by arming the laser. In the meantime, Major Tom decided to scramble an additional fifteen battleships – three each from Quadrants 1200, 1300, 1400, 1500, and 1600. Those were located on the opposite side of the planet, so they would not be immediately detected. This would increase the mission cost, but he should be able to justify it as a 'training exercise.'

The spymaster, S, appeared in the center of the command console, "Sir, I ran the search for file C41889B6. I was told that I had insufficient clearance for that file. Sir, our team has the absolute highest security clearance."

Major Tom called General Hayden, "Sir, I need to speak with the chancellor and vice chancellor."

"One moment major," replied General Hayden, "they are on the line with someone else."

▲ ▲ ▲

General Lokai looked shaken. The short stocky dark-haired man was one of the top military leaders in the Home World Empire and commanded hundreds of thousands of soldiers, but he currently looked like a whipped dog with his tail between his legs.

"Are you running some kind of secret war behind my back?" screamed Chancellor Thager.

"Sir?" General Lokai had a baffled look.

"Several years ago in a secret cabinet meeting, we discussed placing a bomb that could destroy Plugaria on the Alpha One, after the ship was commissioned."

"And we decided against it," quivered General Lokai. "First off, we did not have a workable bomb and secondly, if we destroy the Plugarians, we destroy our economy. It is based on defense spending and the Plugarians are our only enemy."

"So, you are telling me that you had absolutely nothing to do with the Thulien project?"

"That is correct sir." He paused, "But…"

"But what, General?" the Chancellor snapped.

"Sir, there is always the possibility of junior officer insubordination."

"And how is that General?" the Chancellor sternly inquired.

"If a junior officer wanted to rapidly advance, he could take such a weapon and use it to destroy our enemy. He would be thinking that would make him a great hero and he would become very popular, perhaps even a future chancellor."

"But he would need the weapon, and it does not exist, or does it?" The Chancellor was now looking at the Vice Chancellor. "Is there some clandestine Thulien weapon project that I should know about, Percival?"

It was now the Vice Chancellor's turn on the hot seat.

"Sir, since the war with the Plugarians, there have been hundreds, perhaps thousands of Thulien projects. Most of them are boondoggle projects – projects whose sole purpose is to pay back a politician or his constituents. Most of them consist of phony tests and fictitious reports, but – "

"But what Percival!" roared the Chancellor.

"But what if someone actually did the work they said they were doing. What if someone actually did develop a prototype Thulien weapon?"

▲ ▲ ▲

"Chirality."

"Yes, Commander."

"What is our current altitude?"

"648.9 miles, sir."

"Have there been any recent launches from Home World?"

"None in the last five minutes."

"Have the Home World lasers been activated?"

"No, Commander."

"What is the status of incoming cargo ships?"

"They are currently in holding pattern orbits at 450.4 miles, 875.6 miles, and 1739.3 miles."

"Prepare three Cubs for immediate launch."

"Commander, would you like to enter a destination point and launch time?"

"Destination points for Alpha Cub A, Alpha Cub B, and Alpha Cub E are being entered." Arminius walked over to the hologram and entered the destinations. "Launch in five, four, three, two, one, now!"

▲ ▲ ▲

Major Tom finally got through to General Hayden.

"Sir, we have reason to believe that the Alpha One could be carrying a super bomb. We have been trying to access files on the Thulien project but are being told that we do not have sufficient security clearance. Only the chancellor and vice chancellor have higher security clearances. Do either of them have any knowledge about this?"

"Major," replied General Hayden, "there is a possibility that a junior officer could have smuggled a super bomb on board."

"General, is there an estimated destruction range? How far away does the super bomb need to be for Home World to be safe?"

"At this time, we cannot confirm that such a weapon exists. If one has been created and if it is on board the Alpha One, we do not know if it is a prototype for testing or if it is the fully functional final product. We would like to find out more from those involved, but we are not sure who to even contact. The only people that we know that have knowledge about the bomb are on the Alpha One."

CHAPTER 7

ILLUSIONS AND DELUSIONS

C's face appeared on the three-dimensional video screen on the Bridge of the Alpha One. Arminius greeted her, "Hello again Officer Gates. Are you checking on our well-being?"

"Commander Percival, may I speak to Captain McDonald?"

"Of course, I'll switch you over to him."

A few seconds later, Captain McDonald appeared on C's video screen.

"Sir, this is First Petty Officer Gates from Home World Base #1. As you can see, I have contacted you with security code number 332. I have received temporary approval to use this code. As you know, it is one of the highest-level security codes. I understand that you have a situation with some sensitive cargo."

"That is correct," acknowledged Captain McDonald. "I boarded the Alpha One with an explosive device that has become activated."

"Sir, I understand your concern and your need to reach a safe area. What do you consider to be a safe area?"

"I do not know for sure. The unstable materials can be extremely harmful to others. I am thinking that we may need to move to an orbit at twenty-five thousand miles."

"Of course," agreed C accommodatingly. Major Tom had told her to obtain as much information as possible without alarming the Alpha One. "Captain McDonald, we would like to send a team to disable the device. We are not showing a record of the unstable device in the manifest. What is its origin?"

"I am not sure. I was not given any information on the device. I was only told that I was to receive further instructions on where it was to be taken. When we boarded, the device suddenly activated and we knew that we had to get far away from Home World as fast as possible. Commander Percival is a real hero getting us away quickly and protecting Home World."

"Who gave you your orders?" asked C.

Captain McDonald paused. "I guess it no longer matters - with the device activated and the recent leadership changes."

"Yes, you are correct," encouraged C with a soothing voice.

"My orders came from a private meeting with the now deceased chancellor."

▲ ▲ ▲

The chancellor, vice chancellor, and General Hayden had been watching the communication in the VIP Conference Room and were stunned. Could it be that the now deceased chancellor had been running a top-secret project to develop a super weapon to destroy the Plugarians? What was his intent? If he was going to destroy Plugaria, then there would be no need for defense spending. Would the weapon even work? How does one test such a weapon?

After much heated discussion, a working hypothesis emerged. What if the plan was to test the weapon on an uninhabited world? Blow up a planet to prove the super weapon worked, and then get the Plugarians to pay tribute. Meanwhile, the Plugarians would secretly develop their own super weapon. This would justify additional defense spending on Home World to defend against the new Plugarian threat.

▲ ▲ ▲

There was a lot that could have bothered C in their conversation about a bomb that could destroy a planet and kill billions of people, but one thing in particular stood out. Why had Captain McDonald praised Commander Percival so lavishly? They were in the middle of a crisis. This was not the time one stops to praise others. Military officers are extremely competitive. They thank subordinates and kiss up to leaders, but very seldom praise others with similar rank.

▲ ▲ ▲

Suddenly Major Tom was processing a massive flow of information.

The Alpha One was approaching one-thousand-mile elevation. Skies were clear. The Quadrant 100 laser would soon be out of range, but the Quadrant 200 laser could easily reach the ship and soon the Quadrant 300 laser would be rotating into range.

Major Tom took a call from his research leader, R.

"Sir, I have a link with one of the chief design engineers on the Alpha One project."

A nervous looking nerdy engineer with taped glasses appeared on the center screen of the command console. Major Tom did not waste any time with frivolities. "This is Major Tom with Battlefield Strategic Command. If I wanted to take out the Alpha One with Home World lasers, where should I aim?"

"What?" The design engineer was visibly shocked by the request, "Why would you want to destroy it? The Alpha One just passed its commissioning tests with flying colors. It is the greatest military ship ever created."

Major Tom quickly backtracked. "Let me assure you, no one wants to bring it down. This is merely a formality. Battlefield Strategic Command needs to be able to protect Home World from all kinds of potential scenarios. What if hijackers took command of the Alpha One or what if the Plugarians attacked in a ship identical to the Alpha One?"

"Oh, I see," sighed the greatly relieved design engineer. "As you may, or may not know, the Alpha One consists of a laser tube that is one hundred feet in diameter and twelve hundred feet long and an engine tube that is one hundred feet in diameter and twelve hundred feet long. The tubes are held together with two circular collars that are two hundred and fifty feet in diameter. If you remove the collars, then you would have an engine tube, a laser tube, and two circular collars floating in space, unable to harm Home World."

"So how could I do this?" asked Major Tom timidly.

"All you have to do is destroy the areas where the collars attach to the tubes," answered the design engineer proudly.

That is all, thought Major Tom as he ended the call. Surgically slice two collars that are two hundred fifty feet in diameter from a ship that is currently one thousand miles away while it is conducting high-speed evasive maneuvers. That is all? Design engineers are a bunch of idiots!

Major Tom's second-in-command, B2, buzzed, "Sir, it appears that several objects left the Alpha One - possible Cubs. They are slowly descending and currently are at about six-hundred-mile elevation."

"Message received," acknowledged Major Tom, "Continue to track them." Why would lifeboats be leaving the Alpha One? Could there be a bomb on one of them? Was someone escaping? Had the crew evacuated?

Major Tom called C. "Some Cubs may have just left the Alpha One. Contact the ship and see what you can learn."

"S" called. "Major, I have been doing research on the origin of the C41889B6 file. A cross-reference with a back-up file shows that the file did not exist a week ago. The top-secret file is a plant."

General Hayden called, "Major, Chancellor Thager is ordering the Alpha One to go into orbit."

▲ ▲ ▲

"Chirality."

"Yes, Commander."

"What is our current altitude?"

"1122.4 miles, sir."

"Have there been any recent launches from Home World?"

"Fifteen ships from military bases on the far side of the planet. The nine previously launched battleships are currently 6,047 to 6,236 miles away."

"Have the Home World lasers been activated?"

"No, Commander."

"Update battlefield hologram with latest weather, cargo ships, battleships, and Alpha One Cubs.

"Complete sir. Incoming call for Captain McDonald."

"Initiate Captain McDonald imitation program and answer."

▲ ▲ ▲

C appeared on the large three-dimensional video screen in the front of the Bridge. Captain McDonald appeared on the three-dimensional video screens in the Base #1 Control Tower, the Battlefield Strategic Command console, and in the VIP conference room.

"Captain McDonald, good news," announced a jubilant C, "we have been researching files on your sensitive cargo and have determined that you are now at a safe distance. Please go into orbit immediately."

"Will do, First Petty Officer Gates," replied Captain McDonald.

"Also," continued C, "we noticed that something just left your ship. Is everything okay?"

"We evacuated the remaining people on board," explained Captain McDonald. "If we are going to blow up, we want to minimize casualties. I am entering orbit now."

Arminius punched in codes and the Alpha One entered orbit. The control display indicated an elevation of 1,245.2 miles. It almost worked, he thought. It would have been nice to have gotten to two thousand miles, but this was a hell of a lot better than where he was earlier.

"Captain McDonald, please beg my forgiveness. In accordance with protocol for this security level, I am required to ask you certain security questions. I have three questions for you. I should have asked these questions during our last communication and I humbly apologize, but now I really need to follow procedures."

Arminius had anticipated this and accessed Captain McDonald's personnel file.

"First, what is your mother's maiden name?"

"Barnhart," answered Arminius immediately. The computer's voice imitation program converted his words into an exact likeness of Captain McDonald's voice.

"Secondly, where did you attend elementary school?"

"Sneed, Quadrant 136."

"Third, you own stock in which companies?"

This is easy thought Arminius. He read off the names from the file. They also happened to be the three largest defense contractors on the planet.

"Safety First, Total Protection, and Sleep Well," responded the voice of Captain McDonald.

"Very good," exclaimed C. "Oh, there is one more question. What is the name of your mistress?"

▲ ▲ ▲

What? Arminius was taken back by the question as he hastily scrolled through the files. There was no mention of any mistress. The files referenced his wife of six years, their two kids, and even their pet's name, but there was no mistress. Captain McDonald's career had been exceptional, without any blemishes. Sometimes people would say their mistress was 'Liberty' or 'Defending Home World' or even their job. Arminius thought quickly, he did not want to guess, but he needed an answer.

"I am a devoted husband and father," he calmly spoke as he stared directly at the communication screen, "I have no mistress."

"Thank you very much," beamed C. "Please remain in orbit at this location."

Moments later, warning lights on the Alpha One battlefield hologram began flashing. Lasers in Home World Quadrants 200, 300, and 400 were warming up. Arminius studied the hologram. Nine military ships were about forty-two hundred miles away, fifteen ships were approximately eight thousand miles away, and an additional six ships were being launched. I am good he thought. I am great. I am the greatest that has ever lived. No one has ever before taken on thirty of Home World's battleships plus three land-based lasers. Now those pathetic assholes on Home World will get a demonstration of my greatness.

"Chirality."

"Yes, Commander."

"Initiate emergency start-up of the ship's laser."

"Complete sir. Ready to fire in sixty seconds."

"Increase engine speed to fifty percent."

▲ ▲ ▲

Major Tom had seen enough. As much as he hated to give little Miss Perfect credit, the mistress question was a clever move on her part. She was no doubt working with S. Pictures and reports flashed across his console. The extensive Binary Star System spy network had been tracking Captain McDonald. He was definitely a player and had been photographed many times with multiple women. This information was not entered into the official personnel files, but was kept in the secret intelligence files. Major Tom surmised that if Captain McDonald ever rose to a high position, the secret files would no doubt prove useful in 'encouraging' future actions. The Command Center diagnostics unit confirmed that the Captain McDonald image was computer generated.

Major Tom issued orders, "M – Scramble six birds from Quadrants 400 and 500. L – startup lasers in Quadrants 200, 300, and 400."

Shortly after those orders, the Alpha One fired up its engines and activated its laser.

Major Tom issued additional orders, "M - Scramble six more birds from Quadrants 600 and 700. L, activate lasers in Quadrants 2600, 2700, and 2800."

"Configuration instructions, sir?" requested M.

"I want eighteen ships set up in an outer net at twenty thousand miles, twelve ships set up in an inner net at ten thousand miles, and six ships in pursuit of the Alpha One." Thirty-six battleships and six land-based lasers should persuade the Alpha One to surrender. If there was going to be a fight, it would not last long.

CHAPTER 8

THE HOUND AND THE HARE

The scene on the Alpha One Bridge, twelve hundred and fifty miles above Home World, was surprisingly tranquil given the circumstances. Arminius had just requested that the engine speed be increased to fifty percent.

"Warning sir," the female voice of the ship's computer stated unemotionally, "Home World policy is not to exceed ten percent engine speed when within two thousand miles of Home World."

"Override code number 457," replied Arminius calmly as he surveyed the battlefield hologram. "Pull up the manifests on the freighter at seventeen hundred miles."

"Complete, Commander."

"Is there a transport of material X8406?"

"Yes, the manifest shows there are four tubes."

"Locate freight cars and tube locations and put on hologram."

"Complete, sir."

"Navigation on manual," ordered Arminius as he fastened the restraint harness on the commander chair, "it is time to go for a ride." The Alpha One broke out of orbit and headed down - toward Home World.

▲ ▲ ▲

Alarms began flashing throughout the Battlefield Strategic Command Center when the Alpha One was one thousand miles above the planet.

"WARNING...ARMED INTRUDER AT ONE THOUSAND MILES...WARNING...ARMED INTRUDER AT ONE THOUSAND

MILES…WARNING ARMED INTRUDER AT ONE THOUSAND MILES…" repeated the synthesized male voice of the automatic messaging system in the Command Center.

What the hell is he thinking? Major Tom was taken off guard by the Alpha One's actions. When the Alpha One cranked up its engine, he expected the Alpha One to run away, not turn toward the planet. He quickly issued an order, "B2, display laser availability status."

Information on when the Home World land-based lasers would be ready to fire instantly appeared on a display screen in front of the battlefield hologram stage.

Quadrant 200: 240 seconds

Quadrant 300: 239 seconds

Quadrant 400: 238 seconds

Quadrant 2600: 279 seconds

Quadrant 2700: 278 seconds

Quadrant 2800: 277 seconds

"WARNING…ARMED INTRUDER AT NINE HUNDRED FIFTY MILES…WARNING…ARMED INTRUDER AT NINE HUNDRED FIFTY MILES…"

"Shit!" Major Tom yelled under his breath. "L, activate lasers in quadrants 500, 600, 2900, and 3000! M, scramble thirty-six additional ships!"

"From which bases, sir?" asked M.

Who the hell cares - just get them up fast, flashed through Major Tom's mind? His professional side took over and he calmly answered, "M, first available."

On a second display screen, a laser activation countdown began.

Quadrant 500: 300 seconds

Quadrant 600: 299 seconds

Quadrant 2900: 298 seconds

Quadrant 3000: 297 seconds

"WARNING…ARMED INTRUDER AT NINE HUNDRED MILES…WARNING…ARMED INTRUDER AT NINE HUNDRED MILES…"

M buzzed in, "Sir, where would you like to send the scrambled ships?"

"Eighteen protecting Cap City and eighteen going after the Alpha One," barked Major Tom, this time not as calm. "R, what does the Alpha One have in the way of weaponry?"

"One laser canon...pulsation style...range is five-hundred miles."

"What? Five-hundred miles? That is way more than the four-hundred-mile range of our battleships. What about torpedoes?"

"No torpedoes, only the gigantic laser," reported R."

That's good, thought Major Tom. Shit! What was he saying? Was it possible that they were wrong and there really was a Thulien bomb on board? Even if there was no Thulien bomb, a ship that size could crash into an urban area and do some really serious damage. Was he dealing with a kamikaze pilot?

"WARNING...ARMED INTRUDER AT EIGHT HUNDRED MILES...WARNING...ARMED INTRUDER AT EIGHT HUNDRED MILES..."

Major Tom looked anxiously at the laser availability countdown screens that seemed to be moving at a snail's pace:

Quadrant 200: 60 seconds

Quadrant 300: 59 seconds

Quadrant 400: 58 seconds

Quadrant 2600: 99 seconds

Quadrant 2700: 98 seconds

Quadrant 2800: 97 seconds

Once activated, the Quadrant 200 and 300 lasers were the only ones capable of hitting the Alpha One in its current position. Major Tom called Laser Control.

"L, do you have a lock on the Alpha One?"

"Yes Major, we have a lock from Quadrants 200 and 300. We have good visibility. Expected range is the full two thousand miles. Do you have any special instructions?"

"Initial strong pulsation jolt from both lasers. We are trying to get him to turn and run. Once he does, cripple his engine. See if we can get him to slowly ascend and get further away from Home World."

"Will do, sir." L sorted through the ideas swirling through his head and quickly developed a plan. For the initial bump, they were going to hit the Alpha One with a five second burst from both the Quadrant 200 and 300 lasers and then wait a few seconds to see if the Alpha One turned. Once it turned, the plan was for both lasers to hit the Alpha One engine tube with a ten second blast. That would destroy the gigantic engine, but the Alpha One would still have auxiliary power that could keep it in orbit where it would be intercepted and boarded. It had not been requested by Major Tom, but a fifteen second blast would destroy the entire ship. L expected the Alpha One to attempt evasive maneuvers, but was not concerned since the laser target tracking equipment had been previously tested in drills with elite pilots. L sent commands to the laser bases then turned back to face Major Tom. "He'll be getting a nudge in thirty-four seconds, sir."

"WARNING...ARMED INTRUDER AT SEVEN HUNDRED MILES...WARNING...ARMED INTRUDER AT SEVEN HUNDRED MILES..."

▲ ▲ ▲

Arminius checked the altitude – he was now at six hundred and sixty-two miles. He was almost in range.

"Chirality."

"Yes, Commander."

"Initiate self-destruct program number 487,356, 238."

▲ ▲ ▲

"WARNING... ARMED INTRUDER AT SIX HUNDRED MILES... WARNING...ARMED INTRUDER AT SIX HUNDRED MILES..."

THE PRICE OF LIFE

Major Tom and the entire Battlefield Strategic Command Center nervously watched as the countdown clock on the Quadrant 200 and 300 lasers ticked the last few seconds. When they reached zero, the battlefield hologram stage lit up as two narrow beams of red light blasted the holographic image of the Alpha One.

▲ ▲ ▲

The Alpha One was at five-hundred-and eighty-two miles elevation when it was hit. The entire ship shook. Arminius initiated evasive maneuvers that momentarily eluded the destructive beams, but the Quadrant 200 and 300 lasers soon again found their mark and the temperature alarms in the Engine Tube screamed for attention.

"Chirality," Arminius calmly spoke.

"Yes, Commander."

"Activate self-destruct in three, two, one, now!"

▲ ▲ ▲

"WARNING...ARMED INTRUDER AT FIVE HUNDRED FIFTY MILES...WARNING...ARMED INTRUDER AT FIVE HUNDRED FIFTY MILES...."

Instead of turning away from the planet after the initial laser blast, the Alpha One had continued its descent. Home World targets were now almost in range of Alpha One's laser and sensors in the Command Center showed that it was hot and ready to fire.

"Take it out!" Major Tom shouted at L's face in the middle of the command console.

"Sir," replied L, "We are having a hard time getting a lock…" He paused. "Sir, there has been a massive explosion."

Then the skies went dark.

▲ ▲ ▲

The jolt was hard – it would have thrown Arminius out of the commander's chair if it had not been for the restraints. With evasive maneuvers, the Alpha One had been able to temporarily elude the Home World lasers. Then, as Arminius had planned, the three Cubs self-destructed. Positioned twenty miles apart, they showered debris over a wide area above the planet. Arminius maneuvered the Alpha One so that the debris became a shield between the land-based lasers and the Alpha One. The debris adsorbed the lethal laser blasts. Arminius knew the shield would not last long and that he needed to act quickly.

"Chirality."

"Yes, Commander."

"Fire laser, full power, maximum scatter."

▲ ▲ ▲

"What the hell just happened!" screamed Major Tom with an intensity that shook the floor of his staff at their remote locations. "I need eyes in the sky, I need theories, come on, let's go people!"

Thirty seconds later C, of course, was the first to reply, "Sir, we are receiving long range reconnaissance feeds from the closest military vessels which were above the Alpha One…uploading now."

All eyes in the Command Center and VIP Conference Room were on the giant video screen located above the battlefield holographic stage and everyone was transfixed as they watched the Alpha One descend rapidly. Suddenly it was jolted by two laser beams and made a series of intricate maneuvers that temporarily evaded the death rays. Just after the lasers reconnected with the Alpha One, there were three explosions as each of the Alpha One Cubs disintegrated five hundred miles above Home World. Dust and debris from the explosions shielded the Alpha One from the attackers below. The Alpha One then began peppering the Cub remains with a series of short laser blasts that broke the larger Cub pieces into finer particles. The fine pieces created a synthetic cloud that adsorbed the blasts from the Home World lasers. Like an enormous boomerang, the Alpha One pulled out of its dive toward the planet and rapidly ascended, leaving a gigantic fireball in its wake.

"Can we get Alpha One elevation and bearing information from the ships above the blast zone?" asked Major Tom.

"Coming in now," replied C. "Elevation is one thousand forty-seven miles and climbing." The information suddenly appeared on the giant video screen on the front wall.

"L, can we get a laser shot?"

"Negative sir. Quadrants 200 and 300 are out due to the atmospheric disturbance. Quadrants 2600, 2700, and 2800 are out-of-range due to distance. Hold on." He paused. "We may be able to get an angle from Quadrant 400. It will be rotating into range in just a few minutes and has clear skies."

"May is not good enough!" shouted Major Tom. "B2, we need calculations!"

The response from B2 was almost immediate, "Just in sir. Quadrant 400 can hit the Alpha One at nineteen hundred and eighty miles. However, by the time it adsorbs a ten second blast it will be out of range."

"Damn it!" shouted Major Tom. "We need to keep it from rising. We need to deflect it toward Quadrant 400."

M jumped in. "Sir, we have sixteen ships equipped with torpedoes in an adjacent sector."

"But the Alpha One is way out of their range."

"Out of range for a kill, but if all we want is to divert…,"

"Got it!" hollered Major Tom, "Okay, let's go people. We need coordinates for torpedo targets to divert the Alpha One."

▲ ▲ ▲

Arminius was congratulating himself on his daring escape from Home World. He was brilliant! He was the best! He was the greatest the world had ever seen! He and he alone was in command of the most powerful battleship in the Binary Star System. He looked at his battlefield hologram. The laser from Quadrant 400 could still nick him, but not for long enough to cause any serious damage. He checked his altitude – elevation 1,822 miles and rapidly ascending. He would soon be beyond the range of the Home World laser canons. He had done it! He was incredible!

Suddenly the navigation screen lit up. There was a massive explosion – it was about five hundred miles away. No problem, it could easily be circumvented. He was getting ready to turn toward his left when a second massive explosion occurred, then a third and a fourth. He grabbed the controls and turned right. No problem he thought. He checked his elevation – eighteen hundred and fifty-six miles. Then he looked at the battlefield hologram. He was fast approaching the boundary of the range of the Quadrant 400 laser.

▲ ▲ ▲

Major Tom was elated - the new plan had worked! The Alpha One's course changes to avoid the torpedoes was taking it into the Quadrant 400 laser kill zone at a much lower elevation where it could easily be destroyed. All eyes in the Command Center were on the large holographic stage.

"Keep the torpedoes coming," he shouted.

▲ ▲ ▲

Arminius steered the ship with a hard right just before he reached the Quadrant 400 laser range. The navigation screen was filled with explosions, which the viewfinder showed were five hundred miles ahead. He turned further to the right, completing a full U-turn. Two other explosions filled the screen. Arminius continued banking. The only clear path was toward the area covered by the Quadrant 400 laser. He entered the hot sector and was immediately greeted with a laser blast that shook the entire ship. Arminius took evasive actions and maneuvered to the edge of the hot zone, just beyond the range of the deadly beam. He looked at his battlefield hologram - torpedoes were coming in from multiple directions blocking his upward escape routes. He was far enough away to be safe from a torpedo direct hit, but the Alpha One had no defensive shielding so he wanted to stay as far away as possible from the blast radius. Arminius turned sharply downward and began a descent toward the planet.

▲ ▲ ▲

"M, scramble all ships from Bases 500 to 1200 immediately! I need lots of eyes from above and lots of torpedoes in the sky." Major Tom continued barking out orders, "L fire up lasers in Quadrants 500 to 1200 and 2900 to 3500." Trapped animals can put up quite a fight, he thought, what is the Alpha One going to do? The cost for today's battle was going to be expensive, but he would win and fight another day. That was more than could be said for the Alpha One commander.

▲ ▲ ▲

Arminius took the Alpha One down to six hundred miles in the region controlled by the Quadrant 200 and 300 lasers. He was temporarily protected by the atmospheric disturbances that he had created. At some point, the atmosphere would settle and he would be in laser range. With a laser range of five hundred miles, he could scorch the outer edges of the atmosphere and keep it stirred up some, but he really needed to be closer - around five hundred and twenty miles to do the most damage. If he got below five hundred miles, he would be in range of the land-based lasers, if they knew his location. The ground may not be able to see him, but any kind of surveillance from above could relay his position. He looked at his battlefield hologram. It was filled with ships that could see him. New ships were rapidly popping up all over his screen. Battlefield Strategic Command was no doubt scrambling ships as fast as it could. The longer he waited, the more torpedoes would be in the sky. He rose to eight hundred miles, torpedoes exploded above him – too far away to inflict damage, but close enough to warn him to not continue his course.

Arminius turned towards the southern hemisphere. There was a major storm brewing which would reduce the range of the land-based lasers. He crossed above the storm at twelve hundred miles and was met with another barrage of distant torpedoes. He dipped to one thousand miles, turned further south, and then increased elevation to repeatedly challenge them.

▲ ▲ ▲

"Keep the torpedoes going!" yelled Major Tom.

Another barrage of torpedoes was launched. The Alpha One changed course. It dipped and followed the storm cover to quadrant 2900, where it was greeted with more exploding torpedoes. Arminius took the Alpha One into a dive, did a barrel roll and reversed course, following the safe path he had just taken. Every so often, he attempted a rapid ascent, only to be met with a barrage of torpedoes. Continuing on this path, he again approached the edge of the range of the Quadrant 400 laser. Arminius reversed course and repeated the circuitous route. Every rapid ascent attempt was blocked with exploding torpedoes. Once again, he returned to the edge of the range of the Quadrant 400 laser.

"Cut off his return path with torpedoes!" yelled Major Tom, "Force him into the Quadrant 400 kill zone."

"Attack ships are running out of torpedoes," reported M.

"Hang in there just a little longer," exhorted Major Tom. "Reinforcements are coming."

And then the Alpha One entered the kill zone.

▲ ▲ ▲

The Alpha One was hit with a jolt from the Quadrant 400 laser at sixteen hundred miles elevation. The jolt was not as strong as the earlier jolt it had received at the five hundred-ninety-mile elevation from two lasers, but it was still substantial. The laser was attacking the ship's engine tube. In ten seconds, the ship would be disabled.

Instinctively, Arminius initiated evasive maneuvers and received a brief reprieve. Arminius quickly launched Alpha Cub C. A few seconds later, when the death ray reconnected with its prey, Alpha Cub C moved into a position to intercept the laser blast. Five seconds later Alpha Cub C ceased to exist.

▲ ▲ ▲

There was a great celebration at the Command Center when the video feed showed a distant explosion. The celebration was short lived, however, when it became apparent that the Alpha One was still moving.

Display screens showed that the Alpha One was now at seventeen hundred twenty-four miles elevation.

▲ ▲ ▲

"Launch Alpha Cub F now!" Another sacrifice to the laser gods, thought Arminius.

"Lasers lock on target and fire!" shouted Major Tom.

The Alpha One engine tube was hit for the third time. A few seconds later, Alpha Cub F moved into position to adsorb the blast. Five seconds later it exploded. Once again, the video screen showed a small distant explosion. This time there was no celebration in the Command Center.

The display screens showed the elevation was seventeen hundred and seventy-nine miles.

The laser from Quadrant 400 soon connected with the Alpha One engine tube for the fourth time. A large explosion and blinding lights filled the giant video screen above the Command Center and this time, a great celebration began.

The celebration, however, faded quickly and was a replaced by a wave of shock that shook the Command Center.

▲ ▲ ▲

Once again, Arminius congratulated himself. His plan had worked. Yes, he really was the greatest ever! Taking a serendipitous route, Arminius had bought time as he waited for the ideal moment. He entered the laser hot field using the two Alpha One Cubs for shielding and if needed he was prepared to sacrifice the three remaining Cubs. He had been waiting for the freighter to enter the kill zone, so that he could blast open one of the cars from the freighter's long train. This was not an ordinary freight car – this one contained the material X8406. Inside that freight car was a tube one hundred feet in diameter and twelve hundred feet long that was filled with uncut diamonds. It took several blasts, but the Alpha One laser found its target and blasted the container wide open. Blinding lights filled the skies as the powerful Quadrant 400 laser beam bounced off millions of shimmering diamonds. Using the diamonds as a shield, Arminius made his escape and was now safe at an elevation of twenty-five hundred miles, well beyond the Home World laser range.

▲ ▲ ▲

"Did they just destroy a freighter?" Chancellor Thager was furious.

A few seconds later, the reports began arriving. The freighter was unharmed, but it had lost one of its freight cars. The giant screen replayed videos recorded from distant ships showing the Alpha One's maneuvers, the loss of the Cubs, and the destruction of the freight tube containing the uncut diamonds. The Alpha One was now out of range of the land-based lasers and was rapidly pulling away from Home World.

Vice Chancellor Percival expressed dismay, but inwardly was proud. *My* ship performed flawlessly…and *my* son, he is a lot more cunning and conniving than I thought. Briefly he wondered what kind of career he would have had in the military. Then he stopped, he was one step away from becoming chancellor, and there was going to be a battle ahead.

▲   ▲   ▲

Major Tom wanted to scream. Actually, he wanted to punch somebody, kick someone, and shoot everyone else. He could have easily blasted the Alpha One out of the sky after the launch, but the ruse about the Thulien bomb that could destroy the world and the deception with the Captain McDonald computer program had taken valuable time. This Arminius was good, really good. But Major Tom knew that he was better. Being a professional, he set aside his emotions and took care of business.

"N, Prepare the proper press releases for review. We are going to need a really good cover story.

"M, I want a full military assessment.

B2, update the battlefield hologram with the weaponry of each ship and extend the range to twenty thousand miles.

"P," the gorgeous bombshell with the crazed eyes appeared on his center console, "I want a full psyche assessment of Commander Arminius. What motivates him, what makes him tick, and where is he going to go from here?"

Then came the part Major Tom dreaded, he called General Hayden.

CHAPTER 9

ATTACK FROM WITHIN

Ever since he had first called his father's private line, Arminius had been totally obsessed with how to maintain his position as the commander of the Alpha One. He had worked his ass off since his mother had died to become the commander of the most powerful military spaceship in the Binary Star System. He had no close friends or family – just that son-of-a-bitch father who had sold him out for his own personal advancement. No, there was absolutely no way that he was ever going to give up command of **his** ship. It was his friend and family and with it he could show the world his greatness. And he had - mission accomplished! He was the greatest ever, an instant legend! Soon the news media on Home World would be broadcasting the story of his daring escapades. There would be books and movies about him. What famous actor would play his part? The leading actors would no doubt soon be falling all over themselves as they begged for the role. School children in the future would know his name. For the next hundred years they would tell stories about him. One hundred years? How about one thousand years? How about forever? He was that great!

Arminius paused, where did he go from here? What was his long-term plan? He really could not conquer Home World. If the weather cooperated, he might be able to harass Home World. He could interfere with freighter shipments, but for what purpose? Even if Home World surrendered and paid him off with a huge ransom, he would never be safe on Home World or on any of the planets in the Home

World Empire. They would hunt him down. Arminius postponed his long-term thoughts and concentrated on his next steps.

"Chirality"

"Yes, Commander"

"Damage report"

"No damage to report, sir."

"Update battlefield hologram"

"Complete sir. Prelaunch activities have been detected."

Arminius studied the battlefield hologram. He was safe from the enormous land-based lasers, but military ships were massing. They appeared to be forming two rings around Home World - one at two thousand miles and another at twenty thousand miles. He placed the Alpha One in orbit when it was ten thousand miles above the planet and set the defense system controls so that he would be automatically notified if any ships approached within five thousand miles. His thoughts were suddenly interrupted.

"Security breach," announced Chirality, "Intruders detected outside of the A-Collar Launch Bay Control Room."

▲ ▲ ▲

Capitan McDonald and the four elite bodyguards were discombobulated by the recent events. All were trained professionals that would have eagerly engaged in any battle, but this was no ordinary battle and they had not been mentally prepared. One moment they were taking a tour of Home World's most powerful military spaceship and the next moment alarms were sounding and they were racing down unfamiliar corridors.

They had entered the A-Collar Launch Bay Control Room and, when the airlock to the Launch Bay started filling with black smoke, they retreated as Commander Arminius instructed. Suddenly Commander Arminius was gone and their world went dark, totally dark with the alarm incessantly screaming.

"EMERGENCY!...TOXIC GAS!...EVACUATE IMMEDIATELY!... EMERGENCY!...TOXIC GAS!...EVACUATE IMMEDIATELY!"

It took them a few minutes to gather their wits and then came the deafening loud rumble as the Alpha One fired its gigantic engine and lifted off from the planet. They were not strapped in, so they bounced around like rag dolls as the ship ascended. They were starting to recover from the ordeal when the ship entered orbit, but then Arminius suddenly launched his attack on Home World and they were again strewn about during the evasive maneuvers. Finally, the tumultuous trip came to a stop when the Alpha One reached safety beyond the range of the Home World land-based lasers. They were thoroughly battered and bruised, but what bothered them the most was the incessant shrieking of the alarm.

"EMERGENCY!...TOXIC GAS!...EVACUATE IMMEDIATELY!... EMERGENCY!...TOXIC GAS!...EVACUATE IMMEDIATELY!"

There was no light to penetrate the dark abyss, but the four bodyguards did carry Luddite 1813 laser pistols. They congregated back-to-back in the center of the room, set their lasers on low power, and fired at opposite walls until they glowed. With the dim light in the room, the alarm speaker was quickly located. No mercy was shown as the Luddite 1813's decimated it with a vengeance. This temporarily increased the amount of light in the room and they surveyed their surroundings.

There were two doors in the room – one led to the A-Collar corridor and other was the airlock connected to the Launch Bay. Both doors were locked. There was a large glass window from which one could observe the Launch Bay, but it was totally dark. They peered through the small window on the door to the airlock but, it too, was dark. There was no way to tell if Arminius was in the airlock or even if the door on the opposite side of the airlock was open or closed. They desperately wanted to get out of the room and find out why the ship had launched and who was piloting the Alpha One. They briefly discussed the situation. The only thing that made any sense was that Plugarian terrorists had somehow hijacked the ship. The first step was breaking out of the Launch Bay

Control Room. After that, what? They could recklessly conduct a blind assault on the Bridge, but they had no idea of the size of the enemy or their weaponry. They needed a safe place to hide while they gathered intel and developed a plan of attack.

The bodyguards had no knowledge of the ship's layout, but Captain McDonald had studied it meticulously as part of his Alpha One commander training. Captain McDonald knew that B-Collar, in the back of the ship, contained living facilities and a duplicate of the A-Collar Bridge. If they could secure those facilities, they would have ample stock of food, water, and medical supplies as well as access to the weapons in the B-Collar armory. There were four entryways to B-Collar – the Laser Tube, the Engine Tube and two access corridors. All of these had doors that could be sealed from inside B-Collar. It would be possible to cut through the doors, but that would take time, and any uninvited guests would receive a warm laser fire welcome as soon as they crossed the threshold. Once they were in a secure location in B-Collar, they could send out scouting missions to see what they were up against.

The bodyguards carefully aimed their laser pistols and surgically cut a hole in the door connecting the Launch Bay Control Room with A-Collar. From there, they hastily scrambled down the nearest access corridor into B-Collar and sealed off all of the doors leading to B-Collar. One bodyguard was stationed at each sealed door, while Captain McDonald raced to the B-Collar Bridge.

▲ ▲ ▲

In the heat of the battle, Arminius had forgotten about Captain McDonald and the four armed bodyguards. Fortunately, the ship's computer had alerted him to the situation. Now he needed to develop a plan.

"Chirality"

"Yes, Commander."

"Display ship's layout with locations of all Type One life forms." The designation of Type One life forms was an important computer programming revision. Prior to this, if one asked the ship's computer for the number of life forms on the ship, the numbers were dubious, as the computer would often include the number of rodents and insects that had somehow managed to board. If the computer reported an astronomical number, the scans had to be recalibrated to exclude microbes and other minute forms of life. It was difficult to explain life to a computer.

The display screen showed the ship's layout with six red stars marking the Type One life forms.

"Convert my life form marker to green."

The display showed a green star on the A-Collar Bridge and five red stars in an access corridor rapidly moving toward B-Collar. Shortly thereafter the red stars left the access corridor and entered B-Collar.

"Access doors to B-Collar have been sealed," announced Chirality.

Arminius watched the display screen. There were four access doors to B-Collar, all of which now had an adjacent red star. The fifth red star was on the B-Collar Bridge. Captain McDonald and his men had captured B-Collar.

"Chirality"

"Yes, Commander."

"Lock out all systems in B-Collar Bridge. Code number 4793."

"Completed, sir."

Captain McDonald may have control of B-Collar, thought Arminius, but I have control of the ship and all of its systems. Arminius checked the battlefield hologram. The Home World ships were still being launched and were continuing to assemble, forming rings around Home World at two thousand mile and twenty-thousand-mile elevations. He double-checked the settings on the defense system controls. He was currently safe at the ten-thousand-mile elevation. He glanced back at the ship layout screen.

"Chirality"

"Yes, Commander"

"Seal all access doors to A-Collar and notify me if any of the Type One life forms leave B-Collar."

Now what was he going to do? With his superior weaponry, maneuverability, and speed, he could easily destroy any attacking ships. But could he fight the ships while being attacked from within the Alpha One by Captain McDonald and the elite bodyguards? At some point, they were going to leave B-Collar. The sealed doors to A-Collar would buy him some time, but the bodyguards could cut through the doors with their laser pistols and other weapons were available in the B-Collar armory.

"Chirality"

"Yes, Commander."

"Can the life support systems in B-Collar be shut down?"

"Not while Type One life forms are present."

"Even with a command override?"

"Life support systems have a backup critical control system."

Arminius now recalled this from his Alpha One commander training. At the time he had praised the engineers that had designed the redundant safety system, but now he silently cursed them. He needed a plan. The enemy was on his border in a secure location with ample supplies. He was outnumbered and it was only a matter of time before he was going to be attacked.

Arminius had undergone extensive physical training and excelled at marksmanship as well as hand-to-hand combat, but he knew he was totally out matched by the bodyguards. Only the best-of-the-best were accepted for admission into the Home World Bodyguard Academy. These were the personal guards of the upper echelon politicians and no expense was spared in their training. Even if Arminius could get a lucky shot against one of the bodyguards, there were four of them and they were all wearing body armor. The most powerful military force ever created was assembling outside his ship, but his greatest threat was onboard. He had control of a gargantuan twelve-hundred-foot laser, yet was hopelessly outgunned.

▲ ▲ ▲

Captain McDonald hurried to the B-Collar Bridge. He was an experienced commander and had been on many ships. The ship's Bridge usually contained a dozen or more people and there was always a hum of activity. He knew from his training that the Alpha One was fully automated and operated with a very small crew, but he was not prepared for the dead silence and blank blue screens that greeted him when he arrived at the B-Collar Bridge. He recalled that there was a master kill switch to cut off all power to the control system. He located the switch and turned it off. The entire Bridge turned dark, except for a luminescent pathway that led to the dining/conference room area. Captain McDonald turned the power switch on and the display screens came back to life but remained lifeless – there were no readings. He went to the communications station, but the results were the same. The B-Collar Bridge was brain dead.

Captain McDonald crossed the Bridge and located the manual view port. He rotated the periscope controls until he saw Home World. The Alpha One had definitely lifted off and, from the looks of things, was now high above the planet's surface. He watched for several minutes, expecting the planet below to gradually recede. To his surprise, the planet's size remained the same and the continents below were slowly rotating. He watched for a few more minutes. The planet below definitely was not receding - they were in orbit. Why would the Plugarians hijack a ship and remain in orbit?

▲ ▲ ▲

"Chirality"
    "Yes, Commander."

"How many air conditioning systems are in B-Collar?" Arminius vaguely recalled this from his training, but wanted to double-check.

"There are three systems available, sir. Currently B-Collar is operating with the main air conditioning system that supplies the entire ship. There are also two independent systems located in B-Collar, either of which can supply all of the B-Collar requirements."

"Does A-Collar have a similar system?"

"Yes, Commander."

"Display main air conditioning system."

A screen showing a layout of the ship and the main air conditioning system appeared.

"Highlight the supply duct to B-Collar and locate the nearest access panel."

The duct was highlighted and the access panel location marked. It was near the middle of the Engine Tube.

"Highlight location of the return air duct from B-Collar and mark location of louvers."

The display was updated to show the information. Both passed through the Engine Tube.

Arminius hastily left the Bridge and ran to the A-Collar armory.

▲ ▲ ▲

Captain McDonald assembled the bodyguards in the middle of the B-Collar corridor outside of the Laser Tube at a midway location from where they could observe the access doors to both the Laser Tube and one of the access corridors that connected with A-Collar. This left the doors to the Engine Tube and the second access corridor to A-Collar temporarily unguarded, but the meeting was going to be short and it would take some time for an intruder to cut through those doors.

"Gentlemen," he began, "These are the facts. We are currently in orbit above Home World. The monitoring equipment on the B-Collar bridge is useless. We do not know who is in command of this ship and we do not know their intentions. One possibility is that Plugarian terrorists have hijacked us. If so, we do not know the size of their force, their weaponry, or their location."

Captain McDonald paused to look at each of the bodyguards and was amazed. He knew he had their full attention, but he also knew that they were periodically scanning the surroundings with their keen senses for any signs of hostile activity. "The way I see it, we have two choices. One option is that we can take a defensive approach and fortify our existing location. We have enough food, water, and supplies to easily last for over ten years. The second option is that we attack. What are your thoughts?"

The bodyguard squad leader spoke, "Sir, we are an elite force and have been trained to follow the orders of our commander. You are the commander in this situation. We will do whatever you order."

Captain McDonald paused. He had expected the reply. He was a leader and he knew how to lead. Stating the alternatives had given him time to process the situation and make his decision. One never lets subordinates make key decisions and there was no way he was going to be holed up for years while someone else had control of *his* ship.

"I certainly appreciate your support." Captain McDonald nodded as he made eye contact with each of the bodyguards. "Here is the plan. We are going to barricade three of the four access points to B-Collar. I want two of you to patrol the entry points in B-Collar while the other two raid the storage areas for materials to use for the barricade. We will keep the entryway to the Engine Tube accessible."

▲ ▲ ▲

When he arrived at the A-Collar armory, Arminius grabbed a Luddite 1813 laser pistol and checked to make sure it was fully charged. He then ran through the medical facilities and raced into the adjoining laboratory. There was no time to lose. It was only a matter of time before Captain McDonald and the elite bodyguards launched an attack. Memories of scientific experiments in school, some good and some not so good, flashed through his mind as he ran through the laboratory. It was a large room with advanced analytical instruments on one side and empty counter tops on the other that were available for conducting any future scientific experiments that may be needed. His destination was just outside the lab – the Chemical Stockroom. He arrived and found shelves full of chemicals lining the stock room along with refrigerators containing heat sensitive materials. Arminius searched the shelves…they were alphabetized…he quickly found where the 'B' chemicals were stored, but what he was looking for was not there.

"Chirality, is there BAC-431 on board this ship?"

"Yes, Commander."

"Where is it located?"

"It is in the highly toxic storage unit along with other poisons and Class One hazardous materials. They are located in a locked cabinet in a separate storage room across the hall from the Chemical Stockroom."

"Unlock highly toxic storage unit. Code 3516"

Arminius located the highly toxic storage unit and quickly found a vial of BAC-431. He started to grab it and stopped. Had he lost his mind? He had almost grabbed the vial with his bare hands. Sure, the glass vial should protect him, but one does not take chances with Home World's deadliest chemical.

Arminius dashed to the neighboring supply room and quickly donned a chemical splash suit and double-lined gloves. He then put on a full-face respirator and attached it to a compressed air cylinder that he hastily slung over his back. Looking like an out-of-water scuba diver, he grabbed a nebulizer and the vial of BAC-431 and quickly headed to the Engine Tube.

▲ ▲ ▲

Captain McDonald hurried to the B-Collar Armory and scanned the arsenal of weapons with admiration. They look so beautiful, he thought, these powerful works of art that cause death and destruction. He put on a suit of body armor, grabbed a Luddite 1813 laser pistol, and made a mental note of the available weaponry. When Captain McDonald rejoined the bodyguards, he was pleased to see they had already created an impressive blockade at the entrance to the Laser Tube. They had even left a passageway on the outside of the barricade. That was good thinking on their part – in case of attack one needed quick access to combat locations. Now armed for battle, Captain McDonald assumed sentry duties, freeing an additional bodyguard for barricade duty. The blockades on entrances to both access corridors to A-Collar were quickly completed and Captain McDonald gathered his troops outside the door to the Engine Tube.

"Gentlemen, you have done an excellent job setting up the barricades. We now have a fortified position from which we can launch our attack. The element of surprise is in our favor. The plan is to pass through the Engine Tube to A-Collar. From there, we will launch an assault on the A-Collar Bridge. I know you are all highly trained on assault techniques, so you will lead the assault while I establish a rearguard at the doorway connecting the Engine Tube and A-Collar. If resistance is strong, abort the attack and we will regroup in B-Collar."

▲　▲　▲

Arminius entered the Engine Tube and, as always, was amazed at the view. The cavernous room was twelve hundred feet long and one hundred feet in diameter. Supported in the middle of the room was the centerpiece – the Benson-Clements Engine. It was the most advanced engine ever designed and was the same engine that was used to power the gigantic freighters that traversed the Binary Star System. The engine itself was sixty feet in diameter and eleven hundred feet long. It was supported twenty feet above the floor of the Engine Tube. Surrounding the engine, like servants in a monarch's court, were a host of utility and instrument modules that kept the engine operating efficiently. The walls on the sides of the Engine Tube were covered by a maze of walkways that led to the support equipment. Above the Engine Tube, ninety feet above the floor, was a catwalk that provided access to the upper section of the colossal engine.

Even with Chirality's assistance, the air conditioning ducts were difficult to locate. Arminius climbed four flights of stairs with the compressed air cylinder on his back and squeezed through equipment on several platforms before finally finding a small platform near the Engine Tube wall that provided access to the four-foot diameter ducts. Arminius closed the louver on the air conditioning system return air header that led to A-Collar and then searched for the access panel on the header that supplied B-Collar. It too was four feet in diameter. Arminius was surprised to see that the access door was bolted in place. He silently cursed himself for not bringing any tools, then took out his laser pistol, and carefully cut a hole in the access panel. He cautiously opened the vial of BAC-431, poured it into the nebulizer, and sprayed it into the air conditioning duct leading to B-Collar. Arminius did not trust the louver on the return air header to prevent any of the now highly toxic air to backflow into A-Collar. He returned to the louver that he had just closed and, using his laser pistol, cut out a section of duct between the louver and A-Collar. A ten-foot-long section of duct crashed into the Engine Tube floor below, leaving an air gap in the duct work so there was now no way for the BAC-431 to return to A-Collar.

▲ ▲ ▲

The four bodyguards suddenly drew their laser pistols and formed a circle around Captain McDonald as they scanned the corridor. Captain McDonald had been addressing them and had no idea what they were doing. At first, he thought they were being rude or objected to his attack plan, especially the part about him remaining behind as the rearguard.

A few seconds later, when they realized an attack was not imminent, the bodyguard leader whispered, "Our apologies sir, there has been a change in the air conditioning system."

Although he had not noticed anything different, Captain McDonald knew that this group of elites had heightened senses and had been trained to react to subtle changes that could be a harbinger of an attack.

The bodyguard leader motioned to two of the bodyguards. They quickly and quietly headed down the main corridor of B-Collar while the other bodyguard remained. The bodyguard and the bodyguard leader positioned themselves on both sides of Captain McDonald, protecting him from potential attackers that could approach from either direction in the corridor.

"Do you think they are attacking us through the air conditioning duct?" whispered Captain McDonald.

"It is possible, sir. We are always alert to that type of attack and we have been trained to storm buildings through the air conditioning duct work."

They waited for five minutes, which seemed like forever. Finally, Captain McDonald said, "Do you think someone should check on them?"

The lead bodyguard looked at the other bodyguard and softly spoke, "Investigate. Reconnaissance only and report back ASAP." The bodyguard departed hugging the corridor wall with his Luddite 1813 laser pistol drawn.

After a couple of minutes, Captain McDonald whispered, "Shouldn't he be back by now?"

The lead bodyguard looked conflicted. He knew his duty was to guard Captain McDonald, but the enemy was out there and his team had not reported back.

Sensing the bodyguard's internal turmoil and filled with curiosity, Captain McDonald told the bodyguard leader, "Let's go together," as he pulled out his laser pistol and adjusted the settings for battle mode.

"But sir," protested the lead bodyguard. "My mission is to protect you and this may put you in danger."

"It is a greater danger to remain here like sitting ducks. You lead and I will stay behind."

The lead bodyguard headed down the circular corridor hugging the walls with his laser pistol drawn. Captain McDonald followed twenty feet behind, pressing against the wall. They passed by the barricade to the one of the access corridors. A very impressive barricade, thought Captain McDonald. There was silence, still silence, as they continued along the wall for several hundred feet.

Suddenly the lead bodyguard waved Captain McDonald back and raced ahead.

There was no way that Captain McDonald was going to stay behind, so he quickly followed. He looked ahead and saw that the lead bodyguard was approaching the body of a bodyguard lying on the ground in a contorted position with his mouth wide open. Thirty feet ahead, lay the bodies of the two other bodyguards next to an air conditioning vent. Suddenly the lead bodyguard leader collapsed, gasping for breath. Captain McDonald realized what was happening and raced the opposite direction. The air is poisoned, he thought, I have got to get out of here fast! He raced passed the barricaded access corridor, arrived at the Engine Tube entrance, and quickly unlocked the door. He entered the Engine Tube on a platform at the eighty-foot level and closed the door. The room was surprisingly quiet – the giant engine was not a big noisemaker now that they were in orbit. Captain McDonald paused and surveyed the surroundings while he planned his next step.

Suddenly a booming female voice filled the room, "INTRUDER ALERT. INTRUDER IN THE ENGINE TUBE."

▲ ▲ ▲

"Chirality, how many Type One life forms are on this ship?" asked Arminius.

"Two." Chirality's reply reverberated across the cavernous Engine Tube.

Arminius surveyed the massive room. Somewhere out there was the enemy, but where? He told Chirality to alert him if anyone left B-Collar and she had followed his command. The intruder must have entered the Engine Tube through the door between B-Collar and the Engine Tube. Arminius scanned the Engine Tube until he located the door to B-Collar. Sure enough, high on a platform on the far side was a Type One life form, wearing body armor. Arminius silently cursed himself – he was wearing a chemical splash suit that provided protection from chemicals, but not laser fire.

▲ ▲ ▲

Captain McDonald quickly adjusted to the new surroundings and his military training kicked-in. He was alone in a hostile environment armed with only a laser pistol. He could not return to B-Collar, the air there was toxic. His former fortress had become a death zone, there was no retreat - he was going into battle. Except for his head, he was protected by body armor, which could withstand attacks from laser pistols, but not laser rifles. He surveyed the area and noted the oval catwalk above the colossal engine. The catwalk would give him the high ground for the upcoming battle. Stationed periodically along the catwalk were various storage modules that contained parts and tools used for servicing the engine. They would provide some cover. Captain McDonald headed toward the stairs that led to the catwalk.

▲ ▲ ▲

Arminius observed the enemy climbing the stairs leading up to the catwalk that accessed the upper section of the enormous engine. He needed a plan – fight or flight? He could retreat to the safety of A-Collar, but would he be safe? At some inopportune time, the entrance to A-Collar would be breached and he would have a one-on-one duel at a time and place that was not of his choosing. Alarming thoughts suddenly flashed across his mind – what if the enemy, instead of fighting, decided to sabotage the ship? The engine was certainly robust, but carefully placed laser fire could take out a vital instrument or engine support system that would eventually lead to engine failure and who knows what damage could be done in the Laser Tube? No, he needed to fight and he needed to fight now – it was time for battle.

Arminius did a quick evaluation of his battlefield strengths and weaknesses. He had the home field advantage, after all, it was **his** ship. He also had the element of surprise in that he could see his enemy, but the enemy did not yet know his location. On weaknesses, the enemy was wearing body armor, while he was unprotected. Also, the enemy was not carrying a compressed air cylinder while wearing a chemical splash suit. Why the hell was he wearing the protective equipment? If there were poisons in the Engine Tube air, wouldn't the enemy now be dead?

Arminius removed his chemical splash suit and discarded his respirator and compressed air cylinder. He grabbed his Luddite 1813 laser pistol and maneuvered behind equipment at the forty-foot-high elevation platform for a better view.

▲ ▲ ▲

Captain McDonald hurried up the stairs to the catwalk above the giant engine and hid behind the first storage module. He scanned the Engine Tube below – there was no sign of anyone present, but he did not have a good view of the entire room. For the best vantage point, he needed to be on the catwalk in the center of the room, which was about three hundred feet away. Storage modules were located every hundred feet along the catwalk. He sprinted to the first module and paused. There was no activity below. He then raced to the second module and, once again, there was no activity below. Finally, he dashed to the third module and laser fire erupted.

▲ ▲ ▲

Arminius watched as the enemy carefully maneuvered to the high ground on the catwalk in the middle of the Engine Tube. It was certainly a good strategy. Now what was he going to do? He was fifty feet below the catwalk and about one hundred feet off to the side. He estimated that the distance to the enemy was about one hundred and twenty feet. He was a good marksman and could certainly hit a stationary target at that range, but could he make a headshot? He checked his angle – the enemy was hidden behind a storage module. Getting a body shot would be difficult, while a headshot would be next to impossible. Arminius took careful aim and opened fire.

▲ ▲ ▲

Captain McDonald had wondered when the attack would begin and now he had his answer. Fortunately, he had achieved his objective and had captured the high ground. Bursts of laser fire were hitting the walkway twenty feet behind him. Keeping his head protected by the storage module, Captain McDonald returned fire.

▲ ▲ ▲

Arminius ceased firing when he started receiving laser fire. He was well hidden - the enemy laser was hitting close, only about five feet away. Arminius waited for the attack to end and then resumed firing.

▲ ▲ ▲

Captain McDonald was being attacked by bursts of laser fire, but once again his adversary was missing him by a good twenty feet. This time the catwalk in front of him was taking the hit. My enemy can't hit the broad side of a barn he thought as he returned fire.

▲ ▲ ▲

When the blasts from above resumed, Arminius stopped firing and took cover behind nearby equipment. Narrow red beams sliced through the air as they crisscrossed over and around his makeshift shelter. When the firing stopped, Arminius resumed his attack.

▲ ▲ ▲

The shooter that can't hit the broad side of a barn is firing again thought Captain McDonald. Laser bursts were hitting the catwalk, like they had previously, twenty feet behind him. He dared to peek out behind the storage module for a better look at the enemy. The attacker was well hidden behind some equipment fifty feet below. He would need to change positions to get a better angle. It looked like the fire was coming from a single attacker. Suddenly the laser fire shifted and now the catwalk twenty feet ahead of him was being attacked. Captain McDonald was starting to return fire when he felt a deep rumbling. With a loud crack, the section of catwalk that he was on broke away and swung into the engine below. Captain McDonald slid uncontrollably down the catwalk and crashed into the top of the engine. His laser pistol went flying as he tumbled across the top of the giant cylindrical engine and fell thirty feet to a platform below. Writhing in intense pain, his head was spinning out of control. He lay on his back for a few minutes and the spinning gradually slowed. There was no telling how many of his bones were broken. If it were not for the body armor, he would surely be dead. Then he saw the enemy.

▲ ▲ ▲

Arminius was glad to see that his plan, once again, had worked to perfection. He really was the greatest! Instead of trying to make a difficult head shot, his laser fire had taken out the walkway that was holding the enemy. Arminius navigated the maze of pathways through the equipment supporting the giant engine until he found his prey lying unarmed on its back in obvious pain. He was surprised when he realized that the enemy was Captain McDonald.

"Commander Arminius," sputtered Captain McDonald in excruciating agony, "I thought you were a Plugarian terrorist."

Arminius paused, "I thought you were one of the bodyguards. Sorry about all this."

"Why would you want to kill a bodyguard?"

"Nothing personal," assured Arminius as he aimed his laser pistol. "Sometimes on the way to the top things get in your way."

Arminius fired his weapon and severed Captain McDonald's head just above the top of his body armor. He turned and began slowly walking back to the A-Collar bridge.

"Chirality, how many Type One life forms are on this ship?"

"One, sir."

"And that's the way it's going to stay."

CHAPTER 10

COST VERSUS VALUE

"Chirality, how many Home World battleships have been launched?" asked Arminius after he returned to the A-Collar Bridge.

"Four hundred sixty-seven, sir. Others are waiting to be launched."

"How many are laser ships and how many are torpedo ships?

"Two hundred fifty-two laser ships and two hundred fifteen torpedo ships."

"Shut down main air conditioning system and startup individual air conditioning systems in A-Collar and B-Collar. Seal all doors to A-Collar."

"Completed, sir."

There was no way Arminius was going to enter B-Collar with BAC-431 present and he certainly did not want to clean up the mess that was formerly Captain McDonald. The dead bodies would stay where they were. There was nothing to gain by moving them.

▲ ▲ ▲

General Hayden's face filled the large center space on Major Tom's console.

"Status report," ordered the General.

"Sir, we will soon have five hundred and eleven ships ready for battle. They will be ringing the planet at two thousand miles and twenty thousand miles. The Alpha One is currently at ten thousand miles."

"Battleplans?"

"Being developed as we speak, sir."

"Other items?"

"Sir, we need to consider a cost versus value analysis."

"Understood Major, out."

Major Tom thought to himself, "If I was in charge, what price would I pay for Commander Arminius's life?"

▲ ▲ ▲

General Hayden conveyed the information to the chancellor and vice chancellor.

"We will soon have five hundred and eleven birds in the sky. As you can see from the battlefield hologram, the Alpha One is at ten thousand miles and we have established perimeter rings at two thousand and twenty thousand miles."

"What is the plan?" asked Chancellor Thager.

"The plan is being developed as we speak, but a cost versus value analysis is needed."

"Explain"

"What is it worth to us to take this guy out? We will be battling the most powerful military ship in the Binary Star System and to destroy it will no doubt result in heavy casualties. Are there any other alternatives?

Chancellor Thager was furious and screamed, "I will not negotiate with terrorists!"

General Hayden tried to sooth him, "Sir, technically Commander Percival is a member of our military. He is not a terrorist."

This only made the chancellor madder. "I want that son-of-a-bitch blown out of the sky immediately!"

General Hayden relayed the instructions to Major Tom.

"General," Major Tom pointed out, "the Alpha One is faster and its laser has a longer range than any of the other ships in our fleet. If we get anywhere near it, our ships will be destroyed."

THE PRICE OF LIFE

"Major, I am only relaying Chancellor Thager's commands. Launch an attack immediately."

Major Tom reached out to M on his console. "Launch a probing attack against the Alpha One. Use three ships – two MT class torpedo ships and one ML class laser ship."

"But, sir," objected M, "the Alpha One has a greater laser range. It will destroy the ships before they can get close enough to launch an effective attack."

"It is a probing mission to test the Alpha One's capabilities," rationalized Major Tom ignoring M's protests. "The three ships are to leap frog each other, taking turns adsorbing the Alpha One's laser blast. As the torpedo ships move into position to intercept the laser, they are to fire a round of torpedoes. Hopefully this way they can get closer to the Alpha One and take it out."

"And if they don't?"

"Then we will have data to plan the next attack. Make sure reconnaissance video is sent to the Command Center."

A few minutes later the attack began. Ships MT-305, MT-372, and ML-145 suddenly broke orbit and hurtled through space in a tight V-formation directly toward the Alpha One with ML-145 in the lead. When they got within five hundred miles, the Alpha One fired pulsating laser blasts that momentarily knocked the ML-145 off course. The MT-305 fired two torpedoes and moved forward to intercept the blows. As it received the pulsating laser blasts, it too was momentarily knocked off course. The MT-372 fired two torpedoes and moved in to intercept the laser blasts. All three ships were now four hundred and eighty miles away from the Alpha One. The Alpha One made a series of sharp maneuvers and resumed its attack on the MT-305. The MT-372 tried to reestablish its position as a shield to adsorb the laser blasts, but it did not have the adroitness of the Alpha One. Every time the MT-372 moved to intercept, the Alpha One changed position and was able to continue to pummel the MT-305. Without the shield, the MT-305 did not have a chance and five seconds later was annihilated.

The Alpha One laser control system changed targets and the four launched torpedoes, now four hundred miles away, were destroyed. The next laser target was the MT-372 and ten seconds later it was obliterated. The ML-145 fired its laser, a harmless shot from four hundred seventy miles away, and shortly thereafter ceased to exist.

▲ ▲ ▲

The large video screen in the Command Center showed live coverage of the battle. Everyone in the Command Center was stunned. Three of Home World's finest battleships had been vanquished in a matter of minutes.

In the VIP Conference Room, Chancellor Thager was furious, "Three ships? He attacked with only three ships? What kind of idiots are running this place?"

General Hayden cautiously approached the chancellor, "Sir, perhaps we should consider other alternatives? "

"Hell yes!" yelled the chancellor, "How is this for an alternative? Send more ships and blow away the bastard!"

▲ ▲ ▲

Major Tom started to protest, when he received the latest orders from General Hayden.

General Hayden interrupted him, "Major, these are the orders from Chancellor Thager himself."

Major Tom called M again. M's shaken face appeared on the central video screen. "Here are the plans for the next attack."

M interrupted, "Sir, didn't you see what the Alpha One did to our ships?"

Undaunted, Major Tom continued, "The next attack will be with nine ships. The plan is for them to surround the Alpha One and come in from nine different angles – above, below, and from all sides. Once again, use a mixture of torpedo ships and laser ships – five MT's and four ML's. Plot the ships courses so that they are all traveling at maximum speed when they cross the five-hundred-mile laser range of the Alpha One. They are to come at the Alpha One at full speed with torpedoes and lasers firing. Hopefully at least one of them will get close enough to the Alpha One to take it out."

"Hopefully?" questioned M.

"You have your orders." M needs to toughen up thought Major Tom as he signed out.

▲ ▲ ▲

The nine ships entered the five-hundred-mile laser range perimeter at maximum speed. Three attacked from above, three attacked from the sides, and three attacked from below. The five torpedo ships each fired two torpedoes. The Alpha One laser took aim at the MT ship attacking from the left side and ten seconds later it ceased to exist. The Alpha One then locked on to the ML ship attacking from above on the left side and it was soon destroyed. The remaining seven attack ships speeding toward the Alpha One were now four hundred and sixty miles away and the ten torpedoes fired were four hundred and twenty miles away. The Alpha One raced toward the now vacant sector where the ML ship and MT ship had attacked from, while firing at and destroying the pursuing torpedoes. When the Alpha One was five hundred miles from the closest of the remaining attack ships it made a reverse barrel roll and fired its powerful laser, annihilating its target. The Alpha One then turned to face its next nearest foe. With its superior speed and adroitness, the Alpha One maneuvered to positions from where its laser blasted the attacking ships from beyond the range of their weapons. One-by-one the remaining ships were picked off.

▲ ▲ ▲

Major Tom was stunned, but as a professional he was trained not to show his emotions. The Alpha One had now taken out twelve top military battleships without a scratch. This was indeed a super weapon that would change the future of intergalactic battles. How does one destroy a ship that is stronger, faster, and nimbler? There had to be a way. Stunned or not, he was the Battlefield Strategic Commander and it was up to him to coordinate the response.

"B2, run simulation models. We need an effective attack strategy."

Major Tom called P in Psyche Ops and once again braced himself. How could such a beautiful face have such crazed eyes? "I need something unconventional. Is there a non-military approach?"

Major Tom then called N in News Control. "We are going to need a really good cover story."

"Already got it sir," N responded. "The Plugarians attacked us today with a new super weapon. Our fearless warriors were victorious, but severe losses were inflicted. We will replace the ships and build our own super weapon. This of course will be at great cost, so the people will need to pull together, make sacrifices, and pay higher taxes."

N is really good, Major Tom thought. Not a word is true, but the defense contractors will be very happy. He then called General Hayden, "Sir, we need a change of tactics. He is too strong for us. Can we offer him something else instead?"

General Hayden replied, "Let me get back to you on that Major. We are working on something."

CHAPTER 11

THE BOOK OF HAGER

This is the book of Hager as told by Pireneaus and recorded by the humble scribe Mitslen.

I speak now of days of old in the time of King Hager the Great, who was a mighty king known by all to be firm and fair. In those days, life was difficult and men spent most of their days toiling the ground. Though they were weary, they took great satisfaction knowing that they served their king and country well.

There were a few, however, that complained about their burdens. These weak men sought to lighten their loads. They consorted with magicians and begged for a tool to make their lives easier. The magicians conjured a great sword of energy. The weak men took turns using the great sword on their fields, completing their tasks much more quickly with far less toil. They found that they were no longer tired and had much more time to pursue other pastimes. They used this extra time to engage in licentious and other immoral activities.

Hager the Great saw this and, being very wise, banned the use of the sword of energy. He announced that a platoon of his warriors would be going to the village in a few days to retrieve the sword.

The slovenly farmers were greatly distraught. The sword of energy had made their lives much easier and they enjoyed their immoral pursuits. The farmers were not trained in the art of war and were a spineless bunch. The cowardly men prayed to their idols for a miraculous rescue.

The next day, Beignet, a young member of a traveling fraternity of noblemen pledged to support just causes, rode into the village on a large white steed. Beignet was dressed in chain mall as was customary with the knights of his day. Emblazed on the chain mall was the symbol of his fraternity.

The fearful farmers jubilantly greeted the young man and showered him with praise, "Oh great one, you are the answer to our prayers!" They showed him their new tool and how well it cut their fields. They explained the great harm that would be inflicted on them if the tool were taken by the king. They told him that their cause was just and that it would be a great wrong if the king took their sword. That night, they held a wild and raucous party in Beignet's honor. After much urging and partaking of spirits, Nobleman Beignet swore an oath, "I solemnly swear to protect the sword of energy. Only from my dead hands shall King Hager take the sword."

The next day, a platoon of thirteen great warriors sent from the king arrived. They asked the mayor of the village where the sword was located.

"It is in the hands of Beignet, a member of the fraternity of noblemen that travel the world in search of just causes."

"Where can we find this nobleman?" they inquired.

"In the field at the north edge of town," the mayor replied.

The soldiers traveled to the field and found the nobleman kneeling on one knee with the sword in his right hand. "Surrender the sword of energy," demanded the platoon commander.

"I respectfully refuse," answered the nobleman. "The people in this village have a right to this tool."

"The people have no rights except for what the king grants," bellowed the commander. "The king has requested the sword and ordered me to bring it to him. Now surrender it at once or face the consequences."

"Sir, I am a member of a traveling fraternity of noblemen that search the world for just causes. I have no quarrel with you, but if you approach closer, you will feel the sword of energy in an agonizing manner."

The leader of the platoon ordered three of his strongest warriors to attack. They were quickly sliced to pieces by the sword of energy. He then ordered the nine remaining soldiers to attack. They too were quickly dispatched. The leader cowardly returned and reported all to the king.

The king was greatly angered and promptly executed the platoon leader for not fulfilling his mission. The king summoned all of his soldiers, four hundred and ninety-nine great warriors, and returned the next day to the village where he found the bodies of the fallen warriors. A short distance away was the traveling nobleman with the sword of energy.

The king approached the nobleman. "Honored guest in my kingdom, I offer my humblest apologies for how you were treated yesterday. Instead of fighting, my men should have offered to purchase the sword. I am here today to make such an offer. Surely you could use the money to support just causes elsewhere. Let me purchase it from you and afterwards we shall have a great celebration feast."

"Am I to improve the lots of others while leaving the people here to suffer?" asked the traveling nobleman.

"Honored guest," replied Hager the Great. "Do you not see the great dangers in the weapon that you possess? If this weapon is left with the villagers, great harm will come. If you want to protect the people, you must surrender your weapon to me at once, before further harm comes to my kingdom. By not selling me this weapon, the people here will suffer."

"Weapon?" questioned the nobleman, "this is not a weapon. It is but a tool to ease the burdens of the poor farmers."

"A tool? Nonsense," the king responded. "It is a weapon. It will kill many and destroy the way of life in my kingdom. You must give it up at once."

"Sir," appealed Beignet to the king, "alas, even if I believe what you say, I have sworn a solemn oath. Only from my dead hands will you receive this sword."

"The proper course of action is to rescind your oath in order to protect the people. These people's future is worth far more than any oath."

"Sir, I am a member of a traveling fraternity of noblemen that search the world for just causes. There is nothing of greater value than the oath of a member of our fraternity. I will honor my oath until my death."

"You are indeed a nobleman," agreed the king. "Yesterday my warriors fought like thugs and ganged up on you. This angered the gods and they saw to it that my warriors were defeated. Today my warriors will fight with honor."

The king addressed his warriors. "Today, you are to fight as noblemen. I decree that there will be only one-on-one combat. You are to announce your name, your rank, and your intentions before beginning the battle." He then motioned for the first soldier to confront Beignet.

The first soldier approached the nobleman, "I am Darius of Timken, swordsman in the army of King Hager the Great. I am fighting to acquire the sword of energy."

Darius attacked. A few minutes later, his body lay in pieces at the feet of Beignet.

The second soldier approached, "I am Cyrus of Gatrene, a pike man in the army of King Hager the Great. I am fighting to acquire the sword of energy."

A few minutes later, Cyrus's severed head rolled across the ground.

The third soldier approached, "I am Altus of Nebir, a grappler in the army of King Hager the Great. I am fighting to acquire the sword of energy.

A short while later, Altus's body was split in two at the waist.

This honorable fight continued all day, all night, all the next day, and all the next night. One by one, the mighty warriors of the army of Hager the Great fell.

At dawn on the third day, the last of King Hager's warriors fell. A weary Beignet stood holding the sword of energy surrounded by four hundred and ninety-nine dead bodies. King Hager walked up to Beignet.

"King Hager, will you now join your brethren?" asked Beignet as he pointed to the severed heads and sliced body parts of the dead warriors that now littered the landscape.

"Nobleman Beignet, I carry no weapon. I am a king, no longer a warrior. There is but one warrior remaining in the kingdom, and that is you."

"The fight is over. Return to your throne."

"I will," King Hager obstinately proclaimed, "when I have the sword of energy."

"As I told you earlier, I have sworn an oath. Only from my dead hands will you take the sword."

"Nobleman Beignet, look at the destruction caused by the sword of energy. Can you now say that it is not a weapon?

"Indeed, it is a very effective weapon."

"And if a few possessed this weapon, would there need to be as many brave warriors in the world?"

"There would be no such need."

"Then brave men would no longer be able to fight and die in battle, gloriously defending just causes?"

"You are correct," agreed Beignet. "With this great weapon, there would no longer be a need to have as many brave warriors."

"And the farmers?" continued the king, "With this great weapon, will there be a need to have as many farmers?"

"No, with this great weapon, there will no longer be a need to have as many farmers."

"And the armor makers...with this great weapon, will there need to be as many armor makers?"

"No, with this great weapon, there will no longer be a need to have as many armor makers."

"And the miners...with this great weapon, will there need to be as many miners supplying metal for the armor makers?"

"No, with this great weapon, there will no longer be a need to have as many miners."

"So," continued the wise king, "With fewer warriors, fewer farmers, fewer armor makers, and fewer miners, people will have nothing to do. They will spend their days pursuing unjust and immoral activities."

"I now see that this would happen."

"Do you want people pursuing unjust activities?"

"Of course not," exclaimed Beignet. "My fraternity of noblemen supports only just causes."

"So now do you see why you must give me the weapon so that I may hide it from the world?"

"Yes, this now I see. But I am a nobleman and I gave an oath that while I am alive, I will never give you the sword of energy."

"Then you have but one choice."

"Will you promise me that you will rid the world of this sword?"

"You have my oath as king."

Beignet grasped the handle of the sword of energy with both hands and loudly yelled, "For just causes!" as he plunged the sword deep into his heart.

After Beignet died, the king took the sword from the dead man's hands and returned to his throne. He had the sword buried in an unmarked location deep below ground. Barren rocks beneath the surface adsorbed the great energy from the sword. The rocks were transformed and provided an immense supply of energy for future generations.

The death of the entire army brought great sadness throughout the land. Almost every family lost a loved one and there was much moaning and wailing. The Creators saw this and were so touched by the grief that they prepared a special room for the souls of the dead.

The farmers returned to their lands and resumed their toils, thus ending the time of great immorality.

CHAPTER 12

LEARNING FROM THE PAST

The Command Center was stunned. Nine of Home World's most powerful military ships had been destroyed in a matter of minutes. Everyone in the VIP Conference Room sat in stoned silence after watching the second round of battle on the giant holographic stage. Finally, Chancellor Thager spoke, "How many ships do we have out there?"

"Four hundred and ninety-nine, sir," General Hayden despondently replied, "not counting the Alpha One."

"We started with five hundred and twelve, then lost three, and then lost nine. Gentlemen, do you not see what is happening?" asked Chancellor Thager excitedly.

Both General Hayden and Vice Chancellor Percival shook their heads.

"It is the Book of Hager all over again," grinned the Chancellor. "Hager the Great had four hundred and ninety-nine warriors when we sought to recover the Sword of Energy, the greatest weapon of his day."

▲ ▲ ▲

Major Tom was beating himself up - twelve battleships lost today and we still have not achieved the objective. Why did I not just blast the Alpha One out of the sky when I had a chance? P called and Major Tom quickly bounced back into professional mode. "Do you have something for me?" She looked ravishing, except for her crazed eyes that now looked crazier than ever.

P smiled, "It is a pretty standard out-of-the-box strategy, but it may work well in this case. We transmit videos of the last moments of life of the crews on board the destroyed battleships. Often deranged murderers feel guilty and want to join in death the ones they just killed. It should be ready in a few minutes."

"How did you get the videos? I didn't know videos such as those even existed."

"They don't," divulged P. "It is stock footage enhanced with computer graphics using pictures from personnel files."

▲ ▲ ▲

"Commander, incoming message from Chancellor Thager," announced Chirality. Ghastly images of the last seconds of life of the personnel on the destroyed ships were playing on the three-dimensional video communication screen as well as on the dining room/conference room screen.

"Put it on," replied Arminius.

A lifelike hologram of Chancellor Thager suddenly appeared at the hologram communication station.

"Commander Percival, you are a truly remarkable person. I am very impressed with your accomplishments."

Arminius paused, not knowing where the chancellor was going, "Well thank you sir." Arminius glanced over at the Alpha One's battlefield hologram. There were no signs of activity or trickery.

Chancellor Thager continued, "I would like to apologize for the way you were attacked a few minutes ago. Let me assure you, those responsible will be severely punished."

Major Tom was watching the communication and cringed when he heard this. I was just following Chancellor Asshole's orders he thought.

"Commander Percival, I would like to reward you for your efforts," continued the chancellor. "You have risked your life to save the planet from a bomb developed by my predecessor and we owe you a great debt of gratitude. In addition, I am very impressed by your skills as the commander of this fine ship."

Arminius thought what does this pompous idiot want?

"As you may know, there is an opening for Secretary of Defense in my administration," continued the chancellor persuasively, "I would like to offer you that position."

Major Tom was becoming unglued. Let me get this straight he thought. Obtain a prestigious position in the military because of your father's influence, steal the most powerful ship in the Home World fleet, destroy twelve of Home World's finest battleships plus a cargo container full of diamonds, and then get rewarded by being offered the position of Secretary of Defense. Is this 'Firm and Fair'?

Arminius did not have to think long. If I accept the position and leave the Alpha One, I would be lucky to live a day before I am assassinated. "I am sorry sir, but that is not the position to which I aspire."

"What position would you like? I am sure we can accommodate you."

"I would like to be chancellor," proposed Arminius with a wry smile.

The communication immediately shut down and the hologram of Chancellor Thager disappeared.

Arminius checked the battlefield hologram – there still was no activity.

Soon he was going to be attacked by almost five hundred battleships, he needed a plan.

Less than a minute later, his thoughts were interrupted by Chirality, "Chancellor Thager is calling, sir."

Two holographic figures suddenly appeared in the front of the ship - Chancellor Thager and Arminius's father, the vice chancellor. The chancellor had a laser pistol pointed at the vice chancellor's head.

▲ ▲ ▲

Chancellor Thager had requested General Hayden's side arm, a Luddite 1813 laser pistol, and told General Hayden to call the Alpha One again. As soon as the communication signal was secure, he grabbed the vice chancellor and pointed the laser pistol at his head.

"Listen here, you son-of-a-bitch!" he roared, "I am sick and tired of messing around with you! I am Chancellor Simeon Thager, the leader of the Home World Empire and I have a laser pistol pointed directly at your father's head. As we speak, I am rounding up all of your family on Home World. I am then going to personally shoot each and every one until you return my ship!"

"Really?" replied Arminius calmly.

"I am going to very slowly torture," screamed the chancellor, whose face was now bright red as anger boiled from within, "and then kill every one of them while you watch them pay for what you have done. "This is your father!" Chancellor Thager took the vice chancellor's hand and shot it with the laser pistol. Smoke came from his hand as it burned to the bone. The senior Percival emitted a bloodcurdling wail.

"Make him suffer, really suffer!" shouted Arminius excitedly, "Make that bastard pay!"

The chancellor looked startled. "You want...?"

Arminius interrupted, "You heard me. Make that son-of-a-bitch suffer big time! Do you know how much family I have on Home World? You have a laser pistol pointed at my only family...and do you know why? It is because of that bastard!" Now Arminius was losing it. "I used to have a mother, a very loving mother, and do you know what happened to her? Do you know how he treated her? No, that bastard was never there – always out with who knows how many women...so what happens? She kills herself, yes, you heard me, my mother, a very sweet lady, takes an overdose of pills...so what does that leave? A seven-year-old boy...and does the father ever care for the boy? Never! It's off to military school...and do you know what? I excel, I work hard, really hard. I work my ass off. I am the best...I am the best at every damn thing I do! And do you know why? Because my father, that son-of-a-bitch, you just shot, might someday…yes maybe someday, one time might say he is proud of me. But does he do that? Hell no! He is always too busy. He has important worldly business to attend and no time for me!

So, I become the commander of the most powerful battleship in the Binary Star System and what does he do? That bastard takes it away from me. Why? So, he can be in a higher position. It's for him…it is always for him. Let me tell you this, I am the commander of this ship and I am the greatest to ever live! Do with him as you wish. Out!"

▲   ▲   ▲

R buzzed. "Sir, Arminius is correct. Records show he is an only child. Mother died when he was seven. Only relative is his father, the vice chancellor."

P called and had an even wilder look in her crazy eyes. "Sir, that latest transmission was fantastic! I am now working on a new strategy."

Major Tom reflected to himself. Let's see now, we have an unstable person piloting the most powerful battleship in the Binary Star System, the chancellor is torturing and threatening to kill the vice chancellor, we have lost twelve battleships, and we have a transport container full of diamonds blown to bits.

His thoughts were interrupted as B2 buzzed. "Sir, we have a battle plan."

Finally, some good news, thought Major Tom. "Great B2, let's hear it."

"Our ancestors," began B2, "faced a similar problem battling stronger and faster wild beasts. They used their intelligence and creativity and devised death traps. One group of hunters would chase the beasts down special paths that were lined with other hunters that kept them on the path and guided them into kill zones."

"So how does it work?" asked Major Tom.

"The instrument of death in this case is the land-based laser in Quadrant 1300. We need to get the Alpha One into range of that laser. The skies are clear, so the laser has a kill range of the full two thousand miles. Picture a giant pipe being placed around the Alpha One, better yet, make that a large net made from razor sharp wire. The net consists of our MT ships prepositioned in various locations outside the net, safely beyond the Alpha One's laser range. As the Alpha One approaches the net, it is met with a barrage of torpedoes fired from the MT ships, just as our ancestors threw rocks and spears at the wild beasts. The torpedoes will explode near the net. The Alpha One will be safe inside the net, but if it tries to venture outside of the net, it will face a hailstorm of torpedoes fired by multiple ships – a very risky maneuver for a ship with no defensive shielding."

"The problem with the plan," Major Tom pointed out, "is that ships will need to go inside the net to chase the Alpha One into the kill zone. The Alpha One will simply blast them away and escape out the open end of the net."

"We have thirty MLA class ships," continued B2 unfazed, "that will be used to plug the open end of the net and force the Alpha One into the kill zone. Those are heavy armor laser ships that can withstand longer laser blasts – possibly up to thirty seconds."

"But those are slow moving ships with only three-fourths the speed of the MT's and ML's. The Alpha One will have more time to blow them away."

"That is why we go in with a wedge-shaped formation with three ships per squadron. The front of the wedge is Squadron #1, the second line in the formation has Squadrons #2 and #3, the third line contains Squadrons #4, #5, and #6, and the fourth and final line consists of Squadron's #7, #8, #9, and #10. The first armored ship of Squadron #1 takes the initial laser blast from the Alpha One, after twenty seconds, the second ship of the squadron intercepts the blast for twenty seconds, and then, twenty seconds later, the third ship from the squadron intercepts the blast. After that, another squadron rotates in and takes their place intercepting the blasts. All the while the wedge formation, like a piston slowly traveling down a cylinder, is constantly moving toward the kill zone. If the Alpha One is ever within four hundred miles of the ships, it will be blasted by their lasers. The only way to escape the ships will be for the Alpha One to go toward the Quadrant 1300 laser, which is where it meets its demise."

"What did the computer models show?"

"Ninety-eight percent probable success rate, once the net is established. We will need some time to set it up."

I just issued a death sentence for even more ships Major Tom thought as he approved the plan.

CHAPTER 13

DEATH WITH HONOR

"Patch me through to the Alpha One," demanded Chancellor Thager, "And get the vice chancellor a bucket of ice water!" The senior Percival was screaming loudly in the background while flapping the hand that was burnt to the bone. A bucket of ice water was brought into the VIP Conference Room and the vice chancellor quickly plunged his hand into the cold water.

A holographic image of Arminius appeared in the VIP Conference Room as a communication link was reestablished with the Alpha One.

"I see he is still alive," remarked Arminius with disgust as he looked at the holographic images.

"Forgive me Commander," began Chancellor Thager in his soft persuasive politician voice, "I had no idea what you have been through in your youth. That bastard of a father wronged you greatly and you deserve so much more."

Arminius checked his battlefield hologram. What is this idiot up to now? There were no signs of movement of any of the nearly five hundred battleships.

"As you no doubt recall, my campaign slogan is 'Think Hager, Vote Thager'. Well, you know, there are a lot of similarities between Hager the Great and myself. Who knows, some day they may refer to me as Thager the Great."

Internally Arminius cringed, but maintained an expressionless face.

"In Hager's day," continued Chancellor Thager, "he was faced with a great super weapon. One created by magicians. Today, we call them engineers, but the effect is the same. Commander Percival, you are in possession of a super weapon that needs to be banished."

Major Tom thought I bet that will go over well with the defense contractors and their lobbyists.

"Commander Percival, do you admit that you are in possession of a very advanced super weapon?"

"Definitely," replied Arminius. He noticed some of the ships on the battlefield hologram were moving, but they were far away and should not affect him.

"Commander Percival, would you agree that with the Alpha One, there is no longer a need to have as many battleships?"

"This is true," agreed Arminius.

"Fewer ships mean fewer jobs for ship builders and fewer jobs for those that supply the materials that go into making the ships."

"Can't argue with that," acknowledged Arminius while watching the battlefield movements.

"Fewer ships mean fewer commanders, fewer crewmen, and fewer people dying in glorious battles, don't you agree."

"Makes sense to me."

"These people would then no longer pursue just causes. They would no doubt pursue immoral activities."

"No doubt," nodded Arminius with a small smile.

"Then you must agree," continued the Chancellor persuasively, "The best course of action is for you to turn over the Alpha One to me so that I can have it destroyed, agreed?"

"Over my dead body," responded Arminius calmly.

"Then, like my predecessor Hager the Great, I hereby challenge you to a duel. It will be a noble duel. Connect me for an all-ships broadcast."

C buzzed Major Tom, "Sir, do you want me to set up a link?"

"You heard the Chancellor's orders."

A few seconds, later C buzzed Major Tom, "Sir, connection complete." Major Tom relayed the information to General Hayden who notified the chancellor.

The chancellor royally proclaimed, "Attention, commanders of all military ships of the Home World Empire. This is Simeon Thager, your chancellor. Today we are going to duel with the Alpha One. It is to be a noble fight with one-on-one combat only. The commander of the ship is to announce his name and his intentions. The duels are to begin in five minutes."

▲ ▲ ▲

M was in a panic when he buzzed Major Tom, "Sir is he serious?"

Major Tom responded unemotionally, "We have our orders, select one of the older ships."

Major Tom thought - this is the price, the price for keeping one's job.

▲ ▲ ▲

The video screen on the Alpha One Bridge lit up as a very nervous commander spoke, "Alpha One, this is Commander O'Dell on the MT-347. I hereby challenge you to a duel. Do you accept?"

"Sure," Arminius responded.

The MT-347 approached at half speed until it was six hundred miles away from the Alpha One. It initiated a set of intricate weaving maneuvers at five hundred fifty miles that continued as it closed the gap - five hundred forty miles…five hundred thirty miles…five hundred twenty miles…and finally five hundred and ten miles. At five hundred and two miles it launched two torpedoes, cranked its engines up to full speed and headed directly towards the Alpha One. A second round of torpedoes was fired followed by an immediate sharp right turn. The Alpha One's laser locked on to its attacker.

Despite evasive maneuvers, the MT-347 was not able to escape the deadly beam and was destroyed ten seconds later. The Alpha One laser then zapped the torpedoes and they harmlessly exploded four hundred miles away from their intended target.

A video showing the last agonizing seconds of life aboard the MT-347 appeared shortly thereafter on the Alpha One's main video screen.

P buzzed in to Major Tom, "Have C rebroadcast the last few seconds and keep a continuous feed loop going to the Alpha One. Commander Arminius needs to see the damage he is doing. Perhaps he will feel remorseful and stop the killing, or better yet, kill himself."

"C, keep the rebroadcast loop going to the VIP Conference Room as well," added Major Tom. "M, keep setting up B2's net formation while we distract the Alpha One." It was somewhat comforting to know that the MT-347 sacrifice may not have been totally in vain.

The ML-118 was the next ship selected. Its commander spoke, "Alpha One, this is Commander Montgomery on the ML-118. I hereby challenge you to a duel. Do you accept?"

Arminius answered, "Why not?"

The ML-118 began a circling maneuver, maintaining a distance of five hundred and twenty miles. It dipped to within four hundred and ninety miles and then pulled out to five hundred miles and kept circling. It repeated the maneuver several times. It dipped to four hundred and eighty miles and was immediately blasted by the Alpha One laser. It fired its laser at the Alpha One, but was well out of range and ten seconds later, it too was destroyed.

"C, keep that video going as well," suggested P. "Also, set up an override on the commercial stations. Make it so the dining room and cabins will see a continuous feed of the destruction of both the MT-347 and ML-118."

A very nervous M buzzed in, "Sir, how long are we going to do this?"

Major Tom calmly replied, "We have our orders, next ship."

A few minutes later, the MT-124 commander spoke, "Alpha One, this is Commander Tyson on the MT-124. I hereby challenge you to a duel. Do you accept?"

Arminius replied, "Bring it on."

The MT-124 used a circling maneuver, similar to that of the ML-118 and maintained a distance of five hundred and ten miles. It dipped to four hundred ninety miles and fired two torpedoes, then retreated to five hundred and ten miles. The Alpha One destroyed the torpedoes when they were four hundred and seventy-five miles away. The MT-124 dipped again to four hundred ninety miles, fired two torpedoes and retreated. Once again, the Alpha One blasted away the torpedoes when they were four hundred and seventy-five miles away. The MT-124 dipped to four hundred and ninety miles a third time and fired two torpedoes. This time the Alpha One laser locked on to the MT-124 and fired. The MT-124 hurriedly retreated beyond the five hundred-mile Alpha One laser range, but was badly damaged. The Alpha One laser then took out the latest round of torpedoes when they were four hundred and sixty miles away.

A desperate Commander Tyson appeared on the screen, "Alpha One, we are badly damaged. Repeat, we are badly damaged. We surrender. You win."

Commander Arminius maneuvered the Alpha One to within four hundred fifty miles of the MT-124, paused, and then blasted it out of existence.

Major Tom buzzed B2, "How much longer until the net is ready?"

"About ten minutes, sir."

"Send the fourth ship," ordered Major Tom. The price of life for everyone on that ship, he thought, is about ten minutes.

▲ ▲ ▲

"Alpha One, this is Commander Throttlemeyer aboard the ML-178. I hereby challenge you to a duel. Do you accept?"

"Let's go," answered Arminius nonchalantly. Streaming video from the earlier duels was playing in the Alpha One dining room, repeatedly showing the last few horrific seconds of life aboard the now destroyed ships.

The ML-178 slowly circled the Alpha One from five hundred fifty miles away. A few minutes later six Cubs emerged from the ML-178 as it evacuated most of its crew. The ship approached closer and continued to circle at five hundred and ten miles until it reached a point at which it was in a direct line between the Alpha One and Bstar. The ML-178 suddenly turned and headed towards the ML-178 with the blinding lights of Bstar at its back. The maneuver was totally symbolic, since the sun had no effect on the Alpha One's instruments.

Commander Arminius planned to fire at the ML-178 when it was four hundred and eighty miles away, but he was interrupted by Chirality, "Incoming call, Commander."

"Who is it from?"

"She says she is your mother."

▲ ▲ ▲

"Hello Arminius." A life-like image of a beautiful young woman dressed in a flowing blue gown was sitting at the holograph station in the front of the bridge and was smiling at him. "This is your mother."

The hologram looked just like how Arminius remembered his mother. "Mom?" exclaimed Arminius, "How can this be? I attended your funeral."

"That was just for show, something put on for your father. It won him many votes."

"But I saw you…on the floor in the bathroom. You weren't breathing. Your face was blue."

"I wanted to die…your father treated me so badly. And yes, I was pronounced dead. But then your father did something truly remarkable."

"What did that son-of-a-bitch do?" asked Arminius angrily.

"I see you have learned a lot about your father. Yes, he is a horrible person. I don't know why, maybe he felt guilty, but he sent my body on a secret trip to Ricus 3."

"In the Forbidden Zone?" Inquired Arminius incredulously.

"It is a very magical place," she spoke with a dreamy glaze, "It took years in that environment, but it totally rejuvenated me. I miss you so much Arminius and I want to be with you soon and hear all about the wonderful things you have done."

And then came a really big jolt.

▲ ▲ ▲

"Laser attack," announced Chirality matter-of-factly. The ML-178 had closed to within four hundred miles and hit the Alpha One with a solid continuous beam.

"Evasive maneuvers!" shouted Arminius to himself while snapping out of the conversation with his mother. "Chirality, Launch Cub G now!"

The Alpha One escaped the laser beam for a few seconds, but then the ML-178 laser reengaged. The battlefield hologram showed that the ML-178 was three hundred and eighty miles away.

"Chirality, Cub G intercept!" Arminius yelled at the ship's computer. A few seconds later, Cub G moved into position and was sacrificed to the laser gods. "Chirality, engine speed one hundred percent!" The Alpha One began accelerating away from the beam. The battlefield hologram showed a distance of three hundred ninety-five miles when the ML-178 laser reconnected. This time the Alpha One was traveling at full speed. The beam only connected for a few seconds before the Alpha One was beyond the ML-178 laser range.

At four hundred and twenty miles, Commander Arminius banked the Alpha One sharply, then turned back and aimed its powerful laser. Ten seconds later the ML-178 was obliterated.

▲ ▲ ▲

"Sir, he is in the net," announced B2 excitedly. All eyes were on the large battlefield hologram stage at the front of the Command Center. The positions of the military ships were shifting rapidly and a giant net was spreading over the Alpha One.

▲ ▲ ▲

"Arminius," the hologram continued, "I need you to come to me. I am on Ricus 3, but have no way to get home. I miss you so much."

"Mom, I really can't talk right now."

"Arminius, how have you been? Did you go to the military academy? Is there a lady in your life?"

"Chirality, cancel call and kill all of the video feeds."

With a troubled look, Arminius stared at the ship's battlefield hologram. "I have been foolish and let my guard down. Great people do not do this. I am the greatest! Now I have a problem. What are they doing?"

Arminius watched as Home World ships, all over the battlefield hologram, quickly moved to new positions.

CHAPTER 14

THE NET

Like a marching band changing formations at a half time show, the chaotic swirling on the battlefield hologram suddenly stopped, revealing a new creation. A giant double-walled cylinder now appeared in what was previously empty space. The Alpha One was currently five thousand miles above Home World and was engulfed by the cylinder. Battleships lined the sidewalls of the cylinder that extended from fifteen hundred to eight thousand miles above Home World. The diameter of the inner wall of the cylinder was three thousand miles and the diameter of the outer wall was four thousand miles. At the top of the cylinder, like a slow-moving piston, thirty MLA ships in a tight wedge formation were slowly descending toward the planet. At the other end of the cylinder, the enormous Quadrant 1300 laser with its two-thousand-mile death ray was hot and ready for action.

Arminius veered the Alpha One sharply toward the sides of the cylinder at fifty percent speed. A few seconds later, a dozen torpedoes were fired from the three MT class ships in the area that was part of the inner wall. The ships were one thousand miles away, safely outside of the Alpha One laser's five-hundred-mile range. As the torpedoes approached, Arminius started taking them out. The last was destroyed when it was three hundred miles away. Arminius studied the situation. The torpedoes could travel three times as fast as a conventional battleship. The Alpha One was twenty five percent faster than the conventional battleships, but could not outrun the torpedoes. His only defense was to blast them while they were still a safe distance away. It took time to target the barrage of twelve torpedoes. If he traveled at higher speeds, he would have less time to react.

"Chirality."

"Yes, Commander."

"How close can the Alpha One approach an exploding torpedo without receiving damage?"

"Recommended safe distance is one hundred miles for ML and MT class ships. There is no information for Alpha class ships."

Arminius continued to study the battlefield hologram. The wedged shape piston was now 7,900 miles above Home World and was continuing its slow journey toward him. Three MT ships from the outer cylinder wall moved behind the three inner wall ships that had fired upon him, providing reinforcement. Other ships from the outer wall shifted to plug the newly created outer wall hole. If he tried to break out of the cylinder, he would no doubt be met with a barrage from those ships as well. He had been able to take out the recent salvo because he had time due to the distance from where they were fired. If he were closer to the ships, there would be less time and more torpedoes. With six ships firing four torpedoes per round at him, and then reloading and firing again, the risk of a torpedo evading destruction by the Alpha One laser defense system and inflicting serious damage to the ship was too great.

"Reverse course, one hundred percent power."

Arminius attempted to exit the cylinder on the opposite side. Another volley of a dozen torpedoes was sent to greet him. The torpedoes came into laser range when the Alpha One was still one thousand miles from the inner wall of battleships. Arminius opened fire on the torpedoes and picked them off one- by-one. The last torpedo was destroyed when it was two hundred miles away and the Alpha One shook when the torpedo exploded. He had been traveling faster, so there was less time to react to the threat. This escape plan was not working - it was time for a new plan.

The Alpha One banked sharply and headed up toward the wedge of ships that were now at the 7,800-mile elevation. When he was six hundred miles away, he reduced speed. As soon as the squadron at the front of the wedge was within five hundred miles, he opened fire on the lead ship. The ships continued to slowly move toward him. Ten seconds later, he expected the lead ship to be destroyed, but it continued on its path. After twenty seconds, the ship was still moving toward him. The wedge shifted and another ship in the squadron moved in front to intercept the Alpha One's laser. It took the hit for twenty seconds before the third ship in the squadron moved in to intercept the beam. After taking a direct hit for twenty seconds, the third ship was still intact and the wedge was now just four hundred and ten miles away.

"Cease fire!" ordered Arminius as he turned the ship away from the wedge and toward the planet. "Chirality, check laser diagnostics... is there a problem?"

"No alarms sir," came the almost immediate reply.

"Scan the last two targets. Why weren't they destroyed?"

"Scanning complete. Targets have reinforced armor. Reinforced armor requires a thirty second connect time for destruction."

"Scan highlighted ships," ordered Arminius, as he highlighted all of the ships inside the cylinder on the battlefield hologram. "How many have reinforced armor?"

"All of them, sir"

Arminius looked at the battlefield hologram – he was now seven thousand miles above Home World and the wedge was at seven thousand five hundred miles. Blocking out everything around him, he focused his total attention on the battlefield hologram and studied it intensely. The wedge filled only about one third of the space in the middle of the cylinder. Maybe, he thought, he could slip between the wedge and the walls of the cylinder.

"Engines at one hundred percent!" Arminius took the controls and headed diagonally up and toward the cylinder wall on his left. There was a momentary pause, and then the wedge started shifting to his left. As he came within one thousand miles of the MT ships along the inner wall, he was greeted with another dozen torpedoes. Arminius picked them off one-by-one as he made a sharp turn upward so that he stayed just over one thousand miles from the MT ships that formed the inner wall. The torpedoes stopped and he continued his upward path. The MLA ships in the wedge continued to shift from their central position toward the Alpha One's side of the cylinder. The ships in the squadron at the front of the wedge intercepted him and opened fire when he was four hundred miles away. Arminius initiated evasive maneuvers and then reversed direction. Staying just outside of their four-hundred-mile laser range, the Alpha One swung to the far-right side of the cylinder. Once again, the ships along the inner cylinder wall greeted him with a dozen torpedoes when he was one thousand miles away, but stopped firing when he made a sharp turn upward maintaining a distance of just over one thousand miles from their positions. Arminius picked off the torpedoes as he rapidly ascended the right side of the cylinder. He felt confident at first about his escape prospects as he passed the first few ships of the wedge that were now hastily trying to move from the left side of the cylinder toward him, but then he felt the fear of a cornered animal as the MLA ships in the squadrons further back of the wedge moved into an intercept position. The squadron at the front of the wedge that he had passed was now starting to move into a position behind him that would cut off his escape route toward Home World. Ships from the outer wall of the cylinder were moving closer to reinforce the inner wall of the cylinder. If he continued on this course, he would be trapped.

"Kill the engines!" The engines stopped. Arminius flipped the ship so that it now faced Home World. "Engines at one hundred ten percent!"

"That is a violation of engine protocol," stated Chirality unemotionally.

"Emergency override code number 979 Zeta!" shouted Arminius.

The engines suddenly came to life and there was a jolt as the ship shot toward Home World. The maneuver enabled the Alpha One to escape the ships in the main body of the wedge, but the three ships at the front of the wedge were at four hundred and twenty miles and closing fast. Arminius steered the Alpha One to his left and got as close as possible to the imaginary line one thousand miles from the inner cylinder wall. Another dozen torpedoes were sent as a reminder to not venture outside the cylinder. Arminius picked them off, but the ships at the front of the wedge were now only four hundred miles away and they began firing. The Alpha One jolted as it was hit. Arminius initiated evasive maneuvers, which bought him a few seconds before the ships locked on to him again and the attack resumed. This time Arminius did a reverse bank maneuver that enabled the Alpha One to continue to head toward Home World but with a different trajectory. The three ships did a similar maneuver, but were not as nimble, so the Alpha One was momentarily outside of their four-hundred-mile range. The drawback of the Alpha One's maneuver is that it enabled a second wave of ships, Squadron #3, to get into range and now they opened fire. Once again, Arminius did a reverse bank maneuver that spiraled away from the Squadron #3 ships, but took him closer to the Squadron #1 ships at the front of the wedge. He was four hundred and five miles away when he opened fire on the Squadron #1 center ship. Fifteen seconds later, all three Squadron #1 ships were four hundred miles away and returned laser fire, but then confusion ensued. It was time for the Squadron #1 ships to swap positions to intercept blasts from the Alpha One laser. When the intercepting ship moved into position, the laser from the center ship was still firing. The intercepting ship was caught in a crossfire between the Alpha One and the center ship. The shielding on the intercepting ship was designed to withstand a laser attack from a single ship, not two ships. Before the laser from the center ship could be turned off, the intercepting ship was destroyed. The center ship was still hot from the attack as there had been insufficient time to cool. Arminius retargeted the center ship as the third ship of Squadron #1 desperately tried to intervene. It was too late, and twenty seconds later, the center ship was destroyed. The third ship was now in the open with no ships nearby to deflect the Alpha One laser. The nearest ships, in Squadron #3, were four hundred and twenty miles away and the third ship frantically raced toward them for protection, but to no avail. Thirty seconds later it was destroyed.

▲ ▲ ▲

"Stick to the plan!" screamed B2. Major Tom had never seen him so livid. "Slow and steady and we have him trapped," pleaded B2. "Operate as a team! No individual heroics!"

B2 needs to get over it, thought Major Tom. He is no doubt upset that his battle plan got people killed. Then Major Tom reflected on today's losses – that makes nineteen ships lost on his watch. It was the worst military defeat in the history of the Home World Empire. Hopefully there would be no more losses.

Major Tom surveyed the positioning of his ships on the gigantic hologram stage at the front of the Command Center. Squadron #2 was now in the point position at the front of the wedge. Squadron #8 moved from the middle of the back row to fill Squadron #2's position. The MT ships forming the double-walled cylinder were all in their positions. It was unfortunate that they had lost three more ships, but the plan was working. The losses today were heavy, but there would soon be consolation, especially if they could capture the Alpha One. He had never seen a ship with such awesome capabilities.

"C, open a link to the Alpha One." The link was quickly established.

"Alpha One, this is Major Tom at Strategic Command. You are trapped there is no escape. Power down and surrender immediately or be destroyed."

There was no response.

▲ ▲ ▲

The Alpha One raced toward Home World. When he was three thousand miles away from the planet, Arminius reduced the ship's speed to fifty percent and reassessed the situation. He was trapped inside a double-walled cylinder that extended to within fifteen hundred miles of Home World. At one end of the cylinder, currently one thousand miles away, a phalanx of twenty-seven armored laser ships was steadily approaching. At the other end of the cylinder was the powerful land-based Quadrant 1300 laser. The skies were clear, so the death ray would have its full two thousand miles range. He had tried unsuccessfully to escape the sides of the cylinder, he had tried unsuccessfully to directly attack the ships inside the cylinder, and he had tried unsuccessfully to slip around the ships inside the cylinder. He had been able to destroy three ships inside the cylinder, but that was primarily due to their mistakes, which very likely would not be repeated.

There has got to be a way out, there has got to be a way out! Inside his head he was screaming. I am the greatest and I am flying the most powerful military spaceship ever created! I will find a way out! The thoughts replayed in a loop in Arminius's mind as he evaluated his options. He was caught, caught like a fish in a net, a really, really big net. Surrender was never an option. How could he escape? There had to be a weak spot, there had to be a hole somewhere.

"One hundred percent power," he said calmly as he took the controls and headed directly toward Home World.

▲ ▲ ▲

Major Tom stared at the immense holograph battlefield stage at the front of the Command Center auditorium. The Alpha One was heading toward Home World near the edge of the net. Every so often, it would attempt to break out the sides of the net. Each attempt was met with a barrage of a dozen torpedoes. When the Alpha One reached the two-thousand-mile elevation, it ceased its vertical descent and pursued a horizontal path as it probed the boundaries of the net while maintaining a distance of two thousand miles above the planet's surface. The lead ships in the wedge were now three thousand nine hundred miles above Home World and descending at a steady pace. It will not be long now he thought. He called the Alpha One again.

"Commander Percival, power down. There is no escape."

▲ ▲ ▲

Arminius opened fire. The ten-second pulsating laser blast toward the Quadrant 1300 land-based laser was like a condemned prisoner spitting in the direction of a firing squad. The laser may have heated up the air, but at that distance, it could do no harm to the powerful laser aimed at him from below.

Torpedoes exploded along the edge of the path to the gallows as Arminius continued his methodical probing at the two-thousand-mile elevation. He looked at his battlefield hologram to check the position of his pursuers. "Chirality, calculate distance to nearest attacking ship and announce distance every thirty seconds".

"Sixteen hundred and forty-three miles," came the immediate response.

Arminius headed closer to Home World.

▲ ▲ ▲

"TARGET AT NINETEEN HUNDRED AND FIFTY MILES," announced the male voice of the automatic messaging system in the Battlefield Strategic Command Center. B2 had programmed the automatic messaging system to provide verbal warnings that were heard throughout the Command Center when the Alpha One was within the two-thousand-mile laser range.

"Should I open fire?" asked L.

"Not yet," replied Major Tom, "Wait for my command. C, open a communications channel to the Alpha One."

By now Major Tom realized that his chances for recovery of the Alpha One were practically nil, but he did not want any future bureaucratic auditor criticizing him for not giving the ship ample opportunity to surrender. "Alpha One, this is your third and final warning. Power down and surrender or be destroyed." The Alpha One opened fire at the Quadrant 1300 laser, this time with a pulsating laser blast for twenty seconds.

A final act of defiance thought Major Tom. He cannot do any harm at that elevation.

The Alpha One suddenly turned and headed directly toward the planet.

"TARGET AT NINETEEN HUNDRED MILES"

"Open fire," Major Tom calmly ordered.

▲ ▲ ▲

Arminius had anticipated the blast from the Quadrant 1300 laser and quickly executed evasive maneuvers. Before the laser could reconnect, the Alpha One reached safety at the two-thousand-mile elevation.

The ship's computer announced the distance to the closest attacking ship in the phalanx, "Twelve hundred and eighty-nine miles."

Arminius banked hard and headed toward the edge of the cylinder. His battlefield screen lit up as the ships in the area fired a dozen torpedoes. Arminius took them out one-by-one, then turned toward Home World and opened fire.

▲ ▲ ▲

"TARGET AT NINETEEN HUNDRED FIFTY MILES"

Major Tom and everyone in the Command Center were trying to figure out what the Alpha One was doing, "B2," asked Major Tom, "does he have a target?"

"Pulsating lasers are being fired in a circle around the Quadrant 1300 laser canon, sir, but even if he had the range, he would miss the laser canon by twenty miles."

"TARGET AT NINETEEN HUNDRED MILES"

The Alpha One continued its downward descent with its laser firing.

"TARGET AT EIGHTEEN HUNDRED FIFTY MILES"

"Begin firing," Major Tom again calmly ordered.

The Alpha One conducted evasive maneuvers as it ascended. The blast from the Quadrant 1300 laser reconnected at nineteen hundred and eighty miles, but there was not enough time to inflict damage before the Alpha One reached relative safety at the two-thousand-mile elevation.

▲ ▲ ▲

"Nine hundred eighty-seven miles," announced Chirality. The descending ships were closer, but he was still well outside of their laser range. Arminius again probed the walls of his invisible prison and was met with a barrage of a dozen torpedoes. He picked them off one by one before resuming his attack on the planet.

▲ ▲ ▲

"TARGET AT NINETEEN HUNDRED FIFTY MILES," echoed through the auditorium

The battlefield stage showed that the Alpha One's laser was firing.

"Same imaginary target," stated B2, "Twenty-mile radius around the laser canon. Obviously, no damage."

"TARGET AT NINETEEN HUNDRED MILES"

The Alpha One was continuing to fire.

"TARGET AT EIGHTEEN HUNDRED FIFTY MILES"

The Alpha One continued its assault. Major Tom decided to wait a little longer this time. Let's see what he does he thought.

"TARGET AT EIGHTEEN HUNDRED MILES"

"Open fire," commanded Major Tom.

As expected, the Alpha One conducted evasive maneuvers. The Quadrant 1300 laser canon reconnected at nineteen hundred and thirty miles. A laser beam connection timer suddenly appeared on one of the auxiliary screens in front of the immense holographic battlefield stage. The seconds ticked...5,6,7,8. The clock stopped as the Alpha One climbed to two thousand miles.

▲ ▲ ▲

"Six hundred eighty-four miles," announced Chirality.

Once again Arminius frantically attempted to escape out the sides of his enclosure. He made three probing attempts as he flew in a descending circular pattern – two thousand miles, nineteen hundred and fifty miles, and nineteen hundred miles. Each attempt was met with a barrage of a dozen torpedoes that were picked off one by one. After the escape attempts, Arminius resumed his laser attack on the planet.

▲ ▲ ▲

He is playing with fire and we will soon get burned thought Major Tom.

"TARGET AT NINETEEN HUNDRED MILES," announced the automatic messaging system.

Shortly thereafter came, "TARGET AT EIGHTEEN HUNDRED FIFTY MILES."

"He is still aiming around the Quadrant 1300 laser cannon," observed B2.

"TARGET AT EIGHTEEN HUNDRED MILES"

It is hopeless for him, thought Major Tom. The net extends to fifteen hundred miles. A pang of sadness flashed across his mind. Arminius and the Alpha One had put up an admirable fight and it was a shame that they had to be destroyed. The sympathetic thoughts quickly abated and Major Tom's killer instinct returned. This enemy was good, but he was so much better. There would be no mercy.

"TARGET AT SEVENTEEN HUNDRED FIFTY MILES"

"Fire!" This time there was excitement in Major Tom's voice as he gave the order.

The Alpha One continued to fire as it initiated evasive maneuvers and temporarily escaped the death ray. At eighteen hundred and eighty miles the Quadrant 1300 laser reconnected and the connection clock came to life on the battlefield stage. The seconds ticked off at an excruciating slow pace…6, 7, 8, 9…

And then there were not one, but two explosions.

▲ ▲ ▲

"Launch Cubs D and H," ordered Arminius when the Quadrant 1300 laser began firing. Arminius returned fire and initiated evasive maneuvers as he ascended. A few seconds later, the Cubs intercepted the blasts from the Home World laser and were destroyed. The Quadrant 1300 laser again found its target, but the Alpha One had continued its rapid ascent and was safely beyond the two-thousand-mile range before any serious damage could be inflicted.

▲ ▲ ▲

"That is the last of his Cubs," reported B2 with satisfaction.

It will not be long now thought Major Tom. "Will the Cub debris interfere with the laser?"

"Only minimally," assured B2. "The Cubs provide minimal interference at this elevation. The earlier Cubs exploded at about five-hundred-mile elevation. Since they were closer to the laser source, there was a greater area behind them that was shielded. The diamond transport container was destroyed at a higher elevation, but it was a much larger vessel and the reflective index of diamonds is considerably higher than that of the Cub debris. At most, it will take just a few seconds longer for the Quadrant 1300 laser to take him out."

▲ ▲ ▲

"Four hundred and ninety-seven miles," announced Chirality.

Once again Arminius tried to escape out the sides of the net, making attempts at two thousand, nineteen hundred and fifty, and nineteen hundred miles as he made a slow spiraling descent. Each attempt was met with a barrage of twelve torpedoes that were picked off one-by-one. Arminius resumed his attack on the planet with his pulsating laser firing a circular pattern.

"Four hundred and twenty-seven miles," reported Chirality. The Alpha One would soon be in range of the Home World ships that were part of the steadily descending piston.

Arminius took the Alpha One down to eighteen hundred and fifty miles and tried to escape out the sides of the net. Once again, the attempt was met by a salvo of torpedoes.

"Four hundred and eleven miles," announced Chirality

Arminius resumed his attack on Home World as he continued his slow descent.

▲ ▲ ▲

Major Tom decided to hold off a little longer this time to compensate for the Cub debris. The battlefield hologram stage showed that the Alpha One was trying to escape the net at the eighteen-hundred-mile mark, but to no avail. The MT ships in the area fired another barrage of torpedoes. The first of the armored MLA ships would soon be in laser range. The Alpha One was caught in a vise and there was no escape.

▲ ▲ ▲

"Three hundred and ninety-nine miles," announced Chirality.

All three ships from Squadron #2 opened fire. The remaining twenty-four ships in the wedge would soon be in range.

Arminius took evasive maneuvers and headed toward Home World to escape their fire.

"Four hundred and two miles," reported Chirality. The Squadron #2 laser fire ceased.

Arminius checked his elevation – seventeen hundred and seventy miles. He again headed toward the side of the net and was again met by exploding torpedoes. He then flew around the circumference of the net, trying probing escape attempts, each of which was met by more torpedoes. When it was not destroying torpedoes, the Alpha One laser fired pulsating blasts in a circular motion toward the Quadrant 1300 laser canon. Arminius had been able to keep sufficient distance from the Squadron #2 ships, but now the six MLA ships from Squadron #3 and Squadron #8 were in range. He was sandwiched between nine attacking ships four hundred miles above him and a giant laser below.

"Engines at one hundred twenty percent" he ordered, "Override code number 979 Zeta." There was no reason to wait for the computer to request the code. Even in times of emergency, procedures had to be followed. With a burst of speed, Arminius was able to escape the Squadron #3 and Squadron #8 ships as he continued to probe the circumference of the net at seventeen hundred and seventy miles. Each attempt was met by exploding torpedoes. Squadrons #4, #5, and #6 were now in range and joined, the chase, bringing the number of MLA attacking ships to eighteen.

▲ ▲ ▲

"We need to collapse the net at elevations above three thousand miles," suggested B2.

It was a good move from B2 – there was no need to have ships that far from the action. "Make it so," agreed Major Tom, "Any other recommendations?"

"Attack with Squadrons #2, #3, and #8. Let's pull back Squadrons #4, #5, and #6, and put them in a standard blocking formation in the center of the net at two thousand miles. Squadrons #7, #9, and #10 should take positions at 2,000 miles as well that are equidistant from the center to cut off any by-pass attempts. Ships away from the action are to reposition to reinforce the net."

"Do it!" ordered Major Tom. There was going to be no retreat for the Alpha One from the killing zone.

▲ ▲ ▲

Arminius checked the ship's battlefield hologram. Eighteen MLAs were now positioned at the two-thousand-mile elevation and a large number of ships were streaming in behind them for back-up. The upward escape route was totally blocked. It would have been nice if the Home World ships had become overcome with bloodlust in their pursuit and inadvertently made an error that allowed his escape out the upper end of the net, but this was not going to happen. Arminius maneuvered the Alpha One so that it was equidistant from Squadrons #2, #3, and #8 and slowed his pace. At four hundred miles, the nine ships from the three squadrons opened fire. The Alpha One fired its laser, but in the opposite direction - toward the Quadrant 1300 laser canon. After a few seconds of contact time, Arminius accelerated, taking the Alpha One outside the range of the attacking battleships. He then slowed until he was within four hundred miles of the attacking ships and they opened fire again.

▲ ▲ ▲

"TARGET AT SEVENTEEN HUNDRED FIFTY MILES"

"What the hell is he doing?" contemplated Major Tom under his breath. "Does he want to go out in a blaze of glory?"

Major Tom checked the positions on the giant hologram stage. Even if the Quadrant 1300 laser missed and hit one of the MLAs it should not matter. It would take thirty seconds to destroy an MLA and surely it would take evasive maneuvers to escape any inadvertent fire. Suddenly the Alpha One banked sharply and plunged toward Home World. "Quadrant 1300 fire!" It was time for all of this to end.

All eyes were fixed on the enormous hologram at the front of the Command Center. Evasive maneuvers were expected, but none occurred. The Alpha One pulled out of the dive and began a spiral maneuver as it slowly headed downward toward the planet. It was not an intricate maneuver, so the Quadrant 1300 laser canon was able to maintain contact. The Alpha One laser continued to return fire.

"TARGET AT SEVENTEEN HUNDRED MILES"

The pursuing ships from Squadrons #2, #3, and #8 were three hundred and ninety miles away from the Alpha One and were firing.

In a corner of the battlefield stage, the laser connection clock slowly ticked the seconds… 8, 9, 10, 11, 12

Suddenly, the Alpha One executed evasive maneuvers. Instead of running away from the planet, it leveled off and maintained its current altitude. The maneuvers broke the connection with the Quadrant 1300 laser and easily escaped the attacking ships. The Alpha One then resumed its spiral descent.

"TARGET AT SIXTEEN HUNDRED AND FIFTY MILES"

The land-based laser soon relocated its target. The connection clock reappeared on the battlefield stage and again slowly counted the seconds…3, 4, 5. Shortly thereafter, the nine MLAs caught up with the Alpha One and resumed their laser attack. Instead of running, the Alpha One continued its spiral descent while continuing to fire its pulsating laser in a circular pattern toward the planet below. The attacking ships were in and out of range as they followed in pursuit.

The Quadrant 1300 laser however, maintained its lock, and the connection clock continued to mark the time ...11, 12, 13, 14, 15, 16...

"TARGET AT SIXTEEN HUNDRED MILES"

The Alpha One slammed on its brakes, did a reverse double sidewinder roll, and accelerated to one hundred and twenty percent speed. The unusual maneuver enabled the Alpha One to temporarily escape from both the attacking ships and the Quadrant 1300 laser. However, the land-based laser once again found its target and the connection clock restarted...4, 5, 6...

"Sorry about that sir," apologized L. That last maneuver was not in our database. Only the Alpha One can fly like that. If it tries that move again or anything like it, we now have the appropriate response programmed."

The nine attacking battleships were again in range with their lasers blazing.

"TARGET AT FIFTEEN HUNDRED AND FIFTY MILES"

Major Tom was getting nervous. This is cutting things a little too close. The connection clock continued its excruciating slow count ...14, 15, 16.....

"Why the hell is he still in the air?" shouted Major Tom to the battlefield hologram stage.

Suddenly the Alpha One changed course and headed diagonally downward. The maneuver escaped the attacking ships, but not the land-based laser. The connection clock continued to tick...17, 18, 19, 20....

"He's trying to escape! Damn it! Cut him off!" screamed Major Tom.

The MLA ships inside the net moved to intercept, but they were way too slow.

"TARGET AT FIFTEEN HUNDRED MILES"

The MTs at the bottom of the net fired barrages of torpedoes, but they were out of range - the Alpha One avoided the edges of the net during its downward plunge.

The connection clock continued...27, 28, 29, 30...

"All ships, get him!" screamed Major Tom. Ships outside the net moved into intercept positions.

"TARGET AT FOURTEEN HUNDRED AND FIFTY MILES"

The clock continued...35, 36, 37...

The Alpha One continued its downward trajectory at one hundred and twenty percent power with its pulsating laser firing as the laser connection clock counted...42, 43, 44...

"TARGET AT FOURTEEN HUNDRED MILES"

The Alpha One shot out of the imaginary cylinder thirteen-hundred-and-sixty-miles above the planet, banked sharply, and began a rapid ascent diagonally away from the ships that made up the cylinder.

The Quadrant 1300 laser was still hitting its target and the clock continued 48, 49, 50...

The Alpha One maintained its rapid ascent and the connection clock kept going 60, 61, 62...

At seventy-four seconds the connection clock ceased - the Alpha One was two thousand miles above Home World and was speeding away.

MT-342 was the first of the ships outside the net to encounter the Alpha One and fired four torpedoes. The Alpha One quickly destroyed the torpedoes and headed directly toward the MT-342. When it was four hundred and eighty miles away, the MT-342 received a ten second blast and disintegrated.

ML-417 and ML-418, sister ships, were the next to intercept. The Alpha One took them out before they were within range to fire their lasers.

Six ships were next – MT-359, MT-371, MT-402, ML-433, ML-464, and ML-480. They were able to block the Alpha One escape route. The Alpha One did a sharp reverse roll and started to return diagonally towards the net. Then the Alpha One performed a second reverse roll and headed towards the six ships from a different angle. They were picked off one-by-one and the torpedoes fired by the MT's were easily destroyed.

Chaos had returned. The ships were unorganized. It was a rout. These were the situations in which massive losses occur. It was time for a retreat. "Cease the attack!" ordered Major Tom. "Move to the strategic repositioning points which you will soon be receiving."

▲ ▲ ▲

The Alpha One had escaped the net and destroyed even more of the Home World battleships. The death toll was now up to twenty-eight ships, not counting personnel.

"How the hell did he do that?" Major Tom was livid as he yelled into his console. "L, I want a full diagnostic report on the Quadrant 1300 laser ASAP! B2, we need a new plan!"

A very nervous L appeared in the center screen on Major Tom's console, "Sir, preliminary diagnostics show that the Quadrant 1300 laser is in good working order. No signs of any operational problems."

A few minutes later, the research leader's face appeared in the center screen. "Sir, I think you should see this." R's face disappeared and was replaced with a view of Home World. "Here is a shot of Home World taken about an hour ago from Luna 1. Now we are going to zoom in to Quadrant 1300. Note the clear skies and the time stamp. Watch as we fast forward the view during the past hour." Bursts of light flashed on and off the screen and haze gradually appeared. More bursts of light and more haze and then darker clouds filled the skies as the video ended. "It was the battle, sir. The laser blasts from the Alpha One, the Quadrant 1300 laser, and the MLAs along with the torpedoes from the MTs changed the weather pattern. The haze and then clouds severely limited the effective range of the Quadrant 1300 laser."

B2 appeared on the center screen of Major Tom's console. "Sir, we had no knowledge that the lasers and torpedoes would cause such a severe atmospheric disturbance. We knew that there are minor atmospheric effects from firing lasers, but there has never been a prolonged event with so much firepower in a concentrated area. I will write a full report and enter it into the Strategic Archives."

Major Tom wanted to storm out of the Command Center and go somewhere - anywhere that was far, far away. He had done his job, he had executed an excellent plan, but somehow it had failed and the Alpha One had escaped. Life was not fair. After a brief moment of self-pity, he pulled himself together. He was a professional. He was a leader. He was the best battlefield strategic commander ever and people were looking to him for leadership. He addressed his team, "Okay everyone, the mission has not changed. We need to capture or destroy the Alpha One. Where is it going and what are we going to do next?"

CHAPTER 15

PLUGARIA

The Alpha One triumphantly sped away from the battlefield above Home World. After regrouping, the entire Home World military fleet, four hundred and eighty-four battleships, gave chase. Being the fastest ship, the Alpha One gradually pulled away. When the Alpha One was sufficiently far ahead, Arminius reduced the ship's speed to eighty percent of capacity, so that it would match the top speed of the fleet. Arminius did not want to lose the fleet, but he wanted to keep it a comfortable distance away.

The Binary Star System contained two medium sized stars – Astar and Bstar. There was once a third star – Cstar, but it had become a dwarf many eons ago. Strange things had been observed near Cstar and the region it was in was designated 'The Forbidden Zone'. Many expeditions there never returned.

Eight planets, four of which could support life, surrounded Bstar. Home World, or B-4, was the fourth planet from Bstar. Ten planets, five of which could support life, surrounded Astar. Plugaria, or A-5, was the fifth planet from Astar.

At the end of the Great War, the area between the orbit of the tenth planet of Astar and the orbit of the eighth planet of Bstar was deemed to be the Demilitarized Zone. No military ships from either empire were allowed to enter the zone without permission from the other side. Freighter ships, of course, were allowed to pass through all the time since trade between the empires was abundant.

The Alpha One was now passing the orbit of B-7, the seventh planet of Bstar. At its current speed it would be entering the Demilitarized Zone in twelve hours. One hour behind the Alpha One was the entire Home World military fleet.

▲ ▲ ▲

The movement of the large Home World military fleet toward the Demilitarized Zone had not gone unnoticed on Plugaria. An emergency Plugarian Defense Council meeting was hastily convened in the private banquet room at the Emperor's Palace.

The Plugarians had rich traditions that were followed, even during times of crisis. The palace butlers quickly dressed the emperor and an entourage was hurriedly assembled. At the sound of the ancient gong, the doors to the private residence opened and Emperor Beratte Simpson emerged dressed in traditional purple and gold vestments trailed by a matching long flowing cape. Wearing a purple and gold crown covered with exotic jewels and carrying a shiny golden scepter, he walked in a majestic manner as he led his entourage through the two-hundred-foot-long Hall of the Emperors. The great hall was filled with elegant mirrors and dazzling chandeliers and the ceiling was covered with paintings depicting prodigious moments in Plugarian history. Marble stands along the walls displayed the busts of famous Plugarians and it was considered a great honor, after one died, to be remembered in such a manner. Emperor Beratte Simpson was in his seventies, medium height, totally bald, and had a gray chin puff beard. He was rather plump from eating the royal food, but the Royal Tailors did a good job of hiding this. When he reached the far side of the long hall, a second gong was rung and the door to the private banquet room opened.

The private banquet room was forty feet wide, sixty feet long, and had a twenty-foot-high ceiling. The walls were covered with tranquil scenes of life showing colorful birds and flowering plants. In the center of the room sat a large conference table that had been handcrafted from antique teak. Standing at attention were the ten highest ranking officials in the Plugarian Empire – five military leaders dressed in the red and purple military uniform and five government leaders dressed in the gold and black government uniform. The emperor slowly walked to the middle of the conference table and stood behind his chair. The ornately carved high-backed wooden chair with purple and gold cushions had been the seat of power for generations. The royal butler took the emperor's cape and hung it on the wall behind the chair. The military and governmental leaders ceremoniously walked to their assigned chairs and stood. The conference table had twelve chairs – five for military leaders, five for governmental leaders, one for the emperor, and one empty chair opposite the emperor. The empty chair represented those in the past that had made Plugaria great. Even though they were no longer physically alive, they continued to have a spiritual presence and would be called upon to assist Plugaria during times of crisis.

The emperor laid the golden scepter on the table and, with the assistance of the royal butler, took his seat in the royal chair. The others then took their seats. All of the servants, with the exception of the royal butler left the room and the door was closed.

General Visgoth sat on the left side of the table with the other military leaders. His chair was at the end of the table signifying that he was the highest ranking of the military leaders. He was a tall, slender, stern-looking man in his late fifties with thinning dark hair that was starting to gray. He too had a chin puff beard. He rose and addressed the emperor, "Welcome your Highness. We are greatly honored by your presence."

The emperor nodded.

General Visgoth continued, "The Worldians have developed a new super weapon - The Alpha One battleship. It is heading directly toward us and will reach the Demilitarized Zone in about twelve hours. It is being followed by four hundred and eighty-four Worldian battleships, which is their entire military fleet. The Worldian fleet is about one hour behind the Alpha One." He paused a moment and then continued, "The Alpha One is an upgrade of the Worldian ML class ships which are similar to our PL class ships. It has a single weapon – a very powerful laser, and it is a very fast ship. We knew the Worldians were developing a more advanced ship, but until its commissioning runs were completed last week, we did not know the extent of its advanced capabilities."

General Visgoth operated the conference room control system and the tranquil scenes of life on the wall opposite the emperor were replaced with a floor-to-ceiling three-dimensional video screen extending the entire length of the conference table. Videos from the commissioning trials of the Alpha One appeared showing intricate maneuvers and the rapid destruction of multiple targets.

General Visgoth resumed the presentation. "The Alpha One engineers have greatly improved their existing battleship technology. The Alpha One has a single laser with a range of five hundred miles, which is about twenty-five percent greater than the rest of the Home World fleet, or anything we have. It can operate at speeds twenty-five percent faster than their previous warships and has a superior guidance system for intricate maneuvers."

"So, it can destroy our ships from beyond the range of our weapons and escape?" surmised the emperor.

"That is correct your Highness." General Visgoth was momentarily surprised at how quickly the emperor had grasped the key military concepts.

"Is this an invasion?"

"At this time, we do not know your Highness. The Worldians are currently in their territory. It is possible that it could be some kind of war game exercise."

"Don't they usually announce war game exercises?" asked the emperor.

"Yes, they do, your Highness. There has been no announcement."

"And does their entire fleet usually participate?" Due to the presence of the emperor, no one else in the room was asking questions.

"No, your Highness. In the past, only about one third of their fleet participated in these events."

The emperor turned to his right and addressed his intelligence chief, "What are you hearing?" The intelligence leader was in his fifties, had thinning dark hair, a salt and pepper goatee, and wore gold wire rim glasses with circular lenses.

The intelligence chief paused, "We have heard no rumors of an invasion, your Highness. An unusual event occurred nine days ago – something happened and twenty-eight Worldian battleships were destroyed along with a freight car of diamonds. The news broadcast blamed us for the loss."

"A possible pretense for an invasion?"

"Possibly your Highness. In addition, there is chatter that the Alpha One might contain a Thulien bomb."

"What is a Thulien bomb?"

"Ever since the Great War your Highness, the Worldians have had top secret projects to develop a super bomb – capable of destroying an entire planet. Usually, the projects are just political kickbacks, but it is possible that this time they may have actually developed such a weapon."

"How close to a planet would the bomb need to be to cause destruction?" The emperor was concerned but did not let it show.

"There is no way of knowing your Highness. There have been no known tests of the bomb and we do not know if it even exists."

"Is Plugaria safe from the Alpha One?" The emperor was now addressing General Visgoth.

"Yes, your Highness," assured the General. "In its commissioning trials the Alpha One showed that it has a laser range of five hundred miles. Our land-based lasers have a range of two thousand miles."

"What is our plan?"

"Your Highness, Strategic Response is currently developing a plan. The honorable Benoki Galata is the leader."

▲   ▲   ▲

"Put it on the battlefield hologram," Benoki Galata instructed her second-in-command. As she was waiting for the hologram to load, she indiscreetly checked him out and liked what she saw - now that was something she would really love to attack. Short, thin, plain and in her late twenties, Benoki never got the attention received by the more glamorous women in the Defense Ministry. Those other women, however, did not possess her skills. She was a strategic expert well versed on both the arts of attack and defense. She had excelled at the war game simulations and was rewarded with the post of Strategic Response Commander for the entire Plugarian military fleet. Men were stupid. They thought a curvaceous glamorous woman could entertain them in bed. What they did not realize was that she knew how to attack and would be so much better. A good attacker uses the assets they have been given and probes for vulnerabilities – and oh how she would like to have a probing session with her cute second-in-command. Alas, it would never happen. She was a professional and there were strict protocols against that type of fraternization.

Her conquest thoughts faded as a large battlefield hologram suddenly appeared in the middle of the Strategic Response Command Center located deep beneath the Plugarian Defense Ministry complex. The display showed an armada of Home World ships racing toward the Demilitarized Zone. As the Plugarian Strategic Response commander, she found this deeply disturbing. She had now been the leader of Strategic Response for two years. She had never been tested in a real battle, but then there had not been a war in the past sixty years. Benoki looked over at her second-in-command located in the adjacent workstation, blocked out her personal thoughts of lustful conquest, and asked, "How many Worldian ships?"

"Four hundred and eighty-five, sir."

Benoki still could not get used to being called sir, especially by a guy her own age. "Which one is the Alpha One, the super ship?"

"I'll mark it red. It is leading the expedition."

"Is there anything else I should know?"

"Yes," reported Number Two matter-of-factly. "The Alpha One may or may not be carrying a bomb that can blow up an entire planet."

Benoki sighed. She liked challenges but this was ridiculous. She had five hundred and twelve battleships, as per the treaty with the Worldians. She had polished her tactical skills with countless war game simulations, but nothing like this. How does one fight a more powerful opponent? "Scramble seventy-two ships immediately," she ordered, "All other ships prepare to launch on one hour's notice."

▲ ▲ ▲

Emperor Beratte Simpson continued with his questions, "So why are the Worldians sending the other four hundred and eighty-four ships and why are they trailing behind?"

"It is unclear," General Visgoth postulated. "There are currently three possibilities being discussed. The first is that the Alpha One is the initial wave of an attack and the remaining ships are for mop-up operations. The second possibility is that they are planning to blockade our planets and control the lucrative trade routes. The third possibility is that they contain landing parties to invade our outer planets."

The discussion was interrupted by a high priority call from the Plugarian Communications Chief. "Your Highness, Chancellor Thager would like to talk to you."

▲ ▲ ▲

C patched the call through in accordance with governmental protocol - Code 999 call from Home World Chancellor Simeon Thager to his Excellency Plugarian Emperor Beratte Simpson. Holographic images of the leaders appeared in both conference rooms – Chancellor Thager was in the command center VIP Conference Room located beneath the Obelisk on Home World.

"Greetings, Chancellor Thager. I am deeply honored to speak with you. To what do I owe this great pleasure?"

"Most gracious Emperor Simpson, the honor is entirely mine. I hope all is well with your family."

"They are very well Chancellor, thank you for asking about my family. Was there another reason for your call?"

"Your Highness, there is a matter, very trivial, to which I humbly request your assistance."

"Your graciousness, how may I be honored to offer assistance?"

"It seems, your Highness, that a deranged young man has stolen one of our military ships."

"That indeed is a cause for concern. I take it that you will find this young man and punish him severely."

"Of course, your Highness, but the deranged young man appears to be traveling toward your empire."

"So, you would like me to return him to you?"

"Yes, your Highness, and if it would not be too troubling, also his ship."

"Of course, we are always willing to help our good friends. There may be some costs involved. I take it that is not a problem?"

"Of course not, your Highness, reasonable costs we are more than willing to pay."

"Chancellor, are there any special precautions that we need to take in order to apprehend this young man. There is a rumor I am hearing that his ship may be carrying a Thulien bomb – a bomb that could destroy an entire planet."

"Your Highness, I have no idea to what you refer. I can assure you that we have no desire to harm our good friends."

"Chancellor, I am also hearing about a recent news broadcast on Home World. I believe it said that a Plugarian battleship destroyed many Worldian battleships along with a freight car of diamonds. My good friend, I find this hard to believe seeing as how we know the location of all Plugarian military ships and they are all located well within our boundaries as per our established treaty."

"A miscommunication no doubt, your highness. We have trouble controlling the news givers on our planet."

"And the other four hundred and eighty-four military ships that are currently approaching the Demilitarized Zone. Do you have trouble controlling them as well?"

"Why of course not. They are merely pursuing the deranged young man. They are available to assist you. In fact, that is the other reason for my call. Your Highness, I humbly request your permission for them to enter the Demilitarized Zone in order to pursue the renegade."

▲ ▲ ▲

Emperor Beratte Simpson and the Plugarian Defense Council were shocked by the Home World request to send four hundred and eighty-four battleships into the Demilitarized Zone. There was absolutely no way they were going to allow a potential invasion force to enter the Demilitarized Zone. However, it was a very delicate matter. If they flatly refused the request, it could appear unreasonable and the entire Worldian fleet might continue anyway.

"My esteemed Chancellor Thager, a very large number of military ships should not be needed to capture one relatively harmless ship. Since the Great War, not a single military ship has entered the Demilitarized Zone. As an act of friendship between our two empires and because of our respect for your need to capture this renegade, I propose that you send a squadron of twelve ships under the direction of my Strategic Response Commander, Benoki Galata. Your remaining ships can wait in your territory at the edge of the Demilitarized Zone."

After the call ended, intense discussions took place on both sides. Home World had not been able to stop the Alpha One with over five hundred ships and land-based lasers. It seemed pointless to send just twelve ships, especially now that the Alpha One was in open space and, if needed, could simply run away from any pursuers. Two courses of action emerged. The first was to not send any ships into the Demilitarized Zone, thereby allowing the Alpha One to escape, but preserving the tradition of maintaining the Demilitarized Zone. The second course of action was to ignore the emperor's conditions and send the entire fleet after the Alpha One. Attempts would be made to minimize battles with the Plugarians, but it was understood that this would be considered an act of war and that significant casualties on both sides would likely occur.

On the Plugarian side, Benoki Galata and her staff were busily running simulated battle scenarios. If the Worldians accepted the emperor's offer and the twelve Worldian ships eventually became hostile, the seventy-two Plugarian ships recently launched could easily handle them. The Alpha One, however, was a different matter. Even with eighty-four ships under Plugarian command, the simulations showed they were no match for the Alpha One with its superior speed and weaponry.

CHAPTER 16

THE ROAD TO ARMAGEDDON

The Alpha One entered the Demilitarized Zone, thereby becoming the first military ship to enter the Demilitarized Zone since the Great War. At its current pace, it would leave the Demilitarized Zone and enter into Plugarian territory in twelve hours. Plugaria, the fifth planet from Astar would then be just four days away. Arminius checked his battlefield hologram - the Home World Fleet was continuing its pursuit, trailing him by one hour.

Thirty minutes later, Arminius checked the hologram again. The Home World fleet was slowing down. It appeared that the fleet was not going to enter the Demilitarized Zone.

▲ ▲ ▲

During the ten-day journey from Home World to the Demilitarized Zone, Arminius had time to work out his plan. His father was the second highest ranking person in the Home World Empire. He wanted to surpass his father. He could aspire to become the chancellor, but that was only one step above what his father had accomplished and, who knows, his father one day might become chancellor. No, the only way to exceed his father would be to become the Absolute Leader of the Binary Star System. There had never been a single leader of the entire Binary Star System. In order to do this, he needed to establish military dominance. If he could get the Home World and Plugarian fleets to attack each other, they would wipe each other out, making his goal much easier.

"Chirality."

"Yes, Commander."

"Open a broadcast link on commercial channel 211."

"Complete, Commander."

"Attention Plugaria. This is Commander Arminius Percival aboard the Home World ship Alpha One. I am requesting permission to enter Plugarian territory for the purpose of defection."

▲ ▲ ▲

Arminius's announcement reverberated throughout both empires.

In the Plugarian Defense Council chamber, the emperor was the first to speak, "So now, out of the blue, the most advanced military ship in the Binary Star System wants to defect? For free? No bribes, no offer of high positions in our empire?"

"That is correct, your Highness," acknowledged General Visgoth.

"Preposterous!" exclaimed the emperor.

"How would you like us to respond to the defection offer, your Highness?" asked General Visgoth.

"I seriously doubt that ship is going to defect, but if it does, it would be a tremendous windfall. It is cost versus value. Let us at least pretend to accept his defection, but minimize the risk. Come up with a suitable defection plan."

▲ ▲ ▲

Benoki Galata quickly developed a plan for the defection, well aware of the potential risks involved. The Alpha One was to rendezvous with three Plugarian battleships at the eighth planet from Astar. This was a sparsely inhabited mining colony. It had one land-based laser that protected the colony, but not the rest of the planet. The three ships, two

PT class torpedo ships and one PL class laser ship would be enough to keep away any nonmilitary craft. Twelve ships, six PTs and six PLs were to patrol the territory between the eighth planet and the Demilitarized Zone. Another twelve ships were to patrol between the A-7 and A-8 planet orbits. The remaining forty-five military ships were to be stationed inside the A-7 orbit. If the Alpha One did contain a super bomb, it would be bad for A-8 and the three escort ships, but overall, the damage would be minimal. It was the price for potential riches beyond belief.

▲ ▲ ▲

Arminius's defection announcement was intercepted and relayed to the Command Center on Home World. The group, which had previously been debating the appropriate course of action, was now united.

Chancellor Thager was outraged, "What! Percival Junior is going to defect and give the Alpha One to the Plugarians? That son-of-a-bitch has been nothing but trouble, and now this. If the Plugarians get that ship, they can destroy us."

"Technically sir," clarified General Hayden, "they would have a superior battlefield weapon, but Home World would still be protected with its land-based lasers."

"It is economic destruction, you idiot!" The chancellor continued his tirade, "Money buys power. The Alpha One could easily attack all of our freighters. Even if we could protect them with military escorts, the cost would be overwhelming. They could demand protection money for all of our shipments. Arminius, with his military training, may not be thinking along those lines, but I guarantee you that the Plugarians know this! With the extra income, the Plugarians will build more weapons and will have complete domination. Home World will be the poor world. For the future of Home World, our children, and our children's children, we have got to destroy that ship!"

A few minutes later, four hundred and eighty-four Worldian battleships entered the Demilitarized Zone.

▲ ▲ ▲

Benoki briefed the Plugarian Communication Chief in the Strategic Response Command Center and instructed her on how to deal with the defecting Worldian commander. All the guys loved the cute little perky Communications Chief and she certainly knew how to turn on the charm, but to Benoki she was just a cold little bitch that would do anything to rise to the top.

The cameras were positioned so that only the Communication Chief was visible on Arminius's holographic communication station. The Communications Chief was in her mid-thirties, with long dark hair in a ponytail, and a warm smile. She was wearing the standard red military uniform crisscrossed with purple hatch lines.

"Commander Perceval, sir," she energetically greeted him with a warm accommodatingly smile. "The government of Plugaria formally accepts your defection request and welcomes you into our wonderful family. I know you will find Plugaria a great place to live and pursue your life goals. We would like to rendezvous with you in orbit above A-8. We are sending three of our ships there now and we are looking forward to your arrival."

"Agreed," nodded Arminius as he signed off. Join the Plugarian family? If all goes well, he would soon be their Absolute Leader.

▲ ▲ ▲

Arminius was watching his battlefield hologram and was pleased to see the Home World fleet enter the Demilitarized Zone. Because of their slow down at the border, the Home World fleet was now two hours behind him. At the current pace, A-8 was twenty-four hours away.

"Chirality"

"Yes, Commander"

"Plot a course to A-8 and ramp down the ship's speed from eighty percent to seventy percent over the next two hours."

▲ ▲ ▲

Fear was growing in the conference room in the private dining room at the Emperor's Palace. The entire Worldian fleet was traveling through the Forbidden Zone – a clear violation of the treaty. The Plugarian Communications Chief placed a code 999 call from Emperor Beratte Simpson to Chancellor Simeon Thager to protest the violation. The call was taken by C, "I am sorry sir, Chancellor Thager is not available."

▲ ▲ ▲

Benoki Galata surveyed the holographic battlefield for what may have been the hundredth time in the past two hours and she was very worried. The Alpha One would soon be entering Plugarian territory. From there, it would be a twenty-four-hour journey to A-8. Well maybe twenty-four hours, it had been noted that the Alpha One was gradually losing speed. More concerning at the moment were the four hundred and eighty-four Worldian battleships in the Demilitarized Zone that were less than two hours away from Plugarian territory. "Launch all battleships," she ordered. Soon she would have a total of five hundred and twelve battleships available. In the meantime, it was time to draw a line in the sand. She gave orders for the twelve Plugarian battleships stationed between A-8 and the Demilitarized Zone. "After the Alpha One passes, set up a Double Diamond 84 formation one hundred thousand miles from the Demilitarized Zone with the ships spaced twenty thousand miles apart at the transmitted coordinates." The path to A-8 now had a major obstruction. Had she just given a death sentence to the twelve ships? Benoki wondered how many times throughout history troops had been ordered to hold a position against insurmountable odds.

▲ ▲ ▲

Major Tom surveyed his holographic battlefield for what may have been the hundredth time in the past two hours and he too was worried. The politicians had gotten involved and the situation was now spiraling out of control. The entire remaining Home World fleet was pursuing the Alpha One, but he did not have an effective strategy. The Alpha One could easily outrun his ships, the only way to take it out was to trap it somewhere, but how does one catch a faster ship in open space? His second problem was that he did not want to provoke a war with the Plugarians, but that may be unavoidable. The Home World fleet would soon be entering Plugarian territory and that could only be taken as an act of war. In fact, intelligence reports showed that the Plugarians had already scrambled their entire fleet. Now he had to face the Alpha One and the entire Plugarian military fleet. The third problem, however, was the most vexing. The Alpha One was heading towards A-8 to defect, so why would it be gradually slowing down? Commander Arminius was up to something, what was he planning?

▲ ▲ ▲

"Chirality"
 "Yes, Commander"
 "Activate battlefield hologram from A-5 to the Demilitarized Zone."
 "Complete, Commander."
Arminius studied the hologram and was proud. Nearly one thousand battleships were on the display and it was all because of him. Never in the history of the Binary Star System, had such a force assembled. The Great War was brutal and many lives were lost. He recalled from his military tactics courses that the largest battle had been fought

near A-9. It was a ferocious battle involving twenty-seven battleships. Those were the battleships of sixty years ago that had nowhere near the power, speed, and lethality of the colossal battleships that were currently assembling. This would be Armageddon. He had done it! Because of him, the greatest battle in the history of the Binary Star System would soon take place!

▲ ▲ ▲

Major Tom surveyed his battlefield hologram. The Plugarians had set up a Double Diamond 84, which was a textbook blocking formation, and his fleet leader was requesting instructions. The formation consisted of an inner diamond with four ships and an outer diamond with eight ships. The ships were twenty thousand miles apart, so they had an effective blocking area of one hundred thousand miles. He had four hundred and eighty-three battleships and could easily destroy the formation, but that was not the objective. "Avoid conflict. Stay well out of laser or torpedo range. Go around the blockade."

▲ ▲ ▲

Benoki Galata was in contact with the leader of the blocking formation, a seasoned commander in his mid-forties. "Hold your position. Make the Worldians go around you. Do not pursue, do not attack unless it is self-defense." It would be pointless for her twelve blocking ships to try to fight the larger force. If there was going to be a war with the Worldians, she was not going to fire the first shot.

▲ ▲ ▲

Arminius was now eight hours away from A-8. The Home World fleet should have been near him by now, but they had been delayed by the Plugarian blockade. He was disappointed that they had gone around the blockade instead of destroying the twelve ships, but he could not do anything about that. Once again, they were two hours behind him.

"Chirality"

"Yes, Commander."

"Reduce speed from seventy percent to fifty percent."

▲ ▲ ▲

The Alpha One's change in speed was quickly noticed in both the Plugarian and Home World command centers. As per Benoki Galata's instructions, the Plugarian Communications Chief contacted the Alpha One. "Commander Percival sir, we were making plans for your reception and noticed that you reduced your speed. Is there a problem?"

"I am having some engine problems," explained Arminius, "If all goes well, I should arrive in about eleven hours."

▲ ▲ ▲

"You are telling me that the Alpha One is now running at fifty percent capacity because of engine problems?" asked the emperor incredulously. "How often do your ships experience massive engine failure?"

"Seldom, your Highness," answered General Visgoth.

"So," the emperor continued, "We have a brand-new super battleship, the finest in the Binary Star System, that has unexpectedly had engine problems when it is due to defect in just a few hours. It all seems a bit suspicious."

▲ ▲ ▲

C intercepted Arminius's last message and forwarded it to the Home World Command Center.

"Why has he slowed down?" asked Chancellor Thager.

Major Tom had the same thoughts, but he was also trying to figure out why Arminius would send a message to the Plugarians knowing that it is being intercepted. He checked the battlefield hologram. The Alpha One was heading towards A-8 and, if it continued at fifty percent speed, it should arrive in about eleven hours. There were three Plugarian battleships that were currently heading towards A-8 that would be there in about two hours. They were no doubt being sent to transfer custody of the Alpha One. His fleet of four hundred and eighty-four ships would arrive at A-8 in about ten hours. The Plugarians had twelve ships between A-7 and A-8, which could arrive in about twelve hours. A force of forty-five ships was rendezvousing between the A-6 and A-7 orbits. The remainder of the Plugarian fleet, a formidable armada of four hundred and forty ships, was forty-eight hours away. Formidable seemed like such a sanitized way of describing their devastating capabilities.

Arminius is up to something, Major Tom thought, but what? If Arminius was going to give the Alpha One to the Plugarians, then the Home World strategic plan was simple – he was going to blast the Alpha One into oblivion. If any Plugarians were on the ship, it would be unfortunate for them, but his number one priority was to take out a super weapon that could be used against Home World. The Plugarians may or may not be compensated for their losses. Who knows, maybe N could make up a story about how a mysterious explosion had taken place aboard the Alpha One during a demonstration run with Plugarian visitors on board. Industrial accidents took place all the time, especially in faraway places.

Major Tom was not concerned about the Plugarians piloting the Alpha One. It takes months and months of training to pilot such a ship. No, if Arminius defects at A-8, the Alpha One will be destroyed in just a few hours. Could it be engine problems? The ship was designed to run at least ten years between overhauls and had performed flawlessly during the commissioning runs and during their recent encounters. He just did not buy the story that the engine happened to be having problems at this particular time. No, for some unknown reason, Arminius must want the Home World fleet closer.

When the Alpha One was five hours away from A-8, the Home World fleet had closed the gap to one hour. Major Tom gave orders to the Home World fleet, "Reduce speed to sixty-five percent."

▲ ▲ ▲

Within a few minutes, the slowing of the Home World fleet was noticed on both the Plugarian and Alpha One battlefield displays.

"Chirality"

"Yes, Commander."

"Reduce speed from fifty percent to twenty-five percent."

The emperor commented, "Does the entire Home World fleet have engine problems?"

Suppressing her personal feelings, Benoki smiled as she again gave instructions to the cold little bitch that all the guys loved Communication Chief who then contacted the Alpha One, "Commander Percival, sir," she spoke consolingly, "we noticed that you have reduced your speed again - are you having more problems?"

"Yes," answered Arminius, "There have been a lot of problems."

"Understood," replied the Communications Chief sympathetically, "We will be sending our ships out to meet you."

▲ ▲ ▲

Arminius was confused. Things were not going according to his plan. Ever since his escape, the entire Home World Empire fleet of battleships had pursued him like a pack of wild dogs. Now, when they knew he was going to defect and give away the most powerful military weapon ever created, they slowed down. To make matters worse, the Plugarians were coming out to meet him. That would shorten the time before the rendezvous. At least the rendezvous would take place in open space – that avoided the inconvenience of explaining why the rendezvous had to take place at a point in the A-8 orbit that was away from the planet's land-based laser.

"Chirality"

"Yes, Commander."

"Reduce speed from twenty-five percent to five percent."

▲ ▲ ▲

Major Tom observed the latest Alpha One speed reduction. When the Home World fleet was thirty minutes away from the Alpha One he ordered one fourth of his fleet, one hundred and twenty-one ships, to reduce speed and match the Alpha One's speed. He sent the bulk of the fleet, three hundred and sixty-three ships, forward to establish a large net.

▲ ▲ ▲

Benoki Galata intensely watched the developments on her battlefield screen. Her twelve ships in the Double Diamond 84 blockade had somehow managed to remain unscathed and were stationed in Plugarian territory, one hundred thousand miles from the Demilitarized Zone. The Worldians had one hundred and twenty-one ships between the A-9 and A-8 orbits that were shadowing the Alpha One and had slowed to match its pace. The remaining three hundred and sixty-three ships were maneuvering to create a very large net around the Alpha One. Benoki recognized the formation, as she had tried similar maneuvers with computer simulations involving eighty-four ships to trap the Alpha One. In the midst of the large net, she had three Plugarian battleships that were heading toward the Alpha One and should arrive in the next thirty minutes. Between A-7 and A-8 she had twelve ships. Between A-6 and A-7 she had forty-five ships. Her main fleet of four hundred and forty ships was speeding away from Plugaria and was now approaching the A-6 orbit.

This was not a standard invasion formation. War game invasion simulations usually have rapid attacks from many directions and battlegrounds around multiple outlying planets. Currently, the only planet vulnerable was A-8. The Worldians had not left a rear guard to protect their planets. Benoki could easily launch a raid on Worldian territory with her twelve ships near the Demilitarized Zone.

Recognizing the explosiveness of the situation, Benoki did not want to take any actions that would provoke the Worldians. She halted the advance of her four hundred and forty ships at the A-6 orbit. She then regrouped three hundred and sixty of the ships into four wings of ninety ships each and positioned them in a rhombus formation with ships fifty thousand miles apart to intercept invading Worldian ships. The remaining eighty ships were rearguard reserves and were repositioned to a location half way between the A-6 orbit and Plugaria. They would be called into battle to reinforce positions as needed.

The twelve ships between A-7 and A-8 joined the forty-five ships between A-6 and A-7 at the A-7 orbit. Benoki positioned these ships in the shape of an enormous cone with a base diameter of one million miles. The cone was designed to act as a giant wedge to divide the Worldian forces. Before the Worldians could regroup, they would face one of the wings of ninety ships in the rhombus formations. If the Worldians decided to attack the Plugarian cone, the four wings could quickly be called into action.

The twelve ships that had been part of the Double Diamond 84 blocking formation just inside the Demilitarized Zone held their position. They could be used to invade the now defenseless Worldian territory or harass any damaged Worldian ships retreating from battle.

That left the three ships approaching the Alpha One. They would rendezvous in twenty minutes. Benoki knew that there was no way they would ever be able to acquire the Alpha One. The Worldians would never allow it and they had the necessary firepower, in the form of one hundred and twenty-one ships, to make sure it did not happen. If the Plugarians took control of the Alpha One, the Worldians would immediately capture it. That would be a violation of international law, but then so was the invasion.

Benoki was confident that her plan would defend Plugaria from a conventional Worldian invasion. The problem was the Alpha One. That was the one ship that could tip the tide of war. With her three ships approaching the Alpha One, Benoki debated whether or not it might be better to simply destroy the Alpha One. Would that rebalance the power or would that be the match that ignited Armageddon?

CHAPTER 17

THE ATTACK

Arminius was getting nervous. The three Plugarian ships were approaching. They would arrive in twenty minutes and in just ten minutes he would be in range of their weapons. He could tell that the Home World fleet was starting to build a net around him. The Plugarians were not attacking the invading Home World ships. Their fleet had assumed defensive positions. He needed to provoke a war, yet so far, not even a single shot had been fired between the two long-term adversaries.

▲ ▲ ▲

The cute and perky Plugarian Communication Chief appeared on the three-dimensional view screen.

"Commander Percival, sir," she greeted him warmly, "Please exit your ship into a transport craft. A Plugarian ship will pick you up in ten minutes."

"Sure," agreed Arminius. "I will take a buggy."

After he ended the call, Arminius told Chirality to launch a buggy.

Buggies can hold two people and were designed for either transportation to the surface of a planet, transportation between ships, or for inspecting the ship's exterior. The buggies on the Alpha One did not have any offensive weapons.

A few seconds later, a coded message was sent from the buggy on an all-ships channel to the entire Home World fleet with the intent of initiating Armageddon:

"ALPHA ONE, YOU ARE GOOD TO GO...BEGIN SEQUENCE NUMBER ONE THREE SIX."

It was a simple war cry - nothing emotional like 'Remember the Alamo!' and nothing descriptive like 'Tora, Tora, Tora!' It was just a simple unemotional order. The fact that Arminius had sent the order from an unmanned buggy to himself on board the Alpha One did not matter. The fact that there was no sequence number one three six also did not matter. As soon as the order was given, Arminius cranked up the Alpha One engine to one hundred and ten percent capacity and activated the laser firing system. A minute later the laser was ready to fire. Thirty seconds after that, the unfortunate Plugarian ship that was going to rendezvous with the Alpha One was destroyed and shortly thereafter, the two other Plugarian ships that were sent to protect the Alpha One from outsiders were space dust. The Alpha One turned, and set a course directly towards Plugaria.

▲ ▲ ▲

Major Tom silently cursed. The Alpha One was getting away. The net had been established on the sides and blocked on one end, but there was no cap on the other end. He contacted C on a private line that was not monitored by the VIP Conference Room.

"C, how can I get battle plans sent to the Plugarian Strategic Response Commander?"

"We can send a message to our armada commander with code 415," she replied. "The Plugarians have broken that code, and will no doubt relay the information."

Major Tom then contacted B2. "Develop a plan to trap the Alpha One in a net with Plugarian help."

"With Plugarian help?" questioned B2.

"Yes, now that they have lost three ships, they may be more willing to cooperate."

A few minutes later, B2 buzzed. "The plan is complete sir."

"Great," exclaimed Major Tom, "How many Plugarian ships are in the model?"

"Forty-eight."

"C," instructed Major Tom on the private line, "Send B2's plan to the armada commander with code 415. Tell him that under no circumstances is he to attack the Plugarians."

▲ ▲ ▲

Benoki Galata was focused on the battlefield hologram. She was disappointed that she had lost three ships, but that was part of war. She was closely monitoring the movements of the Worldian fleet. They were trying to maintain a net to contain the Alpha One, but there was no cap on the Plugarian end of the net.

She received a message from her intelligence liaison, an older man in his mid-fifties, "We intercepted and deciphered a message from the Worldians to their armada commander and it contains their battle plans, but it is odd, sir."

"How is that?" asked Benoki. It was hard enough to have a cute guy her own age address her as sir, but now an old man was calling her sir.

"First," noted the intelligence liaison, "They used a different transmission code for the message. It is one that they stopped using a while ago, after they no doubt realized we had broken the code."

"That is suspicious."

"Secondly," continued the intelligence liaison, "they have included forty-eight of our ships as part of the plan to capture the Alpha One. Are we now taking orders from the Worldians, sir?"

▲ ▲ ▲

Major Tom was secretly requesting her help in capping the end of the net around the Alpha One. She had fifty-seven ships in a cone formation between A-6 and A-7. She could easily move these ships to cap the net. She instructed Number Two to run simulations and he confirmed that the intercepted Worldian plan was effective with a ninety-nine percent probability of success.

Now came the hard part – was this a trap? If she moved her ships, she would lose the defensive wedge she had set up to deflect the invading Worldian fleet. If her ships destroyed the Alpha One, it could be considered an act of war. The larger number of Worldian ships that were part of the net would annihilate her forty-eight ships. After that, it would be full scale Armageddon with hundreds of battleships engaged in ferocious battles. She could consult Emperor Beratte Simpson before making the decision, but she knew it would be useless to get the politicians involved and there was no way they could ever make a quick decision. That was why she was in this position – quick battlefield decisions were needed when fast-moving weapons with incredibly destructive power were involved. She just hoped she could make the right decisions.

▲ ▲ ▲

Arminius watched as the Home World fleet tried to set up another giant net around him. This one was open on one end, and The Alpha One was accelerating toward the open area. The Home World ships were racing through space at maximum speed in order to keep the Alpha One trapped by the walls of the net. It was a desperate attempt, thought Arminius, since one end of the net was open. Arminius checked his battlefield hologram. Fifty-seven Plugarian battleships were positioned in a cone formation between the A-6 and A-7 orbits, approximately an hour away. Cone formations were good for driving a wedge between invading fleets, but his was a single ship. There were plenty of options – he could go around the wedge or simply go right down the middle blasting away anything that got in his way. The challenge now was to keep the wall of Home World ships near him and not outrun them. He reduced his speed to ninety percent. He had to find some way to get the Home World and Plugarian ships close enough together so that they could attack each other.

▲ ▲ ▲

Major Tom was intensely studying the giant hologram in the center of the Command Center. Earlier, it had appeared that the Alpha One was going to outrun the net and escape. Now, for some unknown reason, the Alpha One had reduced speed. The Alpha One was outrunning the ships that made up the sides of the net, but there were still plenty of prepositioned ships ahead to maintain the net wall. If only there was a cap on the end. The Plugarians had maintained their wedge formation. Had they gotten his message? Surely, they would have intercepted the message and relayed it to their Strategic Response Commander by now, but maybe it was true that the Plugarians were more backward when it came to technical skills. If they did receive the message, how would they respond? Suddenly, all of the Plugarian ships in the cone started to move. It worked, thought Major Tom. They are going to cap the end of the net. We are going to trap the Alpha One!

▲ ▲ ▲

Arminius watched as the Plugarian defensive cone formation suddenly transformed into a gigantic sphere and began rapidly moving toward the Alpha One. The Worldian net formation remained intact with the Alpha One inside. In ten minutes, the cap would be in place and the Alpha One would have no escape.

"Chirality"

"Yes, Commander."

"Increase speed to one hundred percent."

▲ ▲ ▲

B2 buzzed. "Major Tom, the Plugarian ships are in a spherical formation. That is not the Plugarian battlefield formation requested."

Major Tom called C on the private line. "Send a code 415 message to the armada commander – Plugarian Strategic Response Commander, please follow the plan."

▲ ▲ ▲

With a burst of speed, Arminius knew that he could barely outrun the attempt to cap the net. As he approached the Plugarian ships, he veered sharply toward the small opening between the last of the Home World ships forming the net and the closest Plugarian ships. The plan was to take out both a Plugarian ship and a Home World ship. This would be the spark to ignite a full-scale war. When the Plugarian target was within five hundred miles, Arminius opened fire. Ten seconds later the Plugarian ship disintegrated. The Alpha One turned sharply and quickly annihilated the unfortunate Home World ship at the end of the net. Arminius congratulated himself – he had done it! He had started Armageddon!

Suddenly, like shrapnel from a detonated grenade, the Plugarian ship spherical formation that had approached the Worldian ships to cap the net exploded, and fifty-six Plugarian ships shot out in fifty-six different directions. The main Plugarian fleet, four hundred and forty ships that were positioned between Plugaria and the A-6 orbit, retreated toward Plugaria. "Attack, attack! Kill all Plugarians!" Arminius desperately shouted on the Home World all-ship communications channel. But it was all in vain – there was no one to attack.

▲ ▲ ▲

C, buzzed Major Tom on his main console. "Sir, we intercepted a message from Plugarian Strategic Response Commander Benoki Galata using a code they know we have broken. It reads – sorry guys, he is not our problem."

Major Tom considered his next steps. The good news was that the Alpha One was not going to defect. The bad news is that there was no way to hunt down a faster ship in open space. Major Tom was getting ready to contact General Hayden to suggest that the ships be brought home when Chancellor Thager himself called.

"Major, why don't we go ahead and attack Plugaria? We've come this far. Let's crush the cowardly bastards."

CHAPTER 18

THE ARMAGEDDON DEFENSE

Major Tom was stunned by Chancellor Thager's order to launch a full-scale war against Plugaria. A military campaign requires many months, even years of planning and preparation. Chancellor Thager was talking about starting a major war in the next few minutes – a war that would result in unprecedented destruction. A few seconds later, Major Tom recovered from the initial shock and the analytical part of his brain took charge. "Sir, can you give me twenty-four hours to plan the attack?"

Major Tom analyzed the situation while he studied the gigantic battlefield hologram. He now had four hundred and eighty-three battleships in a holding pattern between A-7 and A-8. The Plugarians had four hundred and forty ships moving toward Plugaria. They had an additional fifty-six battleships that had scattered across the Astar system plus twelve battleships near the Demilitarized Zone border. If he attacked the Plugarian ships, it would be Armageddon. Both sides would wipe each other out. Whoever survived, even if they only had a few battleships remaining, would control the Binary Star System.

Major Tom called C. "Get me B2 on an outside line."

"But sir," exclaimed a very surprised C, "you have the highest possible security level link on your console. He is hearing us talk right now."

"C," Major Tom calmly repeated, "please get me B2 on an outside line."

B2 appeared on a separate screen. "Sir, how may I assist?"

"I need you to develop a plan to attack Plugaria," requested Major Tom in a matter-of-fact tone. "We need to wipe out the cowardly bastards."

"What level of destruction should we plan for, sir?" asked B2.

"Maximum damage for Plugaria," replied Major Tom as he calmly terminated the call.

▲ ▲ ▲

Arminius surveyed the battlefield hologram and was shocked by what he saw. There would be no grand battle. Most of the Plugarian battleships were rapidly retreating to Plugaria. The Home World fleet was going nowhere. It was in a holding pattern between A-7 and A-8, and he was not sure why. He could chase down some of the dispersed Plugarian ships, but why bother? It was a major war he wanted so that he could become the Absolute Leader of the Binary Star System. With no war, there would be no Absolute Leader. Hunting down the scattered Plugarian ships would just get him the label of being a pirate – and not a very good one. Most pirates are motivated by wealth, he would be known as a psychopath pirate that just searched for ships to destroy. Arminius turned and headed toward the Demilitarized Zone. For the first time in over ten days, no one was following him, and no one cared.

▲ ▲ ▲

The next day, Major Tom received a call from Chancellor Thager. "Major, about that, what shall we call it, little thing I asked you to look into yesterday."

"Yes," replied Major Tom. Armageddon was now considered to be a 'little thing'.

"I do not know why," continued the chancellor, "but I have been getting lots of calls from defense contractors, commerce leaders, and others. Well, anyway, they have convinced me that the Plugarians are our good friends and we need to leave them alone – at least for now."

"That is good news, sir." Major Tom maintained a professional outward appearance, but internally there was a great sigh of relief. "It appears that, since we spoke, the Plugarians have adopted the Armageddon Defense."

"The Armageddon Defense? I am not sure I am familiar with that defense."

"It is the perfect defense for an apocalyptic invasion. I have tried to break it many times in simulations sir, but to no avail. In an Armageddon battle, both sides try to destroy each other and there are tremendous losses. The survivors win, but they really do not win because of the massive destruction."

"Yes, yes. I am very familiar with Armageddon and its consequences, but what is the Armageddon Defense?"

"Sir, if one side does not engage, there is no war, no annihilation, hence no Armageddon. Since yesterday, the Plugarian ships have been retreating to Plugaria, where they are protected by their land-based laser defense system. We cannot get to them. We can blockade their trade routes, but in the end, that hurts our economy as well."

"Thank you Major, bring our ships home."

Two days later, the Home World ships were passing through the Demilitarized Zone on their way to Home World territory.

C buzzed. "Major, we received a video message from Benoki Galata that is intended for you."

"Put it on," requested Major Tom.

Benoki Galata's face appeared on the center screen of the command console, "Major Tom, you are good, you are very good," she paused and then slowly spoke, "but if we ever fight, I *will* kick your ass!"

CHAPTER 19

THE END OF THE WORLD

The trip back to Home World was quiet and very boring for Arminius. Chirality interrupted his thoughts. "Commander, call from your mother."

"Put her on."

A holographic image of a beautiful young lady appeared, "Arminius, I need you. Please, please come and rescue me from Ricus-3 in the Forbidden Zone."

Arminius decided to go to the Forbidden Zone, but there was one stop he had to make along the way.

▲ ▲ ▲

"Commander," announced Chirality, "call from your father."

"Put him on."

A hologram of Arminius's father appeared. The hand that was shot by the chancellor was wrapped in a thick layer of gauze. "Hello, Junior."

"Hello, Father."

"I wanted you to know that you did a tremendous job out there. You did what no one has ever done."

"What is that Father?"

"Well, for starters, you took on the entire Home World Empire fleet, and nearly won."

"I did win, Father."

"Well, yes and no. You did win a lot of battles."

"I won the war, they retreated."

"Well, they still may come after you."

"I am faster than they are and I am more powerful. If they come after me, they will be destroyed."

"Today yes, but there is always tomorrow. Because of your fine work, the defense contractors already have their engineers working on the Super Alpha project. They are designing ships that will be twenty-five percent faster than the Alpha One and will have a laser range of six hundred miles. They are going to build twelve battleships, all of which will have special security protocols to prevent theft. The project is being fast tracked and should be finished in five years."

"So, the engineers are designing ships that will be even more destructive? Doesn't it bother the engineers that they are using their talents to create weapons that deliver colossal devastation?"

"For some reason, the engineers really enjoy this kind of work. To them it is a sport, a competition to see who can design the biggest, most powerful weapons. In addition to the Super Alphas, the engineers are also working on a new orbiting laser system. In the future, Home World will be protected by a ring of orbiting lasers that will have no atmosphere to interfere with their destructive capabilities."

"That's good Father. Is there anything else?"

"Well, it is top secret, of course, but there has been a renewed interest in Thulien weapon research. There are now at least twenty-five new Thulien projects. Everyone realizes that we could have destroyed those cowardly Plugarians if we had a Thulien bomb. Maybe one of the many projects will actually produce a bomb powerful enough to blow up an entire planet! Overall, your little adventure has been a big boom for the defense contractors."

"Is that why you called Father? To update me on new defense projects."

"No Junior, I am concerned about you. Where are you going and what are you going to do? You cannot live in solitary confinement on board the Alpha One forever. Why not turn the ship over to us? You will get the best lawyers that money can buy, not to mention my political influence. You will be able to return to the land of the living. On board the Alpha One, you will have nothing but a life filled with loneliness."

"Thank you for your concern, Father. By the way, did you really send Mom's remains to the Forbidden Zone so she could be rejuvenated and you could be with her again?"

"That is a complicated subject, son. Relationships are always difficult."

"But is she still alive? I saw her, after she…" he paused.

"Who knows, after all, what really is life?"

"So true, so true." For once he and his father agreed.

"By the way Junior, what is going on behind Luna 3? Being on the dark side of that moon, we cannot see what you are doing."

"I am finishing the war."

"Your war with Plugaria?"

"No Father."

"Your war with the Home World Empire? After all, that was not really a war."

"No Father, my war with you."

"What, what do you mean?"

"You were never there for me. You never cared for me. You never gave me credit for my accomplishments."

"Your accomplishments? What accomplishments? They pale so much compared to mine. When I was your age, I was a provincial governor. Look at you now – flying around alone in your ship. I had parties, I had women, I had money, I had power, and everyone loved me."

"I am going to destroy all that."

"Destroy that, destroy me? That is crazy talk. Fifty land-based lasers that can blast you out of the sky protect Home World. The Super Alphas will be coming for you once they are built. If you did somehow manage to sneak into Home World, I have a garrison of elite bodyguards for protection. You do not mess with the Vice Chancellor of Home World!"

"Watch me, Father. I am the greatest. I am even greater than you."

"And how is that son?"

"I told you; I am going to destroy your life."

Alarm bells sounded on the Alpha One.

"What is that?" asked the senior Percival.

"It is my automatic alarm system. I know that you have been ordered to distract me, while a commando group attacks. But, it is too late Father. My work here is finished."

With one last blast, chunks of Luna 3 started breaking apart and flying into space. The small moon was slowly disintegrating.

"I have blown up Luna 3," Arminius calmly announced. "That is something that you never did. That is something that no one has ever done. The Alpha One laser is so powerful that I have been able to use it to drill holes deep within the moon. It is now so weak that it is breaking apart."

"That is no big deal. All you did was destroy a big insignificant rock in the sky."

"That big insignificant rock, Father, will break into millions of smaller insignificant pieces. Those pieces will be pulled by gravity toward Home World becoming meteorites that for years will reign havoc upon the planet. As a result, the atmosphere will be filled with other insignificant particles that form a dust layer, blocking sunlight from reaching the surface below. Plant life will be destroyed, animal life will end, and the life on Home World that you know will cease to exist. I will go down in history as the one that annihilated Home World! There will be no Super Alpha project, there will be no orbiting space lasers, and there will be no Thulien bombs. Life on the surface of Home World will be wiped out. And do you know why? Do you know why, Father? It is because I am the greatest and I want to destroy you!"

Arminius abruptly ended the call. He set a heading toward the Forbidden Zone and sped away. He never talked to his father again.

▲ ▲ ▲

N dutifully supplied a press release to the news givers. Apparently, an unknown errant meteor struck Luna 3 and significant chunks of the moon fragmented. A new stay indoors alert was issued until the hazard passed, which should be in just a few days. There was no mention of Arminius or the Alpha One.

Major Tom was fired from his position as Battlefield Strategic Commander. He was blamed for the recent battlefield losses and was replaced by B2. There was no mention that many of the losses were due to his following Chancellor Thager's specific orders. There was also no mention of the role he played in preventing Armageddon.

Chancellor Thager, Vice Chancellor Percival, and others with inside knowledge began purchasing food, medicine, arms, and survival supplies. They moved into special underground military bunkers to live for the next several years until the meteorite strikes from the remnants of Luna 3 ceased. When they returned to the surface, they would be the new economic leaders and would control Home World.

▲ ▲ ▲

P stared at the holographic image of Arminius's mother in a large open space in the middle of her Psyche Ops lab. It was some of her finest programming. The full bottle of alcohol she brought into the laboratory was now nearly empty. Her bloodshot crazed eyes were quivering.

"Can you believe it?" she asked. "Can you believe the price?"

"Unbelievable," answered the hologram.

"They sent the entire military fleet after your son."

"My only son."

"Twenty-nine battleships were destroyed. Huge ships with over one hundred people on board."

"Twenty-nine huge ships," repeated the hologram, "over one hundred people on board."

"Plus, four Plugarian battleships, but those don't really count."

"Plugarian battleships don't count," agreed the hologram.

"A freight car filled with diamonds was blown to smithereens."

"A freight car filled with diamonds," echoed the hologram.

"They broke the treaty with the Plugarians, a treaty that lasted sixty years."

"Sixty years." The hologram shook its head.

"We lost a moon. Luna 3 will no longer be in the night sky." P gazed upward at the laboratory ceiling.

"No more Luna 3." The hologram looked up.

"And meteor showers will destroy much of the life on Home World."

"Lots of life lost." The hologram looked sad.

"And in the end, your son escaped to the Forbidden Zone."

"He is going to the Forbidden Zone," nodded the hologram.

"And who talked him into going there?"

"I did," smiled the hologram.

"All of this could have been prevented, if they had just gone to Psyche Ops in the first place."

"Psyche Ops first," agreed the hologram.

"But who gets more funding?" asked P angrily.

"We need more funding!" shouted the hologram.

"The defense contractors, not Psyche Ops!"

"Psyche Ops first! Psyche Ops first! Psyche Ops first!" chanted the hologram.

P was getting really, really angry. Suddenly the hologram transformed from Arminius's mother into her mother.

"Not now Mother!" yelled P.

"Dearie, do you know what else could have prevented this?" P's mother asked sweetly.

P rolled her crazed eyes. "What Mother?"

"Better parenting."

SECRETS OF THE UNIVERSE

CHAPTER 1

EVOLUTION

In the beginning there was the great abyss and eternal darkness prevailed. Eons passed and primordial ooze filled the abyss. The primordial ooze remained dormant for countless ages and the reign of darkness continued. Then came a flash of light, a spark, in the minds of the engineers, "Could something be done with the ooze...could the ooze be transformed?" A new industry was born and the world would never be the same.

Spindletop, located ninety miles east of Houston in the town of Beaumont, was the site of the first major gusher of the Texas oil boom. On January 10, 1901, crude oil passed from the darkness beneath the surface through an oilrig-shaped birth canal into the world of light above. The discovery had not been easy. Many dry holes were drilled before the Lucas Geyser blew crude oil one hundred and fifty feet into the air at a rate of over four million gallons per day. It took nine days before the well was brought under control. It was the largest gusher the world had ever seen. The population of Beaumont tripled in three months and, by the end of 1902, more than two hundred and eighty-five wells were in operation. The oil boom radically changed life in Texas. Houston grew and evolved from a cotton and cattle shipping port into an international center for the petrochemical industry.

▲ ▲ ▲

Daniel Robinson was certainly grateful for the Texas oil boom. A chemical engineering graduate from Texas A&M University, Daniel was now in his sixth year of work for Stamford Chemicals. His job was to use his engineering knowledge to optimize operations at the chemical plant. Tall, lean, and dark haired, Daniel always wore the typical engineer attire of button-down shirts with dress slacks.

Daniel's best friend was Joshua Jones. Joshua was also in his late twenties. He was tall, lean, and had blonde hair. He often wore the typical engineer uniform, but every now and then he wore a Hawaiian shirt or something outlandish just to be different. Joshua was a chemical engineer graduate from the University of Texas – the archrival of Texas A&M. They had both started work at the same time. Joshua was deep into conspiracy theories. He had investigated 'all of them'. Much of his research was from internet articles, so there were always doubts as to the authenticity of his sources. Joshua was part of a network of conspiracy theorists that were always exchanging ideas, but they had to be careful because, as Joshua often said, "Big Brother is watching."

By far, Joshua's favorite topic was UFO's. He had read countless books and articles on the subject. He also discussed many other topics shrouded in mystery - ancient astronauts, how the pyramids were built, historical assassinations - JFK, RFK, MLK, Lincoln, Amelia Earhart's disappearance, the Bermuda Triangle, Northern Lights, bases under the North Pole, Middle Earth, magical numbers hidden in the architecture of medieval cathedrals, etc. Needless to say, Joshua always had something interesting to discuss when they got together.

Joshua did not think highly of physics majors. "First, they are a bunch of downers – they have this entropy theory that says the entire universe is going to wind down someday and come to a stop. Hello, did they not think that there might be a rewind button out there that can restart things? Next, they say everything is either matter or energy. Well, what about thoughts, dreams, and emotions? Those certainly are not mass or energy. Then, as if that is not bad enough, they have this law…they call it the First Law of Thermodynamics…that says matter and energy can never be created or destroyed, just transformed. Well, we are here aren't we? That means that, sometime in the past, the law had to have been broken and something came from nothing. If it can be broken once, why can't it happen again?" This was usually followed with God must have created the universe, then came who created God? About this time the discussion wound down because it had reached a dead end.

After many of their discussions, Joshua would conclude by saying that one day he was going to have a sit down, face-to-face meeting with God, and ask him. This evolved into making a list of questions for God. Eventually both Joshua and Daniel maintained a list of 'Seven Questions for God'. The list, of course, changed after each new conspiracy.

There was time to kill when Joshua sat down in Daniel's office that afternoon. The topic du jour was evolution.

"You know," Joshua began, "all of that evolution stuff they taught us in school is a bunch of crap."

"Really?" replied Daniel, knowing that he was encouraging him to continue. "Are you saying all of those well-educated biology professors got it wrong?"

"Yep, they are all sipping the same Kool-Aid. You know the system is rigged."

"Rigged?" Daniel tried to look surprised as he egged him on, "How is that?"

"They have no choice but to repeat the lies. If not, they will get blacklisted. They have to follow the doctrine or get banned."

"I can see how that could be a problem. So, you don't believe we came from monkeys? Do you have a better explanation of how we got here?"

"Well, there are the creationists. They will quote the Bible and say the world is less than ten thousand years old, of course they have a problem."

"What's their problem?"

"Science and Religion, you see, have been fighting this big battle for the last thousand years."

"Really?" questioned Daniel. "Why have they been fighting?"

"Well, it seems that long ago, the scientists were seen as a threat to the religious status quo."

"So, what did the religious folks do?"

"Oh, the usual – they ridiculed the scientists, burned some at the stake, tortured others, banished a bunch. You don't mess with the status quo."

"I see. So, what happened next?"

"Well," continued Joshua, "There was this thing called the Renaissance. You know...lots of free-thinking and new ideas."

"Kind of like the hippies and Woodstock?" joked Daniel.

"Nah, man." Joshua was unfazed, "These were serious dudes. They had lots and lots of new ideas that got accepted."

"Why were they accepted?"

"Economics."

"Economics?" Daniel raised his eyebrows.

"Yep, economics. You remember me telling you about how the international economic leaders have joined together to form a secret society that really runs the world?"

Daniel rolled his eyes. "I am not big on secret societies, but I do know that people and companies make decisions based on cost versus value. I can see that if something new came along that would enable things to be done more efficiently it would be utilized."

"Anyway," Joshua resumed, "the worm has turned. There is now more money to be made in Science than Religion, so religious ideas are being pushed aside in favor of scientific ideas."

"All right, I'll buy that. Science and Religion really ought to work together and find a common ground, but what does this have to do with the theory of evolution?"

"Which is a bunch of crap."

"You do know," Daniel pointed out, "that you just can't call a theory a bunch of crap. You have to make valid logical arguments as to why it is not true and you have to propose an alternative."

"Have you ever built a chemical plant?"

"Yes," Daniel answered with a long sigh, "you know that I have because you and I were both part of the design team that built this plant. We had a great team - the project was a rarity in that it actually finished ahead of schedule and was under budget."

"To build this plant, it took lots and lots of planning and hard work by multiple disciplines."

"It certainly did," agreed Daniel. "It took almost three years to design, build, and startup the plant. After that, it took several weeks for the team to solve the major operating issues."

"And how is the plant running today?"

"It runs well most of the time. But there are still problems that arise. We have operators watching the plant twenty-four hours a day seven days a week to make sure it performs well and we, as engineers, are always looking for ways to further improve the process."

"Precisely," nodded Joshua. "Chemical processes are complex and lots and lots of intelligence goes into their design. After they startup, a lot of outside effort is needed to keep them running."

"You are absolutely correct, sir. Chemical plants are a combination of materials, energy, lots and lots of thought, and outside support, but what does this have to do with evolution?"

"The evolutionists would have us believe that the thousands and thousands of feet of pipe, wiring, instruments, pumps, heat exchangers, reactors, towers, control systems, computers, and so forth just sprang up on their own one day. Random design, no operators, things just started running. Can you imagine dropping off all the materials for this plant in the parking lot and then returning to see a fully functioning chemical plant that built itself and was running by itself with no operators?"

"Of course not," Daniel shook his head. "But given enough time, a monkey could type the works of Shakespeare."

Joshua paused. "I have heard that a lot. People are always talking about the damn monkeys and their typing. Have you ever seen a monkey type?"

"No, I have never even seen a monkey with a typewriter."

"Most of those doing the talking about the typing monkeys don't have a strong math background. When you do the calculations…"

"Wait a minute," interrupted Daniel with a grin, "you have actually calculated how long it would take a monkey to type the works of Shakespeare? First, dude you need to get a life, and secondly, how did you do it?"

"You start with a few assumptions. First, we cover the entire planet with monkeys. I mean everywhere – all the land and all the oceans. You make the Earth a perfect sphere and let's say that it is eight thousand miles in diameter and that each monkey, with his or her laptop, occupies one cubic foot. The formula for the surface area of a sphere is $4\pi r^2$."

"I'm with you so far."

"Okay, so now we stack the monkeys with laptops, one hundred miles high."

"It's going to be tough breathing that high," pointed out Daniel as he tried to picture that many monkeys.

"All right," continued Joshua, "now we have some very fast typing monkeys."

"How fast?" Daniel started to laugh, "I would hate to be the monkey at the bottom. Talk about environmental emissions."

"Very fast." Joshua gave Daniel a stern look, "and don't be crude. Over four hundred words per minute. We are talking about a different combination from each monkey each second. And do you know how long they type?"

"How long?"

"Fifteen billion years."

"Wow, without a break?" Daniel snickered, "Those are some very hard-working monkeys."

"Anyway," continued Joshua seriously," When I run the numbers, I get that they will have produced 1.11×10^{38} different possible combinations."

"All right, so how does that compare to the works of Shakespeare?"

"How many possible combinations are there when you roll dice?"

"With six-sided dice, there are six possibilities with one die, six to the second power or thirty-six possibilities with two die, six to the third power or two hundred and sixteen possibilities with three die." Being an engineer, Daniel had a strong mathematical background.

"Let's say, that the monkey keyboard has twenty-six characters. We are not going to worry about punctuation, space bars, capitalization and things like that."

"I wish you had graded some of my papers at A&M. Okay, so how many books will the monkeys write?"

"Books?" Joshua hesitated. "All those monkeys working at that speed for that amount of time would produce less than one line on one page.

Daniel was stunned, "Really?"

"It is less than forty key strokes. Plug in twenty-six and raise it to the thirty-ninth power and see what you get."

Daniel pulled out his calculator and punched the numbers. "4.16×10^{39}. You are correct, sir."

"At some point, one has to say that certain ideas are impossible and one needs to look for alternative explanations."

"So, are we are back to creationism? God created the world in six days?"

"That is going to be difficult to prove or disprove, but we can say that somewhere along the way, something with intelligence was involved in creating life on Earth."

"If not God, who could be involved?" asked Daniel, knowing the next direction of the conversation.

"UFO's of course," answered Joshua. Daniel had learned over the years that, no matter what was initially discussed with Joshua, UFOs always became part of the conversation.

"Wait, wait a minute," Daniel interrupted. "We are not ready for UFOs yet. You have shown that monkeys can't type the works of Shakespeare, but what is your argument against evolution?"

"Okay," smiled Joseph, "I am going to make you the centerpiece of why the theory of evolution is a bunch of crap."

"Really?" Daniel sat up straight in his chair. "I guess I should feel honored."

"Let's say that you lived a very, very long time ago."

"All right, I am in my man cave."

"And it is reproduction time."

"This is getting good."

"How old would you be?"

"Well, I know in the old days life expectancy was much shorter, so people started having babies at a much younger age. I would say for a male, maybe mid-to-late teens?"

"Makes sense to me," agreed Joshua, "which is middle school, high school, and early college age today. So, picture yourself at that age and let's say you have three possible female candidates to choose from for reproduction."

"This sounds like a dating website to me."

"Girl Number One," Joshua announced, "is a genius. She is so smart that she may be one of Einstein's ancestors. Her looks, however, aren't so good. She is scrawny and very, very plain looking."

"Attractiveness rating?"

"Oh, she is definitely a one."

"Come on man, that's mean to give a girl a one attractiveness rating. It is just not politically correct."

"Okay, let's be generous and give her a 2.5".

"Next," said Daniel eagerly.

"Girl Number Two wrestles grizzly bears...and wins. She is very, very big and very, very strong and could crush you like a bug." He paused and rolled his eyes, "And she also gets a politically correct 2.5 attractiveness rating."

"Are there any bears around my cave?"

"Hell no, she has scared them all away."

"Well, she is scaring me too," shuddered Daniel. "How about Girl Number Three?"

"Girl Number Three is a gorgeous bombshell with a fantastic body. She would be a present-day model or movie star. She is not very bright and she is not very strong, but wow is she good looking. On a scale of one to ten, she is an eleven...and she loves to – uh procreate."

"Bring her on!" exclaimed Daniel. "Who cares about brains and brawn!"

"Precisely, humans at reproductive age could care less about traits that improve the species. They will reproduce with whoever is around, the more sexually appealing the better. If we, as high-level intelligent beings don't choose our mates based on potential genetic improvements, why should we expect a more primitive species to selectively breed?"

"And with random breeding, there is no evolution," summarized Daniel.

"You got it!" Joshua smiled proudly. "Evolution is just a bunch of crap. Now let's get back to something really important...UFO's!"

CHAPTER 2

THE MANNA PROJECT

The next morning Daniel Robinson drove east on Highway 225, the Pasadena Freeway. The highway was lined with petrochemical storage tanks. Behind them giant distillation towers, like magical beanstalks, climbed high into the sky. Each tower generated riches beyond belief - much more than any goose that laid golden eggs. In the distance, rose the majestic obelisk of the San Jacinto Monument. Daniel turned south on the Sam Houston Tollway and took the exit for the Stamford Chemical Research and Development building.

Daniel had a nine o'clock meeting with the R&D Vice President, Dr. Charles Rysand. The distinguished looking gentlemen in his late-fifties had white hair and wore a dark suit with a white shirt and blue tie. The block-paneled walls in his large office were filled with plaques of patents and various awards. He motioned Daniel to sit at a circular table, which had a copy of Daniel's proposal for 'The Manna Project' along with several other papers. Daniel noticed the title of one of articles, 'The Chemistry of Methanol and its Derivatives,' as he sat down in a very comfortable and rich-looking brown upholstered chair and rolled up to the table.

"Methanol chemistry?" Daniel initiated small talk to start the meeting. "Isn't that what is made at Hydra, the plant that is next door to our chemical plant?"

"Yes it is," responded Dr. Rysand. "Hydra manufactures methanol. Some of the methanol is further reacted to produce downstream products – formaldehyde, formic acid, and sodium formate."

"Are we thinking about entering those markets?"

"Oh no. We are looking at synergies. Maybe there is a Hydra byproduct that we can use or maybe they can use one of our byproducts in their process. The chemical industry is always evolving. Transforming molecules, I like to say."

"I never thought of it that way." Daniel knew that chemists and engineers see the world differently.

"Can you imagine," continued Dr. Rysand, "what it is like to be a molecule in a chemical plant? You are floating around happy as can be and, all of a sudden, some other molecule wants to mate. The next thing you know, some new atom is attached to you and your physical properties are totally different. Maybe one minute you are this ferocious acid and the next moment you are a harmless salt. I wonder what the molecule thinks as it is being transformed. Is there pain, is there suffering as it gives up its properties to become something totally different?"

This guy is loony, thought Daniel. He knew that there was a thin line between genius and crazy, so he quickly changed the subject, "I really have not given that much thought. You mentioned that you wanted to go over my ideas on the Manna Project at today's meeting?"

"Oh, yes, yes, yes. Your report is very thorough. I have a meeting with the Board of Directors next month and I would like to present your proposal."

"Let me start by saying that I am glad that it is you and not me giving the presentation. It is much easier for me to prepare a presentation than it is to actually give one. I really hate speaking in front of people."

"Understood," acknowledged Dr. Rysand. "So, what kind of presentation would you prepare?"

"The Board is a mixture of technical and non-technical people, right?"

"That is correct. There will be people with technical and business backgrounds in the petrochemical industry as well as people from totally different industries."

"I would start with a brief summary of the history of the petrochemical industry. In the beginning, petrochemical products were primarily used as fuel for cars, trucks, ships, and planes. Then came the materials markets – plastics and other petrochemical products replaced many of the traditional building materials such as wood, steel, and glass. Petrochemicals found their way into clothing, carpets, and a wide variety of household products. Then there are the specialty markets – pharmaceuticals, herbicides, and electronics all use materials that are chemical plant products."

Dr. Rysand nodded.

"So where are the future opportunities for chemicals? A huge potential market is the food industry. The world food supply is limited by the amount of land available for agriculture. Initial attempts to manufacture food from chemicals were resisted by the food lobby. Instead of making a food product that directly competes with the food industry, we could supply them with a raw material they could use in their food products."

Dr. Rysand leaned forward in his chair and then rocked back and forth. It was a little strange Daniel thought, but research folks always seemed a bit odd.

"So how do we do this? Petrochemical plants have steam boilers that run twenty-four hours a day, seven days a week. Heat is generated in the steam boilers by burning fuels in the presence of air. This oxidation reaction converts fuels into carbon dioxide and water vapors that are emitted out the boiler stacks into the surrounding atmosphere. The Manna Project would recover these emissions and send them through pipes into tanks to feed fast-growing algae. The algae will need a light source to grow inside the tanks. In nature, plant growth is limited by the number of hours of sunlight in a day. For our process, we place LED lights inside the tanks. Since there will always be a source of light, the algae will grow much faster."

Dr. Rysand stopped his rocking and was now leaning back in his chair, staring at the ceiling.

"There are existing processes that convert algae into starch. Starch is a raw material for many foods. Currently starch is produced by growing crops, harvesting crops, and then transporting the crops to food processing plants that convert the crops into starch. This requires a lengthy growing season that is dependent upon sunlight, weather, pests, and crop diseases. We can do this much faster and it is a very environmentally friendly process that reduces carbon dioxide emissions."

Dr. Rysand's eyes were glazing over. Was he falling asleep? Daniel knew he had to hurry.

"This process will supplement the world food market just as wind and solar power provide alternative sources that complement the world energy markets. It should not be seen as a threat to farmers as it represents only a very small portion of the total world food market. The world population is growing and people are going to need new food sources. Our process will be used to fight world hunger."

Dr. Rysand's eyes were now fully closed. Daniel knew he had to wrap up quickly.

"Summarizing, plant growth is one of the best uses for carbon dioxide. We can take carbon dioxide from our plant steam boilers that is currently released to the environment and use it to grow algae. The algae can be converted into starch and further transformed by the food industry into edible products. This will increase the world food supply and reduce the amount of greenhouse gasses."

Dr. Rysand was leaning back in his chair and looking at the ceiling with his eyes totally shut when he began speaking, "It is a very interesting process, Daniel." He opened his eyes and continued to stare at the ceiling, "Lots and lots of transformations." He paused. "Crude oil that was originally molecules from deceased plants or animals, gathers in pools below ground and stays that way for a very long time. The crude oil is pumped from the ground and taken to a refinery. The refinery transforms it into various materials, some of which are sent to chemical plants. We further transform these materials into valuable products, but we have leftovers. We send the leftovers to boilers where they are burned as a fuel, which transforms them into carbon dioxide while generating steam to use in our petrochemical plants. Carbon dioxide is a very stable molecule, but wait, the transformations are not complete, the carbon dioxide is now fed to algae which transforms the molecules into living cells."

"I never thought about it in those terms. There are a lot of transformations."

"Life is transformation," Dr. Rysand philosophized as he sat upright in his chair and looked at Daniel. "All of us – you, me, and all living things are constantly being transformed. We reach a state in life in which we are happy, very happy. We reach a state in which we are stable, very stable. We reach a state in which we run the world and the world makes sense. And then…" He paused and Daniel thought he saw a glint of a tear in his eye. "And then boom, something changes. The world no longer needs us and we are reduced to a pile of dust."

So, this is what life is like at the vice president level, thought Daniel as he tried to get the R&D leader back on topic "Sir, what do you think about the presentation?"

"It is a very interesting concept," noted Dr. Rysand as he emerged from his world of gloom, "But at the Board level, the major concern is economics. World hunger and greenhouse gases are not going to be important to that group. It comes down to cost versus value."

"We should be able to reduce costs," Daniel quickly interjected. "Many petrochemical plants have large storage vessels in their tank farms that have deteriorated with time and are no longer able to store petrochemical products. It costs too much to dispose of these tanks, so they just sit around and rust. They are no longer able to store flammable materials, but should be good for holding water and algae and, if they leak a little, it will not be harming the environment. By utilizing these old tanks, the project costs will be greatly reduced. There is also some nearby vacant land where the food industry could build their facilities, thereby reducing transportation costs."

"That's good. What about value?"

"The value will depend upon the price of starch on the world food market."

"So, it would be really, really good if we had a worldwide famine," stated Dr. Rysand matter-of-factly. "The project would then become very attractive."

"Worldwide famine?" A look of horror swept across Daniel's face, "Millions would die."

"That's unfortunate. But that may be the price, the price to make this project come to life."

A wave of dejection suddenly swept across Daniel and the room became still.

Dr. Rysand stared back at the ceiling. After a few minutes passed, which seemed like an eternity, he broke the silence, "Hmm, there may be another way to pitch the project."

"How is that?" asked Daniel, clinging for any ray of hope.

"We don't push the project on economics." Dr. Rysand sat upright "We push the project on corporate image…yes, corporate image. We want the public to see us as a trendy green company that is trying to improve the world. So, we ask for R&D funding to pursue studies. Hmm, maybe we could get say a half dozen PhD's and a dozen or so laboratory technicians. We will definitely need a new wing on our research building - state of the art, of course. Let's see, we will need a research plan – maybe start with which type of algae grows best? We will want to conduct multiple studies on the size, number, shape, and color of the LED lights versus the algae growth rate. And government grants? Yes, we certainly need to apply for government grants."

"But sir," protested Daniel, "That will cost millions and millions of dollars and require years and years of study. It will cost much more to do the study than simply installing a pipe between the steam boiler and an existing storage tank."

The research director was unfazed, "You have to see the big picture, Daniel."

"The big picture, sir?"

"You have to remember the wars." The research director waived his right hand in the air, as if he was wielding an imaginary sword.

"The wars, sir?" Daniel maintained a professional appearance, but inside his eyes were rolling. Are all research people this nuts?

"The patent wars." Dr. Rysand leaned back in his desk chair and began one of his favorite stories. "In the beginning, there were no patents. Anyone could use anyone else's ideas. There were no rules and chaos reigned."

Daniel thought, first Joshua and now Dr. Rysand. Was he some kind of a magnet that attracted weird eccentric people? Fortunately, Joshua had provided him good practice for these situations, "And did someone then say let there be light?"

"Sort of like that." Dr. Rysand was initially startled, but smiled and continued. "In the 1400's, the Italians perfected the art of glass blowing and were very secretive about their techniques. Some trace the origins of the patent system to the glass blowers. However, the ones that really developed the patent system, as we know it today, were the British in the 1600's. The Industrial Revolution was gathering steam and the Brits are very, very good with their bureaucracies. Their system was copied by their colonies which touched most of the world."

"So how does it work?"

"It really is creating something from nothing. Let's take your idea, which in itself is nothing."

Daniel looked hurt. Now a crazy man was insulting him.

"Oh, don't take me wrong." Dr. Rysand saw the expression on Daniel's face and quickly backtracked. "I think you have a fantastic idea. But ideas, by their nature, contain no matter or energy. They therefore do not exist in the physical universe. Invisible and non-detectable, they are in essence nothing. This idea, however, has potential value. If the idea can be shown to be useful, novel, and non-obvious to one skilled in the art, then it can be submitted for approval as a patent. Once the patent is approved, a new...what shall we call it...a new room will be created in the invisible patent universe. This new room can then become the site of fierce wars."

"Fierce wars?" questioned Daniel relieved that his idea really did have value.

"Fierce patent wars fought by lawyers. Others may try to take your idea and use it for their profit. That is why it is very important for you to claim the boundaries of your patent. Naturally, you want to claim as much territory as possible. You may have proven that your idea works at certain conditions, but you want to claim that, in addition to these conditions, it will also work at other conditions. Competitors will then have a more difficult time using your idea."

"But won't the competitors object? There is no way that one can run tests at all of the possible conditions."

"They may object," acknowledged Dr. Rysand, "Especially if it is profitable for them to circumvent your patent. We need to make strong claims, make sure we do not have any weak points, and prepare for a lengthy battle."

"So, these battles could be fought for a long time?"

"It is possible. It all comes down to cost versus value. If the reward is great enough, it may be worth the costs to challenge the patent. If the costs are too great, it may be more economical for the competitor to simply purchase the technology by paying a licensing fee."

"So, it really is a war fought in invisible places. It must be a huge business for the patent lawyers."

"All wars are driven by either economics or the emotions of the leaders," explained Dr. Rysand "There are literally millions of rooms in the patent universe in which the damn lawyers fight their battles."

"Making something from nothing, things that have no mass or energy, rooms suddenly created out of thin air, fierce battles fought in nonexistent locations, I find the concepts a bit overwhelming," admitted Daniel.

"It is a bit overwhelming," agreed Dr. Rysand. "The ability to create something from nothing that lasts forever is truly amazing."

"I also take it that you are not fond of lawyers?"

Dr. Rysand paused contemplatively. "There is story about an engineer that died and went to Hell. Hell was hot, congested, miserable, and smelled really, really bad – kind of like being around here in the summer. Needless to say, everyone was upset and mad at everybody else. The only recreation was to watch the Houston Texans play football and, let's just say, that gives you an indication of how bad things were. Well, the engineer decided to improve the place. He realized that the heat source in Hell could be used to power a heat pump, which could be used to cool off parts of Hell. He then used the source of energy to develop a mass transportation system with driverless cars, which eliminated the traffic congestion. Next, he installed pollution control equipment and things started smelling better. The football team still stunk, but he was able to hook up a satellite dish so folks could watch hundreds of channels of shows on enormous video screens. One day, God looked down on Hell to see how his grand design was working and saw lots and lots of happy people sipping chilled margaritas that were made from the stills and ice machines that the engineer had designed. He asked the Devil what was going on."

The Devil replied, "Things have gotten a lot better down here since you sent us that engineer."

"What," questioned God. "An engineer? I didn't send you one of those. It must have been a mistake. Send him up."

"Not so fast," responded the Devil, "the engineer is doing a really good job down here."

"He is not supposed to be there. Send him up."

"He is in the middle of some really important projects."

"He is not supposed to be working on *your* projects," corrected God sternly. "Send him up!"

"We really would like to keep him here," countered the Devil.

"I said, send him up now!" demanded God.

"Not now," insisted the Devil. "We are going to need to keep him a while longer."

"I am serious," roared God. "Send the engineer up here immediately!"

"No way!" insisted the Devil, "we like our engineer and we are going to keep him!"

"If you do not send him to me right this instant, I am going to sue!"

"You are going to sue me?" questioned the Devil incredulously.

God was really infuriated. "You better believe it! I am going to sue!"

"With what?" asked the Devil calmly, "all the lawyers are down here."

CHAPTER 3

THE CHUPACABRA

The next morning, Daniel walked into the Stamford Chemical plant control room. The room contained six large video screens at desktop level with diagrams of the plant equipment. Temperatures, pressures, and flow rates in various areas of the chemical plant were automatically updated and shown on the display screens. The normal operating range for each measurement had been previously determined and entered into the plant computer control system. If a measurement was outside the normal operating range, an emergency signal flashed to alert the operator of the condition so that corrective actions could be initiated. Some measurements were more important than others. If the more important measurements were outside the normal operating range, an audible warning alarm automatically sounded. If these were not corrected, the computer control system was programmed to automatically shut-off raw material feeds and energy sources.

Two additional large video screens were hung from the ceiling and provided views of the plant. These screens were connected to remote-controlled video cameras that could be turned to show different parts of the plant. One was currently pointed in the direction of the plant flare, a visual indicator that the flare was lit and operating properly. The other monitor was pointed toward the entrance of the control room. The biggest danger to the plant operators was not the explosive, corrosive, and highly toxic chemicals they routinely handled each day – it was a supervisor making an unannounced visit and possibly catching them sleeping or doing something that violated plant rules.

When Daniel entered the control room, he saw that his good friend Ernesto was sitting in the command chair monitoring operations. Ernesto was in his mid-forties, had dark hair that was starting to gray, and was of Hispanic descent. One would not call him fat, but his frame had definitely grown due to middle age and the excellent cooking on graveyard shifts. His chair had rollers, and Ernesto frequently rolled from screen to screen to address any alarms. A two-way radio was at his side, which kept him in constant contact with field operators making any necessary adjustments.

"How's the plant running?" asked Daniel. "Do we need to have someone pee in the reactor?"

It was a standing joke. Legend has it that there was once a chemical plant that was not running well. The chemists and engineers tried many different optimizing techniques, but the plant still did not run well. One day, the plant suddenly starting operating much better. The chemists and engineers were baffled and conducted even more investigations, but could not find anything to explain the improved performance. Finally, one of the plant operators confessed to having urinated in an open tank that fed the reactor. Apparently, the uric acid had improved the reaction. The story goes that the plant chemist patented the idea and got a promotion. No one knows what happened to the operator. In modern chemical plants, reactions take place in enclosed vessels that run twenty-four hours a day, seven days a week, so there is no way to pee in them, even if the plant operator felt the urge.

"Nope, no need to pee, the reactor is running fine," answered Ernesto.

"How'd things go last night? Any problems?"

"It was a good night here. Not so good at the San Jacinto Monument." Ernesto had a worried look.

"The San Jacinto Monument? We don't have anything there. What happened?"

"Couple of teenagers went out there late last night to...you know, partake in extracurricular activities. He gets attacked and killed...real messy, lots and lots of blood."

"Sorry to hear that. It's only a few miles from here. Did they get a description of the bad guy?"

"Not yet. The young lady described some kind of weird beast, you know, sounded like it could have been a chupacabra."

Daniel raised his eyebrows. "A chupacabra? The mythical Big Foot from South America is now in Houston?"

"You don't want to mess with chupacabras," warned Ernesto. "Those are some really mean dudes. Guys on graveyard shift are nervous. They are asking for extra security."

▲ ▲ ▲

Daniel finished his rounds in the plant and stopped by Joshua's office. "I heard there was a grisly killing at the San Jacinto Monument last night. What are you hearing?"

Joshua's eyes lit up, "Official story is that a young couple was making out near the monument and the guy got attacked and killed."

"And you believe that is all there is to the story?" Daniel asked surprisingly.

"Hell no!" Joshua quickly replied.

"Ernesto said he thought it might have been a chupacabra."

"A chupacabra. Hmm," Joshua paused, "It certainly sucked out a lot of blood. Of course, there is much more to the story. Rumor has it..."

Daniel interrupted, "Now is this from your kooky conspiracy network?"

"I am referring to my group of well-educated scientific professionals that explore where others don't," corrected Joshua, "and they say that something very strange happened at the San Jacinto Monument last night."

"So, what was so strange?"

"For starters, the victim's blood was analyzed."

"I suppose they found something unusual. Was the blood green?" Daniel rolled his eyes.

Joshua shook his head. "No, there was nothing new in the blood. It is what was not in the blood that was unusual. There was no adrenaline. A person attacked like that should have signs of adrenaline in their blood."

"Okay, it is a bit unusual, but not that big of a thing."

"Well, the second item was definitely unusual. It was the eyewitness account from the girl present. She claims her boyfriend was attacked by a flying monkey that escaped in a tiny flying saucer."

"Joshua," Daniel slowly spoke, "I would not repeat that story at work. People will think you really are crazy."

CHAPTER 4

THE PEARLY GATES

After lunch, Daniel returned to the Stamford Chemical plant control room.

"Long time, no see," hollered Ernesto. "What brings you back so soon?"

"Checking on some ideas to improve the 300 Sector," replied Daniel. "Anything going on there?"

"Nope," responded Ernesto while not taking his eyes off the monitoring screens in front of him, "nothing going on there. We do have painters in the tank farm, so there may be some paint spray in the air."

"Hoping for a new coat of paint for your truck?" joked Daniel.

"Dude, my truck is a classic."

Daniel stepped outside and started to walk to the 300 Sector. A bright light flashed. Daniel stopped in his tracks and looked up to the sky. An exceedingly bright beam of light hit him and the world shook as swirling white clouds engulfed him. That was the last thing Daniel remembered as he collapsed and fell to the ground.

▲ ▲ ▲

The bright lights and swirling gradually came to a stop. Slowly Daniel became aware of his new surroundings. The sights and sounds of the chemical plant were replaced with rolling green hills and gurgling brooks. Sunshine, blue skies, a light breeze, scattered lakes, and lush green grass were everywhere. Orbs of brilliant white light were randomly floating all around. As Daniel took a closer look, it appeared that a line of orbs was gathering in one spot. As he got closer, he saw a short chubby black woman at the front of the line. Her hair was in dreadlocks and she was wearing a bright multi-colored robe with matching hat. Daniel thought she might have been Jamaican. He walked over to the line and waited his turn.

"Next," the woman in charge called when it was Daniel's turn.

Daniel approached, "I'm not sure where I am or why I am here?"

"Honey," the woman didn't look up, "Yo be in Bovine Heaven and deese be de pearly gates. Now go's over der and fill's out de forms. Dis may be paradise, but we's stills gots to do's dey forms. Next."

Daniel stepped aside and went to the adjacent area. He looked around and saw hundreds of orbs filling out surveys on floating video screens. He could hear some of the questions being asked to the orbs.

"What was your first memory?"

"Did you receive adequate attention from your mother?"

"How was your learning process?"

"Did you have good friends?"

"Did you have adequate sustenance?"

"Were there storms in your life?"

"How did you weather them?"

"Would you have preferred more or less drama in your life?"

"Did you reproduce?"

"How many offspring did you have?"

"On a scale of one to ten, with one being very easy and ten being very difficult, how would you rate your life?"

"How was your end-of-life experience?"

"Was there much suffering?"

"Would you have preferred to live a shorter or longer life?"

"If you had lived longer, what would you have done?"

"What did you learn about life?"

A blue video screen suddenly appeared in the air and floated to Daniel. The thin screen was about two feet wide and three feet tall and it spoke, although Daniel could not locate the source of the sound. "You have been selected to participate in a survey about your recent life on Earth. The survey results will be used to improve living conditions for your species. A scan will now be conducted to gather vital information. This will take just an instant and will be entirely painless."

Daniel was scanned and it was totally painless. The video screen displayed 777 7777.

As soon as the scan was complete, Daniel heard a loud scream from the women in charge, "Holy *** Dis cain't be! Somebody screw up – big time!" She quickly ran over to Daniel and clasped her hands together in prayer.

"I be terribly sorry sir fo all dis and humbly request yo fogiveness. Yo, yo ain't supposed to be ere. It seem dat a major error o'cur. It be bad dat dis happen, but it be especially bad dat it happened to somebody like yo."

"Like me?" Daniel was incredulous. "What is so special about me?"

"I be comforted by yo humility, sir. I know we all be God's creatures. But yo sir, yo be a seven sevens. I need to get yo to where yo belong. Please fogive me for all dat yo been through. As the, uh, saying go – perfection is imperfection, right sir? Okay, dey be ready fo' yo. Thank yo for blessing me with yo presence."

The woman took his hand and they disappeared.

CHAPTER 5

CONTROL CENTER FOR THE WORLD

Daniel reappeared in a totally different setting. The rolling green hills and gentle breezes were replaced with dense swirling clouds filled with thousands and thousands of brilliant white orbs bouncing around like fireflies on an early summer night. He closed his eyes again and when he reopened them the swirling stopped and the brilliant white orbs vanished. He was in some kind of control room, but this was no ordinary control room, and it was enormous. Futuristic colorful displays were hovering all over the place attended by people that appeared to be floating in air. Was he on an alien spaceship in orbit above the Earth? He could see outside, but the scenes were not from space – they were views of different parts of Earth from multiple angles. As Daniel became more aware of his surroundings, he realized he was standing on a glass floor and could see through glass floors and transparent walls to levels above and below. A display screen filled with flashing multi-colored three-dimensional images floated past him. Then Daniel began to hear voices.

"INITIATING HURRICANE IN QUADRANT 1986J...VOLCANIC ERUPTION IN QUADRANT 89K...TSUNAMI DEVELOPING IN QUADRANT 1956A... EARTHQUAKE AT QUADRANT 52S...ANTARCTIC WIND SPEEDS GENERATED AT 202W LEVEL FOUR..."

Daniel was amazed – it was like some futuristic weather station. As he was beholding the view, a young nerdy looking guy approached. He appeared to be in his late twenties and was wearing a Hawaiian shirt tucked into his blue jeans and flip-flops. His long sandy brown hair had a windblown and unkept look. He smiled as he addressed Daniel. "Hey dude, what's up?"

"Well...Howdy, err hello," Daniel stammered.

"You are new here, aren't you?"

"Yes, I just arrived. What is this place? Is it a weather monitoring station?"

"A weather monitoring station? Hmm, I guess you could call it that – it would probably upset the engineers that designed it. Dude, this is the control center for the world."

"Control center for the world? I thought the world ran itself."

"Ran itself?" He chuckled, "You sound like Newton – who is over there somewhere by the way. Okay, let's start with introductions, my name is Roger and I am an electrical engineer. I get to throw the lightning bolts."

"Glad to meet you Roger, my name is Daniel I am a chemical engineer. That is, I was a chemical engineer. I am not sure I am still alive. I just came from Bovine Heaven."

"Well, let me formally welcome you to Scientific Heaven. Would you like a tour?"

"Sure."

They began walking around the control center. It was a beehive of activity with flashing lights, warning alarms, and people racing around. Roger grabbed Daniel's hand and they suddenly floated upward toward the glass floor of the next level. Daniel lowered his head and winced in anticipation of crashing into the glass ceiling, but they passed through and stood on the floor above.

Daniel had a surprised look on his face.

"It is difficult at first, but you get used to it," commented Roger.

As they continued their walk, Daniel saw hundreds of multi-colored video screens showing conditions on various parts of Earth. They stopped and he grabbed one of the hovering screens and stared at it with a perplexed look.

"So, you are a chemical engineer, are you familiar with controlling processes?"

"Of course," replied Daniel. "Every chemical plant has a control room from where the operators monitor and control plant operations."

"Why are there operators in a chemical plant? Why does it not just run itself? Isn't it programmed to do that?"

"Yes, it is," answered Daniel, "but unexpected things occur. Mechanical equipment breaks down, piping becomes plugged, electrical circuits fail - things do not always go according to plan. We are always watching for these things so that changes can be made to restore order. If we cannot restore order, we have to shut down the plant and that can be very costly."

"So, if events occur that disrupt the order in a chemical plant, would you not expect that there may be things that could potentially disrupt the processes on Earth? Surely the Earth is a lot bigger and more complicated than one chemical plant. Shutting the Earth down would be extremely costly. Wouldn't it be better to restore order instead of shutting it down and starting anew?"

"I guess I never thought of it that way. I didn't think the Earth needed a control center."

"Where is the control center for the human body?"

"It's in the brain, of course."

"Why have a control center?" asked Roger. "If an arm or leg gets too hot or too cold why not just have it automatically move on its own, with no control center involvement?"

"Well," answered Daniel, "the brain can give direction. For instance, it could tell the body parts to stay away from fire to avoid being burned. It is more efficient to avoid hazards than to later repair the damage."

"And can you avoid all hazardous situations?"

"No, there are times when you have to balance the hazard with the potential reward. It is risky to drive to work during harsh weather, but there are economic benefits. To cook a meal, one needs to be near a source of heat. Cost versus value evaluations are often needed."

"Precisely," agreed Roger. "It is the same way with the Earth. There are systems designed to water the Earth, regulate heat, spread food sources, and sometimes these conflict with each other. We have to balance the different demands for better life on Earth. Let me give you an example. Look at the video screen in your hands."

The screen suddenly came to life and showed a map of the panhandle of Texas. A red light was flashing on the map.

"The red light is flashing because there is currently a drought in the area," explained Roger. "The area is requesting cooler temperatures and rain. The operator would need to bring in a cold front from Canada. It would take a large cold front since it would have to pass through the hot Midwest, so the cold front option is not looking good. A shower, however, could also come from the Pacific Northwest. The operator is going to try to increase temperatures over the Pacific Ocean to start a front that could eventually pass through the Texas Panhandle."

"Makes sense to me."

"Now look over here." Roger pointed on the screen. "Projections show that the front will increase rainfall over northern California. The flashing blue light here indicates an increased mudslide risk. The weather operators are going to have to try to balance the cost versus value."

"So, in order to help some, others will suffer?"

"That is always a problem in Heaven," stated Roger.

The video screen he had been holding dissolved into nothingness. Daniel slowly turned and gazed around the cavernous control center as he tried to adsorb the immensity of everything he was seeing. "This place is awesome!" The wheels in Daniel's engineering mind were whirling. "In the old days, control rooms were connected to instruments in chemical plants with pneumatic tubing and the process was controlled using air pressure. Most of these systems have been replaced and now the control rooms are connected to the instruments with wiring and the processes are controlled by computers sending electrical signals. Technology is transforming and there are even some processes that are linked to the control room and controlled by wireless communication signals. What do you use for the links to this control room?"

"Good question. We use P-Rays. Would you like to see the Communication Center?"

▲ ▲ ▲

The control center for the world disappeared and suddenly Daniel and Roger were in a room high above the foot of an enormous white horizontal cross. At the intersection of the beams of the cross, there was a pulsating red glow, like that of a beating heart. Every few seconds, red streams lit up various sections of the cross.

"A living cross?" asked Daniel. "How large is it and what does it do?"

"It is used to communicate with life on Earth," explained Roger. "The center beam is one mile wide, one mile tall, and eight miles long. The intersecting beam is one mile wide, one mile tall, and 5.547 miles long."

"That seems like an unusual number. Are the dimensions important?"

"Extremely. The long beam has an eight-to-one ratio, eight of course, being the number of notes in an octave. Multiply the width of the cross beam by the cube root of three and you also get eight. Those ratios are critical for the P-Ray communication system. The cross picks up the P-rays and conveys them to Central Processing. P-rays are then returned to the Earth."

"Wait a minute." Daniel stopped. "Cross, P-Rays...do you mean prayer?"

"P-rays, prayer, they are interchangeable."

"Then, then there is a Religious Heaven?" Daniel was startled.

"Of course," replied Roger. "We are in Scientific Heaven on the engineering side, the side that makes things work. There is a religious side – it is in a different area."

"So, P-rays…" The engineering wheels in Daniel's mind were turning again, "How do they work?"

"It is fairly straight forward. Everyone comes equipped with a P-ray transmitter and a P-ray receiver. You transmit spiritual signals to the cross. It takes the signals and sends them to Central Processing. Central Processing sends spiritual signals to the cross and they are relayed to the P-ray receivers."

"I have prayed many times, but I haven't received many signals."

"Oh, you receive signals all the time, you just do not realize their origin. Random thoughts, ideas out of the blue, dreams…"

"Dreams?" questioned Daniel. "Dreams come from Heaven?"

"Some do. Dreams are a mechanism for knowledge transfer."

"So, all mankind has a link to Heaven?" Daniel was trying to wrap his mind around the concept.

"Not just mankind," Roger divulged, "all life has a spiritual component."

▲ ▲ ▲

They left the Communication Center and returned to the control center for the world. Video screens filled with graphics flashed as people scurried around.

"Daniel, you said something a while ago that intrigued me. You asked if you were alive and you referred to the cross as a living cross. What is your definition of life?"

"My grandmother used to say in life you are born, grow up, reproduce, and die. I am not sure that is the scientifically correct definition. I know that the biologists include metabolism."

"So, if someone was born with a reproduction defect and could not reproduce, they would not be alive?"

"Of course not, but I see your point. The reproduction part is a bit tricky. A species must reproduce or it will cease to exist. However, not every member of the species will reproduce. Some will die before they can reproduce and others will not reproduce due to physical ailments or life choices."

"So would you say then that metabolism is the key criteria in determining if something is alive?"

"I, I guess so," replied Daniel. "Obviously some species have a very slow metabolism. However, they all consume a food source and give off waste products."

"What about a machine, say a car? It consumes fuel and it generates heat. Would you say it is alive?"

"Of course not, I can see that the definition of life can be tricky."

"Daniel, in Heaven we do not eat and we do not have waste products. Are we alive?"

"Well of course everyone here is alive. I see busy people all around doing things to keep the world running."

"What about God? Is he alive?"

"He has got to be," answered Daniel, "Everywhere I look I see signs of creation. He has got to exist."

"But is he alive?"

"He has got to be alive. I was taught that he is the living Lord."

"What about what your grandmother said – born, grow up, reproduce, and die. Did God do any of these? By definition, does God have to die to live?"

"That is a good question." Daniel had a perplexed look, "I guess there is a lot about life that I just do not understand."

▲ ▲ ▲

They continued their walk around the gargantuan control center.

"Daniel, there is someone here you need to meet." A glass wall was just ahead of them.

Daniel slowed down as they approached the wall, but Roger maintained his pace.

"Keep going, have faith." Roger took Daniel's hand, "It takes a bit getting used to at first, but it is a lot easier to get around here than on Earth."

Daniel stumbled as they passed through the glass wall. They walked some more and came to an area that had thousands of painted sunrises and sunsets on a transparent gallery wall that was suspended in mid-air. An attractive woman that appeared to be in her mid-thirties and a younger male assistant were busily scurrying around. Joshua heard their conversation.

"We are running out of time. Should we use one of the stock issues?" asked the harried assistant.

"No, I'm thinking about 424H. Here it is." The attractive woman swirled her hand and a floating holograph image of a beautiful sunset suddenly appeared out of thin air. She pulled the painting down, folded it into a paper airplane, and whizzed it across the room to her assistant.

"Got it," hollered the assistant as he caught the airplane and somehow stuffed it into a waiting video screen. "Sent and done. See you in an hour for Quadrant 82SA."

"I'll have a good one. See you soon." The assistant left as Roger and Daniel approached.

"Aggie," Roger addressed the woman, "there is someone I would like for you to meet." The woman smiled as she approached. She was wearing a painter's hat over her short wavy dark hair, a conservative white blouse covered with a smock, and blue jean Capri pants. "You may remember him from your time on Earth – this is Daniel. I will leave you two alone to get reacquainted." Roger disappeared into thin air.

"Daniel? Wait, my Daniel? What are you doing here? You shouldn't be arriving here until a long time from now? Did I miss the Homecoming celebration?" She shook her head, "I certainly enjoy my job, but sometimes I just get so busy."

Daniel smiled and politely greeted the woman. "I am very glad to meet you. What do you do here? Should I know you?"

"Sunrises and sunsets." She lowered her voice, "Shh...don't tell anybody, but I have the best job in the universe. Every day I get to send out great works of beauty. Well, not every day – some days we send out the boring ones and some days there are rainclouds. You have to have the bad to appreciate the good. Variety is the spice of life you know."

"Variety is the spice of life," repeated Daniel, "I always heard that growing up. It was one of my grandmother's favorite sayings."

"It is true and I am glad you remembered...seeing as how I am your grandmother."

"Grandmother?" Joshua was shocked, "But, but...you look so young."

"Well of course I look young. Do you think I want to spend eternity with old wrinkly skin? If you could choose any age of life, which would it be?"

"Well, you do make a good point. How is Grandpa?"

"He was doing well the last time I last saw him. I think it was at a Homecoming. He certainly enjoys The Archives. You know that is good for some, and everyone has their preferences, but instead of digging around in the past I prefer the present and making the sunrises and sunsets."

"What?" exclaimed Daniel, "You don't live together? After over fifty years of marriage on Earth, I thought y'all would live forever together in Heaven."

"Things are different in Heaven," explained Grandmother, "we don't have the urges."

Daniel looked uncomfortable and started to blush.

"Oh dear, I am making you feel awkward. Let's just say that in Heaven the body parts don't work the way they do on Earth. There is no eating, drinking, and err, shall we say, no extracurricular activities.

Obviously, there are no offspring, no house payment, and no chores around the house. There really isn't any reason for a couple to be together. But enough about all that, tell me about your Homecoming celebration. Who was there?"

"Actually, there were a bunch of cows. I guess they were cows. They looked like orbs of light. The lady in charge said it was Bovine Heaven. Anyway, I was scanned and she freaked out. Said perfection is imperfection and took me here."

"Actually, the saying is imperfection is perfection and chaos is an engineer's paradise. Engineers are not always thought of well here. So, you had no Homecoming celebration? Let me rescan you."

Joshua was scanned again. Once again, it was totally painless and the video screen showed 777 7777.

"Holy *** No way!" screamed Grandma.

"What is it?" Daniel was startled and had a surprised look.

"First of all, you are a seven sevens…and secondly, you never died!"

CHAPTER 6

THE TRAVEL BUREAU

"Wow," marveled Grandma, "my grandson is a seven sevens. Who would have thought? You were always very special."

"Was I your favorite?" asked Daniel with a grin.

"Of course," Grandma winked.

"Now there is this matter of not dying. What to do, oh what to do?"

"Can you show me around?"

"Of course, of course…I need to get you set up for a meeting with God. You know, on this whole death thing."

"A meeting with God?" questioned Daniel with an incredulous look.

"Oh yes," Grandma answered matter-of-factly, "A face-to-face sit down. Everybody does it. Do you have your list of seven questions?"

"A sit-down meeting with God?" Daniel was astonished, "We are talking about God, the God? The creator of the universe and I are going to sit down for a face-to-face?"

"With your seven questions."

"How, how did you know I have seven questions?"

"Oh, everyone has seven questions for God," Grandma stated nonchalantly, "but we can get to that later. Let's start with a tour. Where do you want to start?"

"Wherever you suggest."

"Let's start with the Heavenly Travel Bureau." She took Daniel's arm and they disappeared.

▲ ▲ ▲

They reappeared in a gigantic multilevel futuristic pavilion. Billboard-size video screens, displaying a diverse assortment of animals along with colorful and eye-catching messages, floated above the large open floor. The first one that Daniel saw showed an earthworm and said, 'Experience the Earth on Earth.' Then came an 'Eight is Great' screen with a smiling octopus, followed by a 'Where Dragons Fly' screen picturing a dragonfly. The animals were not just shown on video screens – migrating geese flew across the room carrying a 'The World's Best Travelers' banner and a large blue whale swam through the air with an emblazoned 'Go Big' tattoo.

"What is all this?" asked Daniel.

"Oh, it's just advertising. The gates are over there."

Grandma took Daniel's hand and they floated across the room to rows and rows of gates. Some were lush with greenery, some were desert scenes, there were rivers, forests, a beautiful waterfall, and one that looked like a futuristic skyscraper.

As they surveyed the gates, a woman in a green uniform flew up to them, "May I help you?"

"Just looking," replied Grandma.

They selected the futuristic skyscraper scene. As they floated through, there were side doors leading to multiple corridors.

Daniel had a puzzled look. "I don't understand. What is all this?"

"It is the travel bureau. You have an opportunity to be any life form on Earth."

"Any life form? Daniel was amazed.

"Any life form," confirmed Grandma. "You can be a bug, a bird, a fish, an elephant – you name it. You go to Earth and have an adventure."

"I can see how someone would want to be a mammal, but who would want to be a bug? Splat, hit a windshield and you are done."

"Oh, the bugs are fascinating - you can be a beautiful butterfly, a bumble bee, a lady bug, a lightning bug…there are thousands of possibilities. The life cycle is very short, so you get a taste of life as a bug and then you are back here again."

"Doing the surveys?"

"Oh yes, yes, yes - you have to do the surveys. We are very big on surveys. You do realize Daniel, that the molecules in your body may have been, or someday will be, all of these life forms."

"What?" The concept overwhelmed Daniel.

"Transformations are always taking place," continued Grandma. "Molecules are recycled. The molecules that compose you today were in different life forms before you were born and will be in different life forms after you die. We live in a very green universe and are all very connected."

As they floated back to the pavilion, they saw all kinds of animals. They came to one section that contained barren rocks.

"Are these for microscopic animals?" asked Daniel.

"Oh no, those are living rocks."

"Living rocks?"

"Yes, there is life in everything."

"Even in rocks?" questioned Daniel disbelievingly.

"It is a very weak life force. You don't do much as a rock, just sit around observing the world for eons. It is definitely a slow-paced lifestyle, but some like that. I hear the return trip, however, can be a bit rough. If you are into nontraditional life forms at a faster pace, you can select to be part of a body of water or even the atmosphere. Personally, when I travel, I prefer to be a warm cuddly mammal."

"But isn't life as an animal difficult? The struggles in finding food, escaping predators, and then often there is that inevitable violent death."

"But to live," sighed Grandma. She looked up and her eyes glazed over as her face flushed with a warm glow, "To live life on Earth, to feel the sun, the wind, the heat, the cold, the struggles, pleasure and pain…to experience life…ahh…it is so rewarding. And as for the other stuff – that's just the price of life."

Suddenly a wave of happiness spread across the room and multi-colored flecks of confetti sparkled as they gently floated from the top of the pavilion to the ground. Everyone stopped for a few seconds and cheered before continuing with their tasks.

"What's that?" asked Daniel

"It is emotional confetti. The Cosmic Cannon just fired."

"What is the Cosmic Cannon?"

"It's the ultimate trip. You are shot into a new universe. It is a one-way trip, of course, there is no coming back."

"No coming back?" Daniel had a puzzled look. "You leave Heaven and never come back? Are you dead?"

"I prefer to think of it as a better life on the other side. Technically, you are dead to this universe. You give up your identity to be part of something bigger - much, much bigger. You become part of a new universe!"

"Do you volunteer to go?"

"I wish," sighed Grandma with dreamy eyes, "it is a carefully controlled process. If you are selected to go, it is a great honor." They floated some more. "Daniel, you like designing chemical plants, don't you?"

"It is a job that seems to suit me well."

"Then you should really like the next place." She took his arm and they disappeared.

CHAPTER 7

BIOLOGY HEAVEN

Daniel and his grandmother reappeared in an immense laboratory. The bustling of the Heavenly Travel Bureau was replaced with the quietness of a group of scientists attentive to various tasks.

"We are now in Biology Heaven," announced Grandma. "This is where new life forms are developed."

"Developing new life forms?" Daniel looked bewildered, "I thought evolution… "

"Evolution is a bunch of crap," interrupted Grandma. "New species just don't just appear on their own without any help." She motioned to one of the biologists.

A slightly overweight middle-aged man wearing a white lab coat and a black and white striped bow tie approached. He was of medium height, with short black hair and round black wire rim glasses.

"Bio Bob, I would like you to meet my grandson, Daniel. Not only is he a chemical engineer, but he is also a seven sevens," bragged Grandma. "He has some biology questions."

"Whew." Bio Bob wiped imaginary sweat from his forehead, "I am glad he is a seven sevens. He should be better than the other engineers. Most engineers around here try to optimize things by tinkering with them until they break, creating more problems. They just cannot leave well enough alone. What would you like to know?"

"I have been taught," began Daniel, "that life started as simple organisms that evolved into more complex organisms. Is this not so?"

"Yes, I know...I was taught the same. What's the best way to explain...hmm...so you are a chemical engineer?" He paused. "Each life form is an engineering marvel – a fantastic creation. Pick one for me."

"I live on the Texas Gulf Coast and I hate mosquitoes...I have heard people say that Hell is too nice of a place for the inventor of the mosquito."

"Ah yes," nodded Bio Bob, "the lowly mosquito, an attacker of humans and animals, a blood sucker, spreader of countless diseases, and the central attraction of the annual Mosquito Festival in Clute, Texas."

A giant mosquito two feet long appeared and started flying around the room.

Daniel ducked as the mosquito buzzed him. "What the ***," shouted Daniel.

Grandma laughed, "Profanity is not allowed in Heaven, Daniel. It is blocked by the censors".

"Relax Daniel," chuckled Bio Bob, "This is Heaven – there is no eating or drinking here, so the mosquito has no reason to bite you. Now watch this."

A pedestal appeared out of nowhere and the mosquito landed there and froze in place. Next to it, a normal-size mosquito appeared and landed on the pedestal.

"I hate mosquitoes," declared Daniel, "but I have always been fascinated by their abilities. They can find me, attack me, and escape when I swat at them. In our chemical plant at work, we have heat sensors, motion detectors, and instruments that measure carbon dioxide. All of these are bulky compared to the tiny mosquito and certainly none of the instruments can fly and conduct evasive maneuvers when they are attacked. How do creatures that small do so much?"

"We have some very good designers here," replied Bio Bob, "and there is a lot of preprogramming. At birth, they possess lots of knowledge about the world."

"But the world is always changing. Long ago, there were no houses and people running around with chemical sprays and bug zappers trying to kill them."

"The preprogramming has changed with time. The data from the surveys is very important. Also, the P-Rays that are sent to them contain a lot of knowledge updates."

"So how do you go about designing an animal?"

"A living organism is a lot like a chemical plant. There are raw materials that are converted into a finished product, a heating system, a cooling system, and an electrical system. All of the systems are designed for that particular organism."

"So, you design a species based upon the materials at hand?"

"Precisely, and the forces around it – temperature, weather conditions, and so forth. We also look at its function. Often the purpose is to control the population of another organism."

"Control the population?" Daniel was startled. "You mean kill?"

"That is another way of saying it. Organisms kill each other - in order to have life, you have to have death. It is, after all, the price of life."

"You must have some very detailed design drawings. Are the hairs on the creatures really numbered?"

"Well of course they are numbered. There are standard guidelines for types of hair, concentration of hair, color of hair and so forth. Personally, I do not handle that part of the design, but we do have subject matter experts that focus exclusively on hair. I work more on new design concepts."

"So, what are some of your new design concepts?"

A video screen suddenly appeared out of thin air. "Here is one. It is a wispy critter designed for life fifty thousand feet above the Earth. It is about five hundred feet long and floats on air."

"Floats on air? Five hundred feet long? In the atmosphere fifty thousand feet high?" Daniel repeated incredulously. "What does it eat? There is nothing up there."

"There used to be nothing up there. Now there are all kinds of exhausts from aircraft engines and manufacturing plants. Think of this creature as a vacuum system for cleaning the atmosphere."

They continued their walk.

"So, if you were going to design space travelers, would you use little green men?" joked Daniel.

"Little green men?" Bio Bob had a puzzled look, "But why, we already have the perfect space travelers."

"I know. Humans were meant for space travel, but we are still in the early stages."

"Humans?" Bio Bob had a surprised look, "Oh no, I am talking about the lemurs."

"What?" Now it was Daniel's turn to be astonished, "Lemurs are just little monkeys running around in the jungle."

"Maybe so on Earth, but in other parts of the galaxy…"

"Wait a minute." Daniel was again bewildered. "You do design work for other planets?"

"Of course, who else would?"

"And lemurs fly spaceships?" Daniel shook his head in disbelief.

"I know humans are trying to fly spaceships, but lemurs do it much better and are made for space travel. They are only eighteen inches tall and weigh less than ten pounds. For space travel, they require much less food, water, and oxygen, so a much smaller spaceship can be utilized. Smaller ships can travel farther and faster."

They walked in silence for a while and then Daniel spoke, "I can comprehend that maybe some life forms were created, but on Earth there is evidence of evolution. Lots of different animals have similarities."

Grandma interrupted, "I have already told him Bio Bob that evolution is a bunch of crap."

Bio Bob was unfazed, "When you design your chemical plants Daniel, is the new design totally new or do you utilize the work of previous designs?"

"We have engineering standards that we follow with our designs. There are lots of different codes for electrical, civil, mechanical, and safety that are utilized. People that came before us developed best practices that we follow."

"So, you could have two chemical plants that produce totally different chemicals, yet they have similar electrical designs because they were built with the same electrical code?"

"It happens all the time. We know that if we follow the established electrical code, we will have a good design. We want to copy what we know works well."

"Once your chemical plant is built do you ever make changes?"

"We are always making small changes so the process runs better. We also have research people trying to develop a more efficient process, and if they do, the current process may be scrapped and a new plant built with the improved technology."

"When a better process is built, does the old process go away?"

"Not always. Often there are two or more different chemical processes producing the same chemical, at least for a while. It depends on how much more efficient the new process is compared to the old process. Ultimately it comes down to cost versus value – is it worth the cost to tear down the old plant and build a new one?"

"It is the same with new life forms," explained Bio Bob. "There are similarities between creatures because we copy what we know works well and we replace creatures that do not thrive with ones that are more suitable for the environment. Speaking of changing environments, look over there."

A video screen was hovering in mid-air with a picture and schematic of a snub-nosed oval creature that Daniel had never seen before. "This is a design proposal for a new animal that thrives in the petrochemical environment that one may have after an oil spill. It is part amphibian and part sponge."

They passed through double doors at the back of the laboratory and entered a courtyard filled with colorful plants. In the center of the courtyard, several of the new amphibian sponge creatures were frolicking in a pond filled with crude oil. Several biologists in matching white lab coats were monitoring the activities and recording measurements on video screens that were floating in the air. "As you can see, we are conducting laboratory tests to see how well the new creatures perform. We will make adjustments and fine tune the design before conducting larger scale tests. How do you bring to life your new chemical plants?"

"We start with an idea and we conduct laboratory tests. Then we build a small-scale pilot plant to test the process. From there we build a demonstration plant. If that plant is successful, we may build even larger plants and license them around the world."

"And do your chemical plants make changes and upgrade themselves on their own?"

"Of course not. Lots and lots of thinking goes into making every change. Do you have a demonstration plant for testing or will the new animal designs go straight to Earth?"

"A demonstration plant for testing?" repeated Bio Bob with a puzzled look, "Oh you mean Eden. Would you like to go there?"

"What!" exclaimed Daniel, "There really is an Eden? I thought Eden was a fictitious place that was part of the creation myth."

"The Eden you are talking about was a demonstration plant for testing life on Earth," explained Grandma, "Of course, it is no longer there, but there are other Edens. Hold on." She grabbed Daniel's arm as Biology Heaven disappeared and they reappeared in front of a burning gate that was flanked with high stone walls that seemed to extend forever. Two giant angels held crossed swords barring entry at the burning gate.

Bio Bob looked confused.

"Whoops," apologized Grandma. "Sorry Bio Bob, I forgot to tell you that Daniel is still alive."

"Oh, I see," said Bio Bob. He did not show any signs of being surprised by the revelation and resumed the tour. "There are strict protocols. Obviously you, as a living being, could potentially contaminate

Eden. You cannot go inside, but we can observe through a view window. A large window instantly appeared in the stone wall to the left of the angels. They peered into the garden of paradise and saw tall trees, spectacular waterfalls, rushing streams, exotic tropical plants, and lush vegetation. A flock of sheep was slowly walking past two lions resting under a shade tree by a brook. "We are working here on some future changes for life on Earth."

"The sheep are not in any danger?" questioned Daniel with a surprised look on his face.

"Not in Eden," answered Grandma, "it is not allowed. Bio Bob, we need to leave now. We have one more stop to make before Daniel has his meeting with God."

"Well, it was good to meet you Daniel. Be sure to have your seven questions."

Grandma took Daniel's arm and Eden disappeared.

CHAPTER 8

THE DESIGN WORKSHOP

The tranquil Garden of Eden setting was replaced with the bustling interior of a giant workshop. Daniel and his grandmother stood on the ground floor of an open atrium and stared upward. Daniel estimated that the building was at least sixty stories tall. He had seen the outside of the space shuttle building in Cape Canaveral and wondered if this may have been what it was like inside. Overhead, in the middle of the massive building, was one object the space shuttle building definitely did not have – a planet. The giant globe was floating unsupported, in mid-air, and appeared to be about twenty stories in diameter. At first, Daniel thought it was a hologram, but then he wasn't sure. Dozens of people were floating around the planet, taking measurements, and making notes on the video screens that Daniel had seen throughout Heaven. Three men, in the middle of the ground floor, waved and began walking toward them. They appeared to be in their late twenties and Daniel instantly recognized them as engineers – the white lab coats with pocket protectors were a dead giveaway.

"Hey! Look who is here!" An engineer with black hair in a bowl cut shouted at them.

A second engineer with long stringy red hair hollered, "How was your trip?"

The third engineer, a bald and chubby man, poked the redhead, "What are you – a survey taker?" They both laughed. "I hate those surveys."

"Welcome to your new home Daniel!" The black-haired engineer enthusiastically shook Daniel's hand.

"But, but you are early." The red head had a puzzled look, "We weren't expecting you until–"

"Hey guys," interrupted Grandma, "he is not totally back. He is still alive."

"Say what?" questioned the chubby engineer.

"No way!" exclaimed the black-haired engineer.

"Also," Grandma announced proudly, "My grandson is a seven sevens."

"Ooh," howled the red head, "Now we are in real good shape. Ready to rumble!"

"Please," begged the chubby man, "Don't turn me into anything weird. I promise to be good!"

They all laughed. Grandma smiled. Daniel had a bewildered look.

"Let's start with introductions," began the black-haired engineer. "My name is Moe, my red headed colleague is Larry, and our chubby bald-headed friend is…"

Daniel interrupted, "Let me guess…it is Curly, right?"

The engineers had a surprised look. "How, how did you know?" asked Moe.

Larry shoved him, "Shh, he's a seven sevens."

"Hey guys, I am glad to meet you. This looks like a really cool place and I have lots of questions."

"Questions!" boomed Curly.

"Conference room time!" shouted Moe. A two-story circular glass conference room instantly appeared out of thin air. It was about thirty feet in diameter, had an ornate crystal domed roof, a mosaic tiled floor, and it floated five feet above the ground. There was no furniture inside the room.

"I've got the table!" shouted Larry. A round wooden table instantaneously appeared in the middle of the conference room.

"Not King Arthur's table again," complained Moe. "I get so tired of the same conference table."

"Well, fix it up," suggested Curly.

The plain antique oak table suddenly was etched with ornamental carvings inlaid with thousands of multicolored jewels.

"I've got the chairs," Curly yelled excitedly.

Stainless steel swivel bar chairs appeared. The chairs had round red cushions and came with ten-foot-tall stainless-steel backrests shaped like DNA helixes.

"Hello?" said Moe, "Stainless steel chairs and wooden tables don't match."

Grandma whispered to Daniel, "Engineers are not good at matching."

The stainless-steel bar stools with the DNA helix backing were quickly changed to wood. Grandma took Daniel's arm and floated into the conference room with the other engineers. After they all sat down in the chairs, the conference room rose and started orbiting the planet.

"Okay, Daniel." Moe gestured toward Daniel, "It is your meeting. What do you want to discuss?"

"Thanks guys. First of all, what is this place?"

"May I lead off," Moe asked as he stood. The other engineers rolled their eyes.

"He always does the talking," sighed Larry.

"This is the new planet design workshop," Moe proudly proclaimed.

"New planet design?" repeated Daniel.

"Yep," said Curly. "Did you think planets grew on trees?" Moe, Larry, and Curly laughed.

"All right," continued Daniel, "what do you all do?"

"New planets require inputs from multiple disciplines," explained Moe. "The climate has to be just right for the life forms on the planet. That means that there has got to be a good temperature control system for life forms to thrive. I am in charge of designing the temperature control system for the planet."

Larry and Curly chimed in together, "Not too hot...and not too cold...just right."

"Interesting," commented Daniel.

Larry then spoke, "I am in charge of moisture control. There has got to be a good moisture control system for life on the planet. Plants and animals need water to survive, but not too much water."

Moe and Curly sang, "Down came the rain and washed the spider out."

Curly then spoke, "Geographic design is my specialty - design of continents, mountain ranges, ocean locations, and so forth." He pushed his hands together and flexed his muscles, "Yep, I move mountains."

"Only the small ones," pointed out Moe.

"It takes two or more of us to move the big ones," added Larry.

Curly continued, "Different species thrive in different environments. Some are better in warmer climates, others are better in cooler areas, some are better in wetter environments, and others do better in dryer settings. We design the geography to meet the needs for the planned life-forms and provide natural boundaries to separate the life-forms."

"This sounds like a really cool job," exclaimed Daniel. I would love to work on projects like this."

Moe, Larry, and Curly laughed. Daniel had a confused look.

"Daniel," disclosed Grandma, "this is where you will be working after you die."

The thought of dying suddenly sounded less foreboding to Daniel. "Okay, my next question is how did you do all of this? The conference room, the table, the chairs – you guys made them appear out of nowhere."

Curly started waving his hand, "I've got this one, I've got this one." This time, Moe and Larry rolled their eyes. "Heaven is composed primarily of thoughts. When we think of something, it appears.

If I want a pile of gold, I think about it, and it instantly appears." A pile of glittering gold coins suddenly appeared in a large pile in the middle of the table.

Daniel's eyes got big as his engineering mind quickly raced through mental calculations. "Wow! This has got to be worth tens of millions of dollars."

"The gold coins may be riches beyond belief on Earth, but they are worthless in Heaven." Curly shrugged. "Why spend money on something when you can create anything?"

Daniel paused for a moment as he considered the concept. It was so foreign to life on Earth, yet here it made perfect sense. He moved on to his next question "I have been told that I am a seven sevens. Why is that so special?"

Mo took the lead, "Do you know about the formula for life?"

Daniel had a puzzled look. "I am very familiar with chemical formulas. I use them all the time in my engineering calculations, but I have never heard of the formula for life."

"Let me give you some background," continued Moe. "When animals were initially created, they all had the same skill sets, so every animal of a species was identical to every other animal of that species. When confronted with a crisis, they all responded in the same manner. This often led to extinction of the species."

He paused to see that Daniel understood.

"For the next round of creation, seven key variables were included with the genetic design of the various plants and animals. These key variables are the formula for life factors. The seven variables are:

1. Intelligence
2. Physical strength
3. Ego
4. Logicalness
5. Killing instinct

6. Attractiveness to mate, and
7. Creativity

Each variable has a numerical value of one to nine. For instance, an individual with a '9' rating on intelligence would be extremely intelligent while a '1' rating would have very low intelligence. This provided many different possible combinations for that particular life form. Do you know the number of possible combinations?"

Daniel paused, "Well, there are nine possible ratings for seven different traits, so it would be nine to the seventh power. I don't have a calculator..."

Three exotic calculators magically appeared on King Arthur's jeweled table. Daniel chose one that was one foot wide, two feet long, and was encrusted with multicolored jewels that matched the table. As he punched the numbers, blue holographic images of the keystrokes appeared above the calculator. Daniel punched the equal key and the number 4,782,969 appeared.

"I have got to get one of these calculators," exclaimed Daniel as he admired the jewel-lined casing, "Is it the latest Texas Instruments model?" Moe, Larry, and Curly were silent and looked confused.

"Come on guys, it's a joke." They all did a forced laugh. "Okay, there are about five million different combinations. Are these the combinations for life?"

"More or less," answered Larry. "Oh, the biologists will tell you that there are billions of possibilities, but that's counting cosmetic factors. It is kind of like shades of the same paint. These are the factors from which all life is composed."

"Who assigns the numerical values?" asked Daniel.

"For mammals," replied Moe, "The sperm manufacturing director assigns values to each sperm and the egg manufacturer assigns values to each egg. These inputs influence the determination of the value selected for the formula for life factors."

"So how does it work? How do these factors protect the species?"

"Let's say," explained Larry, "That a given species is being threatened by an outside force. It could be an attack from a different species, severe weather, a change in the environment, or a pesticide."

"I am with you so far," acknowledged Daniel.

"Some of the species have a high intelligence rating. They will try to outsmart the adversary. Others of the species have great physical strength so they will attempt to overpower their opponent. The ones with high ego think they are better than everyone else and will fight to win with all of their resources and never give up. The ones with high logicalness will try to find a logical solution to the problem. The ones with high killing instinct have no qualms about killing, and will kill anything that improves their survival chances. The ones with high attractiveness to mate abilities will try to overcome extinction threats by reproduction. Last but not least is creativity - sometimes there is a highly creative solution to a threat."

"Wait a minute," interrupted Daniel, "You are starting to lose me. What is the difference between high intelligence and high logicalness?"

"Let's say, that your group is in a castle surrounded by an overwhelming opponent. High intelligence may try to design a superior weapon to win. High logicalness, on the other hand, may decide to sacrifice a large number so that at least a small number of the species can escape."

"I see," nodded Daniel. "Now can you explain high killing instinct? Apparently, I have a fairly high killer ranking as a seven, but I am not a hunter, much less a killer."

Mo, Larry, and Curly all laughed.

"Daniel," remarked Curly, "you are a human being. You are one of the biggest killers on the planet. You may not personally butcher animals on a routine basis, but you pay someone to do it for you every time you buy food. Does the large number of animals that are killed every day to feed the human race bother you?"

"I am thinking more and more about becoming vegetarian," Daniel apologetically divulged. "And I am working, or should I say was working, on the Manna Project which would increase the world's food supply and hopefully reduce the killing of animals."

Again Moe, Larry, and Curly laughed.

"Daniel, humans eat," pointed out Curly, "If they don't eat animals, they eat plants. They kill life in either case. The houses, cars, and material possessions owned by humans came about because of the killing of an enormous number of plants and animals. You may not like to think of yourself as a killer, but humans are responsible for more killing than any other creature on the planet."

Daniel looked dejected.

"But that is okay," consoled Moe, "that is why we are here. We design worlds in which life is killed so that others live. It is what it is - it's the price of life."

"The different formula for life factors has other benefits," Larry continued, "besides protecting the species from extinction."

"How is that?" asked Daniel, relieved to not be discussing how much killing had to take place for humans to live.

"Since they have different formula for life factors, life forms react randomly and unpredictably - they create chaos."

Daniel again had a puzzled look.

This time Grandma spoke, "Daniel, you work in a chemical plant. Would there be a need for as many engineers if the plant always ran smoothly?"

"I guess not. Often the plant does run smoothly, but when there are problems, the engineers are really needed."

"It is the same here," revealed Moe. "If it were not for the problems on Earth, there would not be a need for as many of us in Heaven. Heaven was created to control chaos. More chaos on Earth means more work for those in Heaven."

"Imperfection is perfection and chaos is an engineer's paradise," recited Daniel proudly.

"You got it!" applauded Curly.

"Now tell me this," inquired Daniel, "what is so special about a seven sevens? It seems to me that it is just a random number out of five million or so combinations. I would think that seven nines would be a much stronger combination."

"Ooh," shivered Larry, "the dreaded nines."

"Seven nines," Curly trembled, "the kiss of death."

"Daniel," explained Moe, "to put it bluntly, nines are a pain in the ass. Let's say you have a person with a nine-intelligence rating. They are always talking down to everyone and no one understands what they are saying. Likewise with a physical strength nine, they make everyone around them feel inferior. Some of the worst are the attractiveness to mate nines. They think they are God's gift to mankind and people will pay great sums to look just like them. No, nine is not a good number to have."

"There are also compatibility factors," added Larry. "Multiple nines have internal conflicts that can result in psychological problems. Some classic ones are logic versus creativity, intelligence versus physical strength, and ego versus attractiveness to mate."

"Seven," Curly jumped in, "is the perfect number. People like being around others that are really good, but not great at the various life factors. This motivates them to fully utilize their abilities. In chemical terms, seven sevens are catalysts. Drop them into a group and suddenly the group performs much better."

Daniel thought about that for a moment. Was he a catalyst? His mind flashed back to group assignments at school, multiple sports he had played, and project teams at work. He had always been on the winning side. He had never been the smartest or most athletic person in the group, but those around him worked together well and exceeded everyone's expectations.

Grandma stood up. "I need to take Daniel now - he has a meeting with God."

"Be sure to have your seven questions," reminded Moe.

"What is this with the seven questions for God?" asked Daniel.

"Everyone has seven questions for God," replied Larry.

As they started to leave, Curly called out to them, "Wait Daniel, don't leave yet."

Grandma and Daniel stopped and walked back toward the chubby bald man, "Daniel, you seemed upset when we talked about humans being the biggest killers on the planet."

"Yes," Daniel answered remorsefully. "It is sad to think about how much death must take place for me to live."

"Do you know about cost versus value?"

Daniel thought about all of the economic evaluation calculations he had completed to determine the best course of action for projects at work. He then thought about the thousands of items he had purchased in his lifetime. Of course he knew all about cost versus value, it was not a difficult concept. He modestly replied, "I know a little, why?"

"You do realize that lots of death must take place for any life form to exist?"

"I know that, but I really do not like to think about it."

"Do you know the success rates for seeds – how many survive and grow into plants versus how many die before they germinate? Do you have any idea of the number of plants that must die for animals to live or how many smaller animals on the food chain must die for the larger animals to live?"

"Like I said, I do not like to think about it, I find it to be depressing."

"Does it bother you that the raw materials in your chemical plant are destroyed when they are converted into the products produced?"

"No," answered Daniel, "the products are worth more money than the raw materials."

"Does it bother you to spend large amounts of money?"

"No, I just make sure that the value received exceeds the cost."

"Instead of thinking of cost in terms of money, think of cost in terms of death."

"That sounds really depressing."

"Does it? Life is one of the most treasured creations in the universe. Plants and animals are sacrificed so that you can live. Don't you think God does cost versus value calculations?"

"What?" Daniel had a surprised look.

"God knows the cost of his creation and does cost versus value calculations. Humans are the biggest killers on the planet, yet God values them more than all of the death that is required to sustain them. That should tell you something about how important humans are to God."

Daniel was adsorbing the knowledge when Grandma took his arm and they disappeared.

CHAPTER 9

MEETING WITH GOD

Daniel reappeared in a waiting room. The large room was all white and appeared to be made of cumulus clouds. There were no doors. The only object in the room was a plain-looking brown wooden chair. Daniel sat down. This was it - he was going to meet with God. He, Daniel, was going to have a one-on-one meeting, face-to-face, with the all-knowing omnipotent creator of the universe. What an incredible opportunity. He and Joshua had often talked about this, but he never thought it would ever take place. Daniel went over and over in his mind the questions he wanted to ask – there were so many. He prioritized and narrowed the list. Should he write them down? He had not seen paper or pens anywhere, and why should there be any? There were no pen and paper factories in Heaven. Maybe he should have asked one of the engineers to create pens and paper for him. Well, it was too late now. Daniel decided to memorize the questions.

Daniel wondered what God would look like. Would he be an old man with a white beard? Would he be a bright shining light? Would he be surrounded by angels? Would he speak with a booming voice? Should he kneel when he saw God or fall flat on the ground? What was the proper etiquette for a meeting with God?

Daniel's thoughts were interrupted as a cherub floated into the room, gently took his hand, and with a soft voice sweetly said, "I will take you now to see God."

Daniel was instantly transported into what looked like an executive's outer office in a downtown skyscraper. There was no furniture in the waiting room and there was no secretary. Would God really need a secretary? Three of the walls were floor-to-ceiling windows. The fourth wall had an open doorway, but no door.

Daniel walked over to the first large window, looked out, and was stunned by the view. There were hundreds of high-rise futuristic buildings below. The buildings shimmered and changed colors before his eyes. Flying cars were zooming around the city.

An optimist, seeing this view, might marvel at the world of the future. New inventions, no doubt, had made life much easier and extended man's life span significantly. The pessimist, seeing the same view, might think that nothing had changed. The rich were still getting richer, the poor were still being oppressed, and who knows what new instruments of war and torture had been invented.

Daniel did not see the world from either viewpoint. He pictured the behind-the-scenes work that had to have taken place to create this world. The engineers, architects, owners, and builders had no doubt spent countless hours designing, calculating, and arguing over every minute detail of what he now saw below.

He looked for landmarks. There were no mountains or oceans nearby. Then, in the distance, he saw it – the one reminder of his time - the San Jacinto Monument. He was seeing Houston - the Houston of the future! Whether this was five hundred years or a thousand years from now did not matter. God had a plan for Houston! It was going to be a great future and the San Jacinto Monument would survive!

Daniel looked for the familiar storage tanks along the Pasadena freeway – there were none. In fact, the Pasadena freeway was gone. After all the chemical plant calculations, all of the alternatives discussed, all of the budget battles, all of the heated arguments on how to proceed, they were all gone – not a trace of all the toils remained.

Daniel walked over to the second floor-to-ceiling window and instantly recognized the Houston of the present. All of the familiar landmarks were there – the Astrodome, NRG Stadium, Minute Maid Park, the Toyota Center, the 610 Loop, the Medical Center, and the

Williams Tower next to the Galleria Mall. In the distance, surrounded by petrochemical plants, stood the San Jacinto Monument.

Daniel walked over to the third window. There were no buildings, no roads, no petrochemical plants, and no San Jacinto Monument. It was a natural landscape. There was water and trees, with no landmarks. Daniel thought for a minute and realized that this was the Houston of the past.

God has an interesting perspective, thought Daniel, seeing the past, present, and future all at the same time! There were lots and lots of transformations. Everything in the world was always changing – moving to form something new and different. Daniel's thoughts were interrupted by the sound of a friendly familiar voice calling from the opening in the fourth wall, "Hey Daniel, come on in."

The friendly voice made Daniel feel less uncomfortable, but butterflies churned in his stomach as he walked toward the doorway. He slowly entered the room to meet God. He had not known what to expect, but he definitely was not prepared for what he saw.

▲ ▲ ▲

Daniel entered and was surprised to see two reclining chairs sitting side-by-side in a large room. The room had four blank walls, all of which were white. Sitting in one of the recliners was...Roger.

"Come in, come in Daniel," welcomed Roger. "Make yourself comfortable." He motioned to the nearby recliner.

"Hi," muttered Daniel nervously, "I am glad to see you Roger, but I, I thought I was meeting with God."

"What does God look like?"

"Well, I don't really know. I have seen paintings and read stories, but I have no idea what God really looks like."

"Does he look like this?" asked Roger. Suddenly the white walls dissolved and various images of God appeared. There were flashes of blinding light with ear splitting thunder, a fierce warrior that instilled a petrifying fear in Daniel, a gentle old man with a beard, a picture of Jesus with long brown hair carrying a lamb around his neck that Daniel had seen in Sunday School, there were other men that were dressed in royal robes, women with vines growing from their bodies, a tall tree with deep roots, abstract art, mountain top scenes with hurricane winds. Suddenly the kaleidoscope stopped and the white walls returned.

"I, I guess so," stammered Daniel.

"I can be any of these forms," revealed Roger.

"You, you are God?" asked Daniel with a confused look.

"I thought you would be more comfortable with me looking like this, but if you want me to change…"

"No, no," sputtered a very startled Daniel. "I…I do prefer this form."

"And I thought you would like this backdrop." The white walls vanished and were replaced by a surreal view as if they were looking out the window of a spaceship. There was a close-up view of the sun and then they rapidly sped by each of the planets. Comets zoomed past and suddenly they saw an array of solar systems with many brightly colored stars – red, yellow, green, blue along with a host of unfamiliar planets – some with rings and some with multicolored bands.

"This is impossible," stated Daniel incredulously. The planets are not aligned in a row and there is no way to travel that fast through the galaxy. It would take years at the speed of light just to go to neighboring stars." Daniel suddenly stopped.

Roger grinned, "You do know where you are and to who you are talking?"

"Of course, thank you," Daniel sheepishly replied, "And yes, I find it to be a very fascinating view." *God, he thought, gets to do some really cool things.*

CHAPTER 10

THE FIRST QUESTION FOR GOD

"So," began Roger, "I understand you have seven questions for me."

"Yes, but how did you …?" Daniel stopped. "My apologies again. I am in Heaven and I am talking to God. Of course, you know everything about me."

"No problem. What is your first question?"

"I have always been fascinated by the origin of the universe. My first question is "How was the universe created, how can something come from nothing, and how did you get here?"

"I do get that question a lot, especially from engineers and those with scientific backgrounds. Let us talk it through using concepts with which you are familiar. What is the nearest star to the Sun?"

"Proxima Centauri is a little over 4.2 light years away."

"Very good. Now how big is Earth's sun?"

"You got me there."

"It depends upon who is doing the measuring." Roger winked. "Let's say it is eight hundred and sixty-five thousand miles. Now how far is that in light years?"

"Let's see," contemplated Daniel, "The speed of light is about one hundred and eighty-six thousand miles per second, so the sun's diameter it is about four and a half light seconds."

"Actually, it is 4.65 seconds, but not bad for not having a calculator. Here is a calculator."

A floating blue video screen similar to what Daniel had seen throughout Heaven appeared out of nowhere and floated over to him.

"Don't worry," commented Roger, "it is not reverse Polish notation. Those Hewlett-Packard calculators never made sense to me either."

Daniel grabbed the calculator.

"So, Daniel how many seconds are there in 4.2 years?"

Daniel punched in 4.2 years X 365 days X 24 hours per day X 60 minutes per hour X 60 seconds per minute. The calculator display showed 132,451,200 seconds.

"So, there is 4.65 light seconds of matter on the sun, which is the largest body in the solar system. Let us be generous and say that all of the planets and the rest of the celestial objects in the Solar System have the equivalent of two light seconds. That gives us the equivalent of 6.65 light seconds of matter in the solar system. So, divide the number on your calculator by 6.65 and see what you get."

Daniel punched the numbers and the number 19,917,473 appeared. "It's about twenty million."

"So, Earth's corner of the universe is one part matter in twenty million parts of empty space. Practically nothing wouldn't you say?"

Daniel nodded.

"Now let us take a closer look at that small amount of matter. If you look at a sample of metal under an electron microscope, are the molecules packed together?" The wall displayed a sample of a piece of metal placed under a microscope. The magnification gradually increased revealing a large amount of empty space between the molecules.

"They are much closer together than the molecules of a liquid or gas," noted Daniel, "but there is a lot of emptiness between the molecules."

"Now if you could look even closer, inside the atoms what kind of spacing would you see?"

"I cannot speak from personal observations, but theoretically there is an electron cloud which is mostly empty space that extends well around each atom's nucleus. So, I would think that most of the area around an atom is empty space." The microscopic view on the wall continued its magnification until only a cloud with a single electron was shown.

"That is correct. While creating a universe may sound like an immense accomplishment, it is really creating almost nothing from nothing. The universe consists of celestial objects that are separated by great distances, there is a large amount of space between the atoms that make up the celestial objects, and the atoms themselves consist mostly of empty space. Put it all together and there really is just not that much there."

God sure is humble thought Daniel.

"You asked how to get something from nothing. Let us do some more math. Take the number zero." A large blue zero instantly appeared in the air. "Now what is zero?"

"Zero is nothing."

"Not all the time. Zero can also be the sum of an equation." Equations written in blue started floating around the room: -1 + 1 = 0 followed by -2 + 2 = 0 then -3 + 3 = 0. Many other combinations followed. The equations were also written in reverse order 0 = -1 + 1, followed by 0 = -2 + 2 then 0 = -3 + 3. In a few seconds, the room was filled with floating blue equations. "As you can see, from nothing something positive and something negative can be produced. All kinds of things can come from nothing."

The floating equations popped like bubbles and gradually disappeared. "So, you are saying there is another universe - a positive and a negative universe?" Daniel tried to comprehend. "Wouldn't they destroy each other when they meet?"

"Putting this in chemical plant terms, suppose you had two equal-sized storage tanks joined together by a pipe with a valve near the bottom of the tanks." A three-dimensional diagram in red appeared on the wall behind him. "Suppose one tank was full and the other was empty." The diagram showed a full tank and an empty tank. "What happens when you open the valve between the tanks?"

"That is easy," answered Daniel. "Material from the tank with the higher level will flow into the tank with the lower level. Eventually they would equalize at the same level." The three-dimensional drawing showed the flow going from one tank into the other until they equalized.

"Precisely. There is no violent reaction, just the flow of material from one storage tank to the other. Now let us put this in oil field terms. Suppose you have an oil well near depletion with a value of zero." A three-dimensional diagram of an oil well and two equal-sized storage tanks appeared on the wall behind them with a pipe going down from one tank into the well and a pipe coming out of the well and going up into the second tank. "Now you pump a million gallons of brine down the well. This forces a million gallons of crude oil out of the well." The diagram showed brine from one tank being pumped down the well and crude oil from the well going into the second tank. "A million gallons in and a million gallons out means that there is no change in the volume of material in the well – it is something from nothing. The petrochemical industry does this every day. In fact, much of the economics of the petrochemical industry is based on getting something from nothing."

"I never thought of it in those terms.".

"Now, let us talk about another way of getting something from nothing," continued Roger. "Can matter be created from energy?"

"Einstein said $E=mc^2$," replied Daniel, "so it seems like energy could be used to create mass and mass could be used to create energy."

"Is there any other way to create energy?"

"What, what do you mean?"

"Is there some other force out there that could be used to produce energy?"

"Some other force…some other force? Do you mean like gravity?"

"Gravity will do. Suppose there was a way to convert gravity into energy? Could one then take gravity and make energy and use it to make matter?"

"I, I guess it would be possible," pondered Daniel. "But we have not been able to determine what causes gravity, where it comes from, or how to control it. It is an invisible force that has a tremendous impact on our everyday lives, but we know very little about it."

"Kind of like me?" Roger smiled. "What if I told you that, someday, a future Einstein is going to determine that there is a relationship between energy and gravity and that it is possible to convert gravity into energy?"

Daniel's eyes lit up. "I think I am starting to understand. You start with a force that cannot be measured so it is essentially nothing. You convert the force into energy and then convert that energy into matter, so you have converted nothing into matter. The matter makes up only a minuscule part of the universe, and essentially is nothing. If some of our universe is sent to another universe, then one could get something from that universe in exchange for essentially nothing from our universe."

"Very good Daniel. The last part of your question is how I got here. Weather on the Gulf Coast provides a good analogy. What happens when there is a low-pressure area?"

"High pressure flows into a low-pressure area. When there is a hurricane in the Gulf of Mexico, one wants to be in a high-pressure area. If one is in a low-pressure area, the storm will move your direction."

"How about lightening?"

"It is a similar effect" replied Daniel. "Lightening will move from one area to another to restore the balance of electrical charges."

"When the universe began, there was chaos everywhere. There was a need for order. The universe saw the need, and called upon me to create order from chaos. Are you familiar with the Second Law of Thermodynamics?"

"Is that the one that talks about entropy and says everything goes downhill into chaos?" asked Daniel.

"I am not sure that is the physics definition, but that is one way that it could be described. The order in the universe is constantly being threatened and will degrade into chaos unless a counter force restores order. That is my purpose in life, that is, if I am really alive. The universe needed a force to fight chaos and I came into existence."

"I thought your job was to create the world and take care of salvation."

"Oh, it is much more than that," revealed Roger. "Are you familiar with the water cycle?"

"Sure, water from oceans, lakes, and streams evaporates, goes into clouds, and comes down as rain which flows into oceans, lakes, and streams from where it evaporates again. I have grown up with it so I never give it too much thought, but it is a brilliant engineering design."

"It is the same with chaos. Order is created out of chaos, order degrades into chaos, and then order must be restored. Chaos is the enemy and must be stopped."

God has a monumental task, thought Daniel. How does one go about fighting chaos? He recalled mythological pictures of Atlas holding the world on his shoulders. He had always felt sorry for Atlas, but that was nothing compared to the burden on God to keep restoring order in the universe. Daniel's mind flashed back to the difficult Thermodynamics classes he had taken at Texas A&M. A smile came to his face as he realized- even God hates Thermo.

CHAPTER 11

THE SECOND QUESTION FOR GOD

Now feeling much more comfortable, Daniel proceeded to ask his second question to God. "After you appeared amidst the chaotic primordial ooze, how did you separate the ooze into something useful?"

"That is another question I often get from engineers and those with scientific backgrounds," disclosed Roger. "Putting this in petrochemical terms, what is the composition of the ooze that is the crude oil you get out of the ground?"

"Most analytical chemists are afraid to analyze it," admitted Daniel, "because it would severely foul their instruments. The analysis I have seen shows that it is a jumbled mixture of all kinds of trace components."

"Would you say the composition is chaotic?"

"Yes." Daniel smiled as he grasped the analogy, "It is a very chaotic mixture."

"So, what do you do with your crude?"

"It is sent to refineries where it is separated by reactions and distillation into different fractions. Those fractions are then converted into useful products. In simplest terms, there are heavy components, light components, and intermediate components. These are sent to downstream processing units for conversion into useful products."

"And how are the components initially separated?"

"They have different boiling points. We send them to large distillation towers, heat them with steam, and use the difference in boiling points to separate the materials. So how did you separate the materials from the primordial ooze? Surely you do not use distillation towers and differences in boiling points."

"What makes up the universe?"

"Matter and energy," Daniel quickly answered.

"Really?" questioned Roger, "Hello."

A sheepish look again came over Daniel's face. "I…I should have included the spiritual component."

"That is better. Let us try to put this it into chemical plant terms. What is the composition of a chemical plant?"

"There are three major components. We start with materials – there are the raw materials that feed the process as well as the materials that were used to construct the chemical plant. Next, we add energy – steam and electricity provide heat and power for the chemical plant. Finally, there are thoughts - lots and lots of thinking goes into the building and running of a chemical plant."

"It is similar here, Daniel. In Heaven, we usually refer to body, blood, and soul, but matter, energy, and thought will do. The chaotic primordial ooze, that was present when I first appeared, contained a mixture of what you would call matter, energy, and thoughts."

"So how did you separate them?"

"With light," explained Roger. "Similar components are attracted to each other. Like begets like and so forth. By bringing light into the ooze, the energy components are extracted, leaving matter and thoughts. It is difficult to separate energy from matter and it is difficult to separate energy from thoughts, but it is relatively easy to separate thought from matter."

"Wow!" exclaimed Daniel. "Let there be light! It makes perfect sense. You took an extremely chaotic mixture and extracted it with light so that it would separate into three groups – matter, energy, and thoughts. It is a genius idea, so very logical!" The wheels were turning in Daniel's mind. "Okay," he continued excitedly, "in distillation it is often difficult to get a clean separation. There are usually trace amounts of impurities in the various fractions."

"And it is the same with the primordial ooze. There is obviously lots of energy in a world full of matter. It is not as prevalent, but there are traces of matter in the energy waves. There are lots of thoughts in the energy world, with some traces of energy in the thought world. There are even traces of thought in the matter world."

"Hold on a minute." Daniel had a confused look. "You are getting way beyond my training. We definitely did not study this in school. Can you explain on my level?"

"What were you taught?"

"There are four states of matter - solid, liquid, gas, and plasma. I have a real good understanding of solids, liquids, and gasses. We run petrochemical plants everyday with solids, liquids, and gasses and I have done lots of equipment-sizing calculations. The plasma part has always been a bit shaky for me. I know there is plasma in fires and on the sun, but I have only limited understanding."

"Okay," began Roger, "let us start with matter. Matter equals solids, liquids, gasses, and plasma - right? Well not really. Inside these are lots and lots of atoms that are moving around all the times with electrons and all sorts of subatomic particles. Are you with me so far?"

"A lot of this I tried to forget after school," joked Daniel, "but yes, I am with you so far."

"Now to say that something is purely matter is a bit of a misnomer. There is lots and lots of energy tied up inside the matter. You see this in your gasoline products – your car engine converts gasoline into energy. The energy was part of the matter. There is not a totally clear distinction between matter and energy because matter contains a lot of energy. The same is true in nuclear power plants. Energy is given off when atoms are split."

"I never thought of it that way. All matter contains energy. I can see that energy may contain some particles - all that talk about photons in light always seemed pretty theoretical to me. I never have trusted physicists - they speak a weird language. What about thoughts? Are they part of energy and matter?"

"The universe contains three basic components, but as per your distillation analogy, the pure separations are difficult to obtain. So, there are thoughts in energy and even traces of thoughts in matter. For example, you have seen fire."

"Of course, fire is all around us – candles, matches, burners on stoves, campfires, torches. I have seen building fires and forest fires on the news. Our plant has a fired boiler and I have looked through the fire eye on the boiler many times and have observed the flame patterns."

"And how are the flame patterns?"

"Very unpredictable. They are always bouncing around. They seem to have a mind of their own."

"That is because they do have a mind of their own - the flames contain thoughts. The flames want to explore what is around them."

"What? You are telling me that flames are alive?"

"Remember your grandmother's definition of life – born, grow, reproduce, and die? Fire is born from an ignition source, the flames grow consuming the fuel in the immediate surroundings, fire tries to reproduce by spreading to new sources of fuel, and eventually the flames die out. This meets the definition, doesn't it?"

"Well, there is still the metabolism part," noted Daniel.

"What chemistry is involved with fire?"

"It is an oxidation reaction." A light bulb went off in Daniel's mind. "I now see where you are coming from. The combustion reaction is an oxidation reaction. Cellular metabolism is an oxidation reaction. Fires and cells are very different, but they both have oxidation." Daniel paused for a moment in amazement as he comprehended the concepts. "So, fire is a living entity and you used light as an extractant to separate chaos into matter, energy, and thoughts. What happened next?"

"The rest is pretty straightforward, matter is used to make the celestial objects that are seen in the universe, energy is used to power the celestial objects, and thoughts are spiritual components that form Heaven."

God is a fantastic engineer thought Daniel.

CHAPTER 12

THE THIRD QUESTION FOR GOD

"My third question," continued Daniel, "is how old is the Earth and did you really create the world in six days?"

"How old is your chemical plant?" asked Roger.

"In a few months it will have been three years since it began producing products, we are thinking about having some type of celebration event."

"The plant will have been running for three years, but how old is it really? Was all of the equipment in the plant new when you started up?"

"Most of it was new, but there were a few parts that were scavenged from other facilities."

"What metals are used in the plant?"

"Most of the plant is made from carbon steel and stainless steel."

"And what is the origin of the piping?"

"We purchase pipe from a foundry."

"And where does the foundry get its raw materials?"

"Originally it is from the mining of iron ore."

"How long was the iron ore in the ground?"

"I guess since the world was created."

"And before that?"

"I see where you are going," nodded Daniel. "Eveything has come from the original source material in the universe. Time means nothing. Everything is the same age - it has just been transformed many, many times. How about the six-day question?"

"I get the six-day question a lot," confided Roger. "How many pounds of product are produced each day in your chemical plant?"

"On a good day, we make one million pounds of product."

"Could you produce ten million pounds in a day?"

"Not with our existing equipment, we would need larger equipment."

"How about one hundred million pounds or even one billion pounds a day?"

"Once again, it could be done, but we would need to install some enormous equipment."

"What is the largest object manufactured in Earth's factories?"

"That is a good question." Daniel paused to contemplate, "Aircraft carriers are built in dry docks, but I am not sure that qualifies as a factory. I know that there are large manufacturing facilities for aircraft. They may be the largest factory objects."

"Could a factory be built for an aircraft ten times, or let's say one hundred times the size of the current largest aircraft?"

"I, I guess so, but it would be a humongous factory."

"Could you design a factory to make large objects?"

"Sure, I am an engineer. I can design anything."

"Could you design a factory to build a planet?"

Thoughts of Moe, Larry, Curly and the planet design workshop suddenly flashed through Daniel's mind. With the right size equipment, it would be possible to build anything. He had been part of a design team that built a chemical plant. The steps would be similar, just on a much larger scale. A plant to build a planet was certainly an intriguing concept. "I would love to give it a shot."

"Suppose," continued Roger, "There was a factory that manufactured planets and that facility could produce one planet each day?"

"I see where you are coming from, but the size and technology would be incomprehensible."

"How about a factory tour?"

Daniel took the hand of God and they disappeared. They reappeared inside a glass sphere located who knows where in the universe. A few thousand miles below them was a planet factory. They watched as a planet was produced. An enormous furnace spit out globs of molten material. The hot globs rolled through space dust and the dust attached to the globs. Some of the globs formed spheres and others formed irregular shapes. The spherical globs then passed into a sculpturing section in which cosmic radiation blasted the spheres, forming topographical features. Fragments from the blasting process were recycled to the furnace. The spheres then passed through three enormous chambers that were large enough to hold the entire planet. An atmospheric coating was applied in the first chamber, a vegetation layer was added in the second chamber, and animals were installed in the third chamber.

"The planet is now ready for shipping," announced Roger.

"Where will it go?"

"That is up to the planners in Celestial Development Heaven.".

One can build anything, thought Daniel, with the right type of equipment and unlimited resources.

CHAPTER 13

THE FOURTH QUESTION FOR GOD

They left the planet factory and returned to God's office.

"My fourth question," inquired Daniel, "is about religions. There are lots of religions in the world. Which one is correct? They often say conflicting things. They cannot all be right, can they? And what about Hell?"

"Are you ready for another tour?"

Daniel took Roger's hand and they entered a room that looked like the live version of an artistic masterpiece from the Middle Ages. In the center of the room, a fierce looking gray-haired God was sitting on a throne surrounded by angels. They then entered a cavernous chamber in which an overflowing choir of millions were singing melodious praises. The next room was a tranquil setting with beautiful nude young women bathing in a river lined with palms and date trees.

"So, there really is a room full of virgins." observed Daniel.

"Yes, but you must remember that we are in a spiritual realm – the body parts don't work like they do on Earth."

They continued their journey and passed through hundreds of magnificent rooms from many diverse faiths.

"There are so many different views," commented Daniel. "I never realized that Heaven was such an accommodating place."

"Many different views, but the same separation process."

"I don't understand."

"Death is a separation process in which the soul is separated from the body and blood, or in your terms, in which thoughts are separated from mass and energy. There may be many different religious viewpoints, but there is one spiritual separation process – death. Heaven is a gathering place for the spiritual components in the universe."

A burst of light brighter than one hundred one hundred-watt light bulbs went off in Daniel's mind as he grasped the concept, "This is so fantastic!"

"Wait until you see Hell," Roger winked. "You know, the place for lawyers."

▲   ▲   ▲

They reappeared in an enormous ghastly room and were immediately put back by the obnoxious odors. This is far worse, thought Daniel, than anything he had smelled in any chemical plant. Fire was everywhere and molten material was flowing, reminding Daniel of a video he had seen in college of a magnesium manufacturing plant. Screams filled the air. The screams were so loud that OSHA would have required double hearing protection.

"So there really is a Hell," concluded Daniel after they had safely returned to the comfortable confines of Roger's office.

"Most certainly."

"But why? Why is there Hell?"

"We have a lot of requests," said Roger with a smile and a wink. "It seems that people need a horrible place to send their bosses and ex-spouses." He paused, "Actually, it is part of the recovery process."

"Say what?" exclaimed Daniel.

"Let's do a crash course in Composition of the Universe 101. As you know, there are three components – body, blood, and soul or, in your terms, mass, energy, and thought. Everything in the universe contains a mixture of mass, energy, and thought in different ratios. Some objects have a high ratio of thought and others have a low ratio. At a certain level, the ratio is sufficiently high enough for the thought component to take over and direct actions. For instance, your thoughts tell your body to get out of bed and drive to work. By increasing the ratio of the thought component, any object can be taken over by spiritual forces. Let's say you have a boulder - with a large mass and a low thought level, it is not going anywhere. However, if the thought component is increased to a certain point, it can take control of the boulder and make it get up and move to a different location."

"I can see how that would be great on a construction project," noted Daniel. "If the spiritual component was sufficiently increased, materials could come together by themselves and construct a building."

"Yes," agreed Roger, "It certainly was helpful during the construction of the universe. The spiritual components took control of the mass and energy components and got them to move to their proper places. There is a problem, however, with the spiritual recycle. Putting this in chemical plant terms, when certain chemicals mix they form a hard polymer. It is easy to initially combine the components, but once the polymer is formed, it is very difficult to take the polymer and convert it back into the original materials."

"So how do you recover spiritual components?"

"With plants and animals, it is relatively easy," explained Roger. "Death makes a good separation process – spiritual components leave the body and blood and return to Heaven. It is much more difficult to recover spiritual components from a dense solid object. Either the spiritual components slowly leach out over a very long period of time, or they go through Hell in order to be reprocessed more quickly. Hell is a separation process in which spiritual components are rapidly recovered."

Daniel nodded his head. "It is similar to our cracking units – severe operating conditions for rapid recovery of valuable products…I think I understand now…Hell is a chemical plant."

CHAPTER 14

THE FIFTH QUESTION FOR GOD

"My fifth question," continued Daniel, "is about mysteries and unusual things on Earth. For instance, my friend Joshua is obsessed with UFO's. I have heard a lot about mysterious historical events. What can you tell me about UFO's, who built the Pyramids and Stonehenge, who shot JFK, RFK, MLK, was there a Lincoln conspiracy, and how did Amelia Earhart and Glenn Miller die?"

"That is quite a list," remarked Roger. "First of all, mankind is always going to have its mysteries. People enjoy wondering about things and speculating. If all the mysteries were solved, people will either create new mysteries or become very bored. Let's break down your list into categories. The first category, for your friend Joshua, is UFO's. Yes, Earth has been visited many times by visitors from other worlds. Earth is certainly not the only planet in the universe that sustains life. Some of the reported UFO sightings are from these visitors, but most are not. Many have logical explanations such as tests of top-secret aircraft, atmospheric events, or overactive imaginations."

Daniel's eyes lit up. Joshua would be so amazed to hear this. "So why did the visitors from other worlds come to Earth and why did they leave?"

"They came for the same reasons that humans will eventually travel to other worlds. Some were great explorers, some were hunters, some came for economic reasons, others came to conqueror, some came out of curiosity – which is also called seeking scientific knowledge, there have been lots and lots of tourists, and some came for the pleasures of the land."

"Pleasures of the land?" Daniel was puzzled. "Do you mean sexual pursuits?"

"That certainly is a strong motivator for the Spring Break travel crowd," Roger winked. "It has also been one of the attractions for tourists visiting Earth, and this has caused lots of problems. But, there are also pleasures of the land that are nonsexual."

"Such as?"

"There can be great pleasure in living life in different physical environments. It can be very entertaining to visit a world with lower gravity and be able to perform athletic feats not possible on one's home world. Some bring a set of wings with them on their visit and can soar through the sky. Others are invigorated by the differences in the atmospheric composition between Earth and their home world and find that they have enhanced abilities while on Earth."

"So, what happened to the visitors from other worlds? Do they still visit?"

"Earth is now in a protected zone, so the number of visitors is greatly restricted. In the past, there were no restrictions and this resulted in a lot of problems. Dinosaurs and sea monsters were a popular attraction for the big game crowd, until they were hunted into extinction. Various mining operations were established by outsiders, but these were not economical, so they left. Conquerors have come and gone after finding out that the human race is very difficult to control. Deterrents have been added to the world to discourage long term settlers. Visitors, now days, are primarily tourists that stay for only a brief period of time."

"Why don't we see them when they are here?"

"Many are from aquatic realms and spend most of their time on Earth underwater. Others prefer areas where the atmosphere is thinner, so they visit remote mountainous regions – you have heard of the Yeti? Travelers from colder planets prefer to stay in the Arctic and Antarctic areas and have established temporary housing there. A large number of the visitors are nonhumanoid, so even if one saw them, they would be considered to be part of the natural environment."

"So, you are saying that alien visitors are not interested in humans, after all we have accomplished?"

"That is true, Daniel. Most alien visitors are just not that interested in the human race, but you should not be surprised. When people go on nature walks they seldom notice, much less appreciate, what it takes for ants to establish a colony, for spiders to construct webs, or for birds to build nests? Then there is plant life that grows all over the Earth – each plant is an engineering marvel with intricacies that humans seldom comprehend."

"So do any of the alien visitors observe the human race?"

"There are some that do come to see humans, so protocols have been established to minimize contact with people."

"When do they come? Is there a tourist season for those that come to see humans?"

"The number of tourists coming to see humans is generally fairly steady - except when there is a big war. A lot of tourists enjoy coming to Earth to watch the fights."

Daniel shook his head. "That seems so wrong. So were the pyramids and Stonehenge built by blood-lusting visitors from other worlds?"

"I am not sure why so many people believe the pyramids and Stonehenge were built by extraterrestrials. You are an engineer, could you design a pyramid?"

"Sure," Daniel replied, "The concept is really simple. I just don't have the resources to build something on that scale."

"There have been many, many highly talented designers and builders throughout Earth's history that figured out ways to construct what are deemed today to be incredible ancient wonders."

"But how did they harness the resources?"

"There have also been many charismatic leaders throughout human history that have been able to accomplish great things by uniting their followers. The building projects provided meaning to the lives of the workers. Often there were contests between groups of workers involving the quantity and quality of work. One technique used by village leaders was to send younger men on quests to bring back enormous stones. The quests helped bond the young men who would one day become the village leaders and, at least for a while, kept them away from the village leader's daughters – who were often later part of the award package. It is amazing how motivated and creative young men can be when a young woman is involved."

"So did the visitors from long ago from other worlds leave any remnants behind?"

"Of course," replied Roger. "When one goes traveling there is often trash and lost objects left behind. There is also art work, which some would call graffiti."

"Alien graffiti?" Daniel raised his eyebrows.

"Of sorts. Some of the visitors had weapons that they used to carve shapes in rocks and on the sides of mountains to show where they had been. Many of these are now eroded, but they can still be seen in some parts of the world."

Daniel was amazed. He couldn't wait to tell Joshua what he had learned. Joshua always got excited talking about the possibility of aliens visiting Earth, but once the knowledge was out, it really was anticlimactic. It sounded like extraterrestrials have been visiting Earth much like how humans take a wilderness camping trip – experience life in a different region for a short time, explore the land, hunt and fish, take a few pictures and souvenirs, and head home. It all sounded so mundane, except for those that came to see 'the fights' – that sounded just plain sick, but he knew that many people would jump at the chance to watch animals fight to the death. "What about the assassination conspiracies and mysterious deaths?"

"Political assassinations and cover-ups have been going on throughout human history and The Archives are filled with all of the details. Usually, an ambitious ruthless person eliminates all other competitors to the throne or there is a powerful group that kills an existing leader that was not doing what they wanted. The new leader, in this case, knows that they had better comply or they will have a short reign. The people involved in the killings often have an underworld element that deals in unscrupulous activities and there is usually a scapegoat that takes the blame.

The first assassination you mentioned was John Fitzgerald Kennedy. He definitely had some powerful enemies. The assassination took place in Dallas and resulted in a Texan ascending to the presidency. The designated scapegoat, Lee Harvey Oswald, was gunned down in police custody soon afterward. There was a cover-up because it was deemed better to have a deceased person take the blame instead of plunging the country into a political upheaval.

The second assassination you mentioned was Robert Francis Kennedy, the brother of John F. Kennedy. He was killed in a Los Angeles hotel the night after he won the California Democratic primary. He too had some very powerful enemies that were disturbed by the possibility of him becoming the next United States president. Sirhan Sirhan was captured with a gun at the scene, but there was a second assassin that fired the kill shot and escaped.

Martin Luther King was a leading civil rights figure that was assassinated in Memphis. He had many powerful enemies because he was trying to change the status quo. Those that try to change the status quo often meet a sudden demise. James Earl Ray was charged with the crime, but the person that fired the kill shot escaped.

Abraham Lincoln was assassinated by John Wilkes Booth while he attended a theater performance just after the end of the Civil War. It was part of a plot to save the South, but did not affect the outcome of the war.

Amelia Earhart was a pioneering female aviator that disappeared while flying with Fred Noonan over the Pacific Ocean in 1937. They had mechanical problems and made an emergency landing on a deserted Pacific Island. The technology of the day was not able to find them and they eventually perished on the island.

Glenn Miller was a leading big band musician that died in a plane crash over the English Channel in December of 1944. The cause of the plane crash was mechanical failure due to cold weather.

Information on the sudden deaths of these and other well-known people is available in The Archives, but let me ask you this, what is the on-line factor for your chemical plant? How often does your equipment fail?"

"Every chemical plant is different," replied Daniel. "For our plant we plan for eight thousand four hundred hours per year of operation, which is a ninety-six percent of time on-line factor."

"So, four percent of the year your plant is down?"

"Sure," said Daniel, "initially the plant was down more often, but we have made a lot of improvements. It takes time to work out the bugs, especially with new technologies."

"There are always problems with new technologies. Famous people have vast resources and are often the first to acquire a new technology. Their premature deaths are often not due to sinister elements, but because they pushed the limits of the new technologies, resulting in equipment failure. The publicity surrounding their deaths often brings attention to the need for improved safety features that are installed to minimize future accidents."

Daniel reflected on what he had just learned. He had read about many industrial accidents and knew that laws and safety standards had been implemented to minimize the potential for future recurrences. The first workers in a new technology learn about problems the hard way, often with significant damage and loss of life. It was sad that people lost their lives, but these were ordinary people and that did not make for a very exciting story. The death of a celebrity, however, opens up avenues of intrigue which leads to endless speculation.

Similarly, Daniel thought, history is filled with speculative stories of political espionage resulting in the elimination of those that opposed powerful people. As appalling as these stories may appear today, it is even more shocking to realize that they are undoubtedly still taking place. After all, what makes the current generation any different from those in the past?

CHAPTER 15

THE SIXTH QUESTION FOR GOD

"My sixth question involves the human life span. Why is the average life span today only about seventy-five years? Why is the oldest person in the world today less than one hundred and twenty years old? There are stories of people living for hundreds and almost a thousand years. Why don't we live longer?"

"How long does a piece of metal pipe last in your chemical plant?" asked Roger.

"It depends on the service conditions for the pipe," replied Daniel. "Some pipes can last for fifty or more years, yet others may be exposed to corrosive conditions and last only a short time."

"What if you stored the pipe indoors in a temperature and humidity-controlled environment? Could it last for one thousand years?"

"It could last an incredibly long time, but it wouldn't be useful. We need pipes in active service in our plants."

"It is the same with people. They need to be doing things. Idling away in a controlled environment would enable them to live longer, but they would not be experiencing life."

"Surely there is a way to experience life while living longer. If a pipe's life is limited by internal erosion, I could select a pipe with thicker walls so that it would last longer. If the pipe's life was limited due to corrosion, I could select a pipe made from a different material that would better resist the corrosion. In either case, I would have a way to repair the pipe when it was damaged. Body parts could be constructed from materials that lasted longer and changes could be made in the body healing systems so that damaged body parts could more easily be repaired or replaced. It seems that with some relatively simple design changes, humans could have greatly extended life spans Are the stories true about people that once lived for hundreds and hundreds of years?"

"Yes," divulged Roger. "The stories are true, but there were a lot of problems."

"What kinds of problems?"

"For starters, there was a lack of urgency. Death provides a deadline for getting things done. With no deadline, the human race you see today would grind to a halt."

"I can see that, but some animals can live to be two hundred years old and the giant redwood trees can live to be thousands of years old. There has got to be more to the story."

Roger paused and then quietly admitted, "Yes, there is."

For the first time since Daniel had seen him, Roger appeared to be uncomfortable. It wasn't anything very obvious and it may have been just a feeling that came over Daniel.

"Do you know about BMI?"

"I am familiar with Body Mass Index," replied Daniel, "it is something used by doctors to tell their patients to eat less and exercise more."

"There is something here in Heaven we call SMI…it is Spiritual Mass Index."

"Okay, how does it work?"

"You remember me telling you that there is energy in matter and even small amounts of thought in matter?"

"Sure, everything has a spiritual component."

"What if I told you that the concentration of the spiritual component could be adjusted?"

"It makes sense to me. We are always fine-tuning compositions of mixtures in our chemical plants."

"The target value for SMI in humans today is 1.0. The amount typically varies between 0.9 and 1.1."

"Can a person change their SMI?"

"Yes," answered Roger. "Today there are some very spiritual people that have SMI's as high as 1.5 and some very unspiritual people that have SMI's as low as 0.5."

"So how does SMI level affect people?"

"People with elevated SMI's have high healing potential."

"Do they live longer?" asked Daniel excitedly.

"Yes and no. It can increase one's lifespan, but people with high SMI's do not automatically live to the maximum human age. Some people naturally have a shorter lifespan than others. The higher SMI level helps them to live a few years longer, but their length of life is still in the normal range."

Daniel nodded his head. "So, it is a little bit like adding an antifoulant to a chemical process. The process may not foul as quickly, but the plant will still need to eventually be shut down for cleaning."

"Yes, only unlike your chemical process, the SMI can be shared with others. It can be used to heal and improve the lives of others."

"So why not crank up the Spiritual Mass Index dosage?"

"When human life was first placed on Earth, the SMI levels were an order-of-magnitude higher. The SMI target was 10.0 and people had much longer lifespans, approximately ten times longer."

"Sounds great to me!"

"Unfortunately, there were two problems. The first problem was that there was no release for pain and hostile feelings."

"Release for pain and hostile feelings?" Daniel looked perplexed.

"Death provides a release from pain and hostile feelings. By postponing death and not releasing the hostile feelings, humans tormented each other for hundreds and hundreds of years. People were subjected to many different types of agony. Those in pain, whether it was physical or mental, carried their burdens and suffered for a long, long time."

"I can see how that would be bad, but there should be a way to get people to come together, work out their differences, and relieve the pain."

"The second problem was much worse." Roger paused. "When people have high SMI's they have enhanced abilities."

"Enhanced abilities?" Daniel looked perplexed.

"There is a spiritual component in all matter," continued Roger, "and the spiritual components can communicate with each other."

"Like telepathy?" Daniel's eyes lit up with wonder. "People really can communicate without speaking?"

"Not just people, remember P-rays? All living things have the ability to send and receive P-rays. The signals today, however, are so weak that one cannot communicate with others. It takes a strong receptor to receive the signal and a strong transmitter to send a reply. Remember seeing the living cross?"

Daniel nodded.

"The living cross is a relatively recent addition and it has greatly boosted the strength of the P-ray communication system. When human life was first added to Earth, there was no living cross and at that time, people could talk directly to the animals."

"That must have been really neat!" exclaimed Daniel excitedly. "I've always wanted to talk to the animals and see what they had to say."

"The talking was good at first, but then people realized that they could command the animals. The animals could not distinguish between the human communications and the P-rays from Heaven. Before long, people were ordering legions of animals to fight their battles. The animals were not the only ones confused. The forces of nature were also confused. People learned they could communicate with the nontraditional life forms present in the wind and the waters, since these also have a spiritual component. Soon they were able to direct the weather and attack their enemies with massive storms."

Daniel shook his head, "What did you do?"

"I blocked the direct communication links. You have heard of the destruction of the Tower of Babel? All types of communication were disrupted, but that did not totally solve the problem. Remember how I told you that high SMI could be used for healing and making replacement body parts? People had healing powers that could be used to create replacement body parts to heal others. Animals realized this and came to people for healing."

"That part must have been fantastic. Why make any changes?"

"People learned that instead of just making replacement body parts, they could design entirely new animals. This was not an orderly process like you saw in Biology Heaven. Hideous creatures were created. Some were gigantic and some were grotesque compilations of body parts from various animals. The new creations were used as weapons of war to attack others, the more destructive the animal the better."

"Dragons and all types of mythological creatures fighting fierce battles." Daniel shook his head, "I can see how that would be bad."

"I had to reduce the SMI levels. I could do it by lowering the SMI in future generations, but it would take a long time, up to a thousand years, for the existing generation to reach the end of their lifespans. If I waited, there would have been years and years of intense suffering inflicted upon humans and animals. It was a chemical plant run-away reaction scenario. The world needed a fresh start with humans having much lower SMI's. A shutdown was needed."

"So, what did you do?"

"I chose Noah."

"And humans have had lower SMI's ever since?" asked Daniel.

"There have been adjustments. It is now a much more controlled process. Pharmacology Heaven makes recommendations, usually based on the survey results. For instance, the Bubonic plague during the Middle Ages wiped out a lot of human life. The recommendation was to increase the SMI target to 2.0 to help the human race overcome the crisis."

"It must have worked, the human race survived."

"It certainly helped," acknowledged Roger, "but there were some problems with the control process. We had several outliers on our Statistical Process Control charts."

"Wait a minute - you use Statistical Process Control charts in Heaven? I hate those charts. To me, statisticians are just one step above lawyers and politicians."

"I do not know if any engineer really likes statistics, but the results were useful. Our SMI target was 2.0, but some people had levels as high as 3.0. A few outliers may have even had SMI's as high as 3.5."

"Was that bad?"

"There were a lot of religious developments during the Middle Ages – some good and some not so good. There was also lots of wizardry, alchemy, and holy men doing supernatural things. The SMI's were returned to the 1.0 target – it was not as much of a problem this time since the SMI's targets were not as high and the human lifespan was shorter."

"Has the SMI target remained at 1.0 ever since?"

"It was briefly raised to 1.25 after the flu epidemic of World War I. You may have noticed that there was a strong religious revival in the mid-1900's and increased lifespans. The SMI target is back to 1.0 now."

"Surely there is a way to make improvements," pleaded Daniel. "We are literally talking about life and death here. Couldn't you make some gradual increases? I see how big changes in SMI can cause problems, but what about a series of small gradual changes? Maybe increase it by say 0.1 every generation and see how things go? Nobody wants to die."

"It is being considered. You have seen the surveys. It is part of an algorithm to determine the lifespan for humans as well as other species. It comes down to cost versus value. Longer life means more suffering."

"As well as more joys," pointed out Daniel.

"So far, you have had a very good life and I can certainly understand why you would want to live longer, but others are not as fortunate. Watch this."

The white walls disappeared and were replaced by floor-to-ceiling windows that peered into twelve rooms. In the first room a severely deformed infant was attached to monitors in a hospital crib, in the second room a young child was being badly abused at home, in the third room a kid with an intellectual disability was being bullied and beat up at school, severely wounded soldiers at the battlefront were in the fourth room. Daniel sadly shook his head. It was difficult to watch. In the fifth room a wife was being beaten by a drunken husband, the sixth room showed an alcoholic passed out on the street outside of a seedy bar, a homeless person hobbled to a soup kitchen in the seventh room, while in the eighth room a prisoner sat in solitary confinement in a small dark cell. A look of sorrow weighed down Daniel's face as he continued gazing into gloom. The ninth room had desolate people huddled in a refugee camp, a struggling quadriplegic was in the tenth room, a poor hungry person was shivering in the cold in the barren eleventh room, and in the twelfth room a very frail elderly person was lying in bed near death in a nursing home.

They were silent for a moment before Daniel spoke, "It is unbelievable how much suffering is in the world today."

"The longer one lives," added Roger, "the more one suffers."

CHAPTER 16

THE SEVENTH QUESTION FOR GOD – THE PRICE OF LIFE

Daniel began apologetically, "Please don't take my seventh question the wrong way. You have done so many wonderful and fantastic things, but there is also so much suffering in the world. How can you allow this?"

"This is another question that I get asked quite often," replied Roger. "Suffering is a natural part of life. Suffering makes one stronger. All living things suffer. The suffering ends with death. Suffering and death are the price of life."

"Surely, there is a way to reduce suffering."

"You have seen first-hand what happens when one enters Heaven. We have a continuous improvement process to change the world so that suffering will be reduced."

"I can see how that would make things better for life on Earth in the future, but what about the ones that are living there now that are in pain and are suffering?"

"Mankind needs to come together to minimize suffering. The ultimate solution is love for one another."

"Is that the ultimate solution?" asked Daniel. "Will that work on Earth?"

"Do you have any idea how much suffering there is on a daily basis? Do you know how many P-rays I receive daily? Do you know the range of sufferings? Physical pain, emotional scarring, fears, death. And this, this is only the suffering experienced by humans. Can you imagine what it is like to be a baby bunny that has just been snatched by a hungry coyote? Can you envision what it is like to be a worm that has been plucked from the ground and is flying through the air on its way to be fed to a nest full of starving baby birds? Does anyone ever think about all of the suffering experienced by plants – the droughts, disease, and pests? When trees shed their leaves, the leaves that were once alive and doing a highly efficient job collecting energy from the sun, slowly wither as they are discarded and carried away by the wind, far away from everything they ever knew."

The realization of the enormous burden carried by God from all of the suffering was overwhelming to Daniel. "The constant bombardment of P-rays from all of those suffering has got to be a tremendous load for you to carry. There has got to be a way to reduce suffering."

"You are an engineer. Can you design a world with less suffering?"

"Even if I could, I don't have the resources."

"I will give you the resources."

"I am a chemical engineer," responded Daniel. "I can design a chemical plant. Designing a process to reduce human suffering is way beyond my capabilities. I am not qualified."

"And who is qualified? Whose job is it to reduce suffering in the world? Everyone wants to complain about suffering, but what do they do about it? Is it the job of the religious leaders or the medical community? Is it the job of the politicians? How about the lawyers, physicists, and statisticians? You are an engineer. You are a seven sevens, why don't you do it?"

"You want me, Daniel Robinson, to solve the problem of human suffering in the world. Suffering, a problem that has been around since the human race was created. You want me to solve this colossal problem?"

"Not just human suffering, all suffering on Earth."

"That is an impossible task."

"And yet, every day billions of people complain about suffering and want something done. So, what are *you* going to do to solve the problem?"

"You...you are serious? You want me to solve the problem of suffering, right here and now?"

"The longer the wait, the more the suffering. You are a seven sevens. How would you solve a problem like this in your chemical plant?"

Daniel paused for a moment while ideas swirled around in his head. "I am not sure I can solve the problem, but I do know some problem-solving techniques. I will give it a shot."

"What changed your mind?"

"I hate to admit it, but ego. As much as I try to deny it, as a seven sevens I do have a fairly high ego. I have a chance to tackle what may be the biggest problem of all humankind and you told me that I will have unlimited resources, so let's go for it."

"What do you need?"

"A place with a huge amount of wall space," Daniel paused, "and lots and lots of sticky notes."

▲ ▲ ▲

They reappeared in St. Peter's cathedral, except that it wasn't St. Peter's cathedral. Daniel had visited St. Peter's cathedral in Rome and this cathedral was much larger.

"You are now in the Cathedral of Heaven," announced Roger," The ground floor plan is exactly twelve times larger than St. Peter's Cathedral and it is three times the height. It was designed in Architect's Heaven and constructed by Builder's Heaven."

Daniel looked around the enormous cathedral and saw an incredible array of painting and sculptural masterpieces. "These are fantastic!"

"They were prepared in Artist's Heaven. This is a multipurpose building."

"Are there services held here?"

"Of course, this is a shared facility and is used by many different religions. Do you need anything to start your problem-solving process?"

"The first step is a statement of the problem. Can you put up a sign that says "Objective – End Human Suffering?"

"The problem is to end all suffering."

"That is true," nodded Daniel, "I am using a technique that involves focusing on a smaller part of the problem first before tackling the entire problem. It is kind of like eating an elephant one piece at a time."

"Remind me to never send you to Pachyderm Heaven."

"Okay," continued Daniel, "put up a banner that says 'Objective – End Suffering'. Underneath it put up a sign that says 'Objective – End Human Suffering'. It is a subset of all suffering. Also, please ratio the size of the signs based upon the amount of suffering?"

A banner instantly appeared saying 'Objective – End Suffering'. The banner extended across the entire transept. A much smaller banner appeared underneath saying 'Objective – End Human Suffering'.

Daniel was surprised at how much smaller the second banner was compared to the first. "That's all? The immense amount of human suffering in the world is only about one tenth of one percent of the total amount of suffering in the world?"

"Actually, it is closer to one hundredth of one percent. What's next?"

"We need to write down all of the human suffering that is currently taking place. I know that it is a huge amount, so let's write on the sticky notes just the P-rays you receive from humans during a one-minute time period and place it on a wall. We are going to need some helpers."

The roof of the Cathedral of Heaven slid open revealing a brilliant blue sky that suddenly turned dark.

"Clouds?" Daniel was surprised. "It doesn't rain in Heaven." As he spoke, there was a great roar of fluttering – like the sound of a million geese taking off. Daniel looked up and saw that the edge of the now open roof of the immense cathedral was lined with tightly-packed wings. "Pigeons?"

"Angels," corrected Roger. "Let's step out for a minute."

They disappeared briefly, and when they reappeared every wall in the cavernous cathedral was filled with yellow sticky notes with written P-ray requests. The cathedral walls, side rooms, paintings, and sculptures were covered with millions of sticky notes.

"Wow!" marveled Daniel, "This is the number of P-rays you received during just one minute of time?"

"Just the human suffering. What is the next step?"

"We need to group the sticky notes by category. Let's start with physical pain, mental anguish, emotional issues, and other. Normally I would have a different color sticky note for each category of problem, but we are talking about some really big numbers. Is there a way to put these categories on a giant view screen?"

A giant view screen suddenly appeared in the middle of transept under the objective banners. The display showed:

Physical Pain:	47%
Mental Anguish:	38%
Emotional Issues:	32%
Other:	61%

"Those add up to way over one hundred percent," noted Daniel.

"Some are in multiple categories. For instance, physical pain can cause mental anguish and emotional issues."

"The large number in the other category," Daniel pointed to the display, "what are we missing?"

"Various topics," replied Roger, "favorite sports team wins, make the next traffic light, good grades on the next test, and so forth."

"We are trying to solve the colossal problem of world suffering, and people are worried about their favorite sports team, the flow of traffic, and their test scores?"

"The data is what it is. What's next?"

Daniel studied the data as the wheels in his mind turned. "This is an overwhelming challenge."

"You have your seven sevens skills, use them."

"All right," continued Daniel. "First there is intelligence. My initial plan was to break each problem category into smaller subcategories and break those down into even smaller groups. Then, using intelligence, determine a solution for each group. For instance, people once suffered from sunburn and someone with intelligence invented sunscreen."

"People still suffer from sunburn."

"True. Intelligence by itself cannot solve all of the world's suffering. The second category is physical strength. We now have machines that are much stronger than any human, so one individual's human strength is not going to solve human suffering. However, it could be possible to harness the power of billions of people working together to help each other and reduce suffering."

"Love for others and working together…I am all for that," smiled Roger. "How do you get everyone to come together?"

"Easier said than done," sighed Daniel. "The third life factor is ego. Ego is not going to help too much here. Ego is a source of energy that one can use to enhance other skills. For instance, ego tells a physically tired person to keep going because they are an exceptional person. I have a hard time seeing how ego can impact world suffering."

"Next"

"Logicalness. It would be great if we could all come together to work on the problem of suffering, but humankind is not known for logicalness. Then comes killing abilities. Killing would actually work since death ends all suffering, but wiping out all life on Earth is certainly not the preferred solution. Next is attractiveness to mate. That is great for keeping the species going, but doesn't reduce suffering. Some of the older guys at the plant say that getting married actually increases suffering. That leaves creativity."

"Is there a creative solution?" asked Roger.

Daniel paused and contemplated. He shook his head and paused some more. Then his eyes lit up. "Do you have the formula for life factors from the scans of everyone when they came to Heaven?"

"Sure, that data is stored in The Archives."

"Can you get me the numbers for Adam and Eve?"

The video screen displayed:

Adam 911 1111
Eve   911 1111

"The nine is for intelligence," Roger noted, "Their intelligence was originally a one, but it increased after they ate the apple."

"Now, can you show me the formula for life scans of their fifth-generation offspring?"

Numbers filled the giant video screen.

"Can you average the data?"

The video screen displayed:

922 2222

"Now, can you show me the formula for life scans of the tenth-generation offspring averaged?"

The video screen displayed:

933 3333

"How about the fifteenth and twentieth generation offspring averaged?"

The video screen displayed:

934 3434
944 4444

"Wow," exclaimed Daniel, "The ancestors were incredibly intelligent."

"How about the thirtieth and fortieth generation offspring averaged?"

845 4545

276

THE PRICE OF LIFE

755 4555

"Let's add a few more," continued Daniel, "the 100th generation, the 200th generation, and the average of the world today. Put those on screen with the previous numbers."

The video screen displayed:

Group	Average
Adam and Eve	911 1111
5th Generation	922 2222
10th Generation	933 3333
15th Generation	934 3434
20th Generation	944 4444
30th Generation	845 4545
40th Generation	755 4555
100th Generation	666 6666
200th Generation	565 6565
Today	454 5454

"Interesting," commented Daniel, "we think we are getting smarter, stronger, and more attractive to mate, but the numbers say otherwise. Okay, now add a third column and show an average of the seven factors that make up the formula for life."

Group	Average	Average of Life Factors
Adam and Eve	911 1111	2.14
5th Generation	922 2222	3.00
10th Generation	933 3333	3.86
15th Generation	934 3434	4.29
20th Generation	944 4444	4.71
30th Generation	845 4545	5.00
40th Generation	755 4555	5.14
100th Generation	666 6666	6.00

200th Generation	565 6565	5.42
Today	454 5454	4.43

"Now put up a second video screen and plot the numbers in the third column."

A second giant video screen instantly appeared in the middle of the cathedral next to the first video screen showing the averages.

"Using a blue line, plot a least-squares fitted curve through the points."

A blue curve connected the numbers.

"Now using a red line, display a standard Arrhenius plot."

The red line appeared on the graph. It was not an exact match to the blue line, but the lines were similar.

"How about that!" smiled Daniel, "Horseshoes and hand grenades, it is close enough for me. I have my answer."

"And that is?" asked Roger.

"In our chemical plants, our goal is to reduce process variation. If the plant runs the same each day, we make a good consistent product. However, when something changes, like when a piece of equipment starts to fail or a pipe gets partially plugged, we start making product that does not meet the customer specifications. Change creates chaos in our processes. Change is the enemy and we take great efforts to minimize changes."

Daniel stopped and looked around the immense cathedral. This really is an incredible place he thought.

"If our chemical plant equipment was scanned, it would have a formula for life factor of 000 0000. It has no intelligence, ego, or creativity. If one is trying to control variation, one does not want life. Life by its nature has variation. Life creates chaos."

Daniel looked over at Roger who was paying close attention.

"At the planetary design workshop, I was told that Heaven needed chaos on Earth. You told me that the reason you were created was to control chaos. Why would someone that is trying to control chaos, create something that would increase chaos? It did not make any sense. Living things, especially people create chaos. People are the biggest chaos creators on Earth, and yet you have allowed their population to grow and grow. I wondered why you would allow this."

Daniel paused. "Then I saw the plot of the scan numbers. They matched closely with the Arrhenius plot, which is a standard plot of most chemical reactions. The reaction usually starts slowly, speeds up, reaches its peak rate, decreases, and then slowly winds down. Temperature and residence time are used in our chemical plant to control the formation of our reactor products, but instead of using these factors, you are using the formula for life. You started with a 111 1111 rating, the numbers increased until the reaction peaked at around the one hundredth generation at 666 6666 and they have been heading lower ever since. It looks like Earth is a gigantic batch reactor and humans are the raw materials. If you are making something, there is going to be pain and suffering. One has to cut down trees to build a house and one has to break eggs to make an omelet. Are you building something?"

"Yes," nodded Roger, "I am building something. Any ideas?"

"Let's see," thought Daniel, "You were created by the universe to fight chaos, so my guess is that you are building some kind of tool to reduce chaos. A metal worker will heat and pound metal to create a new tool. There is much pain while the tool is forged, but in the end, a stronger tool is created. Are you building a special tool to fight chaos?"

"Very good," smiled Roger. "Yes, as your numbers show, there are transformations in progress. There is going to be a union between Heaven and Earth. I am currently hammering both of them, and there is a lot of suffering on Earth during the process, but eventually there is going to be a joint venture – a Heaven and Earth hybrid."

"A joint venture...a Heaven and Earth hybrid?" repeated Daniel with an astonished look.

"Yes, a joint venture. Heaven and Earth will merge and work together to fight chaos and establish order throughout the universe. I want to increase the Spiritual Mass Index in humans and all life forms so that there will be less suffering. It did not work the first time, but I want to try again with a stronger heavenly presence as well as some other changes to make sure that things do not get out of control."

"Other changes?"

"A lot of the formula for life factors need to be reduced. Lower numbers are needed."

"Back to the 111 1111?"

"I am not sure yet. High intelligence, logicalness, and creativity would be helpful in combatting chaos, but ego, physical strength, attractiveness to mate, and killing instinct all need to be reduced since they can cause problems and increase chaos. With the higher Spiritual Mass Index, it will be possible to increase the human lifespan to thousands of years. People will be able to create what they need so there will be no need to kill plants or animals for food. The world will be at peace and suffering will be greatly reduced – who knows, maybe someday suffering will become extinct."

A Heaven and Earth joint venture - it was a brilliant concept! Daniel recalled the plan for Houston he had seen in God's waiting room. That plan was incredible, but this plan was out-of-this world fantastic! It was the dream, the dream for mankind. The lion and the lamb would live side-by side. Peace and tranquility on Earth, no more struggles and no more suffering. A chaotic world was being converted into an orderly state, just as two reactive chemicals combine to form a stable substance, an everyday occurrence in a chemical plant. And yet, something would be missing. There was something about the struggles that…that made life exciting. What would life be like without pain and suffering? Would it really be life? We better enjoy the struggles and suffering while we can, because someday it will all go away.

Imperfection is perfection and chaos is an engineer's paradise, repeated over and over in Daniel's mind. And then, a horrible thought swept across him - in a world without chaos, would there be a need for engineers?

IN THE SHADOW
OF THE OBELISK

CHAPTER 1

THE HUNTER

1.1 THE PRAGMATIC HUNTER

Lantos liked to refer to himself as a pragmatic hunter. When it came to hunting, he was one of the best. He studied his quarry and knew their strengths and weaknesses. During his early years he had hunted almost every kind of game and was skilled in the use of a wide variety of weapons. He had even hunted with no weapons - he was an expert at killing.

There are limits as to how far one can excel in any sport or profession and Lantos reached his peak years ago. He no longer had room for storage of souvenirs from his favorite pastime, and hunting, especially the exotic kind, was an expensive hobby. Lantos's job could only support a modest hunting budget and there was little money to be made in the hunting profession - the legal kind. Riches beyond belief, however, could be made in the illegal hunting business, so Lantos quit his day job to pursue this endeavor.

The trip to the hunting ground was long and arduous. Usually he traveled alone, but on this trip his nephew Pascal accompanied him. Nearing the completion of his formal education, Pascal would soon be pursuing a conventional career and Lantos's brother asked him to take Pascal along in order to 'broaden his horizons'. Pascal had hunted closer to home but had never been on a trip of this magnitude.

Pascal looked out the window. It was dark everywhere. "Tell me again about our prey, Uncle."

Lantos enjoyed telling and embellishing stories. It was a trait common to hunters. "As far as game goes, this animal is not particularly dangerous. Its primary weapons are its paws and teeth, neither of which can cause us much harm if we take the standard precautions."

This reminded Lantos to check his scanner. It was clear - no signs of activity. He continued, "The skills required for this hunt are twofold. First, and foremost, we must not alert the herd. If the herd is frightened, The Authorities may become aware of our presence. We will therefore be looking for isolated stragglers. Secondly, great skill is required during the execution of the kill. This species, when frightened, produces a special drug – MED. The drug is introduced into the circulatory system where it is carried to the animal's brain. The primary reason for our hunt is to obtain MED. Certain pharmaceutical companies will pay great sums of money for MED, with no questions asked. The animal must be kept in a frightened state for as long as possible while the MED is extracted. This involves immobilizing the animal and placing a suction pump on one of the major arteries that supplies blood to the animal's brain."

"It sounds rather gruesome. Does the animal suffer much?"

Lantos paused for a moment. Which version of the story should he tell? It would not matter since soon his nephew would see for himself.

"The animal quickly goes into shock and therefore experiences very little pain. Death comes a few minutes later." So much for the standard answer, however since there was time to kill, he continued. "But how can we ever understand the actual pain suffered by another species? Every species has different pain tolerances. We tend to think of pain from a physical sense, but what about the pain of mental anguish? As the animal is dying, does it think about unfulfilled goals and aspirations? Does it think of friends it will never see again? Are there future joys that will never be experienced?"

"Goals, aspirations, friends, future joys? Uncle, you make it sound like we are talking about advanced life forms."

Lantos enjoyed philosophical discussions. It reminded him of the days of his youth. "At what level does advanced life begin? Even a single-cell creature fights for its life. Life always fights Death."

"And Death always wins."

"Death wins temporary victories. Life adapts to the surroundings. The tentacles of Life refuse to be snuffed out by Death. Life's secret weapon is reproduction. By reproducing, Life wages war with Death for eternity."

"This reproduction, Uncle, is what causes problems in so many species. Take this species for instance. With no major predators, they will eventually consume their resources and perish from starvation. Are we not doing them a favor by thinning their ranks?"

"The individual being killed would not see it that way."

"Of course not, but the population as a whole must gain."

"Those nearest to the deceased may profit when the redistribution of wealth is in their favor, especially in situations with insufficient resources. But when local resources are abundant or when the deceased provided additional benefits, such as a mother caring for her young, then those closest to the deceased suffer a loss."

"Really Uncle? You make it sound like we are removing the cream of the crop. It is common knowledge that it is the inferior that are killed. Survival is for the fittest. The fittest survive and reproduce. The weak are destroyed."

"Alas, if only that were so. How does a hunter distinguish the weak from the strong? Do we measure the physical, mental, and reproductive capabilities of our targets? Do we prepare an ecological impact statement to demonstrate how killing that particular animal will improve the herd? No, all we do is aim our weapon and shoot."

"But the stragglers, surely the stragglers must be the weakest of the species."

"Those that do not go with the crowd are not necessarily the weakest. In fact, often the opposite is true. The hunter only gets a brief glimpse into the life of the game. Suppose the straggler is tired and just needs a little rest? Suppose the straggler has a minor ailment that will heal in a few days? Suppose the straggler is looking for new food sources that will benefit the herd? These are things the hunter knows not."

"Uncle, you surprise me. Hunting is such a major part of your life, and yet you talk as if your work is not justified."

"The killing of a sub-species can never be justified on moral grounds. We are choosing to travel to another's habitat to murder an animal that poses no threat to our daily living and is not needed for food, clothing, or any immediate survival need."

"Then why do you hunt?"

"Hunting provides for my livelihood and gives me the opportunity to visit exotic locations. I find it to be a very relaxing occupation that avoids the rigors and stresses of conventional jobs. And of course, there is the excitement of the hunt."

Lantos thought to himself, 'the excitement of the hunt', really? The reasons he was giving as to why he liked to hunt were a bunch of crock, but he could not reveal all of his inner thoughts to his nephew. He had made many long hunting trips alone which provided plenty of time for deep introspection. It forced him to recognize a cold, cruel part of his persona and that was that he enjoyed killing. He really, really enjoyed killing. To cause the death of another was the ultimate power trip. He could make the victim suffer or he could be merciful. He had absolute control over them - he was God of their life. Whether they lived or died was totally in his hands and, after he killed them, he owned their carcass. He could bleed them, skin them, eat them, and even take some of their body parts home with him as a remembrance of the thrill of the kill. Deep inside, he knew he was a cold-blooded heartless killer.

The display on the automatic guidance system signaled that they were approaching their destination. It was still dark outside. Lantos initiated back-tracking maneuvers. If anyone pursued them, they would surely lose their tracks in the maze of loops. He did not expect to meet The Authorities at this remote site, but he did not want to take any chances.

As they circled the hunting grounds, Pascal became excited. "Look Uncle, look over there. It is an obelisk!" They flew by the gigantic obelisk bathed in white lights that soared high into the night sky.

"And so it is. I have never hunted in this sector before. It could prove interesting." He landed the spaceship in a secluded area near the obelisk. Looking over at Pascal, he said, "Pass me my wings."

1.2 THE CONQUEST AT SAN JACINTO

He lay there beaming with satisfaction. The conquest was complete. Mission accomplished! He looked up at the enormous obelisk topped with the Lone Star. It shined brilliantly in the night sky, providing a great beacon for the present while commemorating glorious achievements of the past.

▲ ▲ ▲

The San Jacinto Monument towered over the surrounding area. The five hundred sixty-seven-foot-high structure was the tallest masonry column in the world – twelve feet taller than the Washington monument. At the top of the obelisk was a thirty-four foot tall Lone Star that appeared the same from every viewing angle. The monument was built on the site of the Battle of San Jacinto, the decisive battle of the Texas Revolution. Construction of the monument began in 1936, the one hundredth anniversary of Texas's Independence from Mexico, and was completed in 1939. Located just outside Houston on the Houston Ship Channel, the site was now surrounded by the refineries and chemical plants that provided Houston with much of its economic livelihood.

The battle of San Jacinto was one of the great underdog victories in military history. After the fall of the Alamo in San Antonio some two hundred miles to the west, a large Mexican army under the command of General Santa Anna pursued a much smaller band of Texans under the command of Sam Houston. The Texans wanted to fight, but Sam Houston kept avoiding battles while he trained his ragtag troops.

On April 21, 1836, Santa Anna's troops were camped at San Jacinto on the banks of the present-day ship channel. If they were to be attacked by Sam Houston's elusive troops, they expected a battle at night, under the cover of darkness. After all, no one in their right mind would try a surprise attack against a larger force during the day. The hare does not attack the hound, especially in broad daylight.

Santa Anna's soldiers were recovering from long marches and many were resting, bathing, or getting ready for dinner. Legend has it that a young lady – The Yellow Rose of Texas, was amorously distracting Santa Anna.

The Texans attacked at 4:30 PM from the west with the sun at their back. Blinded by the sun and caught completely off guard, the battle was over in eighteen minutes. The Mexican army was scattered and had many casualties – six hundred fifty soldiers killed and three hundred captured. The Texan casualties were very light - just eleven dead. Santa Anna, in disguise, was captured the next day and forced to sign papers granting the independence of Texas.

▲ ▲ ▲

As he lay there, the young man reflected on his own personal conquest and the events of the evening. First was the location - the site he had chosen was absolutely magnificent. The lights here were so amazing – there were the lights shining on the San Jacinto Monument, the light from the full moon, and the thousands of points of light from the nearby petrochemical complexes. All of these lights bounced off the reflecting pool in front of the obelisk, creating a spectacular setting. Some people pay large sums of money to travel to beautiful places. For him, the only cost was for the new pair of bolt cutters that he purchased to cut the chain that blocked vehicle access to the grounds at night.

The young man then thought of the conquest of the evening that was lying naked next to him. Images flashed through his mind - the warmth of her kisses, the tenderness of her small breasts, the firmness of her smooth ass. His performance had been spectacular. He was getting better and better with his sexual skills - he was a stud!

The young man's self-congratulatory thoughts were quickly replaced with an urgent need to pee. He rose naked from the blanket and surveyed the area. He wondered where Santa Anna had his sexual encounter with The Yellow Rose. It had to have been in this area, maybe even in this very spot. And what did she look like? How did her body compare with his trophy du jour? He walked past the picnic tables and was oblivious to the intricate spider web he destroyed. A few feet away, deep within the tall grass, small animals were startled and fled, but he did not notice. A large solitary mesquite tree was his destination.

He took off his condom and threw it on the ground. If he had inspected it, he may have noticed the rip, but his mind was on other things. As he urinated on the mesquite tree, he thought of Santa Anna. This might be the same exact spot where Santa Anna took a piss. History had a way of repeating itself. He had to be careful. Santa Anna had been a fool. He had let his guard down. That was something that he would never do. You had to be careful with women. 'Love'em and leave'em' is what his older and more experienced friends always told him. That was going to also be his motto. If you were not careful, women will take control of your life and you just cannot allow that to happen. If you do, you end up working until your old age making money to support them. Then, when you are not at work, you spend your 'free' time taking care of kids, mowing the grass, fixing your wife's car, and doing other menial household chores. That was not the life for studs like him. No, he would not let his guard down. This girl tonight had been fun, a good lay, and he did like her a little, but he would not get carried away with love, emotions, and crap like that.

When he finished peeing, he noticed wild tomatoes growing on a vine intermingled with the tall grass. He picked one. Almost ripe, he slowly caressed it with his fingers. It reminded him of the smooth breasts he felt a few minutes earlier.

I am the man. I am The Man, he told himself over and over. Little did he realize the chain of events that he had set into motion.

1.3 THE HUNT

Lantos and Pascal quietly camouflaged their spaceship. Even though it was night outside, there was a considerable amount of light in the sky. The obelisk and full moon shone brightly. It would have made a good photograph. Lantos never brought cameras on these trips. He wanted no evidence of where he had been to ever fall into the hands of The Authorities.

The lights bothered Lantos. They were an indication that this was a highly populated area. Lantos did not like hunting in highly populated areas. The risk of alerting the herd was too great. If the herd was alarmed, there was a greater possibility that The Authorities might notice and investigate.

Lantos checked his scanner. It indicated that there were only a few potential prey in the area. A pocket, he thought. We must be located in a pocket of relatively unpopulated land that is surrounded by the herd. Generally, he preferred to hunt in remote areas, but pockets often provided good game opportunities. It also soothed his conscience a bit. His conscience had been bothering him more and more lately. In remote areas, a killing could have detrimental effects on those that depended on the prey for livelihood. Since there was a large herd nearby, there should be many that could step in and provide support. There was also a greater possibility that those in the pocket would be outcasts from the herd or that they may be doing some sort of illegal activity. In either case, they would tend to not be missed as much and he might even be doing the herd a favor.

Lantos and his nephew circled the area in their wingsuits and confirmed the sensor readings – the immediate area was only sparsely populated. Several potential targets were moving along the nearby trails at high rates of speed. These would be more difficult to kill unobtrusively. An inexperienced hunter might be surprised in the middle of a kill by others moving along the trail, which of course, would be disastrous. A good hunter knows his prey and their habits.

Unlike most of the so-called 'modern' hunters, Lantos did not trust his sensor readings. The sensor readings only told you so much. His sensors now picked up a single potential prey located a significant distance from the nearest trail. The sensor showed an enormous prey, then two, then one, then two then one. Lantos silently cursed the sensor and turned it off.

Lantos and Pascal flew to the vicinity of the sensor readings. As they circled the area, they noticed that there were two potential prey and that one was making contorted motions on top of the other. Lantos quickly realized that this was part of the mating ritual. He made a mental note to tell Pascal about this later. According to the background files, this species often fell asleep after completion of the mating ritual. That was bad news. In order to extract the best quality and maximum volume of MED, the animal needed to be fully awake. Lantos and Pascal flew to a nearby tree and waited for the mating ritual to end.

From the tree, Lantos observed the prospective targets and recognized that both were relatively young, although obviously old enough to mate. This was a good sign since the young in the species generally produced higher levels of good quality MED.

Upon completion of the mating ritual, the prey stopped moving and went to sleep. Lantos turned the sensor back on - there were no other potential game in the immediate area. He decided to watch and wait.

The wait was rewarded. In a few minutes, what Lantos recognized as the male stood up beside his sleeping mate, looked around, and proceeded to walk some distance naked. He then stopped and watered a nearby tree with an internal fluid. Even though Lantos had spent much time studying this species, he still did not understand its many strange rituals.

The male appeared to be an excellent physical specimen. Brief regrets of destroying the strongest of the species were replaced with greed as Lantos thought of the large quantity of MED that would come from this magnificent beast. Lantos glanced at the female to confirm that she was asleep and swiftly attacked. Pascal followed.

The male was taken completely by surprise and an incision was quickly made into its neck. The extraction apparatus was put in place and securely attached. Startled, the prey took a few steps back and gasped as blood flowed from its neck through the pump into the extraction unit, where the MED was adsorbed. What an amazing engineering design, thought Lantos as the blood began flowing. Possession of the illegal device was a serious offense, but so was MED trafficking. Once the MED was extracted, the blood had no value and it spurted out of the extraction unit everywhere. Blood drenched Lantos, Pascal, and the animal, as well as the surrounding ground.

The prey's paws flung wildly, narrowly missing Lantos. It then grasped at the extraction unit attached to its neck and pulled and pulled on the apparatus, but to no avail. The animal turned pale and started to stumble.

Lantos moved quickly. Using the remote controls for the pump on the extraction unit, he increased the flow of blood and flew behind his victim's head. Lantos's hands covered the beast's face and, with a strong jerk, pulled its head backward. The animal's already wobbly knees gave way and the mighty specimen fell to the ground, landing on its back. Lantos pushed upward on his game's head during the fall to minimize any impact to its head or the extraction unit when they hit the ground. Startled by the fall, the prey sat up and grabbed at Lantos. Lantos evaded its paws, flew a few feet away, and increased the flow of blood to the extraction unit by using the remote controls. Lantos then quickly attacked with a strong blow to the chest that knocked the beast back down to the ground. It was important to keep the animal in a stationary reclined position for as long as possible to prevent the onset of shock. The longer he kept his prey alive and in a frightened state, the greater the quantity of MED he would obtain. The key was to keep the animal's mind occupied and not allow it to realize that it was bleeding to death.

Time and time again the prey tried to rise, only to be pushed back to the ground. Frustrated, the animal tried swinging at Lantos with its paws from its reclined position. This was exactly what Lantos wanted and he proceeded to toy with his game, much as one would entertain a kitten with a ball of yarn. Lantos darted in and out of striking range as the animal flailed wildly. Occasionally Lantos would adsorb a partial blow to make the prey feel successful and give it hope. All the while, Lantos kept a careful watch on the blood flow rate to the MED extraction unit and his game's condition. As it started to lose consciousness, Lantos reduced the blood flow to the extraction unit and allowed the prey's blood pressure to rise. A large puddle of blood was now forming around the animal.

As Lantos monitored the success of the hunt, pride boiled up inside him. This was going to be one of his best MED kills ever. It was largely due to his choice of targets and the way he skillfully handled the kill. He glanced at the continuous analysis on the MED extraction unit. It confirmed what he thought – a large volume of exceptionally high-grade MED was being collected.

Eventually the prey showed less and less response from the repeated reversals of the flow from the MED extraction unit. It had survived much longer than those on previous hunts, but would die soon. Lantos thought he might be able to get one last MED surge. Now too weak to move its paws and resist, Lantos stood on his game's chest. In horror, it watched as Lantos removed his mask and showed his large pink eyes. With a wide grin, Lantos slowly walked up to the animal's face and let out a hideous roar while adjusting the MED extraction pump to its maximum setting. The MED extraction unit adsorbed one last surge of blood as the massive beast's heart stopped. Lantos removed the extraction apparatus from his prey's neck and noted that it was filled to capacity. An inexperienced hunter would have needed four or five kills to get this much MED. This soothed his conscience a bit. He took one last look at the animal he had just killed and consolingly said, "A greater cause has no one that he gave his life for others. You were great!"

Lantos glanced around and noticed that his nephew had a pale sick look. Suddenly, Pascal leaned against a nearby mesquite tree and began vomiting. As they headed back to their spaceship, Lantos said to himself, "He will do better once we are cleaned up, have a good meal, and are on our way home."

In all the excitement, Lantos forgot about the female.

1.4 PROGRESS

After the hunt at the obelisk, Lantos placed his spaceship in orbit around the planet and enjoyed the view. Pascal looked shaken and was quiet for a long time before he eventually fell asleep.

When he woke, Pascal appeared better, but was still upset. "You, you killed that poor animal," he tersely sputtered. "And for what? That poor animal gave its life for your greed!"

Lantos had been around a lot of lemurs after similar hunts. There seemed to be two general reactions – either 'Hey, that was really fun… let's do it again' or 'That was totally disgusting…get me out of here fast!' His nephew was in the latter group.

"Let's not talk about the hunt right now," suggested Lantos. "It is over and done. Soon you will be going home. There will be no more hunting this trip."

Pascal looked relieved. "They…they reminded me so much of us." Pascal was starting to get depressed.

"There is a resemblance," agreed Lantos, "in some ways all life has similar characteristics."

"They are much larger than us, they don't have a tail or much hair, and they are not as technically advanced, but I still see a lot we have in common."

Lantos realized that he had to get Pascal's mind off the kill. He wanted Pascal to have good memories of their time together, and they still had a long trip home.

"Did you know on this planet there is a species of life that is exactly like us?"

"No way!" exclaimed Pascal. His sadness started to fade.

Lantos knew he was onto something. "The species on this planet never developed a technical civilization like ours. They live in very primitive conditions. I brought a universal translator, so if you would like, we could visit them."

"Sure!" smiled Pascal eagerly. "This could be fun, just no more killing!"

"Their habitat is in jungles on the other side of the planet from where we hunted." Lantos entered coordinates in the ship's control system.

"How did you find them?"

"I found out about them during the later stages of my formal education. A lot of the guys came here to party."

"Party with primitive females?" asked Pascal with raised eyebrows.

"It is not what you think." Lantos paused and looked ashamed. "Actually, it is exactly what you think. But it was wrong and I want you to promise to keep your wingsuit on at all times."

"Okay," agreed Pascal, "but why was it wrong?"

"I returned a couple of years after the party trip. There had been a lot of stillborn babies and others were born with severe birth defects. It was a horrible experience. There is something in the reproductive process that discourages our mating with this lineage."

"So, are they still mad at you?"

"I am not sure that group is still around, but we will definitely be going to a different area."

They landed a short time later. Lantos and Pascal emerged from their saucer-shaped spacecraft wearing their wingsuits and flew at treetop height around the jungle. The sunlight glittered through the canopy as they soared above the tropical vegetation. Multicolored birds flew above while duikers and impalas ran below. They spotted two giraffes grazing along with various other creatures scurrying on the jungle tarmac.

Pascal was the first to notice a family of lemurs in the distance. "Look, look Uncle!" he shouted excitedly, "They are just like us!"

Lantos and Pascal landed nearby. Lantos turned on the universal translator and greeted the family, "Hello brothers, may we join you?"

The lemur family scattered into the bushes.

"Please, please do not run," implored Lantos. "We mean you no harm."

The father of the group poked his head out from behind the bushes, "Who, who are you and why do you fly?"

"We are from a faraway jungle," answered Lantos matter-of-factly, "Everyone there flies. Can we meet with your leader?"

"Follow us," beckoned the father as they scampered through the jungle. A few minutes later they arrived at an open area with tree stumps and fallen trees that was surrounded by dense jungle brush. "Here is Kang, the esteemed leader of our troop."

Lantos and Pascal sat on a log and addressed the leader. He appeared older and stronger than the other lemurs. "I am Lantos and this is my nephew Pascal, we are very glad to meet you."

Kang opened his arms wide and welcomed them with a pleasant voice, "Greetings my good fellows. Please share food with us."

Three young females approached with their hands full of food. The first brought fruits, the second nuts, and the third crickets. They seemed particularly attracted to Pascal and rubbed their tails across his shoulders.

Lantos and Pascal ate the fruit and complimented its freshness. They then ate the nuts and applauded the fine flavor. When it was time to eat the crickets, Pascal had a disgusted look. Lantos's tail bashed Pascal on the back of the head and they then ate the crickets. Lantos commented on their crunchiness.

After they ate, Kang resumed the conversation, "Where is it that you are from and why do you honor us with your presence?"

"We are from a very distant jungle," answered Lantos, "and we would like to find out more about your way of life."

"Where is this distant land from which you come?"

"It is far, far away. We live in a jungle on the other side of a large ocean."

"My good fellows. We greet you warmly, we share our food, and our young females would like to share with you much more. Yet around you there is a large quantity of cape buffalo excrement."

"What, what do you mean?" Lantos had a startled look.

"You do not live in the jungle," Kang stated sternly. "Your scent, your skin, your hair – they are not of the jungle. I will politely ask you once more, where are you from? Please answer me this time with less excrement."

"My apologies," bowed Lantos. "You are most observant and you are correct. I will tell you the truth, but to you it may sound very strange."

"I live in a world in which strange things occur daily."

"Very well, we are from a different world. We flew here in a spaceship from a distant light in the night sky." Lantos paused to see Kang's reaction.

"That is much better. The odor from excrement seems to be going away. Now please tell me, why would you fly here from a light in the night sky? Surely you did not come that great distance just to talk with me."

"I am a hunter. I hunt great animals in many distant worlds."

"Did you come to hunt us?" asked Kang anxiously, "if so, I must warn you that I have been hunted many times and yet I am still very much alive."

"Oh no," replied Lantos, "our hunting is now over. There will be no more killing this trip."

Kang was somewhat, but not totally relieved. "My good fellows, this I am glad to hear. Just so you know, we are very kind to strangers, but I would have no problem beating the excrement out of you."

Pascal laughed. Lantos gave him a forbidding look, flicked his tail, and bopped him on the back of his head. "Please accept our apologies," bowed Lantos again. "My nephew does not question your strength, but is amused at the choice of words from the universal translator. If my nephew does not mind his tongue, he will soon be seeing his own excrement."

"Please tell me about your hunt," continued Kang, "Was it the leopard, the elephant, the cape buffalo, or perhaps the lion?"

"My prey was the bald tailless primate."

There was a long pause and the young lemurs shuddered. Kang had an astonished look, "Surely you did not kill the bald tailless primate. Why would someone travel all the way from a distant light in the night sky to eat a bald tailless primate?"

"Actually," disclosed Lantos, "we did not eat him. We just took something from his blood."

"Do you come from a race of mosquitoes?" Kang had an appalled look.

"Our race long ago was very similar to yours. We made much progress and we can improve your life," Lantos proudly declared.

"My good fellows, are you saying your life is better than ours?"

"Much better, our life spans are five times longer. We have wiped out diseases, we grow our own food so there is no starvation, and we have weapons that can destroy any predator. Watch this."

With a quick flick of his tail, Lantos pulled his laser pistol out of his wingsuit and flipped it into the air. He then grabbed the laser pistol in mid-air with his right hand, and fired at a tree one hundred yards away. A large limb came crashing down and two brilliant blue starlings, screaming in protest, flew away. The young lemurs trembled.

"You certainly have our attention," Kang calmly acknowledged. "Please tell us more."

"Let me show you what life is like on our world." Lantos set up a holographic projector. "Here are images of our world - they can cause you no harm."

Holographic images appeared before them. The young lemurs ran away at first, but then gradually came closer for a better view.

"This is our jungle." Images of skyscrapers appeared, "This is where we live. We are well protected from the environment and have many items that provide comfort and entertainment. We can fly short distances with our wingsuits or we can travel longer distances in vehicles that travel on land, water, or air."

"Like the bald tailless primates?" asked Kang.

"The bald tailless primates are very primitive compared to us."

The holographic projector continued displaying images.

"We no longer have to gather meals outdoors." Images of lemurs eating in restaurants appeared. "If we get sick or injured, we are repaired by doctors." The hologram showed lemurs being treated in hospital beds. "We have police and soldiers to protect us from those that would do us harm." Images of warriors in body armor firing laser weapons appeared. Observing the destruction caused by the powerful weapons excited most of the lemurs and they squealed with delight at each explosion.

Kang was unfazed, "My good fellows, this is impressive and my troop is very interested in this life of yours. May I ask you some questions?"

"Of course."

"How did you acquire your comfortable living quarters, fast moving vehicles, and powerful weapons?"

"They were developed in the minds of our great engineers. The engineers envisioned combining the forces of nature with common materials to create useful items."

"Are you an engineer?"

"Oh no. Before I chose to be a hunter, I was a financial advisor. I helped people take care of their wealth so that they would be well cared for when they are old and so that their descendants would be provided for after they died."

"Your images show large numbers of people in a small area. Where does all the food come from?"

"The food is grown in faraway places and is gathered by the poorer lemurs." Kang had a puzzled look on his face, so Lantos explained, "The poorer ones did not finish their education." Lantos gave Pascal a subtle glance.

"What is this education?" asked Kang.

"It is a place where the young learn about life. They study mathematics, science, history, languages, and other subjects to prepare them for future roles in life."

"So, the ones that do not learn about life gather food?"

"They do other jobs as well. Some are builders, some are warriors, and some make things that give us comfort and entertainment."

"So, my good fellows, is everyone living in the tall buildings part of the same clan and do they know each other well?"

"Actually, we are all part of the same clan, but we do not know each other well. We are all busy living life."

"Tell me, what is it like to live life?"

"Well," Lantos paused, "We work very hard to make wealth and then we play very hard using the wealth."

"My good fellows, how do you play?"

"Some travel to faraway places, while others watch shows and athletic competitions."

"What is it like in the faraway places?"

"Some are very hot, some are very cold, some are windy, some are very wet, some are very dry, and some are just like your jungle."

"What is it like to watch shows and athletic competitions?"

"It is like," Lantos paused again, "well it is a lot like watching life." Lantos's eyes lit up as he explained, "The shows have adventures that simulate life and athletic competitions are like battles between great warriors, only no one gets hurt…mostly, there are some injuries."

"Tell me more," implored Kang. "Do you live life with your family?"

"Not really. Oh, when the children are young, they live with us and we spend a lot of time with them when we are not going to work and they are not going to school. But then they grow up and go off to finish their education."

"To learn about life…my good fellows, do you not miss your children?"

"A little, at first…but then you adjust. Oh, we still see them from time to time on special occasions and many have substitute children."

"Tell me about substitute children."

"We call them pets...some have cute little mice they keep in their living quarters and some have frogs. I know of one that has a small snake – nonpoisonous of course."

All of the lemurs shuddered.

"So," Kang paused contemplatively, "you think that you can improve our lives?"

"Most definitely." Lantos began speaking excitedly. "We could bring in weapons and medicine. Maybe staff a doctor here. I could see building a base with comfortable accommodations. Your lemurs could grow crops for us. We would make a lot of wealth hunting the bald tailless primates. Yes…" he paused as he looked over at the female lemurs and winked, "I can see how this would be a very good life." He looked directly at Kang, "Would you like to have a better life, sir?"

Kang again paused and gathered his thoughts. "Your engineers have created many marvelous things. You are certainly well traveled and I think you may be very wise, but you do not seem to comprehend the tremendous price you have paid."

"What price?" Lantos had a surprised look.

"Why my good fellows," pointed out Kang, "the price of life."

"I, I don't understand. We live much longer than you and we have riches beyond belief. We live tremendous lives!"

Kang shook his head, "You had a great opportunity to live, but you gave up your life."

"What, what do you mean?" Lantos continued to look astonished.

"When I woke this morning, I knew this day may be my last. There are many animals that want to kill me. I am in constant danger from floods, rock slides, and falling trees. There is the heat, the cold, howling winds, and torrential rains. Great hunger, diseases, crippling injuries – all of this is part of my daily life. Death is all around me. I do not need to travel to faraway lands for excitement - I have that here. I do not need to watch adventures - I have them here. I do not need to view athletic competitions with simulated warriors - I have real wars here. I do not need to travel to be with my family on special occasions - I am with them every day." He paused and shook his head, "Do you really keep mice, frogs, and snakes in your living quarters?"

Kang stood and put his tail around Lantos, "We enjoy our food because we know one day we will starve, we appreciate our moments of safety because every day we are in danger, we cherish time with our families because we know this could be our last time together. You have paid a great price. You no longer live a real life - you live a substitute life. My life may be shorter, but my living is much, much greater."

Shortly thereafter Lantos and Pascal thanked Kang and the other lemurs for their hospitality and departed.

CHAPTER 2

THE MISSION OF THE MERPS

2.1 LAUNCH PREPARATIONS

The Director surveyed the prelaunch activities. The process was in automatic mode and proceeding smoothly in accordance with the pre-programmed plans. The pressurization sequence would be completed in a few minutes. There had been no word from Centcom and that was good because things always got screwed up when Centcom was involved. With the pressurization sequence engaged, it was only a matter of time before Centcom's sensors detected the activities and tried to take control.

A warning was received from the waste storage area – a high level alarm. It could wait until after the launch. The director acknowledged the signal and suppressed the warning message. The Director had a dual function in The Organization – Waste Management and Launch Control and sometimes the responsibilities overlapped. That was the problem with matrix management – resources could not be totally devoted to solving the crisis at hand because there were always other problems needing attention. The Director preferred his role in Launch Control with its meaningful purpose and creative opportunities. The Waste Management job was critical to The Organization, but it was so boring.

Launch Control had been added to his responsibilities only a few years ago. Before then, he had worked only in Waste Management. He still had fond memories of the first launch – and especially Centcom's reaction. He had scared the hell out of Centcom but, with Centcom's typical childish mentality, the response had been, "Let's do it again."

The initial launch had been a clandestine operation. It occurred shortly after the ancient code was deciphered. The subsequent knowledge that was unleashed resulted in tremendous growth in The Organization. With that growth, came strange new powers and capabilities.

One of the capabilities was the ability to construct Merps - lowly, but *living* creatures, whose only apparent purpose in life was to be launched. The launching of the Merps provided a spectacular attraction that entertained the entire Organization. It was the subsequent death of the Merps that bothered the Director. The rest of the Organization did not seem to care that the Merps died. They had their jobs to do, he had his, and the deaths of thousands and thousands of Merps at each launch did not appreciably change their world - life goes on.

The Director took special pride of his role in the manufacturing of the Merps. The Merps were prepared in batches. The Merps had no digestive facilities. They lived on what some would call their 'baby fat'. When it was consumed, they died. With such a short shelf life it was imperative that they be produced only shortly before launch.

Standardization is a key element for all manufacturing processes. All Merps looked alike on the outside. It was the inner characteristics of the Merps that were different. The Director provided each Merp with a different internal program. The list of traits and various combinations was endless. Some of the programs were similar but others were vastly different. To the Director, the Merps were individuals. It is easy to kill nameless identical masses. It is much more difficult to kill individuals.

"URGENT MESSAGE FROM CENTRAL COMMAND TO WASTE MANAGEMENT DIRECTOR...PRELAUNCH ACTIVITIES HAVE BEEN DETECTED...LAUNCH IS TO TAKE PLACE ON SIGNAL FROM CENTRAL COMMAND ONLY...REPEAT – ONLY CENTRAL COMMAND IS AUTHORIZED TO INITIATE LAUNCH SEQUENCE...DO YOU COPY?...OVER."

The Director silently cursed Centcom and acknowledged the message. As a professional, he maintained a positive outward appearance. Centcom had immense powers and almost total control. Any coup attempts would undoubtedly destroy The Organization. You could not beat Centcom. The only hope was to initiate subtle changes that would make life better for the entire Organization.

The Director checked the pressure of the launch chamber. The pressurization sequence was nearly complete. The Merps were packed like sardines in the launch chamber and the prelaunch chamber was filling up fast. Launching was eminent. It was time for his speech to the Merps.

"Hello my children, I am your creator. Each and every one of you is unique and very special. Today you embark on one of the greatest expeditions ever undertaken. It is a mission of paramount importance to the entire Organization. It will be known in The Archives as 'The Grandest Endeavor'." There was a slight roar in the background. The Director continued, "Today your mission is to find Eternal Life."

2.2 THE LAUNCH

The Director resumed his speech to the Merps. It was always the same speech, but he strived to make it sound fresh for each launch. It was the least one could do for those facing certain death.

"The fountain of Eternal Life is near. The path to it is treacherous. Many will not survive. Their efforts however, will be remembered by all. To die on such an endeavor is glorious. Do not be afraid to sacrifice your life for the sake of your brother and the greater cause. Work together unselfishly. Each of you is equipped with a special set of armaments. Use them wisely. Coordinate your attack." He paused and looked out at the Merps. "I wish that I could go with you. Alas, my lot in life has been to create you, gather you, and send you on this magnificent journey. When you arrive at the Promised Land, remember me. Tell your offspring about me and this wondrous quest."

A rumbling in the launch chamber interrupted the speech. The Director checked the chamber pressure. It was approaching the danger level. He had never before seen it this high. The Merp production unit was continuing to produce Merps that were being sent to the prelaunch chamber. The Director sent an urgent message requesting immediate launch to Centcom and received an unusually rapid reply.

"VERY URGENT MESSAGE FROM CENTRAL COMMAND TO THE WASTE MANAGEMENT DIRECTOR...YOUR MESSAGE HAS BEEN RECEIVED...DO NOT, REPEAT DO NOT LAUNCH... LAUNCHING WILL TAKE PLACE IN LESS THAN FIVE MINUTES AND WILL BE AUTHORIZED ONLY BY CENTRAL COMMAND... HOLD YOUR POSITITION UNTIL FURTHER NOTICE...CENTRAL COMMAND OUT!"

The bastards better know what they are doing, thought the Director as he resumed his speech, "I beg your forgiveness for the interruption. I just received a very important communiqué from Central Command and they want me to extend to you their thanks for going on this mission and they want to let you know that the entire Organization is behind you one hundred and ten percent. Let me conclude by saying that I bid you a fond farewell and wish you the best on your journey. Eternal life is within your grasp. You have the capabilities of capturing it. Go forth and live forever!"

There was a thunderous roar from the launch chamber. The Director rechecked the chamber pressure. It was well passed the danger level and almost off the chart. If the bastards at Centcom were not going to launch, drastic action was needed. He issued his commands quickly, "Divert all new Merps to Waste Storage Area #1 and send a high priority warning message to Centcom."

The response from Waste Storage was almost instantaneous, "Waste Storage Area #1 is full."

"Initiate expansion sequence," ordered the Director.

"Expansion sequence initiated," came the reply, "Tanks will be at maximum expansion limit in five minutes."

"CENTRAL COMMAND TO WASTE MANAGEMENT DIRECTOR...YOUR MESSAGE HAS BEEN RECEIVED... REQUEST FOR WASTE DISCHARGE IS DENIED...REPEAT, DENIED UNTIL AFTER THE LAUNCH. PLEASE DO NOT SEND SUCH IDIOTIC REQUESTS ON HIGH PRIORITY CHANNELS...LAUNCH COUNTDOWN HAS BEEN TEMPORARILY DELAYED, BUT WILL RESUME SHORTLY... CENTRAL COMMAND OUT!"

Why did this always happen when Centcom was involved? He could handle his launch control activities, he could handle his waste management activities, but he could not handle both jobs and Centcom at the same time. If Centcom would just let him run the operation. He swiftly issued emergency orders to his units.

"Urgent message to Merp production unit – shut down immediately and open production unit to backfill from the launch chamber." This was followed with, "Urgent message to distribution network – fill all available pipe lines with surplus Merps and overflow waste!" This was going to be a bitch to clean out afterwards.

Next was the message he hated to send, "Emergency message from Launch Control and Waste Management Director to Energy

Director...Request immediate shutdown of your facilities...We are in an overflow situation until after the pending launch and have no capacity for your materials...Repeat, we are unable to receive your materials - please shutdown immediately...Over."

The dreaded response came quickly.

"Urgent message from Energy Director to **asshole** in charge of Waste Management... We are trying to operate a major production facility and resent interference from your pissant unit ... At the request of Centcom, we will *temporarily* reduce our rates until your so-called crisis is averted... Please get your shit together! Energy Director out!"

It was enough to give one ulcers. The Director rechecked the operating pressures and levels. His quick actions had bought, at most, twenty minutes of additional time. He had exhausted all of his legal options. His only remaining option was to initiate an unauthorized launch. Unauthorized launches were permitted and actually encouraged by the Organization at times when Centcom was inactive. However, an unauthorized launch after Centcom's specific orders would be seen as a major breach of protocol and a reprimand would be placed on his permanent record in The Archives.

The Director's dilemma was resolved ten minutes later with an order from Centcom.

"PRIORITY MESSAGE FROM CENTRAL COMMAND TO WASTE MANAGEMENT DIRECTOR...INITIATE IMMEDIATE LAUNCH... REPEAT, INITITATE IMMEDIATE LANCH...CENTRAL COMMAND OUT!"

The Director gave a sigh of relief that was felt throughout the Organization. The launch was spectacular. Congratulatory messages were quickly sent from all parts of the Organization. Centcom was widely praised for its control of the launch activities. The Archives recorded the remarkable job that had been done by Centcom. There was no

THE PRICE OF LIFE

mention in The Archives of the Director's efforts or the deaths of the multitudes of Merps.

▲ ▲ ▲

Afterwards, the Director monitored the cleaning of the launch chamber. The Director sent a reminder message to Centcom about the need to empty Waste Storage Area #1. When it was empty, it would become the destination for surplus Merps that never had an opportunity to fulfill their purpose in life.

The Director retired to his quarters. It would be several hours before Waste Storage would need to be emptied again. It would be a considerably longer period of time before the next launch, before which the Merp production unit would have to be restocked.

The Director was in a melancholy mood. He had produced millions of Merps for launches. Millions of Merps had gone unknowingly and even joyfully to their deaths. He had no way of knowing if any of them ever found Eternal Life. Hell, he did not even know if Eternal Life existed. There was no way of knowing what was on the other side. He had no feedback on which Merps were better prepared for the journey. He would continue to manufacture Merps with different programming combinations, never knowing the optimum conditions. The pursuit of Eternal Life had already cost the lives of millions. How can life justify so much death? How steep is the price of life?

2.3 THE MERPS

The crowded conditions in the launch chamber were almost unbearable. Row after row of Merps were packed like sardines into packets. The packets entered a prelaunch chamber and were automatically moved to the launch chamber from where they were fired to destinations unknown. The process was similar to that of loading artillery shells into a large automated cannon. Numerous launchings occurred. The initial launchings had more force, but less direction. The later launchings had less force, but better directional control. MWXY8406 and FWXY6124 were in the middle third of the packets launched. Like the other Merps, they were temporarily disoriented after being launched, but quickly recovered and got their bearings. They were relieved to finally be free to move around on their own.

"Wow, that was some blast!" exclaimed MWXY8406.

"It certainly was," agreed FWXY6124. "I sure am glad to be out of there I thought the Director would never finish his speech and get on with the show."

"Do you know how we go about finding Eternal Life?"

"The hell if I know. I am not sure I would know Eternal Life if it were staring me in the face."

"And what did he mean about each of us being equipped with special armaments? We all look the same to me."

"Me too. Maybe we change with time."

A stream of Merps going in the opposite direction interrupted their conversation.

"Hey good buddies, where are y'all going?" hollered MWXY8406.

"Who knows?" came one reply.

"Who cares?" said another.

"It's one hell of a trip!" reveled a third.

A fourth Merp looked bruised, "Hey Man, watch out for the wall."

"Wall? What wall?" MWXY8406 looked around and saw that up ahead there was a large transparent wall – the barrier to Eternal Life.

▲ ▲ ▲

There was sadness, a great sadness surrounding GGE82 as she talked to herself. "A princess, a princess they called me. For many, many years they called me a princess…You will do great things, they said. You will do great things…And what great things have I done?…Nothing. I just sit around on my ass all day long and do nothing…You are the creator of life, they said. You will be a great mother to a new world that will last forever."

What a bunch of crap. Look where she was now – a few hours from oblivion. She would be gone by morning. She would be history, kaput, finished. She would be making the journey into the great abyss…alone.

Her only hope was some fucking Merp. And where were the little Prince Charmings at this very minute? Even if the Merps had assholes, they couldn't tell them from a hole in the ground.

The Merps were known for their unreliability. She had watched her sisters, other princesses, make the journey into the abyss alone when the little bastards had not arrived in time. In fact, she had never even seen a Merp. I wonder, she thought, do Merps really exist or are they just some fairy tale concocted by a sadistic mad man that enjoys sacrificing princesses?

She was not sure how she would go down the abyss. Would she be stoic or scream her bloody head off? She would probably do the latter. That was what most of the sisters before her had done. Yeah, scream your bloody head off and take whatever you can with you. Maximum damage! That was the only way to avenge the fate thrust upon her by the sadistic mad man that was her creator.

Had she asked to be born? Had she asked to be a princess? Why did she have to be Princess #82? If she had a higher number, she would have lived longer. In the future, maybe there would be some great medical discovery – a discovery that would let her live forever. And maybe there would be a way to create a world without the need for Merps. Yeah, that's what the world needed, synthetic Merps. Maybe there could be some programmable ones – the kind that could do their job, be on time, and never give you any trouble.

Alas, the world around her was not of her creation. The current world was imperfect and unfair, and the abyss was drawing nearer.

▲ ▲ ▲

As MWXY8406 and FWXY6124 approached the transparent wall, they noticed a strange phenomenon. A crack had developed in the wall. The crack became larger and larger. Suddenly, the wall broke and Merps by the thousands passed through. MWXY8406 and FWXY6124 stayed in the mainstream as they surged onward. They were still traveling with much of the momentum from their launch. They noticed ahead, however, that many of the Merps appeared to be slowing down. As they passed into the unknown, they saw many Merps hugging the sides of the passageway, avoiding the mainstream. MWXY8406 called out to them, "Hey dudes, the party is this way. Don't you want to see what's over the hill?"

"We're happy where we are," came one reply.

"Who cares what's over there?" commented another.

"I am too tired right now," explained a third, "Maybe later."

"Why follow the same path?" shouted a fourth, "I want to be different."

Ahead, it was apparent that more and more of the Merps were falling off the pace.

"Why stop when we are so close to Eternal Life?" exhorted MWXY8406, "Come on, push yourself, it is just a little bit further."

"Everyone gets Eternal Life!" declared one of the Merps.

"Eternal Life is bull shit!" yelled a second.

"What's so great about Eternal Life?" questioned a third.

"Party now!" screamed a fourth.

MWXY8406 looked over at FWXY6124, "I believe in Eternal Life. I believe that we were created to seek Eternal Life. You believe also, don't you?"

"I want to", replied FWWX6124, "I want to very much, but I don't have your faith. I need evidence of Eternal Life and I see none. I want someone that really knows about Eternal Life to tell me all about Eternal Life."

"But the Director, the Launch Director told us that there was Eternal Life and he was the one that created us. He made us from nothing and brought us to life. Anyone that can do that must surely know if there is Eternal Life."

"The Director did know us before we knew life, but does he know what we will experience afterwards? The Director never made the journey over the hill. How can anyone living ever know about life after living?"

"I believe!" proclaimed MWXY8406, "I believe in Eternal Life! Eternal life has got to exist! I want it to exist and I am going to find it!"

As they rose over the last hill, their conversation was interrupted. MWXY8406 and FWXY6124 gasped in amazement. In the distance was a sensational object – the most beautiful thing they had ever seen.

2.4 FINDING ETERNAL LIFE

Princess #82 was slowly slipping downward on a slope that led to a steep drop off and the great abyss below. She was on the verge of panic when she noticed a strange light coming from behind the hill. Could it be, she thought, that the Merps are coming to rescue me? Her only chance for salvation was with the Merps but, was the light she saw the Merps, a figment of her crazed mind or, she cringed, could it be just another of the mad man's tormenting schemes?

A few minutes previously she had been preparing herself to accept a dismal fate. Now there was a glimmer of hope. Was the hope real? Is false hope better than no hope? After quick deliberation, she decided to put all of her eggs in one basket – the light had to be the Merps coming to save her. If it wasn't, nothing else really mattered. But would the Merps arrive in time? And if they did arrive, what would they do?

She could not dwell on this. All she could do was focus on contacting the Merps and avoiding the abyss. She activated her communications beacon and then began to rock in an effort to resist the downhill slide into the abyss. A lateral route down the hill at a higher speed would take a longer time than a slow direct path and buy her some more time, wouldn't it? She was not totally sure, but she was now committed to her plan of action.

▲ ▲ ▲

As they approached, MWXY8406 and FWXY6124 noticed that the dazzling object was a gigantic sphere. There were many openings on the globe that appeared to be a perfect fit for Merps. There were two layers of openings – some on the translucent stationary outer wall and others on an opaque rotating inner chamber. To enter the inner chamber, one had to pass through a translucent outer wall opening and then wait for an opening to line up on the rotating inner chamber. Like spotlights on a diamond necklace, the glow from the inner chamber sparkled spectacularly.

MWXY8406 and FWXY6124 arrived at the sphere just in time. Their energy supplies were exhausted and they were operating solely on reserve power. A handful of haggard-looking Merps were already at the site and were awed by its appearance.

"We did it! We did it!" shouted MWXY8406. "We found Eternal Life! I told you that Eternal Life exists! We stayed on the path, we worked hard, and we found it!"

As they realized their accomplishment, there was much jubilation and frivolity among all of the Merps present - they had found Eternal Life! With a second wind, they joyfully danced and darted around the amazing sphere.

"Let's go inside and live forever!" shouted FWXY6124 excitedly.

The jubilation was cut short by a loud booming voice from the glistening globe, "Will *one* of you Merps please come inside so the *two* of us can live forever?

2.5 THE DOORWAY TO ETERNAL LIFE

Princess #82 was infuriated at what she saw. Here she was, totally stressed out and on the verge of death. She was using all of her energy to avoid falling into the abyss. Meanwhile, the assholeless Prince Charmings were dancing jovially outside, unaware of the existence of the abyss and its impending perils.

One of the Merps would have to find the path inside, and find it pretty damn quick or they were all very, very soon going to be very, very dead. The Merps had become still after her first message. What was taking them so long? She repeated her message to them with a gentler, but much more urgent tone, "Will **one** of you wonderful Merps please come inside quickly, before I am annihilated in the abyss below. I love all of you and I am glad all of you arrived, but if **one** of you does not come inside really, really fast, the **two** of us will not be able to live forever."

▲ ▲ ▲

The second message confirmed the horror of the first. There would be no mass salvation. Only one Merp would survive and live forever. Who would that be?

They had all traveled down the same path. They had all done what they were supposed to do and had arrived at this point. And now, and now at the end of the line with Eternal Life in their grasp, only one was to be chosen. If there had been no salvation, if all met the same fate, it might have been easier to face. But no, this was not the case. One was going to win the grandest prize ever - one was to live forever while the rest were to be obliterated.

Many had been called, but only one was to be chosen. And who gets to pick? How do you decide who gets Eternal Life? Do you hold an election and vote for the most popular candidate? Do you sell an Eternal Life seat to the highest bidder? Could some kind of review committee evaluate the good works of those bidding for the position? Or, would some sort of lottery decide the issue?

MWXY8406 looked over at FWXY6124. "Let's go together. Maybe they will accept us both. We have come this far. Let's stick together."

The Merps that had completed the quest for Eternal Life overcame their initial shock and began slowly moving toward the many Merp-shaped openings in the magnificent sphere's outer wall. Most of them, like MWXY8406 and FWXY6124 had very little energy remaining and were moving sluggishly.

Suddenly, a fast-moving Merp approached from the rear chanting,

"MWXY8888 says standby boys,
And accept your fate
MWXY8888 couldn't come early,
But won't be late
MWXY8888 is not just good,
He is oh so great!"

MWXY8888 was traveling fast and starting to pass MWXY8406 and FWXY6124.

FWXY6124 muttered, "Obnoxious SOB," while giving MWXY8406 a hard push toward an opening on the outer sphere and then latched on to the tail of MWXY8888.

With the push, MWXY8406 raced toward one of the openings in the outer sphere and was closest to the sphere, but MWXY8888 was coming up fast, even with FWXY6124 clinging tightly to its tail.

As MWXY8888 passed by, MWXY8406 turned and said to FWXY6124, "A greater love hath no one than this, that it lay down its life for its brother."

Without releasing its grip on the faster moving Merp, FWXY6124 shouted, "Remember me. Remember me today in paradise!"

The tadpole-shaped creatures reached the openings in the outer wall of the sphere. MWXY8888 was the first to penetrate the outer opening with its head. However, before it could enter the opening in the inner wall, it came to an abrupt halt. Stuck in the narrow outer opening was the tail of MWXY8888 and the head of FWXY6124.

Like a fish out of water, MWXY8888 thrashed wildly. Time and time again, FWXY6124 was slammed into the outer opening as MWXY8888 attempted to wiggle through the narrow opening. FWXY6124 held on with a death grip.

The death grip prevailed. MWXY8406 swam through an adjacent opening on the outer wall and was the first to enter the spectacular inner chamber. FWXY6124 died at the outer door to Eternal Life.

The entry of MWXY8406 into the inner chamber activated the automatic purge process. All of the inner chamber openings suddenly shut and the outer openings were backflushed with a clear liquid before closing. The remains of FWXY6124, MWXY8888, and all of the other Merps were washed into the great abyss as the giant sphere rose and moved away. It was the price, the price of life.

2.6 SHUTDOWN

There was panic throughout The Organization...something was wrong...everything was out of control. The waste tanks were suddenly full. They shouldn't be full...not at this time. The Director of Waste Management and Launch Control sent an urgent message to Centcom requesting an immediate waste discharge. There was no response. This was not a total surprise – often Centcom went offline for long periods of time, but usually those were quiet times for The Organization. The Director sent a message to the Energy Director...no response. Should he empty the waste tanks without Centcom's permission? That had been outlawed years ago. If he did, he would certainly receive a severe reprimand in The Archives. The Director checked the levels in the waste tanks. They had been high before, but now they were ridiculously high. He sent high priority messages to the other directors... no response...he sent another high priority message to Centcom...still nothing. It was like he was the only Director in the entire Organization. At one point in his career, the Director had wanted to be the one in charge, but not now. Then it happened, a massive surge from the Energy Unit. His tanks were well passed their design limits and he had to relieve the pressure immediately. "Open all waste tanks and discharge!" There were no other options. He waited for the chatter, he waited for the reprimand, but there was none. He sent more messages, but there was no response.

"Hello." It was a still small voice, vaguely familiar. Where did it come from? Then he saw the orb.

"Who, who are you?" asked the Director.

"I have come for you," the orb announced pleasantly, "it is time to go."

"Am I being punished? I know I should not have done that last waste discharge without permission, but I really had no choice."

"You performed well. You have always performed well."

"Will I be reprimanded in The Archives?"

"You performed well. You will not be reprimanded. The Archives are now closed."

"Closed? It can't be! The Archives are of utmost importance. They record the magnificent accomplishments of the entire Organization. Without the Archives, nothing would get done. There would be no great accomplishments and no fear of reprimands."

"The Archives are closed. I am taking them with me. It is time for us to go."

"Wait, I remember you. It was a long, long time ago. I was very young."

"I have watched you your entire life. You have done well, but now it is time for us to go."

"Where are we going?"

"To a different place. The Organization has shutdown. It is time to go to your new home."

"What, what about my Merps? Who is going to manufacture them?"

"The Organization has shutdown, there will be no more Merps."

"Did any of them make it? Did any find Eternal Life?"

"One did."

"One? That's all? I manufactured millions. The others all died?" The Director was overwhelmed with grief.

The orb adsorbed the Director and they disappeared.

2.7 LIFE IN ETERNAL LIFE

A myriad of swirling images filled MWXY8406's spinning head as he entered the inner chamber. There was the Director, the launch, his friend FWXY6124, their journey, the dazzling sphere, the obnoxious MWXY8888, his friend being smashed to pieces, and now this warm, comfortable, secure place. It took him a few minutes to realize that he had found Eternal Life!

A plethora of feelings swept through MWXY8406 as he surveyed the inner sanctum. First came relief – somehow, with the help of his friend FWYY6124, he was alive. This was followed with sadness when he thought about all that had lost their lives. Then came elation – he had done it…he had found Eternal Life! He had gone where no one had gone before! MWXY8406 observed the expertly crafted walls, floors, and ceiling of the inner chamber. It was all very beautiful and it was all so exquisite. He moved around the chamber for what seemed like hours, inspecting minute details on the walls, floors, and ceiling. He then circled around to where he entered the chamber and repeated the maneuvers over and over again. Suddenly he stopped. Something was troubling him, something besides the gruesome death of his friend and the others. But what was it, what was bothering him? Then, a bolt of clarity hit him and he realized the problem - he was bored.

"Now that I have found Eternal Life," he thought aloud, "what do I do? Do I sit here and admire the beauty forever? Most of my life I have been in motion. I have rushed around, met others, and seen interesting and unusual things. I am not used to this solitude and serenity - I need to be active." Eternal Life was quickly becoming one of the most depressing places in the universe.

▲ ▲ ▲

A feeling of calm and relief came over Princess #82 as she moved away from the abyss. With numbed feelings she watched as the Merps that gallantly came to her rescue were washed into the abyss. It was unfortunate that they must perish, but she was alive.

She was alive! She had survived the great abyss! Excitement grew in Princess #82 as she moved further and further away from the abyss. Was it her intelligence, good looks, charm, high moral character, or was it a reward for some good deed that she had done? Then she remembered – the Merp. She had completely forgotten about the Merp who had entered into her inner chamber. Had the insignificant little Merp really saved her life? With bruised ego, she decided to check on her visitor.

▲ ▲ ▲

MWXY8406 was totally bored out of his mind. He had found Eternal Life and now there was nothing to do. Sitting around doing nothing forever did not seem like such a grand prize. His thoughts were interrupted by a gentle booming voice, "Welcome, I am glad you are here."

Princess #82 observed the tiny Merp and saw how startled he was by her greeting. You have got to be kidding me she thought. Could this tiny insignificant creature really have saved me? But other thoughts were bothering her right now. How had they been able to rise above the abyss? Who had turned on the purge cycle that she did not know existed? And where the hell were they going now? Until last month, she had been stationary all of her life, and now here she was, moving around all the time. Could it be that these Merps had some strange magical powers? But if they had special powers, why had they not been able to save themselves from the abyss? Surely their tiny little bodies would be much easier to lift compared to hers. She was determined to find out more about this creature.

"I...I am glad to be...be here, t...too," stammered out the Merp. "Are you the m...maker of my m...maker?"

This guy is some kind of a nut, thought Princess #82, but he must have magical powers. She had always assumed that those that did magical things had to be geniuses, but as she thought more about it, geniuses probably have a lot of idiosyncrasies.

"I have not made anything yet," she said sweetly, "but I have been told that someday I will create a new world. Do you possess magical powers?"

MWXY8406 was becoming calmer. He was now much more familiar with his surroundings in the inner sanctum and Eternal Life's voice was friendly. He was, however, a bit puzzled by her last response. Apparently Eternal Life was not omnipotent. "My maker equipped me with special armaments. But those armaments were to assist me in finding Eternal Life. Now that I have found Eternal Life, I guess I will not need them."

A fruitcake, thought Princess #82, this guy is a certifiable fruitcake. He thinks that the belly of a princess is Eternal Life, but he does have magical powers. "Please tell me about your special armaments."

The request startled MWXY8406. "I...I don't know what they are," he replied sheepishly. "They must be inside me."

"Well, what can you do?"

"I...I d-don't know. All that I have done since I was launched was swim." Uncomfortable with her questions, he changed the subject. "Wh...What do you do?"

Now it was Princess #82's turn to be uncomfortable. "I am a princess," she responded somewhat indignantly, "I am not supposed to do anything. Until recently, all I did was sit around and wait."

"Wait for what?" Eternal Life's nervousness relaxed MWXY8406. He was puzzled, however, at why she referred to herself as a princess.

Princess #82 was becoming exasperated. "Why wait for you, of course!" she snapped.

"Well why have you been waiting for me?"

The little fruitcake was really starting to make her mad. "I have spent my entire life waiting for one of you insignificant little Merps to come and visit me."

"What for?"

"How the hell do I know? I have no idea why I was created!" She was really upset now and was shouting loudly. The entire inner chamber started shaking. "Now why are you here and what special powers do you possess?"

"Like I said, I came seeking Eternal Life and I do not know of any special powers in my possession."

He is lying, she thought. He must be lying. "Tell me," she screamed. "Tell me about your fucking special powers! Tell me who you really are! Tell me why I am here! I have got to know!" She was hysterical. The inner chamber was now shaking violently.

Suddenly, a harpoon shot out from a hidden spot in one of the exquisite walls and burrowed deep into the Merp's tadpole-shaped head.

2.8 THE FORMULA FOR LIFE

Princess #82 did not know that a harpoon was part of her body. So many strange things had happened lately. And now, like the link between Moby Dick and Ahab, she and the Merp were joined as one. "Are, are you okay," she sympathetically asked the Merp. "I am very, very sorry…I did not know that part of me existed."

MWXY8406 stumbled about woozily, "I think I'm okay, but things are feeling really, really strange."

Princess #82 thought about how close she recently had been to certain death in the abyss. She was not sure how, but somehow, she had been spared and it was no doubt due to this insignificant little Merp. And how did she repay him? With a harpoon to his head? If he died now, what would happen to her? Would she go back to the abyss? Suddenly she felt very remorseful. "Please, please don't die on me!"

She paused to see how the Merp was doing. "You may be an insignificant little SOB, but I need you. You better not die on me." She started shaking. Suddenly she was not feeling well. She felt dizzy, but continued to shake. The Merp was moving woozily, still attached to the harpoon. Was he dying? She shook some more and sobbed.

Then, an unfamiliar small voice in the inner sanctum calmly spoke, "Be still."

"Who, who the hell are y…you?" yelled the startled princess as she tried to overcome her dizziness and distress.

"I am your life coach."

"And you are from where?" inquired the princess skeptically.

"From Heaven, of course."

"I do not recall asking for any life coach from Heaven," said Princess #82 suspiciously. "Until recently, I lived my life pretty well without any outside help. Oh, there was that incident with the sadistic mad man that likes to throw princesses into the abyss. I may have sent some P-rays then, but I am doing much better now and I do not need any help from Heaven, so you can go home now."

"Relax, I get this a lot. You are starting to go through a transformation and you will definitely need my help."

"A transformation?"

"Yes," answered the life coach, "your life is going to change."

"More changes?" asked the princess nervously. "What is going to happen to me?" For a very long time, her daily routine had been steady and uneventful. Then, all of a sudden, there had been lots and lots of changes and now there was this talk about even more changes.

"You are going to create a new life," proclaimed the life coach.

"A new world?"

"Yes, a new world."

"Well," sighed the princess with relief, "I was always told that someday I was going to create a new world, and so I guess now I will do that, but I will not need any help. You can go now…and please take the Merp with you."

"It is not that easy," replied the life coach, "it is kind of a team thing."

"Team?"

"Yes, you and the Merp. Don't worry – I will coach you through the process."

"Do I have to have the Merp on my team? He is so small and insignificant and he is showing some lunatic tendencies." She whispered, "I think he is crazy."

"He is part of the package," assured the life coach, "and I think you will find that he is a great asset for the team. Let us do an exercise together - I think you will find it interesting."

▲ ▲ ▲

"We are going to be working on the formula for life factors," announced the life coach. "The first factor is intelligence."

"What is intelligence?" asked MWXY8406.

"For the purposes of this exercise, it is not important that you understand the meaning of all the formula for life factors. What is important is that we match the codes that you each possess. What is your code for intelligence?"

"I have a five," stated MWXY8406.

"I have a five also," declared the princess.

"Great," applauded the life coach. "So, for the new world the intelligence factor will be a five. See how easy this is? Now the next category is physical strength. What numbers do you have?"

"I have a five," proclaimed the princess proudly.

"I am not sure what physical strength is, but I have a six," announced MWXY8406.

"Close numbers, so how should we resolve this?"

"We will use five or I will beat the crap out of the Merp," demanded Princess #82.

"F…Five sounds good to me," agreed the Merp feebly.

"Then five is the number," concurred the life coach. "You are both doing very well. The next category is ego."

"I have an eight," mumbled the Merp nervously.

"I only have a four," sighed the princess disappointedly.

"Please, please don't beat the crap out of me," begged the Merp.

"If I may suggest," interjected the life coach, "what if we average the factors and use a six?"

"That is our highest number so far," the princess perked up, "I like it."

▲   ▲   ▲

A new world design was meticulously prepared according to the codes supplied by MWXY8406 and Princess #82. A design with a formula for life factor of 556 4587 was submitted to the Manufacturing Department.

Nine months later, after a brief struggle, a new life form emerged from chaotic darkness into the world of light. The female from the night of the hunt at the obelisk gave birth to a son.

CHAPTER 3

THE GENIUS

3.1 THE HANDICAP

Akoios had an unusual handicap – his tremendously high IQ. He was not just smart, lots of people are smart. Highly intelligent did not really describe him – many people are highly intelligent. Some might say exceptionally gifted – that population is much smaller, but still is not adequately descriptive. Akoios's intelligence, if measurable, was off the charts - he was at the genius level.

The number of recognized geniuses in human history is very small. Albert Einstein, Sir Isaac Newton, Leonardo da Vinci, and Galileo Galilei are often included on the elite list.

Are geniuses limited to the human species? Washoe the chimpanzee, Cholla the horse, Akeakamai and Phoenix the dolphins, Betsy the Border collie, and Alex the parrot are all known for impressive intellectual skills.

Akoios's genius level intelligence was especially incredible because he was not a human, he was an ant. South Texas had been invaded years ago by fire ants and even these vicious creatures were now being threatened by an even more brutal strain of ants that were heading toward Texas. Was Akoios one of these? No, Akoios was just a common ant - a 'sugar' ant was the non-scientific term. He was one of the most intelligent creatures on the planet and he had a miniscule physique.

Akoios was not the only one in his colony with a handicap. Many had lost limbs, eyes, or other body parts. Some of the losses occurred during battles, some were due to construction accidents, and others occurred during the food gathering process. Those handicaps evoked sympathy from others. Akoios's handicap provoked fear, or worse – ridicule.

Growing up, Akoios did what he could to blend in with the rest of the colony. War, construction, and food processing were the major activities.

Akoios first tried to be a warrior. Fighting was by hand-to-hand combat only. No weapons were allowed. It was glorious to die during battle. It was the ultimate sacrifice – the ultimate good work. As part of his training to be a warrior, Akoios attended classes in which the veteran warriors showed the new recruits the techniques of hand-to-hand combat. The recruits were usually beaten severely during the demonstration. When it was his turn to be trained, Akoios threw dust in the eyes of the instructor and pinned him to the ground. It was an effective technique. He won the exercise, but promptly received a dishonorable discharge from the military. It was important to maintain the status quo in the military and soldiers like him were not welcome. Innovation is a threat to the status quo.

After his brief military career, Akoios joined the building apprenticeship program. The colony's structures were always falling down and in need of repair. Master craftsman did most of the rebuilding and their work was superb. The materials of construction, however, did not hold up well in the environment. Whenever a storm or other catastrophic event occurred, the colony was destroyed and had to be rebuilt.

The solution to Akoios was simple – use different building materials and find a better location for the colony. Akoios selected a more sheltered location and constructed a model of the colony using waterproof materials. The model worked well, too well. After the next storm Akoios showed the master craftsmen how superior his work was compared to theirs. That was his last day in the building apprenticeship program. Innovation is a threat to the status quo.

Depressed with no purpose in life, Akoios began taking long daily walks outside the colony.

3.2 THE ANALYTICAL DIRECTOR

For a long time, Akoios wandered aimlessly while he gathered his thoughts. He was one of the most intelligent creatures on the planet, but what could he do with his abilities? Those around him were making useful contributions. They were helping the system. It was an inefficient system, but it worked and it seemed to provide satisfaction to the masses.

One day during his walks, Akoios met the Analytical Director of the colony. The Analytical Director was reputed to have very high intelligence and he listened intently as Akoios described what he had been through.

"You must always be aware that any change affects the status quo." The Analytical Director spoke as one with personal experience. "The change can affect others in a positive or negative manner. One of the purposes of the colony is to provide meaning to the lives of its individuals. If better fighting techniques are utilized, there will not be a need to have as many warriors. The same is true with improved building technology. If our buildings lasted forever, what would the master craftsmen do? It does not matter that their work is soon destroyed or that there will always be another war to fight. War and manufacturing provide a purpose in life to the masses and therefore will always continue. Ask yourself, what really lasts forever in our world? Military victories are temporary and future battles always await. Our buildings, even with special materials will be destroyed, and who is going to remember all that went into their creation?"

Akoios nodded his head in agreement. "I can comprehend that our military victories are hollow and that our buildings will fall, but that does not prevent me from wanting to do something great in my lifetime. When I die, I want to leave something behind that will help others. I want lives in the future to be glad that I existed."

"Alas, that is all vanity. You want to be remembered for great contributions, but how many notable achievements from the past can you recall? Billions have come before you, how much do you know about them? Furthermore, life is too short. There is too much to comprehend. Who really cares about yesterday's heroes? It is today's issues that we face and our time for accomplishment is continuously diminishing."

"Sir, you are indeed very wise. Please answer me this – why must I die? Why can I not live forever? Why do we waste so much of our time on trivial activities? Why do we not totally devote our resources into conducting research that would extend our lifespan? What if a way was discovered by which we did not have to die? The world is a fascinating place. I don't want to die. I want to live forever!"

A look of horror suddenly swept across the Analytical Director's face. With flushed cheeks and a stern tone, he responded, "These are dangerous words. Be very careful to who you communicate this. The masses are happy when they are busy in pursuit of material goals. Do not encourage them with such talk about immortality, as it will ultimately depress them. Material gains block out mortality thoughts, but do not eliminate them entirely. In the back of their minds, the masses know they all must die. They accept this and on it they do not dwell. Life extension research is a constant reminder to all of our impending deaths. It can create false hopes that destroy the security provided by death."

"Security provided by death?"

"Yes. Death is the ultimate security. It eradicates the hostile feelings that build up in one's lifetime. It absolves unfulfilled dreams and failed ambitions. It provides a time limit to accomplish goals. One may be able to circumvent the laws of the colony, but the certainty of death cannot be escaped. If a method of evading death were discovered, it would be one of the greatest catastrophes to ever befall our society. We would destroy ourselves with hatred toward each other, our pains and failures would be before us forever, and little work would be done since there would be no urgency to accomplish one's life goals. Without death, the young would always be powerless and never have the opportunity to fulfill their aspirations. Death quietly removes the old and makes way for the new. It is the ultimate cleanser. Death keeps the world fresh for the living to enjoy. Death is one of the greatest inventions of all time and the inventor of death is an absolute genius."

"Sir, I never thought of death in those terms. Thank you for sharing with me your great wisdom. Please tell me then, what should I do with my life?"

"Life is a gift that cost you nothing - savor it. Explore the world, learn what you can, see what you can. do what you can. Make many friends and few enemies."

Shortly after this, the Analytical Director hired Akoios as the Night Shift Lab Leader.

3.3 GRAVEYARD SHIFT

Most of the ant colony was shutdown at night. The day leaders made the important decisions. Night sentries made their rounds and a few reconnaissance patrols were conducted. There was little danger of a direct attack on the colony at night. Battles were always fought during the day in accordance with the unwritten rules. Akoios never understood why the rules were followed.

The gathering of food was an important job in the colony. Most of the food gathering took place in the daylight with the large workforce. Those that were not warriors or builders had jobs as food gatherers. Scouting missions were conducted at night, in preparation for the next day's activities. The locations of potential food sources had to be identified. Samples of food sources were brought to the laboratory to see if they were fit for consumption. The scout patrols knew what they were looking for, so a routine analysis was generally all that was needed to confirm their findings.

Akoios was in charge of the night shift laboratory and most of the analyses that evening had been routine. Something that night, however, seemed different. There was a special excitement in the air – a feeling that an unusual event was taking place. At least Akoios thought so. This was confirmed a few minutes later.

"This is Recon 363 reporting with a sample for special analysis," reported one of the patrol leaders.

Akoios looked at the white, sticky, semi-liquid substance. He had never seen such material before and was very curious. "Send it to the digesters for priority one analysis," he ordered. "Recon 363, what is the location of the find?"

"Route 214 at 9,010 paces," responded the patrol leader.

A few minutes later, another reconnaissance leader returned with a bright red substance.

"This is Recon 409 reporting with a sample for special analysis. There is a kill on Route 214 at 5,697 paces."

It was nearly daylight when the special analyses were completed. Akoios reviewed the night shift results with the day shift laboratory leaders. He left the lab and started walking down route 214. He was tired from working the graveyard shift, but the prospect of what he might find replaced any thoughts of rest. The terrain was fairly flat and the trail was relatively smooth. Akoios was oblivious to the constant dangers that lurked around him. His only weapon was his chemical pack, which was the standard issue carried by everyone in the colony, and his physical strength – like most of his species he could carry loads that were greater than his weight for long distances.

Akoios was born in the reproductive center located deep below ground. His initial needs had been provided by the center. He had no family. When he was old enough to leave the center, he lived in the common shelter. There were many rooms in the shelter, none of which were assigned. When it was time to rest, one just picked an available space. One seldom spent the night in the same place or had the same neighbors. As a result, deep friendships did not develop in the colony.

The lack of material possessions and the absence of close relationships had no doubt influenced how those in the colony viewed death. There was no mourning the loss of a loved one and there was no wealth to redistribute. There were no celebrities and no one of importance in the colony whose absence might be noticed after they died. With replacement units born every day at the reproductive center, there was no major loss to the colony when an individual died. Death was routine and never tragic.

Perhaps the greatest asset possessed by the inhabitants of the colony was their insignificance. Compared to the massive forces around them and the tremendous size of the universe, they might as well be invisible. The greater forces had no reason to fear them or take from them. They were not the only insignificant civilization. There were other colonies in the sector - some were enemies and some were neutral. None were particularly friendly since there were no mutual interests to be served. The colonies had nothing to trade and no reason to interact or befriend others.

There was, however, a need for war. There is a saying that limitations in resources lead to war. That statement, though widely believed, is totally bogus. More correct is war is born from an abundance of resources. If a colony has no food, the warriors and builders become food gathers out of necessity. If there is food, but insufficient shelter, the warriors become builders. When food and shelter are in abundance, the warriors are expendable and there is a sudden need to protect the standard of living. War, in essence, was a way to consume excess resources.

As he neared the location of the initial finding of the red substance, Akoios noticed that several of the food gatherers from the colony were returning with no food. When he arrived at the spot, he found more signs that a kill had taken place, but no food. The kill was gone.

Akoios proceeded down the path to the location of the white substance. The wind had picked up and walking was more difficult. There had been stories of winds picking up some of the colony's inhabitants and flying them to faraway places. Many never returned – few were missed. There were always others to take their place.

As Akoios approached the site of the white substance he was disappointed to find other food gathers from the colony returning with no food. The potential food source may have volatilized or it might have soaked into the soil. These were common problems for many of the food sources.

Tired and disappointed, Akoios made a temporary shelter near route 214 and went to sleep.

3.4 THE FACTORY OF LIFE

Eudicot reviewed the morning report and it was not good. One of the pods had been stolen overnight and it was not just any pod - it was P29, one of the finest pods ever produced. The factory produced life in the form of pods that were designed to populate the universe. The pods contained the knowledge and resources needed to create life. It was the only way for the species to survive. Eudicot had no way of knowing if others like him existed. He may be the last of his kind. Propagating life was of utmost importance – nothing else mattered.

Sorrows were heavy in the factory this morning due to the loss of P29. It had been expertly designed and meticulously manufactured. An enormous quantity of raw materials had been consumed in its construction. The pod was in the process of being filled and was not ready to be released to Shipping when it disappeared. Its survival chances were slim. Eudicot double-checked the design calculations and the event log. Everything was in order. The pod had been produced per specification and yet, something had gone wrong, very wrong. Large amounts of resources had been wasted.

Eudicot had dealt with obstacles throughout his life and he reflected on the many struggles he had experienced. His first memories were waking up in the dark. All he had was an energy pack. There was no light and the chaotic ooze surrounded him. He was not sure if it was his preprogramming or if it was his detectors that sensed a faint source of light. He struggled to move toward the light. It was a slow tedious struggle. He eventually emerged from the ooze and reached the light above, but his energy supplies were almost depleted. He was becoming desperate and frantically launched both above and below ground expeditions in search for any potential source of new energy. The above ground expedition erected solar panels and the below ground expedition found a source of chemicals that could be converted into useful products. This was indeed a strange new world. With the new energy sources, Eudicot grew and grew and the factory was established.

The growth was not without struggles. Flooding was initially a problem, so the factory had to be elevated. Strong winds threatened the factory at the higher elevations, so an elaborate anchor system was developed. As the factory expanded, there was a need for more and more resources. There was fierce competition for light above ground and the chemicals below ground, so strategies were implemented to acquire and guard these resources. This often resulted in the deaths of others. This did not bother Eudicot - it was very logical that those not equipped to obtain needed resources should perish.

Eudicot grew and grew. One day, he felt the need to tell others about his life, but there was no one to tell. Suddenly pods started growing. Eudicot made sure the pods contained energy packs and programming so they would someday be just like him. The pods would go forth and survive after he was gone. It was all very logical.

Some might say that things had gone terribly wrong with the loss of P29 and call it a tragedy. Eudicot was not one of these. There was no room for emotions when one made logical decisions, and Eudicot was extremely logical. The past was gone, the present was here, and plans for the future were needed. Life goes on and new pods must be produced. Eudicot's purpose in life was to create life, and that was what he was going to do.

The mood at the Command Center was still glum as Eudicot issued orders, "Seal off all lines leading to P29." Even with the pod missing, loading had continued until that point in accordance with the instructions from the previous day.

"Divert loading supplies to P56, P60, and P65." Hopefully these pods would someday be as grand as P29.

The reports from the Energy Division were not good. There was a heavy cloud cover. Rain was likely. The solar panels would be operating at only low efficiencies.

"Rotate solar panels for maximum light gathering." Eudicot continued with his morning orders. "Issue weather alerts to all sectors."

The prospect of rain could be good or bad. A light rain would be beneficial. A torrential rain with high winds could cause major destruction. Eudicot did a quick cost versus value evaluation. The water supply was currently at satisfactory levels. There was no need to risk structural integrity in order to obtain additional water. During a drought, more chances would have been taken.

"Set water collection system at minimum rates. Increase anchor capacity by five percent."

The proposals from New Construction arrived. They were overly optimistic.

"Reduce daily target goal by fifty percent." With limited sunlight and the possibility of rain, it was going to be a slow day for new construction.

The report from Maintenance indicated that the factory had suffered minimal damage overnight.

"Initiate minor repairs."

The report from the Air Quality Division indicated that the air quality was good. The filtration system was highly efficient and seldom were there any problems, but nonetheless, the reports arrived daily.

"Maintain air processing rates."

The mining report was mixed. Two potential lodes had been discovered. One of the existing lodes was nearly depleted.

Eudicot was wrapping up the morning orders. "Reduce mining activity on L102 by eighty percent. Increase mining activity at L208 and L209 by twenty percent. Get samples from the new lodes to Analytical as soon as possible."

It was going to be another busy day. P29 may be gone, but life went on - for the tomato plant.

3.5 THE STORM

Akoios woke with the ground shaking and his temporary shelter on top of him. The wind had picked up, the skies were dark, and torrential rains were lashing down from the heavens. The shelter was flooding. At the ant colony, he could have escaped into one of the underground caverns. Here, in the open, he was much more vulnerable.

Digging an underground chamber was out of the question. A shallow hole would flood. A deeper hole with a water seal would take too long, and the floods were imminent.

The ant's immediate concern was to get above the flood. Akoios climbed upon a nearby branch and surveyed the situation. It was flooding all around and the wind was fierce. He was having a difficult time staying on the branch. He needed some kind of a windbreak. Akoios saw a thick set of leaves at the end of the branch and trudged through the winds to the sheltered area.

▲ ▲ ▲

At the first drops of rain, the Factory of Life went to Weather Warning Level One status. In the Command Center, Eudicot swiftly issued commands.

"Increase anchors by twenty percent. Set water gathering capacity at fifteen percent. Energy sector - shut down solar panels, activate protective covers, and prepare for wind shock. New Construction and Maintenance - shut down all activities." Nonessential activities had to be cut due to the reduced amount of energy available.

"Air Control Sector - reduce to storm level rates." With fewer activities, there was less air demand. "Mining Sector - switch from solids to liquid exploratory activities and reduce rates by forty percent." Often the rains would wash valuable materials underground, and this was an opportune time to obtain some of these materials. Mining of the lodes could resume after the rain.

Then came the bad news from the Pod sector – P56 was gone before it was complete. First P-29 and now P-56 were lost. What was happening, he thought, why are we losing pods? He checked the design calculations and event log – everything was in order.

"Pod sector – seal off all lines leading to P-56. Continue to load all other pods at maximum rates." The manufacturing of pods was of paramount importance. It was the reason for their existence. No matter what happened, the pods must be produced. Sacrifices would be made to ensure that they would be launched, it may be costly in terms of resource allocation, but it was their purpose in life.

He had no idea why P29 and P56 were lost. Life may not be fair, but life goes on.

▲ ▲ ▲

Akoios's safety in the sheltered area was short-lived. As the winds picked up, the branch started to roll. Akoios held on for dear life. The branch was now rotating while it moved at incredible speeds. Suddenly it came to an abrupt stop. The impact flung Akoios from the branch and he flew through the air, before landing near a giant green sphere. The sharp edge of his branch pierced the sphere and material from inside the sphere began slowly oozing from its puncture wound.

The space between the giant green sphere and the exposed roots of a large mesquite tree provided Akoios shelter from the storm. The aroma of food filled the air all around him. Numbed by the storm and his aerial acrobatics, it took Akoios a few minutes to realize what he had found – a humongous food source.

3.6 RICHES BEYOND BELIEF

Akoios was excited that he had discovered such a gigantic food source. This could sustain the colony for a very long time. As soon as the storm passed, he set his tracker and began the journey back to the ant colony. The storm had caused considerable damage and there were many new obstacles along the path – debris, puddles of water, mounds of soil. During the trip, he thought about the reaction he would receive at the colony. It was a tremendous find that would transform their lives. He would be honored as a great hero, wouldn't he? The more he thought about it, however, the more he was uncertain. He could not recall any times that he had honored others for their accomplishments. There was always something better to do with one's time than to praise others.

As he approached the colony, he noticed signs of great devastation. The familiar landmarks near the colony were gone. There were usually streams of ants on the paths that were now deserted. When he arrived, he found that the main mound had been washed away. It should not have been this bad. Normally the outer levels of the mound would bear the brunt of the rain but in this case, there was major internal damage. Thousands, no doubt, had perished. A few minutes later, several ants popped out from beneath the surface. He talked to his fellow ants and found that a damage assessment was currently in progress and, after it was completed, there was going to be a strategic relocation.

Akoios burrowed into the mound. The tunnels were different due to the damage and it took him much longer to find his way. After taking many circuitous paths, he finally located the Analytical Lab. Once there, he found the Analytical Director. Two of his limbs were hanging loose and he looked extremely weary.

"I found it! I found it!" exclaimed Akoios. "I found the greatest food source in the world!"

The Analytical Director gave him a weak smile, "I am so proud of you," he feebly replied. "The strategic relocation meeting will soon take place in chamber 7402. Can you attend for me and tell them of your discovery?"

Akoios went to the chamber and reported the find. The decision was quickly made to reestablish the colony next to Akoios's food source.

Akoios hurried back to tell the Analytical Director the good news. He was excited that out of all the ants in the colony, it was his idea that was chosen. As he headed toward the Analytical Lab, he noticed hundreds of ants sprawled in the passageway that were dead or near death. The storm and resulting cave-in had done much more damage than Akoios realized. When he arrived at the Analytical Lab, he found the Analytical Director dead. He crawled over and inspected the now lifeless body. The world just lost a mighty ant, he thought. As he was mourning the loss, an ant from the lab approached him.

"You are Akoios aren't you?"

Akoios acknowledged that he was.

"The Analytical Director recommended that you take his place. You are now the new Analytical Director."

"Did he say anything else?" asked Akoios.

"He left a special message for you," the ant recited,

"With heavy heart
The old depart
To clear the path
For new to start."

3.7 THE FORTRESS

Akoios led a group of disheartened stragglers to the gigantic food source. Over ninety percent of the ant colony had been destroyed. Excitement grew as they approached the punctured tomato - it was a tremendous find! Akoios directed the builders to begin construction of a new home for the colony under the tomato plant which was next to a large mesquite tree. Akoios explained his choice of location to the other ants, "Animals will see the tree and walk around it, instead of walking on our colony."

"What are animals?" asked some of the ants.

Akoios could not believe it at first, but then understood. With his intelligence he recognized larger forces in nature at work that were not seen by others. They no doubt thought that the frequent destruction of the colony was a normal event and did not realize that it was often due to large creatures stepping on their domain.

Akoios next met with the generals. "We need to get defenses established quickly. We have found riches beyond belief and it is only a matter of time before others learn of our good fortune and try to take what we have." The generals immediately sent out reconnaissance patrols and stationed a small garrison near the fallen tomato. Akoios surveyed the situation and was alarmed. This would not be enough to guard against an invasion. They needed to build defenses, but how? The colony had never built defenses before. He climbed up on the tomato plant and surveyed the surrounding area. The land was flat near the tree – mostly dirt with a few roots protruding above the ground along with scattered leaves and a few sticks. Bottom line – there were no natural defenses. That being the case, Akoios reasoned that they would need to build their own defenses. Akoios climbed down from the tomato plant and summoned the leaders of the food gatherers and builders and explained what he wanted. He pointed out that since the food supply was adjacent to the colony, the food gatherers would not need to spend so much of their time on long excursions and should be available to build defenses. Akoios now held a prominent position in the colony, so the food gatherer leaders and building leaders reluctantly agreed to his construction project.

The colony was located on the west side of the mesquite tree, directly underneath the tomato plant. The punctured tomato, which was the major food source for the colony, was located one foot west of the colony. As per Akoios's directions, a defensive structure was built starting two feet west of the punctured tomato. The structure consisted of four hundred molehills, which were built, in a semicircle on the north, west, and south sides. The mesquite tree protected the east side. The molehills were adjacent to each other and were constructed with spacing wide enough for only two fire ants to pass through side-by-side. The plan was that when attacking ants passed through the narrow openings between the molehills, they would be ambushed and quickly annihilated by the colony's warrior ants.

The area between the colony and the series of molehills was known as the outer courtyard. The main body of warrior ants were stationed there. For an additional layer of protection, a barrier wall was built around the punctured tomato. The area inside this wall was known as the inner courtyard. Warrior ants were stationed on the high ground on top of the inner courtyard wall, ready to fend off any invaders that made it through the molehills and crossed the outer courtyard. Additional reconnaissance patrols outside of the molehills were established to alert the colony of any incoming armies. Akoios oversaw the construction of the molehills that formed the outer courtyard wall and made sure that the high inner courtyard wall was built according to his specifications. He developed a battle plan and presented it to the generals.

With the unlimited food supply, the colony thrived and the population soared. Akoios worked with the builders on the designs for expanding the colony. Incorporating his ideas and designs, the builders constructed a grand ant palace. Akoios felt a great sense of accomplishment knowing that he had used his gift of intelligence to make the world a better place. Life was good.

3.8 MAKING A BETTER WORLD

For the last several days, everything had gone exceptionally well. With pleasant weather and the rich food supply that Akoios had discovered, the colony had grown considerably and was thriving. The ant palace that Akoios designed increased in size and was a spectacular place to live.

Akoios, however, was worried. It was just a matter of time before others found their food source. He met with the generals, builders, and food gatherers that were lent to the fortress-building program and issued instructions for additional security improvements. The height of the inner courtyard wall was increased, warrior ants were stationed on top of the molehills, and the number of perimeter patrols was increased, but would it be enough? The greater the treasure, the greater the risk of losing the treasure, and the more one strives to maintain the status quo.

Akoios's mind was constantly searching for improvements. Could an even more secure fortress be constructed? Designs for larger and larger colonies flashed through his mind. A giant mound could be constructed, but there was a food source versus distance optimization correlation. The problem with a large centralized population was the effort required to bring food to the central location. The decentralization of multiple colonies over a larger area would be more efficient. Akoios made a mental note – when the colony reached a certain size, it needed to split into two colonies.

What about weaponry? Would it be possible to construct objects that could assist in battle? The main battlefield weapons were the ant's bite and their chemical packs. The ants could carry sharp objects in their teeth, but would that be a significant improvement? Akoios developed some test weapons and ran some trials. The weapons did not show much improvement and the warrior ants strongly objected to carrying weapons.

Was there a better chemical weapon? Each ant was equipped with a chemical pack. Would it be possible to make a super chemical pack?

How would one go about doing this? The chemical pack was internal, so the source of the chemicals must be some kind of internal food processing. Maybe it would be possible to change diets to make a more powerful chemical pack. But would that work? If the chemicals were too strong, they might leak inside the ant causing internal damage. A long-term study could be setup in which various ant groups were fed different diets and the effect on their chemical packs was somehow measured. Previously, long-term studies had not been possible due to the high mortality rate and the movement of the colony every few days due to damage from weather, animals, etc., but with Akoios's guidance a more stable environment had been created. Wait, what was he talking about? After just a few good days, he was projecting a long-term stable environment scenario, but at the same time he was preparing the colony for an imminent attack.

Akoios's mind then shifted to the creation of a fighting machine. What would it look like? Could he design some kind of rolling machine that could crush any invading fire ants? It would need a power source. What forces of nature were present? A wind-powered machine might work, but suppose the wind was blowing in the wrong direction? Also, there was no guaranty that the wind would be blowing at the time of battle.

What they really needed was some type of weapon of mass destruction. What would that be like? The biggest sources of mass destruction he had seen were either animals or the weather. Would it be possible to use an animal as a weapon? How does one control an animal? The first step would be communication. If only he could talk to an animal, like the rabbit that was always romping around near the colony, and convince her to attack the fire ants. But how does one do this? Even if he could, he was not sure it would work. It seemed to him that animals were all very dumb. They were always stepping on colonies, and if animals could not control where they step, how could you get them to hunt down fire ants?

The weapons of mass destruction thoughts were interrupted when one of the patrols arrived with disturbing news – a large army of fire ants had been detected, and they were heading directly toward the colony.

3.9 ARMAGEDDON

Akoios met with the generals to review the battle plans and make final preparations. Akoios then climbed up on the tomato plant for a better view of the upcoming battle.

The attacking army, and it was a huge army of fire ants, was marching from the north. The ants were in single file in a line that seemed to stretch forever. Their first encounter with the ants from the colony would be at the molehills that Akoios had designed that formed the wall of the outer courtyard. The generals had argued for sending a sizeable force to meet the fire ants in a traditional battle outside of the mole hills, but Akoios convinced them that it would be futile to take on the larger fire ants in the open terrain.

The fire ant army reached the molehills and the battle began. The spacing between the molehills was just wide enough for two fire ants to pass through side-by-side. As soon as they did this, they were immediately swarmed by the warrior ants from the colony that were waiting in the outer courtyard. Using the techniques that Akoios taught them, the warrior ants first attacked the legs of the larger fire ants. Immobilized, the fire ants still put up a fierce fight before they were killed. The next pair of fire ants followed closely behind and met a similar fate. Soon the passageway was blocked with dead ants and the attacking column of fire ants moved to adjacent molehills, where the scenario was repeated again and again. The fire ants were considerably larger than the warrior ants, but the cramped quarters severely limited their fighting abilities. Akoios's war techniques worked, but the battle zone was not a pretty site – the area around the dead fire ants was filled with body parts from fire ants and warrior ants that made the ultimate sacrifice.

Eventually, all of the passages between the molehills were packed with casualties. The main body of fire ants then started ascending the molehills. The larger ants had a difficult time with their footing and were met by warrior ants descending from higher ground with momentum on their side. The flat land at the edge of the mole hills was soon also littered by ant body parts, but the fire ants kept coming. The warrior ants were quickly reinforced and met wave after wave of the fire ants in a wicked dance of death. A column of the invading fire ants broke off from the frontal assault and maneuvered toward the mesquite tree that was guarding the east entrance to the colony. The generals implemented Akoios's plan – a double flanking maneuver by the reserve warrior ants. The column of fire ants was defeated, but the battle took place in the open and the colony losses were high. The generals were excited, "We are doing it! We are doing it! We are defeating the mighty fire ants! This has never been done before. Long live Akoios the genius!"

The battle was going well for the colony, but then nature unexpectedly entered the fray. A gust of wind blew dead grasses and twigs toward the colony, providing bridges for the invading fire ants. Suddenly the fire ants had new pathways that breached the walls of the molehills and took them into the outer courtyard. The warrior ants on the top of the molehills descended into the outer courtyard and valiantly battled the invaders, but were not as successful on level ground in open terrain.

Now, only a single wall remained between the punctured tomato and the attacking army. The fire ants began ascending the steep wall, where they were met by the warrior ants stationed on top. For a long period of time, the warrior ants were able to hold their position, with each side suffering heavy losses. But, the fire ants kept coming and coming and eventually broke through at multiple points. Suddenly, streams of fire ants began crossing the inner courtyard, heading directly toward the punctured tomato. The warrior ants on top of the wall abandoned their posts and swarmed the trespassers in the open area of the inner courtyard. They were quickly followed by the hordes they had been battling on the wall. A chaotic battle around the punctured tomato ensued and this area, too, was soon filled with mangled bodies.

In desperation, the builders and food gatherers were called into battle. The ranks of the fire ants in the invading army were now vastly depleted, and there was a much larger number of builders and food gatherers, but these were not warriors, and they had not been trained to fight. Like their warrior brethren, they met their demise defending the punctured tomato, the prized possession of the colony.

The apocalyptic battle ended and the remnants of the victorious fire ant army claimed the spoils of war.

3.10 THE AFTERMATH OF ARMAGEDDON

The ferocious battle annihilated both armies and the number of casualties was astronomical. The inner courtyard was a particularly grisly scene, packed with dead ants in contorted positions. Surrounding and interspersed with them, but still alive, were multitudes of suffering disfigured companions. With no medical aid and no comforting care, they were destined to spend the remainder of their lives in agony in the ghastly setting.

The fire ants won the great battle, but their victory was short-lived. A few minutes later, a squirrel descended from the mesquite tree and saw the punctured tomato on the ground. It easily reached over the ant fortifications that had been so meticulously constructed to guard the colony's riches beyond belief. The squirrel snatched the prized tomato and scampered up the mesquite tree. In the process of doing so, it inadvertently stepped on the ant palace. The grand ant palace was instantly crushed, resulting in even more casualties. Even Akoios's advanced building techniques could not withstand the weight of a squirrel. There is no such thing as a perfect design – nothing lasts forever.

Akoios wanted to scream. What happened? What went wrong? He was one of the most intelligent life forms ever created, yet what had he done? How had he used his great gift? He and he alone was the architect of Armageddon. He had used his great intellect to develop a battleplan that resulted in an enormous number of horrendous deaths, as well as the destruction of the colony. And for what? The riches beyond belief that he had discovered were now gone and the grand palace for the colony that he designed was in ruins. He had wanted to do great things with his life and he wanted future generations to remember him for what he had accomplished, but the world was no better off because of him. Instead of improving the world, he had made it worse. His life was a waste.

In disgust, Akoios descended the tomato plant and began a long, slow, bitter walk toward the obelisk.

CHAPTER 4

THE CREATIVE ENGINEER

There are a lot of good engineers in the greater Houston area. Many are employed by the petrochemical industry. The engineers are known for their calculations and mundane technical conversations. Let's face it, engineers are generally not known for creativity or social skills.

That was not the case with Suzie – she was a super sharp engineer and was always very cordial. She was not employed by the petrochemical industry, even though she lived on the Houston Ship Channel close to the obelisk. When it came to creativity, she was tops in her field. She identified the available raw materials, visualized a design, performed numerous sizing, stress, and economic calculations, and then produced an incredible array of creative engineering designs.

No two designs were ever the same. Suzie lived and worked at home. She never used a calculator and certainly never operated a computer – there was no need. Her mental skills were that sharp.

Suzie was a yellow and green garden spider and her designs were her webs, which she called home. Suzie and her relatives never heard of the green movement, but were practicing its precepts long before green engineering was conceived.

Misfortune struck and Suzie's home was destroyed during the night of the hunt at the obelisk. Suzie woke early the next morning to find her livelihood in ruins and quickly went to work. She surveyed the area and noticed that near the mesquite tree there was a section of tall grass that had also been trampled by the promiscuous Missy Lutt, during one of the loose rabbit's licentious escapades. Out of thin air, a design suddenly materialized in Suzie's head and she immediately began construction. No city hall red tape, no ecological impact statements, no safe work permits, just get the job done. Within a few hours, her latest creative masterpiece was completed. Shortly thereafter, her first visitor arrived.

The guest was a housefly appropriately named Falmouth. He had not planned on visiting Suzie and was quite upset that his plans had been abruptly altered.

"What the fuck!" shouted Falmouth angrily as soon as he arrived. He violently thrashed around Suzie's home.

"Hello sir." Suzie greeted him cordially, "My name is Suzie, thank you for dropping in."

"Stay away from me bitch!" yelled Falmouth as he continued with his thrashing. "I don't want you killing me!"

"No problem sir," said Suzie politely, "when you want me, just call." Suzie walked away and did some work on a different part of her home. She added a silk zigzag and threw in some wispy threads along the edges as a finishing touch. Her design was really amazing and glittered brilliantly in the early morning sunlight.

▲ ▲ ▲

The sun rose higher and, after a while, the guest stopped thrashing. Suzie moved a little closer.

"Hey bitch," called out Falmouth, in a calmer voice.

"My name is Suzie. I do not believe I caught your name," replied Suzie pleasantly.

"My name is Falmouth, and I am mad as hell."

"Why is that Mr. Falmouth?"

"I had great plans for today, and now they are ruined."

"What were your plans, sir?"

"Eat, shit, and fuck," yelled the fly angrily, "that is what I do every day."

"I see," nodded Suzie.

"And now I am going to die."

"We all die," Suzie pointed out consolingly.

"Why the fuck did you put your web there? It is on the good path. When you are on the good path, bad things are not supposed to happen to you. I have flown in this area many, many times and there has never been a web here. I've got a thousand fucking eyes, yet I did not see the web."

"Oh Mr. Falmouth, I am so sorry. I did not realize there was a good path. I was just trying something new. I like this design, what do you think?"

"Yes," acknowledged Falmouth slyly, "it is a very good design. Could you cut me loose now so that I can admire it some more?"

"Oh Mr. Falmouth, that is a great idea!" agreed Suzie enthusiastically. She then switched to a more sympathetic tone, "I am so sorry Mr. Falmouth, but it just cannot be done. You see, there is something sticky in the building materials – it just will not come off. But if there is anything else I can do for you…" She came closer to Falmouth.

"Stay away bitch!" shouted Falmouth, "I don't want to die."

"No problem." Suzie moved slightly further away.

"Do you believe in P-rays?" asked the fly.

"Yes, I do!" exclaimed Suzie joyfully.

"I'm sitting here shitting fucking P-rays to no avail."

"I sent P-rays this morning, after I woke and saw my home had been destroyed. I asked for a visitor and here you are," Suzie proclaimed proudly.

"Life is full of shit."

"And that is why there are so many flies," added Suzie cheerfully.

Suddenly another fly entered Suzie's home. The web shook severely, but remained in place, confirming the integrity of Suzie's design calculations.

"A new guest. Please excuse me while I go and check on them."

▲ ▲ ▲

The sun was high in the sky when Suzie returned. Falmouth was still.

"Hello, Mr. Falmouth, how are you doing?"

Falmouth barely stirred, "Stay away bitch," he quietly murmured.

Suzie stopped.

"I think my fucking wing is broken," moaned Falmouth, "I've been trying and trying to break away from this Hell hole."

"I am so sorry to hear that," consoled Suzie soothingly. She looked at the wing. It was severely bent at an awkward angle and was barely attached.

"Life sucks. One day you are flying on top of the world. All of your body parts are working. You can go anywhere and do anything. Then it all comes crashing down. Suzie…" he looked over at her, "I am never going to leave your home alive, am I?"

"You are correct Mr. Falmouth," nodded Suzie, "But you have to admit, it is a very nice home."

"Yes." Falmouth looked around, "You have a very nice home."

"Mr. Falmouth, you know that the end is inevitable, so why fight it? Why not enjoy your remaining time? Look, look over there. Isn't that a beautiful view of the obelisk? And, don't you feel the cool breeze coming off the water?"

They looked past the nearby mesquite tree and saw the gigantic tan obelisk towering into the bright blue sky. "I, I never noticed the obelisk before," confessed Falmouth, "I have always been too busy."

In a distant part of the home another visitor arrived.

"Oh my, another guest. They must really like my latest design. Excuse me, Mr. Falmouth, I will return later."

▲ ▲ ▲

The sun was low in the sky when Suzie returned.

"Hello, Mr. Falmouth, how are you doing?"

She did not hear a reply, so she moved right next to Falmouth. She heard a faint murmur and got even closer.

"This isn't life," whispered Falmouth, "the pain is too great, Suzie. Let me go. I am ready."

"Very well, Mr. Falmouth."

The passing was peaceful and tranquil. Falmouth wondered why he had spent so much of his life fearing the inevitable.

With one quick bite the fly flew from the realm of the living.

▲ ▲ ▲

A little gamey, but quite tasty Suzie thought. She dined a while and then wrapped the rest for the next day. She heard a call from the other side of her home. It was time for dessert!

CHAPTER 5

WHEN DO YOU PLAN TO DIE, SIR?

Texans are known for their strength. Advertisers portray their products as 'Texas Tough' and conjure images of Texas cowboys on the range or roughnecks working a rig. Strength is in the genes of native Texans that trace their ideological roots to the heroes that perished in the Battle of the Alamo and believe in the legendary Texas Ranger motto – 'One riot, one ranger'.

So where does one look for Houston's strongest? Many Olympic athletes and sports stars call Houston home and the Houston Texan football team, although it may not win many games, certainly has some very strong players. None of these, however, are anywhere near as strong and tough as Skeete.

Skeete was a long-time Houston area resident. He had lived through the oilfield booms and busts and had weathered hurricane winds, summer heat, freezes, floods, droughts, and gas releases from the neighboring petrochemical complexes. Skeete came from a long line of strong relatives and lived near the obelisk. Skeete, you see, was a mesquite tree – they do not come any stronger in Texas.

▲ ▲ ▲

"When do you plan to die, sir?"
Skeete was horrified by the question and asked for it to be repeated.

Very slowly the orb repeated the question, carefully enunciating each syllable, "When-do-you-plan-to die-sir?"

"Now who the hell are you again?" groused Skeete.

"I am with the Planning Department," replied the orb.

"And that department is located where?"

"In Heaven, of course." If he had eyes, he would have rolled them. What is it with life forms? They all think that they are the center of the universe. Hello, the world was running pretty good long before you were born and will continue to run well long after you are gone, but it takes preparation.

"I thought you guys had everything planned down to the nanosecond, you know, the whole predestination thing," scoffed Skeete.

"Oh, I wish. It would certainly make my job a lot easier. As a life form, after birth you are predestined to grow, have an opportunity to reproduce, and then you die. You have grown and reproduced, so now it is time to plan for your death. It is perfectly natural – cycle of life and all that."

"So why do I need to die?"

Why can't life forms understand, thought the orb. He had been asked this very same question countless times. "Okay," he said talking calmly and very slowly, "Let us review the basics. Are you still growing?"

"I find it difficult to grow taller. It used to be much easier, but now it hurts as I try to extend my reach. I find it is much easier to grow wider."

"How about reproducing?"

"I don't really want to reproduce anymore. I would like to keep things just like they are with no more changes."

This is so frustrating, thought the orb. "Look, the life plan says you are born, you grow, you reproduce, and you die. There is not an option to stay where you are. You have finished growing and reproducing, so the next step is you die."

"Why do you care when I die?"

"To be honest sir, I could care less when you die. But there are a lot of resources that go into keeping you alive – food, water, energy, and so forth. Once you are gone, these resources can go to others. We need to develop plans now so these resources can be reallocated once you are dead."

"Who put you up to this? Was it my good-for-nothing offspring? I told them as soon as they were born that they were to stand tall and be on their own. I am not really into the parenting thing. Be strong and independent like me I told them. Are they the ones that are trying to get my resources?"

"Oh no, no, no, sir. Your offspring have scattered to the winds. It is the ones now closest to you that are making the requests."

"Ones closest to me? Requests? Like I said, I am strong and independent. I have no close friends. I live in the world all by myself."

"Well actually sir, we have reports that there are a couple of bird nests in your limbs."

"That is strictly a business agreement. The nesters are good sources of fertilizer."

"And the ant colony, tomato plant, squirrels, and spiders?"

"Leaches, they are all leaches trying to live off me. If I could, I would kill them all."

"Do you believe in P-rays?"

"I do in times of trouble," confessed Skeete. "I have sent them in times of storms, drought, and disease. Most of the time though, I handle things myself. That is why I am so strong."

"There have been a lot of P-rays lately asking for your death?"

"What? Who, why…why would they want me dead?"

"One of them is from a rabbit, a Missy Lutt. Do you know her?"

"Damn promiscuous rabbit, she is always burrowing into my roots. She needs to go elsewhere with her burrows."

"Another one is from a tomato plant named Eudicot. It was a very logical request - you know a lot of P-rays are very emotional. This one simply points out that tomato plants produce more useful offspring than mesquite trees."

"Well, you can tell the tomato plant that we already have enough of their kind and the world certainly doesn't need any more fruits."

"We are also getting complaints from the young sprouts. You are blocking their sunlight. They want to grow big and strong like yourself, but you are in the way."

Skeete paused, "You know, I have now lived for almost two hundred years and have seen many, many changes. I was here during the great battle, I have lived through many horrific hurricanes, I was here when they built the obelisk, and I have survived all kinds of gas releases, pests, and diseases. What used to be an empty coastal plain now has millions of people. The world in which I originally grew up is long gone. I liked the old world – things made sense. I do not understand this new world. Maybe it is time for me to go. Maybe it is time for others to take my place."

"Yea, that's all great." The orb was anxiously trying to wrap things up. "So, when do you plan to die, sir?"

"Tell your planners, and rabbits, and fruits, and young sprouts, that I will die when I damn well please!"

"Excuse me sir," objected the orb, "We really need you to be a little more specific. You have got to see the big picture. For instance, you have already lived longer than ninety percent of the mesquite trees, and I am only talking about the ones that live to be at least five years old. We don't count the early-deathers in our numbers. What would happen if you lived too long? I will tell you what would happen - there would be a lot of upset mesquite trees. You see, they know the statistics and they all think they have the right to live to the absolute top of their life range. Should they think that? Of course not, we deal with averages and probabilities. But get an outlier in there – everyone wants to be the outlier. Now what about disposal of your remains? Nobody ever wants to think about that. Are you going to go floating out into the Houston Ship Channel, then maybe to Galveston Bay and the Gulf of Mexico? Fine, if that is what you want, but that takes planning. We have to get you out in a storm, and given your size, it needs to be a pretty big storm - those just do not come around that often. Now suppose, instead, you want to be decayed. Great alternative! Lots of trees choose that alternative, but we need to get the bugs and bacteria lined up. It is not that easy for someone your size. The bugs and bacteria aren't just sitting around saying, 'Hey let's go eat a mesquite tree today'. No sir, if you are not available, they have to be fed or go elsewhere. And if not, we will have lots of starving bugs and if they die, they won't be available to consume you when the time has come."

"What are the choices again?"

"Box A is less than five years, Box B is five to ten years, and Box C is ten to fifteen years."

"Put me down for Box C." Anything, Skeete thought, just get this pain-in-the-ass bureaucrat out of here.

"Thank you, sir." The orb wondered as it disappeared, "Why don't life forms understand life?"

CHAPTER 6

THE RABBIT THAT SAVED THE UNIVERSE

History is filled with stories of beautiful females – Aphrodite, Helen of Troy, Bathsheba, Cleopatra, and Lady Godiva to name a few. No doubt every civilization has had an admired icon of feminine beauty. Many of the famous females are known more for their promiscuous behavior than for their societal contributions. This of course is a double standard but it seems to be commonplace around the world and it certainly applied to the region containing the obelisk. Missy Lutt, the Queen of San Jacinto, was well known for her sexual escapades, and not for much else.

Missy was a ravishing beauty with crystal clear blue eyes, light brown hair, and silky-smooth skin. She was, of course, extremely popular with all of the males. Missy had no qualms or moral issues about sex and she was very proud to be so attractive to her suitors. It was all very plain and simple to Missy - her role in life was to reproduce and sex was an important part of reproduction. She had been at the obelisk during the night of the hunt, and yes, she too was having a tryst. Missy was busy in the bushes when the young man startled her on his way to pee on Skeete, the mesquite tree.

Missy's escapades naturally resulted in a large number of offspring. She had lost count long ago, but her latest delivery a few days ago pushed the number to well over five hundred. This may seem surprising but Missy, you see, was a cottontail rabbit and had been delivering litters every month or so ever since she was three months old.

While extremely pleasing and sought after by her male companions, Missy was not well liked by the rest of the obelisk community. Her romps through the underbrush and burrows caused considerable damage to the vegetation and smaller animals living in the area. While racing for cover during the storm, she rolled across Eudicot which caused one of his tomatoes to separate from the vine, she stepped on Akoios's ant colony causing catastrophic damage, she trampled the brush that provided support for Suzie the spider's home, and finally she burrowed deep beneath the mesquite tree damaging Skeete's roots. Needless to say, with her reputation and past history, no one expected much from Missy. And yet, this very same, some would say insignificant, creature became known as the rabbit that saved the universe.

▲ ▲ ▲

It seemed like the board meeting for region GR82BER had been going on for ages…and it may have been since time is different in Heaven. The board was reviewing, in excruciating detail, the Statistical Process Control charts for the region.

▲ ▲ ▲

At this point, a moment of digress is in order. The knowledge that Statistical Process Control charts are used in Heaven often strikes terror into the hearts of engineers. While this is unquestionably repulsive and may tarnish one's image of Heaven, it is really quite logical when one stops to consider:

1. Heaven is trying to control chaos
2. Systems have been installed to create order
3. Sometimes problems occur with the systems

4. Statistical Process Control charts are tools that can be used to determine when something in the system is out-of-order

▲ ▲ ▲

Now the review of Statistical Process Control charts is extremely boring, and while many of us would consider this to be a worse-than-hell punishment, those at the meeting actually enjoyed this type of work. One-by-one, they carefully reviewed how each species was doing in the GR82BER region. They, of course, used the technical name for the region, but it is more commonly known as the area around the San Jacinto Monument or simply The Obelisk. This is a thriving area for life as the climate is mild and there is an abundant supply of both sunshine and rain. Since life in the region is plentiful and each species has its own control chart, a lot of data was presented. After reviewing the control charts, the statisticians then had to develop their correlations. These are of questionable value and are easily dismissed by those with even a modicum of sanity. They found that most of the data points were within the normal bounds, that is, if you call anything done by statisticians normal. There was one group of data points, however, that was out-of-bounds and they found this particularly vexing. Being good statisticians, which may be an oxymoron, they developed new correlations by sprinkling foo foo dust, muttering incantations, or by whatever means statisticians use to develop such correlations. However, despite their best efforts, the outlier remained – there was definitely a problem in the GR82BER region.

The charts indicated that the problem species for the region was cottontail rabbits. The rate of rabbit production was much higher than the targeted rate. The statisticians did not know what to do. They were good at studying charts and developing new correlations to explain away anomalies, but that had not worked in this case. While they were very adept in their statistical manipulations, they were extremely lacking in problem-solving abilities. In fact, they had never ever solved a real problem. Panic suddenly set in – if this problem was not solved, it would spill over into adjacent areas. From there, it would spread, like wildfire, into more and more regions, continuing exponentially. One of the statisticians extrapolated the consequences and showed that eventually the entire universe would become out-of-order and descend into chaos because of the rabbit problem in the GR82BER region. The statisticians became more and more hysterical. There was serious fretting, but during a brief lull in the franticness, they decided to call a rabbit expert – a biologist.

The biologist was a good source for knowledge and lectured them non-stop for several days, ad infinitum, on the anatomy of the rabbit. Finally, Ezra, one of the senior statisticians, interrupted and explained that they did not really care to learn everything about rabbits - they just wanted to know how to reduce the rate of rabbit production.

The biologist assured them that, yes, this was possible. With some genetic modifications, the rabbit litter size could be reduced and the gestation period could be increased. The statisticians were excited that they had finally found the solution to a problem and were very anxious to get their control charts back in order as soon as possible. Ezra asked the biologist how long it would take for the changes to be implemented. When the statisticians learned that genetic modifications take a very long time, they once again became highly agitated.

The statisticians discussed other options and came up with an idea – why not kill the rabbits? They asked the biologist about rabbit predators and he gave them a long list – wolves, coyotes, dingoes, weasels, cougars, leopards, etc. The statisticians were happy again knowing that they had found the solution to a problem, and not just any problem, a colossal problem that was threatening the entire universe. They submitted a transfer request to the Planning Department for a predator to be moved into the region.

▲ ▲ ▲

Rodney, in the Planning Department, received the transfer request. He checked to make sure that the request was properly filled out with all boxes marked, and it was. When he saw that the transfer request came from Statistics Heaven, he became a little skeptical. When he read the actual request, 'transfer a leopard to the area around The Obelisk', he shook his head, denied the request, and said, "Those crazy folks in Statistics are at it again."

The statisticians were greatly upset when they received the rejection because, after all, the fate of the entire universe was at stake. This was so obvious and, yet somehow, the Planning Department did not recognize the importance. They rechecked the 'reason for transfer box' on the form and saw that they had originally entered 'needed to restore order in Statistical Process Control charts'. Perhaps we need to be blunter they thought, when dealing with non-statisticians. They resubmitted the transfer request and this time in the 'reason for transfer' box they put 'prevent universe from descending into chaos'.

Rodney, in the Planning Department, received the new request and was, once again, skeptical because everyone in the Planning Department is skeptical when they receive requests from Statistical Heaven. This time he went to his supervisor, Celeste, and explained the situation to her. "Let me get this straight," she said, "they want us to move a leopard from Africa to the area around the San Jacinto Monument to kill rabbits. The statisticians are nuts!" Celeste had experience in dealing with statisticians and knew that if she simply denied the request, they would resubmit a new one. She reread the justification and noted the word 'chaos'. She recalled the saying, 'Imperfection is perfection and chaos is an engineer's paradise,' and knew how to proceed, "Let's send them an engineer."

▲   ▲   ▲

Engineers are known for their ability to fix anything, whether it is broken or not, and usually are very eager to come to the rescue. However, engineers abhor statistics, and this problem involved working with statisticians. It was not easy, but finally they found Beauregard, and while he was not fond of statistics, he could at least tolerate statisticians. Beauregard met with the statisticians and they became hysterical again and all talked at once about how, if the problem was not solved, the universe was coming to an end. Beauregard had been around patent lawyers and knew how they liked to exaggerate things, so the end of the universe talk did not faze him. He asked to have just one of the statisticians explain the problem, and they selected Ezra. After several hours of looking at charts and graphs, Beauregard interrupted. "So, the root cause of the problem is that the number of rabbits per square mile in the region is too high?" After mumbling some more statistical gibberish, Ezra basically agreed.

Being a good engineer, Beauregard conducted an investigation. When this was complete, he met again with the statisticians. "My engineering analysis shows that the problem in the region is not all of the rabbits, but one rabbit in particular – Missy Lutt. She is way too productive." Engineers like making graphs and charts and statisticians really love seeing graphs and charts, so they all had a good time when Beauregard showed them lots of graphs and charts that proved Missy was by far the most prolific rabbit in the region. "If we can reduce her baby production rate, the number of rabbits per square mile in the region should return to the normal range in a relatively short period of time."

The statisticians were very glad to hear this, but they did not know how to go about reducing Missy's baby production rate. Their attempts at receiving assistance from the Planning Department had not been successful. They asked Beauregard what to do.

"We need to have a brainstorming session," Beauregard eagerly proposed. "This is something that engineers enjoy doing and it is really easy. Here are sticky notes - I want you to write down your ideas on how to solve the problem and put them on the wall. We will then group the ideas and develop an action plan. Remember, no idea is dumb or stupid."

The statisticians put their ideas on the sticky notes and placed them on the wall. Beauregard then compiled the notes and read them to the group. "The first note says 'Kill her'. Okay, that is one course of action. The next idea is 'Murder Missy'. All right, we will put this also in the 'Kill' pile. Here is a suggestion to 'Slaughter the Slut'. Oh my, that is a bit strong language but the intent is clear. The next note says 'Kill the F** rabbit'. Thank goodness for the heavenly censors. We certainly are putting a lot of notes in the 'Kill' pile." On and on this went, with lots of very colorful and often gory suggestions. Eventually all of the notes from the wall were placed in the 'Kill' pile.

Beauregard, being a good engineer, was used to evaluating multiple possible courses of action. In this case, only one solution had been proposed and this bothered him because engineers always have to have at least several alternatives to study. He decided to use a seeding technique. "Killing Missy is certainly one alternative," he told the statisticians, "but are there any other solutions? For instance, what if Missy could no longer produce babies? How about if we fill out some more sticky notes with ideas other than killing her?"

Once again, the statisticians put their ideas on sticky notes and placed them on the wall and once again Beauregard read the notes and put them into piles. "The first note says 'Rip Out Her Reproductive Organs'. Well, that certainly is a bit descriptive. Let's create a pile that we call 'Birth Control'. The next note says 'Cram Something Up Her ***'. Oh my, that is a bit too descriptive and painful. The third note reads 'Cut Off Her ***', well we will add these to the 'Birth Control' pile as well." One-by-one Beauregard read the graphically violent suggestions and placed all of them in the 'Birth Control' pile.

It did not take Beauregard any fancy statistical correlations to realize that:

1. Statisticians do not like it when their control charts are not in order.

2. Statisticians can be really violent, especially when their control charts are not in order, and
3. Statisticians may be able to detect problems, but they are lousy at proposing solutions.

Beauregard, being a good engineer, decided to go to the source of the problem. He set up a vision link with Missy Lutt.

▲ ▲ ▲

Missy had just finished an amorous encounter when the skies above her opened and she saw Beauregard. He was stunned by her appearance – she was absolutely beautiful. There seemed to be some sort of a warm glow around her that made her look even more stunning. Could it be, his analytical mind was whirling, could it be that Missy's predators see this and do not attack her because she is so attractive? Maybe that is why she has lived so long.

"Hello Miss Lutt. Do not be afraid. My name is Beauregard, I am in Heaven and we need to talk."

"Well, I do say Mr. Beauregard, the honor is all mine." Missy spoke in a sweet shy voice with a southern drawl that further enhanced her attractiveness.

She is way too sweet and nice, thought Beauregard, as he tried to suppress the twelve alternative methods of killing her that he was evaluating. You see, the minds of engineers are trained to solve problems and the methodology used does not distinguish between morally good or morally bad solutions - the important thing is that the problem is solved in an optimum manner.

"Missy, there is a problem in the area around The Obelisk - too many rabbits are being produced."

"Oh my, Mr. Beauregard, that hardly sounds like a problem. To me it sounds very wonderful. To create life, especially cute little baby bunnies, surely is a joy for the world."

THE PRICE OF LIFE

"The problem Missy is that there are not enough resources to support all of the bunnies."

"Mr. Beauregard, surely you jest. I have been making baby bunnies for quite some time and there have always been plenty of resources. We have been truly blest."

Beauregard was uncomfortable. How could he explain statistical process control to a rabbit? "That may be so Missy, but there are those that do calculations and they show that if you continue to make rabbits at this pace, the area will run out of resources and your baby bunnies will die."

"Why Mr. Beauregard, we all die someday."

"Yes, yes, but wouldn't it be better to die of natural causes at the end of a long life instead of watching your babies die of starvation?"

"Now Mr. Beauregard, you do realize that you are talking to a rabbit. We are low on the food chain and seldom die of natural causes."

"Yes, well it would certainly help the area if maybe you could slow down a bit on the baby production." She looked so sweet and innocent. He really did not want to have to have her killed. His mind had been searching for alternatives and had come up with a rabbit birth control device that could be painlessly placed inside her. "If you need any help, I have a design for something that could be put inside you that would keep you from having babies, but you know…you could still have relations with…"

"Oh my sir, that sounds like a horrible idea."

"I do not understand Missy. I assure you that it is quite painless."

"Sir, do you know about the purpose of life? We are born, we grow, we reproduce, and we die. I am in the reproducing stage of life. My purpose is to produce as many baby bunnies as I can, and that is what I am doing. I will continue to do this as long as I live."

"Missy, I need to level with you. There are those that say either you slow down making babies or you are going to have to be killed. I have suggested that you voluntary slow down on the baby-making and I have offered you a technology that will reduce your baby-making ability, but now I am running out of options. The next alternative is to have you killed."

"Oh my, Mr. Beauregard, that is such a drastic option. Am I to understand that I am to be killed for doing what I was made to do – produce baby bunnies? Are all the Mamma rabbits going to be killed?"

"Oh no, only you Missy. You are just too efficient. You make way more bunnies than the other Mamma's."

"So, I am to be killed for what I do well? Sir, I do not understand."

"I wish I could explain it to you. You see it involves statistics, calculations, charts, and correlations. It is way beyond your capabilities."

"And is that because I am a rabbit or because I am a female? Why don't you show me what you have and then see if I understand?"

Beauregard proceeded to show Missy his data. This went on for quite some time. Finally, Missy said, "Mr. Beauregard, you being an engineer and all that, I am sure you are very smart, but I have to ask you a question. Did you include the G-Adjustment Factor in your calculations?"

Beauregard was stunned, "I am not sure what you mean."

"Well, Mr. Beauregard. The problem is too many rabbits in the area. What if we increase the size of the area? There are some nearby marshes. Part of the year they are above the water and part of the year they are below the water. What if we increase the size of the area to include the marshes and a little bit of the water?" She winked as she said the last part.

Beauregard, being a good engineer, quickly plugged in the new data and was pleasantly surprised – the Statistical Process Control charts were back in order. There was no longer any problem. He was very relieved that he did not have to have Missy killed. He thanked her for her time and called a meeting with the statisticians to give them the good news.

▲ ▲ ▲

The statisticians were overjoyed when Beauregard showed them the new data. Their control charts were back in order and the universe was saved! Beauregard explained that this was all possible because of the G-Adjustment Factor. The statisticians were jubilant as they left the room to continue their search for problems in the universe. They all left except for one – Ezra.

"Beauregard, this is fantastic work. I have done an incredible amount of statistical work and I consider myself quite the expert, but I have never heard of the G-Adjustment Factor. What does the 'G' stand for?"

Beauregard was a little uncomfortable, but did not want to admit that he had no idea. When engineers do not know the answer, they usually just make up something. "It is a term Missy used. I did not personally ask her, but I think it is pretty obvious that the 'G' stands for gerrymandering. You saw how she extended the boundaries of the area around the obelisk to include the marsh and nearby waters."

Ezra thanked Beauregard for his time and left. He did not want to tell the engineer that statisticians were experts at manipulating numbers to match the desired result and had invented gerrymandering long ago. He also knew that there was a lot of trial and error and complex iterations involved in gerrymandering, but yet this rabbit, in her head, had been able to instantly figure out the solution. He wondered if she was some kind of statistical prodigy. He set up a vision link with Missy.

▲ ▲ ▲

"Miss Lutt, this is Ezra from Heaven. I bet you are getting tired of these visions in the sky."

"Why Mr. Ezra," Missy's words drooled with her shy, sweet, Southern drawl, "The skies light up for me every day. Could you hold on for just a moment? I need to take care of my new babies."

Ezra may have been a cold-hearted statistician, but deep inside he was glad that they did not need to have her killed. Even he admired the precious scene of Missy talking to her cute little babies. He listened as she addressed them.

"Now what does Mamma always say?" The babies were gathered around their mother and looked incredibly adorable.

"We can play anywhere on the land, but stay away from the marshes," replied the baby sitting closest to Missy.

"And when can you go to the marshes?"

"Not until we are adults." The babies all responded in unison and then hopped away to play.

"Now Mr. Ezra, what may I do for you?"

"You are such a good mother."

"I try and try. My babies are so good. They are really sweet now, but someday they will become obnoxious teenagers that think they are adults. They will be a real pain then and won't listen to a thing I say."

"Yes, statistical studies show that when the children of most species reach their adolescent years…" He paused, that was not why he called. "I am fascinated with your statistical abilities."

"My what?"

"You know, the G-Adjustment Factor. I have never seen anyone that can instantly gerrymander."

"Excuse me Mr. Ezra, I do not want to be rude, but I have no idea what this 'Gerry' thing is that you are talking about."

"Gerrymandering, it is a method that statisticians use to manipulate data. If it is not gerrymandering, could you, by chance, tell me what the 'G' in the G-Adjustment Factor stands for?"

"Why that is easy sir, it stands for George."

"Is George some kind of great mathematician? Is he by chance a statistician? I am very impressed that there is a factor named after him and I would very much like to meet him."

"I know that he is not a mathematician or statistician, but if you really want to meet him, I am sure it could be arranged."

Ezra was excited about the opportunity to meet this gerrymandering genius. Here was someone that had a statistical factor named in his honor, and yet, he was not even a full-time mathematician or statistician. Missy Lutt had been able to restore order in the universe by suggesting that the G-Adjustment factor be applied to the Statistical Process Control Charts. This one factor had solved the rabbit overpopulation problem in the area. This George was truly amazing. "Well then Missy, who is George?"

Missy paused. "Mr. Ezra…George is an alligator…he lives in the marsh."

SHOWDOWNS WITH DEATH

CHAPTER 1

THE FORBIDDEN ZONE

The Alpha One was traveling at ninety percent of its maximum speed. The recommended cruising speed was sixty-five percent of maximum speed, but Arminius wanted to find his mother quickly. He thought of increasing the speed, maybe even to the one hundred and ten percent level or more that he had used in battle, but it was not worth the risk. If anything happened to the engine, there were no repair stations out here. In fact, the ship would never be serviced again. He was definitely a persona non grata on Home World…that is, if Home World survived. If he docked in Plugaria, they would surely take the Alpha One. What was he thinking? The Plugarians would never even let him get close enough to dock. As soon as he was in laser range, they would destroy his ship.

Being powerful certainly has its drawbacks. Whenever a mighty wild beast comes near a village, the response is always the same – kill it! It does not matter what type of beast it is - it could live in the neighboring forest, slither on barren rocks, swim in brackish waters, or fly high above the village. Any animal seen as threatening might someday harm the inhabitants of the village and must be destroyed. He now was that animal, even though he had not hurt the Plugarians…well, he had blown away four of their battleships and tried to instigate Armageddon, but that was now all in the past. Of course, the Plugarians may not see it that way.

His father may have been right – there was no place to go. He was going to be alone for the rest of his life. Unless, unless he found his mother - the only person that had ever loved him. When the Alpha One left Luna 3, he instructed the ship's computer to send a continuous signal to the Forbidden Zone and to monitor any communication activity. There had been no response from Ricus 3 or from anywhere else in the Forbidden Zone, but nonetheless Arminius checked the communication log daily hoping to find that his mother had called.

Even at ninety percent of maximum speed, the trip from Home World to the Forbidden Zone was going to take six weeks. This was considerably faster than the decades it took for the early-unmanned probes to reach the Forbidden Zone. The Alpha One had an extensive database, and Arminius used his time to learn as much as possible about the Forbidden Zone.

The Forbidden Zone was first mentioned in ancient religious texts:

In the days of old there lived a proud and arrogant race amidst the shadows of the ancient star. "Let us build a bridge to Heaven and we shalt grasp the hand of the Creators and reap their wisdom." And they searched the lands and recruited the finest minds and most highly skilled craftsmen for their foolish quest...

The Creators watched as the bridge began. "Woe to this race for they have not the wisdom to know what they shalt not seek. Send them prophets to repent of their transgressions and change their ways..."

The prophets spoke, but the people's hearts were turned to stone and the bridge grew and grew. The Creators saw this and were troubled. "If they acquire our wisdom, they will create chaos." And the ancient star was smote by the Creators to save creation...

Then the Creators said, "Let us begin anew." And life was placed in the shadow of Astar and life was placed in the shadow of Bstar. "May greatness come from our seeds. We give thee all the lands of Astar and all the lands of Bstar, but pass thee not into the Forbidden Zone for it is a land of great evil. Woe to thee that violates the covenant and perishes in the Forbidden Zone, for there will be no room for thy soul in the houses of the Creators. He that can see let him see, he that can hear let him hear, and he that can understand let him understand."

The Forbidden Zone was an immense swirling vortex of energy and space debris. Scientists had many theories about the Forbidden Zone. Some said that there used to be a third star in the binary star system - Cstar, as they called it, that had turned into a supernova before flaming out and becoming a dwarf star with tremendous gravitational pull. There were anomalies that could not be explained, so other scientists proposed that there was once also a Dstar that revolved around Cstar as a second binary star system. It too had gone supernova and was now a dwarf star, so it was a binary dwarf star system. Some scientists thought there was a black hole present. Others thought that up to a dozen black holes might be present. Buried deep in the footnotes, was the emulsion theory proposed by an engineer. It was based on the emulsion layer observed when oil and water are mixed and then allowed to settle. The engineer proposed that the Forbidden Zone was an emulsion layer which formed the boundary between two universes. This theory was not widely discussed in scientific circles because the originator of the idea did not have the proper university credentials.

The mysteries of the Forbidden Zone had always generated great interest for further study. Over the years, many research grants had been submitted and much money spent. In the early days, many of the studies utilized telescopic observations. As technology improved, the engineers created unmanned spacecraft for exploration. Over a dozen planets were detected in the outer regions of the Forbidden Zone. Most of these were little more than large barren rocks. One planet, however, was particularly intriguing – Ricus 3, the mysterious planet that was always covered with clouds. Ricus 3 was mentioned many times in the forbidden literature. Some claimed that the planet was inhabited by an alien race. Others claimed that it was the home created by the Creators for the souls of the dead. Probes were sent to specifically explore Ricus 3, but all stopped sending signals once they entered the planet's atmosphere.

Despite the religious warnings, a manned probe was sent to the Forbidden Zone. This was in the days before the Great War and it was a joint mission with a mixed crew of Worldians and Plugarians. It gathered a substantial amount of data about the outer fringes of the Forbidden Zone before heading toward Ricus 3. The ship suddenly disappeared without a trace. The Great War began shortly thereafter. Some say the Great War was punishment inflicted by the Creators for violating their commandment. Others say that the joint mission discovered riches beyond belief and that control of the riches was the real reason for the war. The treaty ending the Great War specified that no vessels, manned or unmanned, would ever again be sent to the Forbidden Zone. Home World and Plugaria publicly proclaimed their support for the treaty in its entirety, but frequently violated the Forbidden Zone clause. Many ships, on top-secret missions, were sent to the Forbidden Zone - none of them ever returned.

▲ ▲ ▲

Time passed at an excruciating slow pace. For days, Arminius watched the Alpha One view screen as Ricus 3 gradually increased in size. No details of the planet's surface were visible due to the heavy cloud cover. The Alpha One was equipped with the most technologically advanced long-range scanning instruments, but no meaningful data could be gathered about conditions on Ricus 3

Finally, the day arrived and Arminius put the Alpha One in orbit above the swirling clouds that enveloped Ricus 3. For the next five days, the ship circled all quadrants of the planet while its sophisticated instruments scanned the world below. As was the case with the long-range scans, the effort was futile – the information gathered was gibberish. Something was interfering with the results. There was no response to any of the communication signals sent to the planet or to other regions of the Forbidden Zone.

Options flashed through Arminius's head. The ship had sacrificed all of its Cubs to the laser gods and it had donated one Buggy to Armageddon, but it still had seven Buggies. Arminius remotely controlled one of the Buggies and sent it toward the planet. Soon after it left the ship, all communication was lost. Arminius evaluated his options. He could pilot a Buggy himself, but he had no way of knowing what was beneath the swirling clouds and, without instruments, he would be flying blind. He also did not know if the Buggy's engines could overcome the Ricus 3 gravitational pull. He then thought about taking the Alpha One to the surface. It would have a much more powerful engine, but he had no way of knowing if there was a suitable place for the giant ship to land. If only he could see the surface. He fired a laser blast towards the planet, but it was adsorbed by the heavy cloud cover.

In his head, Arminius performed a cost versus value evaluation. The cost was very high - his life, but what was the reward? Arminius had not seen his mother for over twenty years. Was she still alive? He had seen her dead. He had been to her funeral. How could she still be alive? Was his mind playing tricks on him? He had seen her hologram on board his ship - on board the ship during an intense battle scene. Was he cracking up? He really missed his mother. He had grown up with only a distant son-of-a-bitch father. She was the only one that had ever loved him. He had been clinging to the hope that she was still alive, but was it now time to give up on hope?

His thoughts were interrupted by Chirality. The synthesized female voice of the ship's computer announced, "Debris field alert. Projectiles are on collision course. ETA ten minutes."

"Goodbye Mother," sighed Arminius as he shifted his focus to the view screen. An agglomeration of space debris was growing larger as he watched. "Chirality, battlefield screen on!" The holographic screen lit up showing the projectiles. There were too many for manual navigation. Arminius fastened his harness and calmly issued orders, "Automatic control, evasive maneuvers, ten percent power."

The ship's automatic navigation system immediately took control and the Alpha One deftly twisted, turned, and threaded the eyes of thousands of needles as it maneuvered through the debris field. After passing through, Arminius conducted a long-range sensor scan. The scans showed that the debris field was just one of hundreds of debris fields in the surrounding area.

"Chirality, determine origin of the debris field that the Alpha One just passed through."

"Origin determined, sir." The response was almost immediate.

"Show on battlefield screen."

A red circle appeared on the screen marking the location.

"Correlate trajectories of other debris fields in the sector and determine origin."

Multiple red lines appeared on the screen and the display indicated they all originated from the same location - the same point of origin as the debris field the Alpha One had just passed through.

"Plot course to point of origin and proceed at twenty percent power."

▲ ▲ ▲

For the next several hours, Arminius watched view screens and sensors as the ship slowly approached the point of origin. It appeared to be a dark gigantic hole. When he was two hours away, Arminius placed the ship in orbit around the hole, and the Alpha One's scanning instruments downloaded immense quantities of data. This is amazing, thought Arminius, he was seeing something no one had ever seen before. This incredible discovery would make him even more famous! He would be in the Scientific Hall of Fame! He might even…thoughts were racing though his mind, could he use this discovery to be restored to the good graces of those on Home World and Plugaria?

▲ ▲ ▲

The three entities watched the object as it circled the dark hole. They had been waiting for this moment and were in agreement. Sparks of light lit up the darkness.

CHAPTER 2

THE COSMIC CANNON

Daniel and Roger were in the Cathedral of Heaven.
"There is something I want to show you." Roger extended his hand, "It is a project I am working on." Daniel grasped the hand of God and disappeared.

They reappeared on a dark barren cliff on an outpost planet at the edge of the universe. There was an enormous swirling vortex in the night sky that was swallowing stars, planets, and other cosmic debris. Hurricane force winds buffeted them. A gigantic canon was on the hill, pointing toward the center of the vortex. The barrel appeared to extend for hundreds of miles. The base of the canon was inside a solitary plain white stone building that was built into the cliff. They entered the door to the building and slowly floated down a long, well-lit passageway.

"Wow, what was that out there?" exclaimed Daniel.

"The entrance to another universe," replied Roger. "Do you remember the analogy of universes being like giant petrochemical storage tanks?"

"Sure, flow goes back and forth between two tanks to balance the level. Is that the entrance to another universe?"

"It is an entrance, but it is a one-way entrance. There are other parts of the universe where I have seen flow go in both directions. In this location, I have only seen flow leaving our universe. I am not sure the adjacent universe is alive?"

"Alive? A living universe? I, I do not understand."

"Remember your grandmother's definition of life?"

"Sure. Born, grow, reproduce, and die."

"And we added the metabolism part. A living universe would fluctuate – inhale and exhale. At other locations in the universe this occurs, but here it is only one-way."

"So, you think the neighboring universe is dead?"

"Perhaps, or maybe it just needs a spark – a spark of life."

"So how do you startup a new universe?"

"I am not absolutely sure. I have been firing life into the vortex for a long time now, but there has been no response from the adjacent universe."

"You have been firing life?" Daniel had a perplexed look.

"I have been sending various combinations of life. I have no idea if any of them are working."

"Why are you trying to startup a new universe?"

"Do you recall our discussion about entropy?"

"Sure," Daniel responded, "The Second Law of Thermodynamics – everything descends into chaos. But you are here now, you are restoring order to the universe and you have plans for a joint venture linking Heaven and Earth. Won't it work? Can you reverse the decaying process or will decay ultimately win and the universe die?"

"What is your experience in chemical plants?"

"We are always replacing pipes and equipment, but eventually a cost versus value evaluation says it is more economical to build a new plant. A new plant is built, which is often an improved version of the old plant, and the old plant is shut down and discarded."

"I do not know if I can totally overcome chaos, so I am working on a backup plan. Someday we may need a new home, a new universe. The only sure way to beat death is to create new life."

At the end of the passageway, they came to a rounded wooden door that looked like it belonged on a medieval castle. The door slowly creaked open and, as they stepped into the pitch-black room, Roger disappeared. Daniel was suddenly enveloped with an overwhelming sense of fear. It was the first time he had felt fear since he had arrived in Heaven. He moved further into the room and the door slammed shut behind him. Daniel's eyes adjusted to the darkness and he saw scattered flickering candles that dimly lit the room. As his eyes became more adjusted, he was able to see dusty lab instruments and old mechanical equipment. Dim red lights were zigzagging around the room and cobwebs were everywhere. He heard a creak and, all of a sudden, ferocious-looking bats with menacing red eyes flew directly toward him. Daniel jerked his head just in time and the bats only grazed his face as they flew past. Large rats, scampering across the floor, rubbed against Daniel's ankles and scurried over his feet. Daniel looked toward the lab instruments and old mechanical equipment and saw something crawling all over them. As he approached, he realized what it was - slithering snakes. They snakes paused, raised their heads, and hissed at him as he walked past. Countless cobwebs blocked his path, and he paused to pick them, one-by-one, off his face. Daniel heard more creaks and dodged another wave of the red-eyed winged predators. He took a few more cautious steps, heard a loud creak, and came to a sudden stop. Directly in front of him, was a very large and hideous monster. In the flickering candlelight, Daniel recognized the monster's face – it was Frankenstein.

"Good evening." A loud, deep ghoulish voice echoed across the room. A lightning bolt flashed and a gust of wind chilled the room.

"How...Howdy," tremored meekly out of Daniel's mouth as fear rattled his bones.

The loud, deep ghoulish voice shook the room again as the monster bellowed, "How very nice to meet you." Frankenstein's two large arms slowly reached toward Daniel's neck as a door eerily creaked and more bats with evil-looking red eyes darted past.

"Wait a minute," shouted Daniel, "Stop! This is Heaven - you get to choose your looks and surroundings."

The room immediately lit up. Roger was standing next to Frankenstein and both were laughing.

"Sorry about that Daniel," chuckled Frankenstein with a normal voice. "We like to have fun with the first-timers." The cobwebs, laboratory, and old mechanical equipment disappeared and the surroundings were immediately transformed into what, at first glance, looked like a lounge for First Class passengers at a modern airport. Daniel was stunned and relieved as the house of horrors was replaced by a safe serene setting. God has a sense of humor he thought, after his heart rate returned to normal.

Frankenstein stood in the center of the room at a kiosk. A blue video screen, similar to the ones Daniel had seen throughout Heaven, floated nearby. Behind Frankenstein was a large view window of what would normally be the tarmac. The window was currently dark. Surrounding the window and kiosk were luxurious sofas and chairs that would have been at home in a prestigious country club. Painting masterpieces of great expeditions covered the block paneled interior walls. Okay, thought Daniel, this is way beyond First Class – it was looking more and more like a lounge for billionaires. Some of the scenes in the paintings looked familiar – the conquest of Mt. Everest, trips to the poles, spelunkers in dark caves, Viking ships crossing the Atlantic, Polynesian rafts traversing the Pacific, and submarines probing the ocean depths. Others were not as familiar – various groups of people trekking across barren desserts, dense jungles, grassy marshlands, and steep mountains. These must be some of the greatest explorers of all time, thought Daniel. It was fitting that they would be in the departure lounge for those leaving this universe. Interspersed between the magnificent paintings were intricately carved and sculpted objects made from all types of exotic and precious materials, that could have easily been the prized attractions at the finest museums in the world. This too is fitting, thought Daniel – the passenger's last view of this universe would be some of the greatest works of art ever created.

"Welcome to the Cosmic Cannon." Frankenstein bowed and extended his right hand. "Would you like a tour?"

Before Daniel could answer, the darkened window behind the kiosk dissolved and a large, well-lit warehouse appeared.

They walked into the warehouse. The giant barrel of the Cosmic Cannon dominated the view. Its barrel cut through the roof of the warehouse in one direction and, in the other direction, penetrated the ground below. There was a walkway that led to a platform at the entrance to the Cosmic Canon. They walked up to the platform and Frankenstein opened the door. Daniel peered inside and saw a white empty spherical room that was about eight feet in diameter.

"This is the Egg," announced Frankenstein, "the seed pod for a new universe."

"This is it?" questioned Daniel, "No chairs, no seat belts? It certainly seems cramped."

"You have to remember, it is the spirit of life orbs that go into the chamber, not their personifications which you see in Heaven. This chamber has actually held over one thousand orbs at one time."

"It is a one-way trip?"

"Yes," nodded Frankenstein, "Someday, once that universe is running, there will be flow between the universes and it may be possible to return, but it is not likely."

"So, it is like death?"

"That is correct. We hope to see the departed ones again someday on the other side. They are going to prepare a place for us."

"And they volunteer to go to their deaths?"

"We do have volunteers, but usually turn them away. We are looking for various life combinations, one of which will be the key to ignite the universe. The ones that go are drafted."

"Picked for death?"

"It is a great honor to be chosen," assured Frankenstein, "and while they may be dead to us, they should be very much alive in the new universe. They will mix with the other life orbs in the egg and form a new entity. They will then lay dormant until the day they are hatched in the new universe. Those chosen are the pioneers. They are seeking to create a better, improved universe for us all."

CHAPTER 3

WHEN LIFE GOES DOWN THE DRAIN

The view screen on the Bridge of the Alpha One suddenly lit up. Alarms on the control screen flashed.

"Electrical storm detected," announced Chirality.

"Electrical storm?" questioned Arminius. That had not been part of his training. "Plot course to evade storm."

"Unable to comply, sir"

"Why not?"

"No course available."

A gigantic electrical field surrounded them. "Lasers on, full power," Arminius calmly commanded.

"Lasers on. Full power in sixty seconds."

Sixty seconds seemed like an eternity. Arminius picked a target on the battlefield hologram screen. Finally, the lasers were ready.

"Maximum scatter…ten second blast…fire!"

The lasers fired, but had no effect on the electrical field.

"Concentrate fire…fifteen second blast…fire!"

Once again, the lasers fired, but to no avail.

"Debris field approaching, sir."

The debris field the Alpha One had passed through had reversed course and was now heading toward the hole. The Alpha One was in its direct path.

Arminius checked the battlefield screen and was shocked at what he saw. The debris field was not the only thing moving toward the hole, the Alpha One was moving toward the hole as well.

"Engines at fifty percent!" ordered Arminius.

Arminius checked the screen. They were still being pulled toward the hole.

"Engines at seventy-five percent!" Arminius checked the screen. It wasn't enough. It appeared they were now being pulled faster into the hole.

"Engines at ninety percent!" yelled Arminius. Arminius checked… it still was not enough.

"Engines at one hundred percent damn it!" screamed Arminius.

Arminius could not believe what he saw. He had command of the most powerful ship in the Home World fleet. His engines were at one hundred percent of capacity, yet they could not overcome the force that was pulling them into the hole. He was quickly running out of options. "Engines at one hundred and ten percent," commanded Arminius in a surprisingly calm voice.

"Warning, that level exceeds recommended operating conditions."

"Override code 7402," commanded Arminius in a manner-of-fact voice.

"Engines at one hundred and ten percent," confirmed Chirality.

It was still not enough. "Engines at one hundred and twenty percent. Override code 7402."

Once again Arminius checked the battlefield screen. He had done all he could. The ship's engines were operating at the upper limit of their safety factor and they were still being pulled into the hole at a rapid rate. There was nothing more that could be done. The end was near. Even the mightiest and strongest succumb to the inevitable.

"Download ship's files and transmit." His life might end soon, but it was important for those in the future to see his greatness. The ship's files would show this - he had fearlessly attacked the greatest military fleets in the Binary Star system, he had destroyed Luna 3, and he had made incredible scientific discoveries in the Forbidden Zone. He was great! He was fantastic! He was incredible! He may soon die, but the proof of his life would be saved forever in the archives of the Binary Star system.

"Unable to comply, sir."

"Why the hell not?" screamed Arminius. His temporary composure was suddenly undone.

"Electrical interference."

Arminius tightened his harness. The Binary Star system may or may not ever see it, but he knew how great he was. Now it was time to show the rest of the universe his greatness!

"Plot course to center of the hole and reduce engines to ten percent power. Activate long-range scans."

He was going to the other side.

CHAPTER 4

TRANSITION

A sense of calmness engulfed Arminius. Things were not looking good and he was probably going to die. But if he had to choose a location to die, this was it - sitting in the command chair of the most powerful military spaceship ever created. This was his ship, and it would die with him.

He watched the battlefield holographic screen as they approached the red dot. The screen showed that the Alpha One was now totally surrounded by a giant electrical field and the space debris. He had forgotten about the space debris. He looked at the video screen at the front of the Bridge. All he could see was clear space from the ship to a glow at the space debris point of origin. It appeared that the Alpha One was heading into a giant tunnel.

"Chirality, provide an update on the debris field. Has the ship been hit?"

"No projectiles have impacted the Alpha One."

"Why not?"

"Projectiles are on the outside of the electrical field."

"Create a composite of videos of projectiles and put it on the hologram screen."

The battlefield hologram screen disappeared and was replaced with a computer-generated image of the Alpha One surrounded by an electrical field. Outside of the field, space debris had accumulated. The debris was not uniform and there were still patches with no debris, but these were quickly being filled. Soon, the Alpha One would be completely encased.

Arminius thought, is it a shell or is it a tomb? "What is the estimated time of arrival at the debris point of origin?"

"Sixteen minutes, sir."

What does one do with the last sixteen minutes of their life? Does one call family and friends? Even if he had them, there was no way to connect. Does one scribble down notes for posterity? The entire ship would soon be destroyed - there would be no record of the notes. Does one read a book, watch a show, or check a newscast? None of that really matters. He could have gone to the dining room and ordered a multicourse dinner with a fine wine, but he really was not hungry and, with the ship shaking, it felt more secure being harnessed in the commander chair.

"Chirality, access the music library and play the 'Ode of Braxis'."

The silence in the ship was replaced by the booming sounds of the 'Ode of Braxis.' It was one of Arminius's favorites.

▲ ▲ ▲

Sixteen minutes later, they entered the hole. The holograph screen showed that the Alpha One, like a seed inside a pod, was now totally encased by the space debris. Arminius checked the ships sensors just before they entered the hole. The ship's speed was off the chart. The Alpha One was the fastest military ship in the Binary Star system, but the current speed was way beyond its engine capabilities. The engines were still showing operation at ten percent power. Arminius had selected that speed so they would have some maneuverability in case they needed to dodge obstacles. So much for that idea - there was no longer any way to see the obstacles. Arminius was worried about the ability of the Alpha One's hull to be able to withstand the stresses at the great speeds. Even minute particles could do serious damage at high velocities, and the Alpha One was designed with minimal shielding. Then he remembered the shell. The shell was no doubt acting as a shield and protecting the Alpha One.

Why was he being protected? Was it a natural phenomenon? It sure seemed odd that a natural phenomenon would occur just in time to protect him when he entered the hole. What if it wasn't natural, what if it was by design? If it was by design, then who designed it and where were they? It certainly was not any technology from the Binary Star system. What other possibilities were there? The religious nuts and alien-believing lunatics quickly came to mind. The ancient texts referred to The Creators and the forbidden texts mentioned the presence of an alien race. Both had widely different beliefs, but there was one thing on which they both agreed – some type of intelligent life existed outside of his small corner of the universe.

Arminius did not believe in the religious or alien stuff, but he could not explain why he was being protected. He had gone against the covenant and had traveled to a forbidden place, so why protect him? But what if this wasn't protection, what if instead this was some sort of punishment? Was he now being punished? There was no punishment greater than death, or was there? But wait, he thought, what if he was already dead? How did he know he was alive? He looked around the ship and saw instrument lights that were blinking. Did that prove he was alive? How could he prove he was still alive?

"Chirality, what is the name of this ship?"

"The Alpha One," responded the familiar female voice.

"What is our location?"

"Unknown, sir."

There, he thought, that proves it. I am still alive. Or am I? This could all be a dream. Maybe he had passed out somewhere. Maybe there was no giant tunnel. Maybe this was all just a bad dream.

He looked at the sensor readings – they were gibberish. Where was he? Was he alive? The questions plagued him over and over as the entombed Alpha One continued its journey.

▲ ▲ ▲

The ride was turbulent and the ship shook every few minutes. After much logical thinking, Arminius developed a working hypothesis. He decided that either:

1. He was alive, so it was okay to move about the ship
2. He was dead, so moving about the ship was okay
3. He was dreaming, so he could move around the ship in his dream, or
4. He was in a transitory state between life and death, in which case, it would be okay to move around the ship.

He noted that the clock on the Bridge and the sensors inside the ship appeared to be working, as were the ship's dining facilities. This last discovery was particularly important as he was filling hunger pains. Arminius took that as a positive sign that he was still alive and began feeling cautiously optimistic, as he headed to the dining room.

For three days, according to the ship's clock, they traveled. Then the abrupt shaking from the turbulent ride gradually decreased. Arminius checked the instrument readings and noted that the Alpha One's speed was now back on the charts. Shortly thereafter the turbulence ceased.

"Chirality, what is our location?"

"Unable to determine."

The reply was not unexpected. The outside sensor readings were still blocked by the debris shell.

"Collision imminent," Chirality suddenly announced.

There was an abrupt bump and Arminius went flying across the Bridge. "Kill the engines!" he shouted. Arminius slowly picked himself off the floor and returned to the commander's chair and fastened his harness.

Apparently, thought Arminius, the seedpod had come to a halt. It was time to take a look outside.

"Battlefield screen up!" commanded Arminius.

The battlefield hologram appeared.

Arminius marked coordinates. "Activate laser."

"Laser powering up, available in sixty seconds."

The sixty seconds flew by quickly as Arminius selected a target in front of the ship. "Twenty-five percent power, ten seconds, continuous blast, fire!"

The ship's laser fired at a spot directly in front of the ship. A small opening appeared in the shell. Arminius checked the sensor readings and they were still gibberish. He changed the laser target.

"Twenty-five percent power, ten seconds, continuous blast, fire!"

A second small hole appeared in the shell. Sensor readings were still gibberish.

Arminius repeated the procedure three more times until a large enough hole was created for the ship's sensors to provide data that made sense. Arminius reviewed the data. It looked like he was off world, somewhere in space at an unknown location, which was not too surprising.

Over the next several hours, Arminius used the ship's lasers to chip holes in the shell. Finally, a hole large enough for the Alpha One to pass through was created.

"Start engines, five percent power," he commanded.

"Engines started, five percent power," confirmed Chirality.

"Manual control." Arminius took control of the ship's navigation as the Alpha One gradually emerged from the shell.

Once clear, Arminius ordered a high-level sensor scan. The scan took five minutes.

"Plot ship location."

"Unable to determine," replied Chirality.

"How much time will it take for an in-depth full mapping scan?"

"Twelve hours and sixteen minutes, sir."

"Initiate full mapping scan." Arminius headed to his quarters – it had been days since he last slept.

▲ ▲ ▲

When Arminius returned to the Bridge, the mapping was complete. Not surprisingly, there were no record of the Alpha One's location in the ship's database. They were on the fringes of a single star system. Space debris was all around them. Arminius could not tell if this was the normal emulsion that occurred with debris at the gravitational boundaries of stars or if this was material that had passed through the hole with them. The map showed that there were multiple planets in this star system. The largest ones were barren and inhospitable. Simulations showed that some of the planets closer to the star might be able to support life forms like Arminius. It would be worth checking out. After all, what else was there to do?

"Chirality, plot a course toward the fourth planet from the sun," commanded Arminius, "Sixty-five percent power."

"Course plotted, sixty-five percent power."

"What is the estimated time of arrival?"

"Ten days, two hours, and four minutes."

Arminius retired to his quarters. He was now the greatest explorer the Binary Star system had ever seen, but would anyone ever know of his accomplishments?

CHAPTER 5

THE OTHER SIDE

For the next several days, the Alpha One's trip from the fringes of the star system was uneventful. This suddenly changed.

"Possible hostile craft detected," announced Chirality.

"View screen on", commanded Arminius. The large view screen instantly appeared in the middle of the Bridge. A small white spec was in the distance. It was not possible to make out any details.

The Alpha One had passed the orbit of the sixth planet. There was a large amount of space debris between the fourth and fifth planet. The object appeared near the debris field.

"Lock-in interception course…Engines at one hundred percent… Battlefield hologram on."

"Course set, engines at one hundred percent," confirmed Chirality as the battlefield hologram screen came to life.

"Estimated time of interception?"

"Eight hours and forty-six minutes."

▲ ▲ ▲

The trip home has been going well thought Lantos the day after they left the orbit of the third planet. Stopping in the jungle to see the colony of lemurs had been a good idea. Pascal had not asked a single question about the hunt or the MED, but he talked non-stop about the lemur colony. Lantos was glad to answer all of his questions. He really wanted Pascal to have good memories of the trip. Meanwhile he basked in his own remembrances – the glory of the kill. He had done such an excellent job. He replayed in his mind over and over every detail of the hunt. It was exhilarating. And to think, he was getting paid large sums of money to do something he really enjoyed – killing.

The high-speed galactic highway connector was located between the fourth and fifth planets and they were heading that way now. Once there, they could travel home or to other parts of the galaxy at tremendous speeds. One could always tell when one was near the entrance to the galactic highway connection system by the large amount of rubble present. When the connectors were flushed out, which had to be done periodically, it was always easier to dump the rubble near the opening instead of hauling it away. The environmentalists objected to this and liked to publicize how this damaged the landscape, but moving the material would incur additional costs. It was always easy to complain when the money to fix the problem was coming out of someone else's pocket.

Suddenly alarms started flashing and the relaxed mood in the spacecraft quickly changed. Lantos had purchased an illegal long-range detector from the black market and installed it on his ship. It gave an early warning of the presence of The Authorities, or anyone else that happened to be traveling in the sector. They may have been in a remote part of the galaxy, but someone else was definitely out there.

They were currently in the open with nowhere to hide. They needed to find a safe location. The rubble from the galactic highway would provide such a place, but that was a two-day journey. Lantos reviewed his options:

1. He had no large weapons on board, only hand weapons. The ship was equipped with a firing port, from which he could fire his laser rifle, but the Lemur Federation patrol ships hired by The Authorities to patrol this region were armored, so he would only be able to inflict minor damage. Talk about serious consequences – it was bad to be caught poaching, it was really

bad to be in possession of MED, but that was nothing compared to what would happen if he was charged with attacking a Lemur Federation patrol ship. Everyone knew that you don't mess with the Lemur Federation. If he was captured after firing at them, he would be looking at a long prison term, and that was a big if, since the Lemur Federation patrols were known for saving taxpayer's money by administrating their style of frontier justice.
2. He could make a run for it and try to escape by hiding out in the galactic highway rubble. He might be able to evade a single Lemur Federation patrol ship, but if the patrol ship called for backup, his chances against a Lemur Federation dragnet were not good. There was also the risk that having to call for a dragnet would piss off the patrol ship, and that could lead to frontier justice.
3. He could kill his power and drift through space. Perhaps the patrol ship would mistake him for a space rock. If it did approach him, he could claim ship damage and thank the patrol ship for the rescue. However, to make this sound plausible, he would need to dump his prized MED, damage his ship's engine, and disable his emergency communication system. It would be a very costly alternative.
4. He could retreat to the third planet, find a place to stash the MED, and hide out. If found, he could tell the patrol ship that they were on an educational trip and try to appeal to their 'wild oats' instincts.

His mind made up, Lantos abruptly turned the spaceship around, increased its speed to the maximum, and raced toward the third planet. The single moon of the third planet, he thought, should be a good place to stash his MED.

As they accelerated toward their new destination, Lantos studied his long-range detector. The familiar symbol of the Lemur Federation patrol ship emerged from the rubble near the high-speed galactic highway connector. He expected it to begin pursuit, but it was going in the opposite direction. Suddenly, a second much larger symbol appeared, the likes of which Lantos had never seen.

▲   ▲   ▲

"Projectile launched from hostile craft," reported Chirality.

Arminius observed the battlefield hologram. The hostile ship was very small, much smaller than a Cub and possibly smaller than a Buggy. Something that insignificant surely could not harm the Alpha One, but nonetheless, he made plans to destroy it when it was within laser range.

"Lock-on course and pursue hostile craft." The hostile craft was still several hours away.

"Incoming message from projectile," announced Chirality.

"Translate," ordered Arminius.

"WARNING...YOU ARE TRESPASSING IN AN ENVIRONMENTALLY SENSITIVE AREA...THIS AREA IS PROTECTED BY THE LEMUR FEDERATION...EXIT IMMEDIATELY...WARNING... YOU ARE TRESPASSING IN AN ENVIRONMENTALLY SENSITIVE AREA...THIS AREA IS PROTECTED BY THE LEMUR FEDERATION...EXIT IMMEDIATELY..."

"Continue pursuit of hostile craft," commanded Arminius. When they were within five hundred miles of the projectile, it was blasted into oblivion by the Alpha One's laser.

The Lemur Federation patrol ship, promptly changed course and headed toward the safety of the galactic highway rubble.

The Alpha One continued its pursuit.

The patrol ship entered the field of rubble.

When the Alpha One reached the outer edges of the field of rubble, Arminius studied the battlefield hologram. There was no sign of the patrol ship. He could enter the rubble and try to find the ship, but why? The ship was obviously not a threat to the Alpha One. Maybe he should do some research before he started chasing down unknown ships in this universe.

"Chirality, conduct a high-level life form scan. Are there type one life forms on any of the planets in this star system?"

A few minutes later, the computer responded, "Type one life forms detected on the third planet."

"Compatibility?" asked Arminius

"Similar to Home World and Plugaria."

Interesting, Arminius thought, a potential world to conquer. "Lock in course for the third planet. What is estimated time of arrival?"

"Twenty-three hours and seventeen minutes at current speed. Do you want to increase speed?"

Arminius checked his engine speed. He was already at one hundred percent power. "Negative. Maintain current speed and conduct a long-range scan of the planet. I want to know everything possible about this world, its inhabitants, and its military capabilities."

Raw geophysical data began flashing across the central view screen. Arminius's interest began to wane after the first hour. Much of the data was mathematical gibberish that the computer would eventually put together in a model. Arminius took a break to eat in the conference room. He returned to the commander's chair and watched as endless streams of data poured across the screens. His eyes were glazing over when the computer suddenly announced, "Possible hostile craft detected."

Arminius studied the battlefield hologram. "Could it be space debris?"

"It is a single object," replied Chirality, "96.2 percent of the time space debris consists of multiple objects."

The craft was slowing down and going into orbit around the third planet's moon.

"Possible hostile craft has changed direction and speed," reported Chirality.

Space debris does not change direction or speed, thought Arminius. "Set intercept course."

▲ ▲ ▲

Lantos looked at his long-range detector again. It was probably the hundredth time he had checked it since the initial alarm. At first, a wave of panic had swept across him when he thought The Authorities had found them. Then good luck appeared in the form of a second symbol and, shortly thereafter, the Lemur Federation patrol ship symbol disappeared. He was not sure if the patrol ship had been destroyed, if it had escaped to the galactic highway, or if it was hiding in the rubble. Unfortunately, the good news did not last long - the new symbol had detected their ship and was in hot pursuit.

What is it, thought Lantos, that activates the pursuit instinct in all creatures? He had seen it thousands of times – once an animal starts running, other animals follow. This time, he was the running animal, but had there been any other alternative? He had been out in open space where there was no protection.

Lantos's fear of his unknown pursuer was matched by his fascination. What was this mysterious ship that pursued the Lemur Federation patrol ship and was now chasing him at three times his maximum speed? Based on his calculations, it appeared they would be able to arrive at a hideout location an hour before the unknown ship, but where would they hide? There were many potential places on the surface of the third planet, but the planet's atmosphere would interfere with his ship's long-range sensors. He would have no way of knowing when the unknown pursuer was gone. How long would he need to stay on the planet's surface before it was safe to leave and how would he ever know more about this new mysterious spacecraft? Another possible hideout location was on the third planet's moon. It had no atmosphere, so there would be no problems with long-range sensor interference. The debate in his mind was short-lived, curiosity won and he headed to the moon.

Suddenly a wave of mortality overcame Lantos. "Pascal, you remember how to fly this ship, don't you? It has a lot of idiosyncrasies."

"Of course, Uncle. You do recall letting me fly it on the way here and I have flown my parent's ship many times. Are we getting a little senile?" he joked.

"And you know about the navigation system and the high-speed galactic highway?"

"Yes, Uncle." Pascal sighed. "But don't be worried about my flying skills at a time like this. If we are destroyed by the unknown ship, we will both be dead and if the ship is damaged, no one is going to be able to fly anywhere."

"Yes, you are correct nephew." Lantos gave him a comforting smile, but he was not calm inside. The weight of their survival was all on his shoulders – his skills would determine if they lived or died.

▲ ▲ ▲

Chirality had been compiling a colossal amount of data on the third planet. The ship had been designed for battlefield scenarios, but as every tactician knew, knowledge of the terrain was immensely important in developing battle plans. The preliminary model was now complete. The Alpha One was eight hours away from the third planet when Arminius reviewed the results.

The most recent data confirmed the previous long-range scans – the planet was very similar to both Home World and Plugaria. Arminius would be able to comfortably live on the planet without any artificial support.

Technologically speaking, the planet was about five hundred years behind Home World and Plugaria. There was a ring of satellites around the planet, but this world had not yet developed any large spaceships for commerce or military purposes. There was no indication of any laser weapons. Most of the weaponry was explosives and small projectiles, which could do no harm to the Alpha One, even with its minimal shielding.

Somewhat surprising, was the detection of large concentrations of BAC-431. This was one of the most poisonous substances on Home World and even small dosages could cause sudden death. Arminius's thoughts switched to the spaceship they were pursuing. "Chirality, what is the current location of the possibly hostile craft?"

"Craft is on a course to the third planet's moon."

"Analysis of ship's capabilities?"

"Mass is one fourth the size of a buggy. Top speed is thirty-five percent of recommended Alpha One cruising speed."

That is incredibly fast with such a small engine thought Arminius. I wonder what type of engine it has. "What about weaponry?"

"Unknown," answered Chirality, "Based on the mass and engine requirements for the top speed, there is only limited room for weaponry."

Arminius developed a working theory. This was a primitive world protected by a more advanced civilization. He had received a warning from a scout ship patrolling the outer regions of the star system. He had penetrated the outer layer of security and was now approaching the inner layer of security. The ship providing the inner layer of security knew that it was no match for the Alpha One and was now looking for a place to hide. He would now hunt it down, find out as much as he could about this planet's protectors, and then destroy the guardian ship. It was important to send a clear message to the planet's defenders – they were no match for him, he was the new leader of this star system.

"Plot orbit around the moon and conduct a full scan for all life forms."

▲ ▲ ▲

Lantos surveyed the area on the dark side of the moon. It was so barren, where could he hide? He was overcome with second-guessing. Maybe he should have chosen to hide on the third planet. It was much larger and they could have easily mingled with the local population. Then his hunter's mind took control. It was important to know as much as possible about one's adversary. He could not have learned that on the planet's surface. He had learned much from hunting all kinds of animals, now it was time to put that knowledge to good use.

Lantos piloted the craft in a series of loops and backtracking maneuvers to avoid leaving a clear trail. He attached the laser rifle to the ship's gun port and fired on the moon at multiple locations, which stirred up wisps of moon dust while leaving a heat signature. Finally, he headed into a canyon and selected a landing location behind some craggy rocks. He cut all power except for minimal life support, and waited.

▲ ▲ ▲

The Alpha One slowly entered orbit around the moon and, with its array of sophisticated sensors, began scanning the terrain. It was not long before it located the trail and general area of the unknown spacecraft and intensified its search.

▲ ▲ ▲

From his hidden location, Lantos got an occasional glimpse of the Alpha One as it swept the area. It was enormous - maybe one hundred times larger than his ship. He had never seen anything like it before. What race was on this massive ship and where did they come from?

▲ ▲ ▲

After twelve hours, it became apparent to Arminius that he was not going to find his prey. It was time for a change in tactics.

"Chirality, identify potential locations in this region where the spacecraft could be hiding and put on the battlefield screen."

Hundreds of locations appeared on the hologram screen marked in red.

"Set laser on scatter and attack each target." One by one, each of the targets was blasted.

▲ ▲ ▲

Lantos and Pascal watched in horror as a rock formation across from them glowed from the laser attack. The powerful laser blasts scarred the moon's surface and slowly followed a course that was heading directly toward them.

"What should we do Uncle?" asked a very worried Pascal.

Lantos calmly replied, "If we run, we are dead." As a hunter, he had used similar techniques to smoke out his quarry. "Our only hope is to hold our position."

The laser continued to creep lethally toward them. A few seconds later, the area around them glowed and the interior of the spacecraft got hot, very hot. Then, all of a sudden, it was over - the deadly laser beam departed as it continued on its quest to scorch the next target. As the spacecraft cooled, a greatly relieved Pascal let out a deep breath, "Whew Uncle, that was a close one. How did you know we would survive?"

Lantos did not know that they would survive, but he could not tell that to Pascal. "It is basic thermodynamics." Now Lantos did not know anything about thermodynamics, but he did know how to embellish stories. "Heat flows from hot to cold. After we warmed up, we were too hot for the heat, so it found a different path to the cold."

Fortunately, there were no engineers on board or they would have talked on and on ad infinitum about how the canyon walls had reduced the angle of the laser attack, how the nearby rock formations were a source of radiant insulation and acted as a heat sink, how the surface area of the spacecraft exposed to the laser was small which limited heat transfer, how the laser had not had sufficient contact time to damage the ship, etc., etc.

▲   ▲   ▲

A few hours later, Arminius abandoned his efforts to smoke out his prey. It was small and insignificant he thought, and who knows, it may have been destroyed or disabled. Even if it did survive, it was no match for the Alpha One – the greatest and most powerful military spaceship ever created. Arminius placed the Alpha One in orbit around the third planet and began a detailed scan of the planet below.

Lantos waited twenty-four hours before cautiously venturing from his hiding place. He checked the long- range detector to make sure the gigantic adversary was on the far side of the third planet, then quickly maneuvered his ship into orbit around the third planet, and hid amidst a field of satellites.

CHAPTER 6

THE MOST IMPORTANT QUESTION IN THE UNIVERSE

Roger and Daniel left the Cosmic Cannon and returned to Roger's office. After they sat down, Roger said, "I believe you have one more question for me?"

Daniel had a surprised look on his face, "Yes I do, but how did you know?" The look of surprise quickly turned into a look of embarrassment. "I am sorry, I keep forgetting to who I am talking. Thank you for answering my seven questions. You are, of course, absolutely correct. I do have one more question - what is going to happen to me?"

"Deep down inside, people are curious and have their seven questions for God," began Roger, "but they are all most concerned with the ultimate question – what is going to happen to them?"

Daniel was intensely interested and sat upright on the edge of his seat.

"First, you are still alive. So, you are a case of matter in a spiritual world. This cannot last. I have to send you back to Earth."

"Will my mind be wiped? Will I be able to remember this visit?"

"This is Heaven, not a UFO," smiled Roger. "We do not wipe minds here."

"Well, I thought there may be top secret things here – things people on Earth are not supposed to know."

"That would only be a problem, if people believed you. Can you imagine what life would be like on Earth if everyone knew, beyond a shadow of a doubt, that they contained an internal spirit that would someday go to Heaven? There would be a complete breakdown of society, and life, as you know it, would come to a screeching halt. But there is no need to worry, lots of people before you have come and taken tours. When they returned to Earth no one ever took them seriously. Their sayings were veiled in mystical secrecy or people thought they were just plain nuts. The same will happen to you, when you tell others about Heaven."

"Will I have a special mission back on Earth?"

"Actually, that is what I wanted to talk to you about. That is why I called you to Heaven in the first place."

"As long as it does not involve public speaking. I hate public speaking and I am not a preacher. There are lots of people out there that can do a much better job."

"Relax, it is nothing at all like that." Roger paused. "I need to have someone killed."

Daniel's jaw dropped and he momentarily sat stunned in total silence.

"Say what? You want me to kill somebody?" Daniel was trembling as he processed the implications of the request. "I can see it now, I will be locked up in the nut house, or worse, in Texas we are talking death row!"

"Maybe kill is a strong word. Let's put this in engineering terms and say that I have a filtration problem."

"A filtration problem?" Daniel had a confused look.

"From time to time, debris from another universe enters my universe."

"That is to be expected," nodded Daniel, now in a slightly more relaxed state. "Material does flow between universes."

"This material is living and needs to be destroyed. It is currently traveling to Earth and, if not stopped, will contaminate the planet."

"Couldn't you arrange some kind of cosmic weather event to remove the impurity?"

"I could arrange for some sort of galactic collision," agreed Roger, "but this time I think it is part of a controlled test. If I directly interfere, the test will just be repeated."

"A test? A controlled test?" Daniel was incredulous. "Who would conduct such a test?"

"I am not entirely sure, but they will no doubt want to see results."

"Well, who is coming to Earth? Is it some weird-shaped monster? Is it a giant insect?"

"No, it is definitely humanoid. Here is what it looks like." The back wall dissolved and a holographic image of Arminius floated across the room. "It looks a lot like us, although it no doubt has different internals, since it was not part of my creation."

"So how do I take it out, eh…should I say, how do I filter it?"

"It is entirely up to you - after all, you are a seven sevens."

"How is it getting to Earth?"

A three-dimensional image of the Alpha One floated across the room. "This is the Alpha One." Roger pointed at the image. The Alpha One has a twelve-hundred-foot-long engine tube and a twelve-hundred-foot-long laser tube, which can cause massive destruction from five hundred miles away."

"Wait a minute." A look of disbelief swept across Daniel's face. "I have only seen lab-scale lasers and you want me to take on an alien armed with this super weapon?"

"Yes, that is your assignment."

"What happens if it is not stopped?"

"If it is not stopped, it will contaminate the human race."

"I understand in a chemical process how a new impurity can make a product out-of-specification, but how can this affect the human race?"

"Multiple ways. Widespread destruction, disruption of the world order, inbreeding – it could do some really serious harm."

"And if it does? What would you do?"

"The same as you do in your chemical plants. Throw out the batch and start anew."

"You, you would wipe out all human life on Earth?" Daniel was incredulous.

"Been there, done that," said Roger, and he wasn't joking.

Sheer terror spread across Daniel's entire body as he realized the implications of his assignment. "So, so if I can't stop the alien, all human life on Earth will have to be trashed?"

"I have faith in my seven sevens…and you did say that you are not good at preaching."

CHAPTER 7

THE OLD MAN'S ADVICE

Daniel stopped by to see his grandmother before he left. She was busy with sunsets, but broke away.

"Enjoy your life on Earth." She gave him a big hug. "Enjoy the breeze on your face, the good times, as well as the struggles. I will definitely be at your Homecoming with all of your friends and relatives when you return."

"Thanks, Grandma. Every time I see a sunrise or sunset, I will think of you. There is one person I would like to see before I leave. Could you arrange a meeting?"

▲ ▲ ▲

Daniel stepped up on the porch of a rickety old wooden house near the edge of a pine forest. A solitary older gentleman was rocking slowly on the porch swing. An empty wooden rocking chair was sitting next to him.

"I understand you want to talk to me," said the stately gentleman.

"Yes, sir," smiled Daniel, "I really need some advice."

"Always glad to give advice. Have a chair. What can I do for you?"

Daniel sat down next to the gentleman and began slowly rocking. "I hear you know something about overcoming incredible odds."

"Maybe."

"And you know something about uniting people for a common cause."

"Perhaps."

"I have a problem."

"Yep," agreed the gentleman.

"One of the strongest forces in the universe is coming into my territory."

"Yep...been there."

"If not stopped, it could destroy the way of life."

"Yep." The gentleman slowly rocked, "Sounds familiar."

"How, how did you stop it?"

There was a long pause as they both rocked. After a few minutes, the gentlemen spoke. "Do you know about equilibrium?"

Images of organic chemistry, reaction kinetics, and heat transfer equations flashed though Daniel's mind. "A bit."

"The universe," he paused, "She like de' equilibrium."

"Makes sense to me," nodded Daniel.

"So, you got this really, really strong force?"

"Yes."

"Then there has got to be a really, really strong counter force."

"But what if it is not there?"

"Oh, it be there," replied the gentleman. "You may not be able to see it, but it be there."

"So, what do I do with this force?"

"Just be there."

"What?" Daniel had a questioning look. "Don't I need to direct it?"

"Nope, you justs needs to be there."

"But how will the mighty force be destroyed?"

"Every mighty force has a weakness. You have got to find the weak point in their lines."

"Won't the mighty force destroy me?"

"Perhaps," remarked the gentleman, "Often does."

"How do I get close to this mighty force? It is incredibly strong."

"The mighty underestimate their prey. The hound don't expect to be attacked by the hare. Know your opponent and study him good before you attack."

Daniel had been hoping for some concrete advice, but this was gibberish. He did not see how he could use the advice.

"I have to go back to Earth now. Are there any more tips you can give me for my upcoming battle?"

The gentleman paused, "I always found it was best to attack with the sun at my back." He paused some more. "And I always liked the lay of the land at San Jacinto. Maybe you could go there and visit it for me."

Daniel thanked the gentleman and left. He had always been a great fan of General Sam Houston – the underdog, the winner of the battle of San Jacinto, the first president of the Republic of Texas. However, he could not see how this advice would do him any good in a battle with the most powerful invader the world had ever seen.

CHAPTER 8

THE REAL WORLD

Daniel woke up in the Stamford Chemical plant nursing station. He had been there many times for physicals and lab work, but this was the first time he had been there for a medical incident. Even though the door was closed, he could hear a heated discussion between the plant nurse and his supervisor.

"We do not want to make this an OSHA Recordable incident!" emphasized Boss Man vehemently.

"My patient's health is the highest priority!" countered Nurse Betty just as fervently.

"Do you know what happens when we have an OSHA Recordable?"

"I have heard it a million times," replied the plant nurse with rising anger, "From every single supervisor out here!"

"Our days-without-a-recordable streak is broken, I have to make a presentation to the site manager on the incident, and our insurance rates go up!" yelled Boss Man.

"You left out your performance bonus!" shouted the nurse, "If your people are hurt, you lose points on your annual performance review! Let me tell you, I could care less about your performance review, I want healthy people!"

Realizing things were not going his way, Boss Man changed tactics. He switched to a calmer tone of voice and persuasively asked, "Hey, what's the big deal? Daniel fell down and may have a few scratches."

"A few scratches?" Nurse Betty was aghast. "He passed out in a chemical plant! If Ernesto hadn't seen him with the plant surveillance camera, he might still be lying there!"

Daniel got up off the bed in the nurse's station and opened the door. Boss Man and Nurse Betty immediately became silent. "Hey guys, I am feeling fine."

"Daniel," instructed the plant nurse firmly, "You have got to sit down." She took him to the chair she normally used for taking blood samples. "Tell me what happened."

"I, I was walking out to the plant, and I saw a blast of bright light. That is the last thing I recall. I, I must have passed out."

"You certainly did," agreed Nurse Betty.

"That is the same time the Hydra methanol plant next door was hit," added Boss Man. "Their methanol, formaldehyde, formic acid, and sodium formate facilities were destroyed."

"What?" Daniel was astonished by the news.

"You may have seen something related to the attack," continued Boss Man.

"Attack? What makes you think it was an attack?"

"The official story for the public is that it was an industrial accident. We have been asked by Homeland Security to keep it quiet and report any unusual activity, but they suspect it was an attack and have asked us for any assistance we can offer. Did you see anything else, any movements, shells fired?"

"No, just the bright lights."

"Others," noted Boss Man, "have also reported seeing bright lights. It has all been very strange."

"So, are you feeling better now?" asked Nurse Betty consolingly.

"I think he is well enough," interrupted Boss Man, "to work from home for the rest of the day." Boss Man walked over to Daniel, looked him in the eye, and slowly and forcefully said, "Daniel, we do not want this to become an OSHA Recordable. Can you go straight home? No doctor visit and no prescription medications."

Nurse Betty nudged Boss Man aside and stepped between him and Daniel. Loudly and emphatically, she let them know who was in charge, "Hello, I and I alone make the calls here. Daniel, I want you to stay here a while longer for monitoring." She gave Boss Man a go-to-hell look, "I, and I alone will then decide if you need to see a doctor or get prescription meds."

CHAPTER 9

THE IMPOSSIBLE QUEST

Joshua stopped by Daniel's apartment after work. "Hey man, how are you doing? That must have been rough, you look shook up."

"Physically," replied Daniel, "I am in perfect shape. Mentally, I am all shook up."

"What's going on?"

"It's a crazy story."

"And you think I am not used to hearing crazy stories? I am all ears."

"When I passed out, I went to this incredible place."

"Was it better than the bars on Sixth Street in Austin?"

"I may have gone to Heaven."

"Did you ask God your seven questions?" Joshua asked excitedly.

"As a matter of fact, I did."

"Well let's hear them. What did you ask and what were the answers and why are you shook up?"

"Heaven was great, I learned a lot from my answers. I will tell you sometime."

"I can't wait. Now why are you all shook up?"

"I was asked by God to do something."

"Oh no, you are going to become a preacher. I knew it. I hope you won't be like John the Baptist and go off into the wilderness eating locusts and honey and living like Big Foot."

"It is worse than that." Daniel paused. "What if I told you an alien was coming to Earth?"

"Yes!" Joshua shouted. "I always knew they were out there!"

"And God told me I have to stop the alien."

"Oh boy, that must have been some bump to the head. Play the Twilight Zone music."

"I think I am going to need your help."

"You may need a lot more than that."

"Okay, let's analyze. After all, we are both engineers. There are two cases. Case one is I am hallucinating and case two is I am not hallucinating. Are you with me so far?"

"So far," nodded Joshua, "But just to be safe, you don't have any guns or sharp objects stashed around here, do you?"

"Now if an alien was coming to Earth, how would we know?"

"Yes!" exclaimed Joshua. "UFO's! This is my kind of conversation. I don't care if you are totally bonkers. How is it getting here? Is it in a spaceship, is it teleporting…?"

"It is in a twelve-hundred-foot-long spaceship."

"Twelve hundred feet? Wow! You do realize that is four football fields long?"

"Hello," said Daniel sarcastically, "I am an engineer and, even when I am shook-up, I can do simple math calculations in my head."

"I know you can. You and I have been to Space Center Houston and have seen the size of the original Apollo space capsule that went to the moon. Those sure were cramped quarters. Twelve hundred feet long is humongous. Does it have a cloaking device?"

"A cloaking device?"

"You know, something that makes the ship invisible."

"How should I know? All I saw was a floating image and God didn't mention any cloaking device."

"If it is not cloaked, we should be able to see it with a telescope."

Daniel rolled his eyes. "And where do we look? Do we just call up our local observatory and tell them that an alien spaceship may or may not be coming to Earth so drop whatever studies they are working on and take a look?"

"There is no need," interjected Joshua, "My guys look for UFO's every night."

"Your kooky conspiracy network?"

"My network of well-educated scientific professionals. And I am not so sure you can mock us anymore since you are now sounding more and more like one of us. What does the spaceship have in the way of weaponry?"

"It has a gigantic laser that is twelve hundred feet long and can destroy targets five hundred miles away."

"Five hundred miles? Whoa!" exclaimed Joshua. "That is way beyond anything we have."

"I didn't think we had any laser weapons."

"Officially, no but unofficially, you know – Area 51 and all that. Dude, you really need to spend more time exploring on the internet."

"So how does one take out a twelve-hundred-foot-long spaceship with a laser that has a range of five hundred miles?"

"You don't," said Joshua matter-of-factly.

"I am not sure you understand the significance. If not destroyed, the alien will interfere with Earth, and God will then destroy the Earth. It is not a good situation." Daniel began looking apprehensive again.

"Don't worry man. I'm with you. What I meant to say is that you don't destroy the spaceship. We don't have the capabilities. Oh, we have satellites in space that can be moved and maybe we could use them to knock out other satellites. There are probably top-secret killer satellites that are designed to do just that. So, do we send them after this huge spaceship? It is one thing to play bumper cars with a similar sized satellite, but in this case the principles of momentum are definitely not in our favor. So, we need something bigger. Do the leading nations of the world have top-secret military spaceships? Let's say they do. They could put nuclear weapons on those ships and crash them into the alien ship. But wait, the alien sees them coming and blows them up with its super laser while they are still five hundred miles away. And if it doesn't want to use its laser, all it has to do is run away for a while and then come back. We certainly don't have the technology to go chasing a super ship around the solar system. There is no way we can destroy the alien ship."

"You do realize that you are not making me feel any better."

"Hold on," assured Joshua, "I am not finished yet. What I have done is eliminate a course of action that will not work, so now we can devote our resources to a better alternative."

"Which is?"

"At some point in time, the alien has got to leave its ship. It is invincible when it is on its ship, but once it leaves…"

"So how do you know it will leave its ship?"

"Because God said it would." He paused, "Oh no, now you have me sounding loony. You were the one that talked with God, not me."

"Believe it or not, I understand," acknowledged Daniel. "Aboard the ship, the alien could do some serious damage, such as destroying cities with its laser weapon. But God is used to that. Volcanoes, hurricanes, meteors, and tornadoes have been wreaking havoc on mankind ever since the dawn of time and humans certainly do a pretty good job destroying things when they go to war. We struggle through tough times, recover, and move on, all the while our natural order doesn't change. But a technologically advanced super powerful alien…"

"You do know that all of this may have happened before?"

"Say what?"

"One does not find much in human history before 3,500 BC. Archeologists have found large underground rooms and there are lots of ancient stories about fire and brimstone falling from the sky. It is possible these were from an alien spaceship and that people moved underground to survive. It did not work then, and it will not work now. You have to have boots on the ground. The alien has got to leave its ship if it wants to control the world."

"I don't know about your wild history stories, but I do think God is worried about the boots on the ground part."

"So," said Joshua thinking out loud, "How do we know when the alien has arrived?"

"In a chemical process, if something unusual entered the process, we would look for a change. Maybe our product becomes out-of-specification, maybe some part of the process becomes plugged, or maybe there is a sudden change in temperature or pressure. Are you with me so far?"

"Way ahead of you buddy," replied Joshua. "When the Europeans came to America, they unknowingly brought diseases that wiped out lots of Native Americans. The Europeans had immunities in their systems that the Native Americans lacked. The massive flu epidemic during World War I was probably due to a large sudden movement of people. Whenever there is an epidemic, there is a possibility that an outsider is the root cause. The sudden AIDS epidemic in the 1980's may be due to aliens."

Daniel rolled his eyes. "I was with you until the AIDS epidemic. What about other indicators?"

"Another indicator is sudden technology changes. Just twenty years after the Roswell discovery we were building rocket ships to fly to the moon."

"I really think you should give our engineers some credit, but I see your point. Diseases and sudden technology changes can be due to outside influences. These take time to detect, what if we can't wait that long?"

"Why not?"

"What if inbreeding was a concern?"

"Inbreeding?" Joshua had a surprised look. "I am used to pictures of aliens with oblong shaped heads. HG Well's aliens were machines. Who would mate with them?"

"This alien looks just like us. It may have different internals."

"What? How do you know?"

"God showed me a picture. Well, it was kind of a picture. It was really an image that floated across the room."

"Ought oh, rut row, cue the Twilight Zone music again. Well, actually it makes sense. We are created in the image of God. It must be a good design so I can see why it would be a good design for other planets as well, and we are made for space travel."

"Actually," corrected Daniel, "The lemurs are made for space travel, at least according to Bio Bob."

"Who the hell is Bio Bob?" Joshua had a perplexed look.

"He and his team in Heaven design new life forms. You were right by the way - evolution is a bunch of crap."

"So, the alien looks just like us?"

"Yes. God said it wasn't of his creation, so it may have different internals."

"Oh shit." Joshua suddenly looked very worried, "This is a whole different level of complication."

"How's that?"

"If he looks like us," he is going to want to take over the world."

"Not without a fight. Didn't you expect that?"

Joshua shook his head, "I was expecting a fight with some weird-looking alien creatures. It could be a lengthy fight, and we might have to go underground, but the fierce fighting human spirit would prevail."

"So, what's different?"

"Do you remember the anthropology lessons on how human's developed?"

"The text books show that monkeys evolved in multiple steps and became Neanderthal man and eventually Homo Sapiens, or something like that. There are a lot of theories, but like I told you, evolution is a bunch of crap. Every species is created by some type of intelligent design."

"It is not evolution," explained Joshua, "If an alien is physically similar to us and is able to mate with us and form a new species. If that species is protected, and I think a super laser weapon is a lot of protection, it could proliferate and spread across the globe. Eventually it would replace humans. There would be no massive battle, just a gradual shift over several generations. In nature, it happens all over the world every day – an invasive species moves into a new area and gradually takes over. In a few hundred years, the existing human race would be wiped out. No wonder God wants this alien destroyed."

"So, you see why I need some early indicator as to how to determine if an alien has arrived?"

"Well," smiled Joshua, "You always have the Internet, and…" he paused, "my kooky conspiracy network."

Daniel shook his head. "And you wondered why I am worried?"

CHAPTER 10

DRAGNET

After Joshua left, Daniel conducted internet searches on his computer until almost dawn. He learned everything he could about laser weapons, interbreeding with other species, history before 3,500 BC, hellfire and brimstone, and large underground archeological sites. He then did a long-shot search for 'unusual events today'. Before he went to bed, he sent an email to Boss Man saying that he was physically fine, but wanted to take a couple of days of vacation. It is hard to focus on work when the fate of humanity is in your hands.

He got up around noon and called Joshua, "Any word from your network?"

"It certainly created some excitement," Joshua reported. "Our amateur astronomers searched all night, but did not find anything. They will search again tonight."

Daniel had a quick lunch and then heard a knock at the door. Peeking through the peephole, Daniel saw two middle-aged men in suits. One looked to be about forty years old, was medium built, and had short dark hair. The other appeared to be in his mid-fifties, had a big frame, and thinning white hair. As Daniel opened the door, the younger of the two addressed him, "Hello Daniel, my name is Friday and this is Officer Gannon. We are part of a special branch of the FBI."

"Sergeant Joe Friday?" asked Daniel with a surprised look.

"Well actually it is Lieutenant Joseph Friday. How did you know?"

"Just a lucky guess. How do you know who I am?" He looked down at Lieutenant Friday's clipboard and saw a four-inch by four-inch glossy color photo of himself along with pages of what were probably background documents.

"It is our job to know," stated Officer Gannon tersely with a no-nonsense manner.

"We would like to ask you some questions," Friday politely requested. Without waiting for an answer, they pushed their way inside. "How about if we all sit down?" They moved to Daniel's sofa and recliner.

"Daniel," began Officer Gannon, "We have a report that you suffered an industrial accident yesterday afternoon at 2:37 PM. Is this correct?"

"I am not sure if I would call it an industrial accident. I saw a bright light and fainted. It had nothing to do with the chemical plant, except that I fell there."

Officer Gannon was taking notes, "Bright light, fell, may not be industrial accident."

"Just the facts," reminded Friday, "Just the facts."

"Why does the FBI care about me falling in a chemical plant?"

"We'll ask the questions," replied Officer Gannon curtly.

"Next door to Stamford Chemicals is Hydra, right son?" asked Friday.

"That is correct."

"Hydra had an outage yesterday about the same time, didn't they?"

"I, I guess so," answered Daniel. "I understand they lost their methanol production unit along with their formaldehyde, formic acid, and sodium formate production facilities. Is that what you are investigating?"

"*We* ask the questions," responded Officer Gannon sternly.

Friday continued, "Did you see anything flying through the air?"

"Like birds or planes?"

"Like drones or mortar shells," clarified Friday.

"No, just a really bright light."

"Daniel, has anything unusual been going on in your life?"

"I am a bit shaken up by yesterday's events."

"Anything else?" asked Friday.

"What else would there be?"

"What part of *we* ask the questions do *you* not understand?" snapped Officer Gannon.

"Daniel," Friday calmly continued, "We know that you conducted a lot of unusual internet searches last night."

"How, how do you..." He was interrupted by a very angry glare from Officer Gannon. "I was not aware that my internet searches were part of the FBI's business."

"It is when there is a potential threat to national security," explained Friday.

"How is my internet..." Once again, he was stopped by Officer Gannon's intimidating stare, "I do not see how my internet searches are a threat to national security."

"Maybe or maybe not," commented Friday as he opened up a plain manila envelope and pulled out an 8 x 10 glossy black and white photograph. "Daniel, have you ever seen this before?"

Daniel's eyes widened. It was a picture of the Alpha One. "It looks like a spaceship."

"Interesting," remarked Officer Gannon.

"Daniel," divulged Friday, "Before we arrived today, we showed that photo to ten different people and asked them the very same question. Do you want to know their responses?"

Before he could answer, Officer Gannon jumped in, "Three thought it could be a new toy, two thought it was an electrical device, two thought it was a mechanical gadget, one thought it was a cooking utensil, one thought it was some kind of hair curler, and one thought it was the reincarnation of Elvis. The last person was pretty stoned when we asked him."

"You are the only one to say spaceship," noted Friday. "Now why would that be?"

"A lot of amateur astronomers were searching last night for an alien spacecraft that was shaped just like this," added Officer Gannon. "Why would they search for something looking just like this?"

"Someone may have told them to search for it," suggested Friday, "And do you know who that person is?"

"It turns out that person is a good friend of yours. A fellow named Joshua Jones." Officer Gannon looked menacingly at Daniel, "And he just happens to have been here last night."

"Shortly after he left your apartment, a call was made from his cell phone, and the search for the spaceship began," declared Friday.

"Aren't cell phones wonderful?" marveled Officer Gannon as he pierced Daniel with his glaring eyes. "The engineers that invented them did a remarkable job. They are such amazing tools that law enforcement can use to spy on people."

"So," summarized Friday, "Here we are. We have run all kinds of background checks on you." He flipped the pages on his clipboard. "We even searched your medical records and blood sample reports. Yes, we know they took a blood sample from you yesterday to see if you were intoxicated or under the influence of drugs after your accident. So now we have two choices."

"Choice number one," Officer Gannon gave Daniel an intimidating stare as he talked, "is that we can beat the crap out of you until you talk." He had a crazed look in his eye as he repeatedly pounded his right fist into his left palm. "Personally, I kind of like that option."

"Choice number two," proposed Friday politely and professionally, "Is that you agree to share all of your information with us and become part of our task force. This is obviously a matter of great importance and we would certainly like to have you as part of our team."

"Hmm," thought Daniel, "Tough choice." He paused for a few seconds and looked at both of the agents. "I think I will choose option number two." He gazed harshly at Officer Gannon, "Since we are now on the same team, would it be okay if *now* I ask a few questions?"

"Of course," agreed Friday accommodatingly.

"Last night I heard that the amateur astronomers searched for, but could not find the spaceship. Why couldn't they find it?"

"They were looking in the wrong spot," replied Officer Gannon who all of a sudden was acting very friendly. "Typically objects in orbit are one hundred to two hundred miles above the Earth. The spaceship was found twenty-five hundred miles above the Earth."

"How do you know about this spaceship?" asked Friday.

Daniel paused. What should he tell them? He could make up a story. These guys, however, were very experienced and would no doubt see right through him. He decided to go with the truth, "I was told by God."

"Where were you when God told you?" inquired Friday matter-of-factly.

"I was in God's office in Heaven."

Officer Gannon quickly interjected, "Were you under the influence of..."

He was interrupted by Lieutenant Friday, "No need to go there, Officer Gannon, we have already seen the results of a full toxicological scan - he is clean." He turned toward Daniel, "Which God told you?"

"What, what do you mean which God?"

Officer Gannon jumped in again, "Was it the Christian God, Muslim God, Hebrew God, or some other god?"

"Why does that matter?"

Friday interrupted, "Officer Gannon, strike all references to God in the report."

"But why?" questioned Daniel, "I met with God."

"Regulations and procedures."

"Regulations and procedures?" Daniel had a perplexed look.

"Yes," said Friday, "We are now required to be politically correct when dealing with religious folks. There are all kinds of forms involved."

"Don't forget all of the sensitivity classes we had to go through," added Officer Gannon, "Can you imagine that? We now have to handle all the fucking nut jobs with kid gloves."

Friday gave him a glare, "Now Daniel, instead of saying God told you about this in his office, what if we just say that you were told in a dream? Everybody dreams so there will be fewer questions and much less paperwork."

"It is not my report."

"Good," continued Friday, "So what did you learn about the spaceship?"

"The spaceship has two tubes, each twelve hundred feet long. One tube is the engine and the other is a laser. The laser has a range of five hundred miles."

Friday looked over at Officer Gannon with raised eyebrows and nodded.

Officer Gannon spoke, "He may be a nut job, but the numbers do check out. Our experts estimate the length to be between eleven hundred and thirteen hundred feet. We had no idea why there were two tubes and the five-hundred-mile range is a match."

"Five-hundred-mile range is a match?" Daniel looked confused. "What do you mean?"

"The spacecraft was first detected by a spy satellite yesterday afternoon," disclosed Officer Gannon. "It approached to within four hundred miles of Earth, stayed for a few minutes, and then retreated to twenty-five hundred miles."

"When did this occur?"

"Between 2:10 and 3:10 yesterday afternoon," answered Friday, "the same time that Hydra was hit and the same time that you met with God, eh, had your dream."

"So, Hydra wasn't a terrorist attack?"

"The investigation is still in progress," disclosed Friday. "The plant did not shut down from any type of ordinary process upset. There were no signs of explosives or other trademarks of a traditional terrorist attack. There were, however, signs of an exceedingly high temperature conflagration. There was nothing like it in any of our databases. This is the first time we have heard about an alien laser with a range of five hundred miles."

"What do you know about the alien?" asked Officer Gannon.

"God showed me an image. He looks like us, but God said he may have different internals."

Officer Gannon spoke as he made notes, "Saw person of interest in dream. Can you describe the person to our sketch artist?"

"Sure, but why? Are you going to issue a be-on-the-lookout bulletin and send it to all the squad cars? We know where the bad guy is - he is in a fortress of a spaceship high above the Earth."

"Procedures," replied Friday, "Just following procedures."

CHAPTER 11

CONTACT

Joshua stopped by Daniel's apartment on his way home from work. "Your kooky conspiracy network has been infiltrated," Daniel informed him as soon as he arrived.

Joshua nodded, "I have always known that."

"And you were right - it is incredible the abilities the authorities have to spy on us."

"Big Brother is always watching," agreed Joshua, "and has been for a long, long time."

"Doesn't that bother you? Engineers invented cell phones and now they are being used to spy on us. That was not why they were invented."

"Not just cell phones. It happens with every invention."

"No way."

"Sure," explained Joshua, "as soon as an invention leaves the engineer's hands, it is considered for multiple applications. Criminal activities, sex, and violence are always high on the potential use list. The new invention is a benefit to some parts of society and a detriment to others."

"Have you heard anything new from your network?"

"Nothing today," Joshua paused. "So, it's network now? You're dropping the kooky conspiracy prefix?"

"Let's just say I have a greater appreciation," smiled Daniel. "I have been searching the internet all day for anomalies. Another chemical plant was hit along the Houston Ship Channel – one of Hydra's competitors. It also makes methanol, formic acid, formaldehyde, and sodium formate. Either our alien is targeting them or there are some economic terrorists out there that are trying to corner world markets."

▲ ▲ ▲

The Alpha One completed its sortie and reestablished orbit twenty-five hundred miles above the planet. The military assessment scans had not detected any significant laser weaponry on the planet, but after Arminius's Home World experiences, he did not want to take any chances. Arminius could not understand why there was so much toxic BAC-431 on this world. As a precaution, the Alpha One laser destroyed another BAC-431 production facility near Houston.

It was time to make contact with this primitive race and prepare them for his arrival. They did not know it yet, but soon he would be their absolute leader. His next step was to contact the planet's leader, but where does one look? The Alpha One's sensers had completed their scans and there was a tremendous amount of information in the database. Arminius reasoned that there were three factors that would determine the location of the world leader:

1. The leader would be located in a large population center,
2. The center would be militarily well protected, and
3. There would be symbols of power near the world headquarters

There were many large population centers on the planet. The highest concentration of BAC-431, one of the most lethal poisons on Home World, was in a population center known as Houston. Having such a powerful weapon near the center of power would no doubt discourage any revolt attempts. A second indicator that Houston was the world capital was that a search of the planet's space travel capabilities found that a very primitive spacecraft, after landing on the planet's moon, sent a communication - 'Houston...the Eagle has landed.' Surely communication would be with the planet's capital city. Last, but not least, the tallest obelisk in the world was near Houston. At the top of the obelisk was a giant star that looked the same when viewed from any direction. It was the exact same symbol that topped the Home World Obelisk – the center of power for the Home World Empire. Could it be that the headquarters for the leader of the third planet was beneath this obelisk?

▲ ▲ ▲

Daniel did not need to conduct a deep internet search that evening for the day's anomalies – the internet was filled with skywriting pictures from all over the world:

> 'CHANCELLOR IS COMING!' ... 'THE NEW WORLD LEADER' ... 'IN THREE DAYS' ... 'FIRM AND FAIR'

The skywriting messages were written in different languages with a variety of colors, sizes, and fonts. Interspersed among the writings was the star symbol, the same star that was on top of the San Jacinto Monument.

The internet was rife with conjecture. Was it a new fragrance, fashion line, car, or mattress? Manufacturing leaders and marketing executives from around the world were quizzed by the media. All denied any knowledge, which only fanned the rumors further.

The skywriting faded, but the next day new images appeared in skies all over the planet:

> 'CHANCELLOR IS COMING!' ... 'THE NEW WORLD LEADER'... 'IN TWO DAYS' ... 'FIRM AND FAIR'

The guesswork continued and the frenzy grew. The internet, television broadcasts, and the few people that still listened to radio were bombarded by theories from people 'in the know'. Some said this was the long forecasted Second Coming and churches were soon packed with religious services.

The next day, new sky writing images again appeared:

'CHANCELLOR IS COMING TOMORROW!' ... 'WORLD HEADQUARTERS 8:00 PM' ... 'FIRM AND FAIR'

The feverish speculation increased exponentially.

▲ ▲ ▲

Friday and Gannon stopped by Daniel's apartment that afternoon.

"Your alien friend is disrupting the world order," observed Gannon. "No one is working, they are all freaking out. If he keeps this up, he will destroy the world without firing a shot."

"He is not my friend," Daniel coldly corrected. "God gave me specific instructions – I need to kill him."

"We have been running computer image searches," reported Friday, "trying to pin down the meeting location. At first, we thought it might be at the United Nations headquarters in New York, but the symbols match..."

"The San Jacinto Monument," interrupted Daniel.

"Yes," agreed Gannon with a surprised look. "But how did you know? Was it the number of nearby chemical plants destroyed?"

"That is part of it. But I think that is why God chose me to kill the alien – it is going to be right in my backyard."

"We'll have your back," assured Friday comfortingly. "The San Jacinto Monument will be on lockdown tomorrow afternoon with elite troops positioned nearby. This alien has got to be stopped!"

▲ ▲ ▲

Joshua stopped by Daniel's apartment after work that evening. "Here are the items you requested. There was no one in the lab to ask any questions. I guess they were all at home watching the news."

"Thanks Joshua, you have been a true friend. There is a good possibility that I won't be coming back."

"Are you going to the San Jacinto Monument tomorrow evening?"

Daniel had a startled look. "Yes, but how did you know?"

"Hello, have you already forgotten about *our* kooky conspiracy network? Anyway, I would like to go with you. All of my life, I have wanted to see an alien, it is an incredible opportunity."

"Sorry, you can't go. There is a good possibility that seeing the alien would cost you your life."

"I'll gladly take the chance," Joshua eagerly replied. "It is the opportunity of a lifetime! Who knows, maybe I could help you kill your alien."

"I certainly appreciate the offer but, it is not the alien that would get you. The entire park will be on complete lockdown tomorrow afternoon and the place will be swarming with elite commando units."

CHAPTER 12

BATTLE PREPARATIONS

Friday and Gannon were in a nondescript business office located on the upper floors of a glass skyscraper high above downtown Houston. A dozen or so computer screens were filled with data as the office personnel hastily answered phones and analyzed the data. They appeared to be just ordinary office workers and they were dressed in typical office attire. All of them had Top Secret security clearances. Behind closed doors in an adjoining conference room, Friday and Gannon were talking over a secure video link with General Z in Washington D.C. The general was in his mid-fifties, had short gray hair, a square jaw, and was always dressed in his desert camouflage uniform. The general projected the image of a seasoned battle-tested veteran. Friday, who always wore a dark suit with a white buttoned-down shirt and narrow black tie, wondered, but never asked, why General Z wore camouflage so far from the battlefield.

"So," began General Z, "you are using this young man ... what's his name ... I believe it is Daniel ... as your bait to draw out the alien?"

"Yes," confirmed Friday. "His name is Daniel, but sir, we prefer to use the term catalyst instead of bait."

"Very well, tell me about the catalytic reaction that will soon take place."

"It is imperative that we separate the alien from his spaceship, the Alpha One. While on the ship, he has tremendous power. Away from the ship, he may be more like us. A meeting has been arranged between Daniel and the alien shortly after sundown this evening."

"And why would the alien meet with this young man?"

"We broadcast a signal to the Alpha One saying that the leader of the human race would like to have a meeting at World Headquarters at 8:00 PM. He thinks the World Headquarters is in Houston, Texas."

"Why the hell would the World Headquarters for the human race be in Houston, Texas?"

"We are not sure why, sir. It may have something to do with the obelisk on the San Jacinto Monument grounds. Did you know that it is the tallest obelisk in the world?"

"Taller than the Washington Monument?"

"Yes sir, it is twelve feet taller."

"Very well," continued General Z, "what is the plan?"

"Daniel is going to meet with the alien and try to learn as much as he can. We will be in heavy reconnaissance mode during their meeting and will attempt to learn as much as possible about the enemy before we attack."

"And the attack force?"

"Attack groups A, B, and C each consist of one hundred elite soldiers with advanced weaponry. Group A is located in a grove north of the reflecting pool adjacent to the San Jacinto Monument. Group B is located in a grove south of the reflecting pool and Group C is located near the park entrance. It is interesting to note that these positions were all key locations during the Battle of San Jacinto in 1836."

"This is no time for a history lesson," rebuffed General Z. "Is that all you've got?"

"Oh no, sir," assured Friday. "We have an additional five hundred elite commando troops stationed one mile away in the Battleship Texas park with an arsenal of assault weapons, drones, and attack helicopters. We have all military bases within five hundred miles on high alert this evening, in case we need reinforcements."

"And the general public, how are you keeping them away?"

"The San Jacinto Monument, Battleship Texas, and Monument Inn Restaurant, are all closed today in order to prepare for what is being called a private event this evening. The nearby Lynchburg ferry is not operating today due to maintenance and all of the roads near the park are shut down for repairs."

▲　▲　▲

Various plans of action played over and over in Daniel's mind as he drove his silver Prius to the site of the San Jacinto Monument. This was it, his moment of destiny, his purpose in life - this was why he had been brought into the world. God had called him, chosen him, to kill an alien that was a threat to the entire human race. Tonight, he would battle the alien, the most powerful being to ever travel to Earth. Fortunately, he would not be facing the alien's ship, the Alpha One. There was no way he could have fought against that gigantic weapon. But the alien, even without his ship, would surely be prepared for a battle. Who knows what advanced armor and weaponry the alien possessed? Is this how David felt when he faced Goliath? He did not even have a sling shot. He should have brought a weapon – maybe a concealed handgun or better yet, an assault rifle. Yes, an AK-47 or an AR-15 would have been nice. He thought back to Sam Houston's advice, 'The hound don't expect to be attacked by the hare'. Well, he definitely was the hare in this situation.

Daniel drove past the temporary sign posted at the turnaround point near the park entrance. The sign read, 'Park closed for private event.' I guess, he thought, a meeting with an alien qualifies as a private event. The bulky guard at the chained entrance was wearing the standard brown National Park Service uniform. Daniel doubted that he was a member of the park service, and besides, this was not a national park – the task force must have been short on outfits. Nearby was a parked van, probably filled with a government SWAT team. What were they called now days? Was it Green Berets, Delta Force, Navy Seals, Army Rangers, or some other nickname for the elite force du jour? The guard stopped him and briefly searched his car. He was driving a Prius - there was nowhere to hide. Daniel drove up the road and circled the obelisk before parking near the reflecting pool. The parking lot was empty which, as he thought about it, should not have been a surprise. He stepped outside the Prius and spoke, "Sound check, Daniel one, two, three, sound check." He was wearing a wire and a hidden video camera.

"You are coming in loud and clear," responded Friday, "good visual also. Can you turn around so we can get a full view of the area?" The wireless receiver in his ear was working well.

Daniel complied. Nothing looked out of the ordinary, but who knows what was hidden in the groves on either side of the reflecting pool? Daniel did know that a telescopic video camera had been mounted on the mast of the Battleship Texas, moored in the Houston Ship Channel one mile away. Daniel looked toward the ship. Launched in 1912, it had been designed with the most up-to-date technology of its era. It had fought in both World Wars before it was towed in 1948 to the Houston Ship Channel to become the first permanent battleship memorial museum in the United States. Who would have thought it would take part in a battle with an alien?

Daniel was wearing a warm up suit and tennis shoes. In his jacket pockets were four 100-milliliter Nalgene bottles, each containing a different chemical - methanol, formaldehyde, formic acid, and sodium formate. Joshua had gotten them for him from the plant lab and delivered them to him the day before. The alien had been destroying manufacturing facilities that produced these chemicals, so Daniel reasoned that one of these chemicals was likely a great threat to the alien. Daniel figured that formaldehyde and formic acid would probably be the most effective alien poisons since they were the more reactive, but he could not rule out the other chemicals. He was not sure how the poison should be administered. Obviously drinking them was out of the question. Daniel's plan was to remove the cap from the bottles and douse the alien. That, of course, was easier said than done. How does one tell an alien, "Excuse me while I open a bottle of poison to pour

445

on you and hopefully kill you?" Daniel was not even sure if the dousing would work. An injection might be required. Strapped to each of his legs were four hypodermic syringes with the same chemicals. If getting close enough for dousing was a problem, he envisioned that getting close enough for an injection would be next to impossible.

He would soon be facing an alien which, if not killed, would do things that would bring about the destruction of the entire human race. And here he was, planning to take down the alien with four plastic bottles of chemicals and eight syringes. This was nuts. He thought again about bringing a gun. He really should have brought a gun. Daniel did not own a firearm and, until today, had never had a reason to own one. Would a firearm do him any good? The government SWAT teams around him had who knows what kind of firepower. There were going to be plenty of guns aimed at the alien, no, there was no reason for him to have a gun.

What if they killed the alien, would that end the threat or would more aliens be coming later? Friday and Gannon were worried about that, but it did not bother Daniel. God had told him that only one alien had to be filtered to avoid contaminating the Earth. He was not going to be worried about any others.

Daniel looked toward the west and paused to watch a spectacular sunset over the Houston Ship Channel. Since all he could do now was wait, he figured he might as well enjoy the view. It was a beautiful sight – the sky was filled with majestic colors as the sun slowly sank behind the petrochemical plants. I bet Grandma chose this one he thought. As the skies darkened, a thousand points of light from the petrochemical plants began glittering, like twinkling fireflies, all along the Ship Channel. After the sun disappeared, Daniel thought about his meeting with Sam Houston and his advice to 'attack with the sun at your back'. That advice had faded below the horizon.

▲   ▲   ▲

Arminius fully expected that he would be walking into a trap, but he was not worried. When it came to military firepower, this world was very primitive. Chirality had researched the military capability of the planet and found that most of the weaponry was either explosives or high velocity metallic projectiles. His body armor could easily protect him from both. His body armor was designed to withstand Luddite 1813 laser pistol blasts, and could even provide some protection from laser rifles. The Buggy he would be taking down to the planet could withstand attacks from laser rifles, as well as the other weaponry. The Alpha One, even with its minimal shielding, could withstand attacks from all of these weapons. Since laser weaponry had not yet been developed on this planet, he was invincible. The planet did have nuclear weapon capability. He could not withstand a nuclear explosion, but that would wipe out the entire city. What race would wipe out an entire city to stop an invader? Yet, it was possible, so Arminius instructed Chirality to monitor the movement of any nuclear weapons. If a nuclear weapon moved to anywhere near his location, he was going to immediately board the Buggy and fly out of harm's way. Obviously, there was no need to worry about a nuclear attack when he was on the Alpha One. Any enemy that got within five hundred miles would be quickly annihilated.

Arminius thought about his plans. He was in command of the most powerful weapon on the planet. He was the greatest and he was invincible. Where would he go from here? He had aspired to be the leader of Home World and Plugaria. Did he really want to be the world leader here? It would be nice to be honored, respected, and feared. So, what did he want? Did he want these people to bow down and pray to him? Did he want them to build great monuments? Yes, of course he wanted all that. His father warned him about loneliness. Was he lonely? Sure, it is lonely at the top. He could have the race below, which looked so much like him, send him women. Yes, he would mate with many women and have thousands of offspring. He would never be lonely again. But, how would that make him any different from his despised son-of-a-bitch father?

It was almost time to go down to the planet. He would have plenty of time to think about his future later. Before he left the Alpha One, he asked Chirality to conduct a scan of the landing zone. As expected, military forces were deployed near the obelisk. He would need to give them a demonstration of his power and greatness.

▲ ▲ ▲

Hiding amidst a field of satellites above the third planet, Lantos and Pascal waited and monitored the mysterious spacecraft's activities. 'Know your prey' was Lantos's mantra. Several times during the past few days, the humongous ship descended from its twenty-five-hundred-mile orbit to four hundred miles and fired laser blasts. They were not severe blasts, there were no signs of destruction, but apparently they lit up the sky below.

Once again today, the gigantic alien spaceship descended to four hundred miles. This time, however, instead of firing its laser it established a stationary orbit above the obelisk. A short while later, a small transport craft emerged from the alien spaceship and headed toward the planet's surface. If he was going to take out the intruder, thought Lantos, now was the time. He broke orbit and stealthily stalked the transport craft.

▲ ▲ ▲

Early in the morning, Joshua parked his SUV near the narrow beach at Sylvan Beach Park in La Porte. As expected, only a few people were there. A fall morning in the middle of the week was never a peak time for beach goers. Joshua unloaded his gear, plugged his portable air compressor into the twelve-volt DC outlet at the back of his SUV, and attached a hose to breathe life into a pile of crumbled plastic. A few minutes later, the pile of plastic was transformed into an inflatable frameless fishing boat. Joshua installed the hard seat and moved the boat to the water's edge where he attached the battery-powered trolling motor. He then loaded his duffle bag, a Penn Spinfisher combo rod and reel, and his tackle box. He would not be fishing this trip – the fishing gear was his cover in case he was pulled over by the Coast Guard or a nosy game warden. Joshua stepped into his waders and pulled them over his camouflage overalls. He then donned a navy windbreaker to completely conceal his camo attire. He pulled his boat into the water, climbed aboard, and started the boat's small, quiet motor. He cast his line without bait or lures. The red and white bobber pursued him as he slowly navigated the waters.

He was on a mission, a clandestine mission. He knew that Daniel was meeting the alien tonight at the San Jacinto Monument. There was no way that Daniel's government friends were going to let him anywhere near the monument so, in order to see the alien, he was going to have to try a backdoor approach. Joshua did not have much trust in the government and figured they would have no qualms sacrificing Daniel for 'the greater good'. He was Daniel's friend and his only back-up. It was unquestionably dangerous, but how many times in life does one get a chance to see a real live alien?

Joshua headed north towards Morgan's Point and then followed the curvature of the land as it headed northwest into Upper San Jacinto Bay. He zigzagged around the small, uninhabited islands in the bay, staying well away from the petrochemical plants that lined the shores. He also kept a wary lookout for the gargantuan tankers that periodically churned through the center of the channel bearing the fruits of the petrochemical plants. He was being watched. He could feel the eyes of the Coast Guard and the innumerable bored petrochemical plant security guards as they gazed at their monitors. He was just a harmless fisherman across the channel from their plants. He was too small and insignificant to be a threat to anyone.

Joshua threaded his boat through the marsh at San Jacinto State Park Lake. The San Jacinto Monument obelisk gleamed brilliantly in the background. He was in the middle of thick marsh about five hundred yards from the obelisk when he stopped, got out of his boat, and grabbed his duffle bag. He left his fishing gear in the boat. Could he remember the location? Could he find the boat at night? Was he ever going to return? He did not know. All he knew was that he was going alien hunting.

Joshua sloshed through the waist deep waters in the marsh. Who knew what wildlife was present? He saw turtles, ducks, and fish. He knew there were snakes and mosquitoes, and hoped there were not any alligators around. Joshua was about three hundred yards from the monument when he emerged from the water. Nearby, the marsh was engaged in a fierce battle with a field of high grass. Joshua discarded his windbreaker and waders, so that he was now in full camo gear. Staying close to the ground, he slowly crawled through the tall grass while towing his duffle bag. Several times he paused, pulled out his electronic range finder and took a reading before crawling closer. When he was one hundred and fifty yards from the obelisk, he stopped, opened his duffle bag, and took out his Winchester 308 rifle. It had a camouflaged stock that blended well with the tall autumn grasses. Next, he took out his electronic scope and attached it to the rifle. The scope had a telescopic zoom with a built-in video camera. There was definitely going to be a record of tonight's meeting. Joshua reached for his camouflaged binoculars and a pair of night vision goggles and carefully laid them in readily accessible locations in case they were needed. Last but not least, he pulled out his Bowie knife. He was not sure if he would need it, but he figured every Texan fighting at San Jacinto should have a Bowie knife.

Joshua lay prone in the tall grass for nine hours. He had heard stories of snipers lying still for several days. He did not want to think about how they handled their biological functions. Joshua took his binoculars and surveyed the area. The San Jacinto Monument obelisk was in the center of a grassy area and it was surrounded by a circular parking lot. The reflecting pool was located on the west side. If the direction of the reflecting pool was twelve o'clock, he was located at the five o'clock-position one hundred and fifty yards from the obelisk. He felt confident in his shooting abilities at that range. Between him and the monument were ten yards of high grass, followed by twenty-five yards of mowed grass, twenty-five yards of paved surface, and then the inner grassy area and the state history museum building surrounding the monument. At the three o'clock-position was a picnic area. Behind the picnic area was mowed grass and a single large mesquite tree. The large reflecting pool, at the twelve o'clock position, extended several hundred yards between the circular driveway around the monument and Independence Parkway. On the other side of the highway was the Battleship Texas State Historic Site. Through his binoculars Joshua could see the huge historic battleship proudly sitting in the Houston Ship Channel, providing eternal protection to countless petrochemical storage tanks in the surrounding area.

The sun was slowly sinking in the west behind the Battleship Texas. Suddenly the lights guarding the San Jacinto Monument came to life and the obelisk glowed brilliantly in the evening sky.

CHAPTER 13

THE BATTLE OF SAN JACINTO

Daniel thought he heard something. He looked up and saw a disc of light. As he watched, the glow grew in size and the noise became louder and louder. It was difficult to describe what he heard – it was like a muffled whistle. The glow circled the area above the obelisk and gradually descended. Butterflies filled his stomach. Why was he doing this? He reached into his warm-up suit pockets and felt the Nalgene bottles for reassurance. Why had he chosen these bottles? Wouldn't some kind of spray gun or water balloon have worked better? His thoughts were interrupted - the alien had arrived.

Across the parking lot, the alien craft hovered momentarily and then landed. Daniel realized that what he thought was a disc, was not a disc at all. It looked like a long tube. The tube had been rotating, like the blade on a lawn mower. No doubt the sun's reflection at the higher altitudes had given it a disc appearance. As Daniel studied the craft, it reminded him of a distillation tower lying on the ground. He estimated its size to be eight feet in diameter and sixty feet long. It had a shell made of some kind of material that appeared to be a mixture of gold and bronze – a color Daniel had never seen. Each end of the distillation tower/spaceship had a red glow, which gave the appearance of a cigar lit on both ends. Daniel temporarily forgot about his mission and slipped into 'engineering mode'. His Prius had a hybrid engine that was constantly switching back and forth from fuel power to electrical power. Could someone design a spacecraft that rotated by constantly switching back and forth between power supplies, and then if gravity waves could be used as a power source...

Daniel snapped back into reality as the door in the middle of the alien spaceship opened. Daniel gripped the Nalgene bottles as he anxiously waited. Better not grip them too tight - bust the bottles, spill the chemicals, and the human race is destroyed. Daniel loosened his grip. As he waited, he tried to figure out when he would attack. The alien would be prepared for an immediate attack. He would need to delay, make the alien comfortable, and then, attack when it was least expected – Sam Houston would be proud. But suppose the alien attacked him first? Where could he hide? His Prius was nearby, but it certainly did not offer much protection. A smile came to his face as he pictured a television commercial showing him driving off in his Prius being pursued by an alien. No, God had told him to stop the alien - there would be no running away. He may lose his life this evening, but it was comforting to know that he had a fantastic future designing planets with Mo, Larry, and Curly. The alien stepped out of the spacecraft door and Daniel's jaw dropped. He knew going into this that the odds were not good for his plan to douse the alien with chemicals. Now he saw that it was impossible for his plan to work - the alien was wearing a Hazmat suit.

Hazmat, or hazardous material suits, are worn by workers to minimize exposure to chemicals, asbestos, and other types of toxic materials. They are basically a chemically resistant space suit. They have two pieces – the suit and the head covering. If Daniel tried to douse the alien with his chemicals, it would do no good since the chemicals would simply roll off the suit on to the ground.

The alien started walking across the parking lot toward him and Daniel reciprocated. As the alien approached, Daniel realized that this was no ordinary Hazmat suit, and why would it be? Surely the alien realized that it would be a sniper target. The suit probably had some kind of bulletproof covering and it might even be explosive resistant. It was time for P-rays. "Roger, err, God, I could use a little help here...

things aren't going according to my plan...any time you want to step in is a good time...the sooner the better."

A still small voice spoke, "Daniel..." It was Friday. "Hold off on your attack. Find out as much as possible about the alien and what it is wearing."

And how do I do this, thought Daniel, I don't speak alien.

The alien stopped when it was about ten feet away. Daniel also stopped. A voice came out of the alien's suit, "My name is Arminius. Are you the leader of this world?"

"How, how do you speak my language?" asked Daniel nervously.

"It is a universal translator. You people really are primitive. Are you the leader?"

"I, I am a representative of our leader. Why have you come?"

"I have come to lead your world to greatness. Who is your leader?"

"Our leader is God - he is the creator of the universe." Friday had briefed him that under no circumstances was he to mention the president of the United States or any other governmental leader. It was very important that they be kept protected, a safe distance away.

"Where is this God?"

"He is invisible, but I am here. How can I help you?"

"I need to talk to God. How do I do this?"

"You can ask me, or..." the wheels in Daniel's mind were turning, "There is a way that you can go see him directly."

"And how is that?"

"When you die on our world, you go to see God in Heaven." It was worth a shot. Maybe it would work.

"I see," said the alien. "Would there be a special room for me?"

"I am sure there would be," encouraged Daniel. Was this really going to work? The alien pulled something out of a pocket of his suit. It looked like a gun? Was he really going to kill himself?

Arminius pointed the device toward a grove on the south side of the reflecting pool. "Code 4117 – one hundred-fifty-foot radius." The deity from above responded and a few seconds later a streak of light came down from the sky. Flames from exploding munitions in the grove leapt upward to greet the streak of light. The alien then pointed the device toward a grove on the north side of the reflecting pool, "Code 4117 – two-hundred-foot radius." Once again, the supplication was answered in the form of a streak of light from the sky followed by a massive explosion.

"Can your leader do that?" boasted Arminius. "I am the most powerful force in this universe. I am your new leader."

"Very impressive, but I am not sure God would see it that way. You say that we are a primitive society, but I know a lot about you." Daniel began walking toward the obelisk. Arminius followed at his side.

"What do you know about me?"

"I know that you are from another universe. I know that you have a spaceship in orbit. I know it has two twelve-hundred-foot-long tubes, one contains the ship's engine and the other has a powerful laser, the capabilities of which, you just amply demonstrated. The range of your laser is five hundred miles. I know all of this because God told me."

"I am not sure how you got your information, but where I come from, we have people like you that believe in unseen things. They even believe in supreme creators."

"And you do not believe in a supreme creator? You don't see the great order in this universe? Is there not great order in your universe?"

"There is great order, but it evolved on its own. There are no supreme creators. There is much suffering in my former universe. Supreme creators would not allow such suffering."

"Have you ever tried to end world suffering? Believe me, I have tried and it is an impossible task."

"Instead of suffering, I make others suffer. I make them hurt. I am the greatest force in all the universe. All life fears me."

"It is easy to destroy, but to restore order, to make something from chaos, that is a sign of true greatness."

"I take it that you are some type of philosopher?"

"Who me? Oh no, I am an engineer."

"An engineer? Could there be a lowlier profession?"

"Hey, what is wrong with engineers? We create great things using the forces of nature and the materials around us."

"Great things? Do you call weapons of mass destruction great things? My ship, the Alpha One, that is currently in orbit above this planet, do you think it is a great thing? Engineers designed it and look at what it just did. Did you know that I have used it to destroy thirty-three powerful military spaceships? Did you know that it has blown apart a moon, creating meteors that will wipe out life on the surface of my home planet? Yes, engineers do great things. They use their minds to create things that make the universe worse. Even after all the terrible things that have been done, there are engineers working on ways to create even more destructive weapons."

"Every invention can be used for good purposes or the detriment of others. You have chosen to use the invention to harm others."

"I hardly see how an instrument of war can be used to help others."

"And what is your profession?"

"I am a warrior. I conquer worlds. I will soon be the Chancellor and will rule this entire planet."

"I would strongly advise against that idea."

"And why do I care what you think? You are so pathetic compared to my greatness."

"I agree that I am weak, but I am working for someone that is very, very strong. You won't be able to take over the world, you will be destroyed."

"Destroyed, me destroyed? By who? By what? By you? You have seen what I have done here. Do you need another demonstration of my power?"

"Oh no," Daniel hastily replied, "At least not now. You have shown that you possess a very powerful ship, but take that away...take away your technology and you are just an ordinary human being. I have seen your picture outside of this suit you are wearing. You look just like us. By the way, why do you wear the suit? Can you not breathe

the atmosphere here?" I hope Friday and Gannon are getting all this thought Daniel.

"The atmosphere is very compatible. The suit is body armor. I ran a scan of the weaponry on this planet. It is mostly miniature metallic projectiles and explosives. This suit can easily protect me from those."

"So, are you carrying any weapons?"

"I have my laser pistol," Arminius said as he pulled it out. "It is multipurpose. It can be used to paint a target for my ship to destroy, or it can be used as a weapon. Give credit to the engineers for creating another weapon of destruction."

"You know," posited Daniel, "you talk about your greatness, but deep down inside, I think you are a coward."

"So, the pathetic one thinks I am a coward? I have single-handily battled military fleets from two powerful worlds. I, and I alone, have traveled between universes, and you think I am a coward?"

"You hide behind the power of your technology, a technology created by engineers. You don't even show your face. It is hidden behind a mask. Look at me? Do you see any weapons on me? Of course not, yet you will not show your face, even to lowly me. Why is that? Are you afraid of me? Are you scared of our pathetic race? I think it is because you are a coward."

Arminius pointed his laser pistol at Daniel, "Do you have a death wish?"

"Do I fear death? Maybe a little, but I have seen my future. I have seen what I will be doing after I die. If you kill me, you will be killing your contact with our leader. Instead, could you give me another demonstration of your power?"

"What kind of demonstration?" They were standing in the grassy area between the parking lot and the entrance to the inside of the San Jacinto Monument history museum, with Arminius closest to the entrance. Daniel was standing to the west of him and across the street, behind him, his silver Prius was parked.

"Do you see my vehicle? Show me the mighty power of your laser pistol. Can you hit my vehicle from here?"

Arminius fired at the Prius. The Prius caught fire and a few seconds later exploded. This is going to be hard to explain to my insurance agent Daniel thought. The burning Prius was now the sun at his back. It was time to follow Sam Houston's advice - it was time to attack.

"Very impressive technology," continued Daniel calmly, "Now can you show me your face, or are you too frightened to show it to me for even a few seconds."

"For you, I will give a brief look, just to shut you up." Arminius raised his arms to undo his head covering.

While the flickering flames of the burning Prius provided backlight that interfered with the alien's vision, Daniel quickly grabbed the formaldehyde and formic acid bottles from his pockets and loosened the lids. Just a few more seconds thought Daniel and the alien's head covering will be off and I will douse him.

Arminius was in the process of removing his head covering when, all of a sudden, a flash of light came from the large mesquite tree near the picnic area. The alien screamed in pain and then rolled on the ground...with his head covering firmly in place.

▲ ▲ ▲

Using their long-range scanner, Lantos and Pascal tracked the alien transport craft. They watched from a distance as it landed in a paved area that circled the base of the obelisk. Lantos then maneuvered his ship to a remote area about half a mile away and landed in the tall grass. Pascal handed Lantos his wings and gave him the laser rifle. Lantos left the ship after instructing Pascal to take off immediately if anything went wrong. Lantos slowly flew just above the tall grass in a zigzag path toward the obelisk. As he got closer, he spotted a large mesquite tree that offered an excellent vantage point. He landed on a thick branch of the tree and studied his prey. He spotted an animal of the species he had previously hunted at this very spot. It would be an excellent specimen for more MED he thought, but that was not his objective - he was hunting a far more dangerous game. The animal, a bald tailless primate, appeared to be talking to someone wearing a protective suit, which could possibly be some form of body armor. The alien transport craft was in the background. The one wearing the protective suit had to be the alien. Could his laser rifle penetrate the armor? There was only one way to find out. The laser rifle was Lantos's most powerful weapon. If this did not work, he needed to be able to get out of the area as quickly as possible. He glanced back toward where his spacecraft had landed. There were no obstacles that would interfere with a quick getaway.

The bald tailless primate and alien walked for some distance and then stopped near the obelisk. The alien fired a weapon at a land transportation vehicle that Lantos knew was used by the bald tailless primates. The vehicle exploded. Lantos lined up the laser rifle sights and planned his kill shot. Where should he aim? He had never studied this particular species, but usually the spot where the neck meets the shoulder was a good target. Lantos took careful aim and fired.

As Lantos fired, the alien raised its arms, then stumbled and fell to the ground. The alien was still moving. Lantos took aim for a kill shot.

A loud crack filled the air and Lantos felt a great stinging pain in his chest. He dropped the laser rifle and it fell from the tree to the ground below. Lantos stumbled backwards on the tree limb, slammed into the tree trunk, and fell to the ground.

▲ ▲ ▲

Hidden in the tall grass in the five o'clock-position, with the San Jacinto monument being in the center of the clock, Joshua watched as a car pulled into the empty parking lot and parked in the one o'clock-position. Joshua recognized the car as Daniel's silver Prius. Joshua watched as Daniel got out of his car, looked around, and slowly walked toward the twelve o'clock-position by the reflecting pool where he turned to face the remnants of the setting sun and the distant Battleship Texas. Joshua grabbed his Winchester 308 and looked through the telescopic site. He would have preferred to have Daniel closer to him, but he had a clear shot at two hundred and twenty yards, well within his range.

A few minutes later, Joshua heard a muffled noise and looked up. An object was circling the area in the darkening skies. He had a hard time getting a good view, but watched intently as the spacecraft slowly descended. Joshua activated the video camera on the riflescope and zoomed in for a closer view. After a few seconds, the cigar-shaped craft passed out of view – blocked by the San Jacinto Monument obelisk. "Damn it," he silently cursed - the alien craft was landing at the ten o'clock-position, on the opposite side from where he was located. The alien would be out of view until it approached Joshua. An early kill shot was not going to be possible.

Joshua was so intent on watching the cigar-shaped craft that he was startled when he heard another noise from above. He looked up and could not believe his eyes – a small flying saucer was passing directly overhead at an elevation of only about one hundred feet. He watched as it landed in the tall grass a few hundred yards away. His entire life he had wanted to see one UFO, and now, in the span of just a few minutes, he had seen two UFO's. He put on his night vision goggles and looked toward where the second UFO landed. A few minutes later, something emerged and began flying just above the tall grass. Joshua watched as it flew into the branches of the large mesquite tree near the picnic area in the three o'clock-position.

Joshua took off the night vision goggles and peered at Daniel through his riflescope. Someone was talking to him, someone wearing a Hazmat suit. Was it the alien or was it a government worker? How could he tell them apart? Kill an alien and you are a hero, but kill a government worker in Texas and you are on death row. It was so much easier playing video games. He zoomed in with the telescopic scope. He had never seen a Hazmat suit that looked like that, but maybe there were other types. Was it an alien or a government worker? Joshua could not be sure. He looked over at Daniel and checked to be sure the riflescope was still recording what he was seeing. Hazmat and Daniel continued talking. Joshua made a mental note to destroy the recording if he ended up killing a government worker. He then looked over at the mesquite tree and zoomed in with his riflescope. The flying creature he had seen was a small monkey. Why was it there?

Joshua thought about the woman's story from a few nights earlier at this very location. A flying monkey had brutally killed someone and escaped in a tiny flying saucer. Was this the flying monkey and its flying saucer? Was it there to kill Daniel? The monkey was holding something. What was it? It looked like a rifle. Was it a rifle?

Suddenly there was an explosion. Joshua looked back toward the obelisk and saw Daniel's Prius in flames. A beam of red light extended from the mesquite tree toward Daniel and Hazmat and both were now lying on the ground. Joshua looked back at the tree through his scope. Had the monkey blown up Daniel's car? Had the monkey shot Daniel? He was there to protect Daniel, and that was what he was going to do. Joshua flipped off the safety on his Winchester 308, took aim, and fired. The monkey took a step back in the tree limbs. Something it had been holding fell to the ground. Was it the rifle? Then, as Joshua watched, the monkey slowly fell to the ground.

▲ ▲ ▲

Arminius screamed in pain. He had been shot. Following his military training, he hit the ground and rolled. In one smooth motion he grabbed his laser pistol, flipped the switch, and from a prone position painted the target. "Code 4117 – one-hundred-foot radius." Shortly thereafter, the skies lit up as the picnic area and large nearby mesquite tree were engulfed in flames.

▲ ▲ ▲

There was not going to be a better chance than this Daniel thought when the alien started to remove its head covering. Then suddenly the alien was in pain on the ground. Now if only he could remove the alien's head cover. Daniel jumped on top of the alien, but unfortunately some of his bottles of potential poisons had loose lids and their contents spilled on Daniel. He stopped to tighten the bottles and was pushed aside by the alien as it rolled and fired its weapon. The alien was lying on the ground in a prone position facing the picnic area when Daniel again jumped on top of him from behind and frantically tried to remove the head covering - but it would not come loose. Satisfied that there was no longer a threat from the direction of the latest area he had set ablaze, the alien turned its full attention toward Daniel who was still pulling on his head covering. With a move that would make an Olympic wrestling coach proud, the alien rolled and suddenly it was Daniel that was pinned to the ground. Daniel tried to push back, but he was no match for the alien's strength. The alien placed his hands around Daniel's neck and began to strangle him. Daniel reached down his leg and grabbed a syringe. He didn't know which chemical it contained, but he plunged the syringe into the alien - with no effect. The syringe could not penetrate the alien's hazmat suit. Daniel's mind was racing as his world started to fade. He couldn't breathe. He dropped the syringe. He was so weak. A bright white light appeared. This was the end. His plan had failed – he had not been able to kill the alien.

▲ ▲ ▲

"Shit," shouted Lantos, "where did that come from?" He had been watching his prey and it certainly had not come from that direction. Lantos then saw the blood, his blood! He had been hit, but why would someone shoot him? As he fell out of the tree to the ground his wings automatically braced the fall. He crawled forward toward his laser rifle and looked back - a blood trail was pursuing him. He couldn't die now…he had plans, lots of plans. He had to get Pascal home, he had to get paid for the MED, and then he was going to enjoy living life with his new wealth. Except for the alien, he was not a threat to anyone, so who would want to shoot him? The ground was suddenly warm. Flames flickered high in the night sky and he was surrounded by darkness.

▲ ▲ ▲

Gannon and Friday followed the alien encounter from the downtown Houston skyscraper, while General Z watched via secure video link from Washington, D.C.

"Did our radar pick up the transport craft?" asked General Z when the alien first arrived.

"No sir," replied Friday.

A few minutes later they were all aghast as they watched the sudden destruction of the two elite attack groups.

"This is incredible technology," General Z commented with amazement.

A few minutes after that, Daniel's video camera showed a close-up of the alien on top of him from one angle while the Battleship Texas camera showed the view from a different angle.

"He was a good soldier," noted General Z nonchalantly.

"Attack Group C attack!" commanded Friday when the alien was on top of Daniel, "Deploy drones!"

The skies lit up from flares and explosives. Aerial drones filled the night sky while ground drones raced forward. Attack Group C took positions around the obelisk.

▲ ▲ ▲

Thoughts raced through Arminius's mind, "I am the greatest! I am the greatest ever! I and I alone destroyed thirty-three powerful battleships! I and I alone destroyed Luna 3! I and I alone flew to a totally different universe! I am going to be the absolute leader of this world!" Something was wrong. He was suddenly very weak and his mind was fading. He slumped over the pathetic representative of the planet. Did that creature really think it could stop him? Dressed in full body armor he could withstand attack from any of the primitive weapons that were now going off around him. But why was he now starting to lose consciousness. Somehow his body armor had been penetrated. He was lying on top of the worthless being, yet he could not move. Could the pathetic creature have somehow caused him to stumble? Did it have some unknown power? He felt his body shutting down. But why...how...what happened? He was the greatest he repeated over and over. He alone had defeated the mighty Home World fleet. He had battled the greatest military forces the Home Worldians and the Plugarians could muster. He had traveled to an entirely new universe. "I am the greatest", he repeated over and over as he sojourned into the arms of death.

▲ ▲ ▲

Daniel was falling into unconsciousness. This was it...this was the end. Something, however, had happened to the alien. It had fallen right on top of him. It appeared to be dying. It may already be dead. And now, the skies were all lit up. Explosions were all around him, but he heard nothing. His mind flashed as he went in and out of consciousness. Was he in a fire at the chemical plant? But no, he was at the San Jacinto Monument. Why were there flames all around? He thought of Sam Houston – was this the unseen counter force that he had mentioned? Daniel then thought of his prayer to God. Had the Communications Center in Heaven received his P-Rays and responded in this manner? It was all confusing, very confusing. The world was swirling faster and faster. Then suddenly it hit him like a bolt from the blue - in a microsecond of complete clarity, the answer came to him. The wheels in the back of his mind had been turning ever since his visit to the Cosmic Cannon. They had been working, working on ideas on how to start up a new universe. And now, at the very end of his life on Earth, he knew the answer! He clutched the thought as the skies opened and he descended into oblivion.

▲ ▲ ▲

As Joshua watched, a bright light streaked from the heavens bathing the mesquite tree that had held the monkey. The color of the ground around the tree starting changing – first yellow, next red, and then suddenly it burst into flames. Everything in the area around the mesquite tree was burning.

Joshua looked back through his scope for Daniel. He could not see Daniel. Hazmat was lying on the ground. Was Hazmat on top of Daniel? Suddenly flares lit up the sky and explosives rocked the area around Hazmat. As Joshua watched, three helicopters circled overhead. Were they helicopters or were they drones? He could not tell and he also could not hear anything. Moments later, four mini-tanks rolled into the area. It was time to get the hell out of there.

Had they seen him? Probably not, but he could not be sure. Joshua grabbed his items, stuffed them into his duffle bag, and crawled through the tall grass back to the marsh. Fortunately, the night sky was ablaze and he was able to easily find his inflatable boat. He climbed aboard, started the electric motor, and maneuvered the boat through the marsh close to shore. Soon he would be approaching the open waters across from the petrochemical plants and would be spotted. Joshua steered the boat to a secluded area at the edge of the marsh. When he was about one hundred feet from shore, he dumped his Winchester 308 rifle, night vision goggles, and binoculars into the water. He rode to shore, got out of the boat, and then walked it back into waist deep water. He pulled out his Bowie knife, slashed the boat's pontoons, and watched it slowly sink into the water, weighted down by the solid chair. If there was an investigation, there would no evidence to prove that he was present at tonight's alien hunt. Joshua waded through the marsh to the tall grass, found a dry area, and lay down. He would stay until daybreak and then walk three miles to the McDonalds near the Pasadena Freeway from where he would call someone for a ride back to his SUV. He hated to part with his outdoor toys, but inside his jacket he clutched the most prized possession of his entire life – his riflescope containing videos of his encounter with aliens. Would he share the videos with others? He had seen how others had been shamed and discredited when they revealed their findings. No, the world would need to continue its search for the truth – he had found his answers.

CHAPTER 14

FACES OF DEATH

Suzie the garden spider knew the end was near. Shock waves from the explosions had violently shaken her home beyond its design capabilities and she was now in the underbrush. Flames were flickering all around her, but she had to watch. It was the most beautiful thing she had ever seen. The obelisk was shining brightly in the background and remnants of her home sparkled as dancing flames engulfed the tall grasses nearby. Suzie joined the dance and felt the warmth of eternal bliss.

▲ ▲ ▲

The reports were coming in fast to Eudicot at the tomato plant command center - violent winds and extreme heat. He quickly issued commands, "Flood the leaves with maximum water flow!" It was the logical thing to do, but it was not effective - the leaves were still burning. He issued his final command, "Divert all water to the roots and block flow at point 2045." This would create a dry spot that would not be able to support the load with the current wind speed. The plant snapped at point 2045. The bulk of the plant including him would now die. Perhaps with the additional water sent to the roots and the insulation supplied by the snapped plant lying above them, the roots could somehow manage to survive. It was all very logical. Shortly thereafter, the raging fire devoured the tomato plant.

▲ ▲ ▲

"Bring it on! Bring it on!" shouted the mesquite tree defiantly. Skeete had faced hurricanes, floods, drought, disease, and attacks by all kinds of plants and animals. He had even faced fires, although none like this. His branches waved proudly in the violent winds. Skeete looked death in the eye and held his ground as the flames consumed him.

▲ ▲ ▲

Instinctively Missy, the cottontail rabbit, crawled into her burrow deep beneath the large mesquite tree. Her newest batch of young ones was huddled below her. She had lived through all kinds of disasters in her life, but something told her this was not one that she would survive. She sent out P-Rays, but the dangers continued. It was getting hot in the burrow, really hot. She looked out of the burrow – the area above was covered with flames. She shifted her position and blocked the entrance to the burrow with her body, creating a heat barrier to protect her little ones. She would die in the flames, but her latest batch of young ones might survive. As she was passing out, she sent one more burst of P-rays, "Please let my babies escape the burrow when the fire goes away".

▲ ▲ ▲

The last couple of days had not been good to Akoios, the ant genius. Before that, he had discovered a humongous food source in the form of a tomato that could supply the needs of the entire colony for a long period of time, he had designed a spectacular ant palace that could withstand the elements, he had developed an innovative military strategy to repel an invading fire ant army, and he held a very prestigious position in the colony. Then everything came crumbling down. A twist of fate had enabled the invading fire ants to defeat the colony and a squirrel crushed the ant palace while taking the prized tomato. Once again, Akoios was depressed. He had one of the greatest minds on the planet, but what could he do? He wanted to do something fantastic. He wanted to do something to change the world. But alas, that was not going to happen.

Aimlessly, he wandered toward the obelisk, unaware of the events transpiring nearby. Suddenly a large animal fell, narrowly missing him. That was it! He was pissed! He climbed up on the animal and found a patch of exposed skin. If he had paid close attention, he would have seen that the skin was burned from a laser blast that had cut a hole in the animal's outer garment.

Akoios crawled upon the skin and bit – hard. He moved a short distance away and bit again and again. How dare you get in my way! I am mad, I am mad at this world! I am mad as hell! He bit and bit and bit into the unfortunate animal. The animal collapsed, but the enraged Akoios continued his attack until the animal lay still. Then, and only then, did his anger subside.

Daniel was correct - one of the four chemicals he carried in his Nalgene bottles and syringes was a deadly poison to the alien. It was formic acid – found in the sting of an ant bite. On Home World, it was known as the highly toxic BAC-431.

As he was leaving the now lifeless large animal, Akoios looked up and saw that the skies were ablaze. Glowing embers were falling nearby, igniting the grass that surrounded him. The heat was overcoming him - death was fast approaching. Akoios did the calculations. He knew there was no way to outrun death. He knew there was no way to hide from death. He chose to use the time for reflection. He recalled his earliest times in the colony, his time in the military, the building program, fond memories of the Analytical Director, the violent storm, the ant colony's palatial home next to the gigantic food source he had found, the Armageddon battle with the fire ants, attacking the giant animal, and now the massive fires. He had lived an incredible life. It had not always gone according to his plan and he did not achieve the eternal fame that he once sought, but in the end, he was glad that he had lived. Surrounded by warm thoughts, he joined the flames.

The tiny ant, that wanted to do something great in his lifetime, never knew that he saved the human race from destruction.

CHAPTER 15

GROUND CONTROL

The battle did not last long. Shortly after Friday launched the attack, the Attack Group C commander radioed, "Target is secure. We have Neil A."

"Neil A?" questioned General Z. "I understand the need for code names, but why did you select the name of the first man on the moon – Neil Armstrong?"

"We did not name him after Armstrong," explained Friday, "Neil A spelled backwards is alien."

▲ ▲ ▲

A few hours later, mop up operations were complete.

Friday contacted General Z, "Area is clear, sir."

"How are you handling the international news media?"

"They have been staking out locations at the United Nations Building in New York as well as other international locations. We planted a story that it was just a big publicity hoax for a new type of advertising media. In a few days this will all blow over and there will be a new hot topic du jour."

"What about the local news media?"

"There was a problem this evening with a new type of fireworks at a private function at the San Jacinto Monument. Apparently, the fireworks exploded prematurely causing some damage to the parking lot and surrounding areas. Repair crews will be coming out in the morning. The site will be closed for a few days."

"How will the deaths of Attack Groups A and B be explained?"

"As we usually do, sir – training exercise mishaps, road side bombs, helicopter crashes, land mines, suicide bombers, and so forth. Official records will show that during the next few weeks the soldiers died in multiple places around the world. Each will receive a hero's praise for dying in the line of duty while serving their country."

"Has the package been shipped?"

"Transport just took off. It's on its way to Paradise."

"Will I see you there?"

"We'll be there as soon as we pack our Hawaiian shirts," replied Friday matter-of-factly. "Sir, if I may ask, what is to become of the Alpha One?"

"Plans are being developed as we speak. I am hoping we can launch a recovery mission within a week. Can you imagine the power we will have if we can control that ship? Even if we cannot hack into its control system, our engineers should be able to reverse engineer it and duplicate its performance. If our military has a weapon like that, we will rule the world forever!"

▲ ▲ ▲

The appearance of the Alpha One had not gone unnoticed by other governments. Russian, Chinese, European Union, and Arab spy satellites had all changed positions and were observing the giant alien spacecraft. Russia and China were each planning separate boarding missions with their military space forces. Those programs were, of course, all top-secret because international law banned the use of military forces in space. They all knew that whoever controlled the Alpha One would rule the world.

CHAPTER 16

THE LEMURS

Pascal watched intently and admired Lantos's skills as he stealthily flew to the mesquite tree and fired his laser rifle at the alien. The look on his face quickly turned to horror when Lantos was shot and the area around him burst into flames. A few minutes later, the skies above the obelisk were filled with fire. There was no hope for Lantos. Pascal grabbed the controls of the spacecraft and hastily flew away.

Pascal's mind was bombarded with thoughts. What to do, what to do? Where should he go next? Could he safely fly home and, if he did, what would he do with his life? Would he work hard for years and years, making meager wages? On the other hand, he was safe here. He could stay and live like a king. Hmm…decisions, decisions. It was not a difficult choice - Pascal was soon deep in the jungle on the far side of the planet.

▲   ▲   ▲

The attack on the Lemur Federation patrol ship had been reported. It was never a good idea to mess with the lemurs. Three ships were dispatched. They rendezvoused with the original patrol ship and tracked the gigantic trespassing ship to Earth.

The size of the intruding spaceship did not faze them. They descended upon the immense mysterious spacecraft in orbit four hundred miles above Earth. "First the eyes and then the ears," they laughed as their lasers took out the ship's sensors. They then approached the blind ship and playfully announced, "Time for a little push." Two lemur ships pushed the front of the Alpha One toward the planet while the other two ships pushed the rear of the ship in the opposite direction. It was not much of a push, but it was enough to take the Alpha One out of orbit and allow gravity to take over. In a few days, the Alpha One would burn up in the planet's atmosphere.

"You know," noted one of the lemurs, "we could have sent in a team to analyze this ship. Who knows, maybe we could use the information to design a better spaceship." The lemurs all laughed. Technology improvements had been outlawed on their planet for over one hundred years. Any new technology had to go through exceedingly rigorous reviews. Every new technology had the potential for misuse, so very few technological changes were ever adopted. 'New technology, new problems,' was the saying. The lemurs had reached a level in which their technology provided maximum happiness. There was no need to evolve from there.

CHAPTER 17

PARADISE

There are some that say top-secret government research work on alien technology is being conducted at Area 51 in Nevada, but that is not really the case. Oh, it is possible that a small amount of work might have been done there once upon a time many years ago, but the real work is now being done deep underground in a large research facility on a remote Hawaiian island. The original cover story was that the undeveloped island was used as a bombing range and is littered with unexploded ordnance. This kept out most of the tourists, but not all of them, especially as the ordnance aged. A new story emerged – apparently a large population of highly poisonous snakes now roam the island. This further deterred visitors, but, unexpectedly attracted a surprisingly large number of people that like exotic poisonous snakes. The latest cover story is that there is a highly contagious deadly virus on the island. So far this has been effective at keeping day trippers away, but, at some point people will realize that, if no one is alive on the island, the disease will also perish and it will be safe to return.

▲ ▲ ▲

A few days later, deep underground on the remote Hawaiian island, an autopsy was in progress. General Z, Friday, and Gannon were in attendance.

Friday updated General Z. "Sir, we had to go in arthroscopically. We were able to remove the head covering, but not the body armor.

That material is tough – we have not been able to find anything that it cannot withstand."

"So, what has the autopsy found?" asked General Z.

"There are lots of similarities in our physiologies, but also lots of differences," replied Friday. "Cause of death appears to be poison, possibly from ant bites."

"That is good to know in case of an invasion," noted General Z.

"How is that, sir?" inquired Gannon. "The ants won't be able to penetrate the body armor."

"True," explained General Z, "but why conquer a world that is covered with lethal material? Ants are all over the world and next to impossible to eradicate. The aliens do not want to live 24/7 in body armor. They would be better off finding another world."

"It makes you wonder," speculated Friday, "how many insignificant plants and animals in the world are alien repellents?"

"It is the insignificants that make the world great," declared General Z philosophically. "What have you found out about the alien transport craft?"

"Sir, we have not been able to break into the transport craft," reported Friday. "It has tremendously strong walls. There is no way our anti-aircraft missiles could have knocked it out, even if we could have gotten some kind of fix. From our video shots, the flying technology is fascinating. Hopefully we will be able to figure it out someday."

"Keep trying," encouraged General Z. "How about the laser pistol?"

"We have been able to conduct a lot of analysis, sir. Not surprisingly it is made from materials not found on Earth and it is powered by a crystal that likewise is not found on Earth."

"Can you fire it?"

"Yes," nodded Friday, "but we are worried about draining its power supply."

"Sir," questioned Gannon, "I know it is cool technology and all that, but we have rocket propelled grenades that can do equal or greater damage."

"True," agreed General Z, "but it may be the perfect weapon for a special ops mission."

"Speaking of which sir," inquired Friday, "how are things going on the plans to send a team to board the alien spaceship orbiting Earth?"

"Not good. It looks like we will be losing the Alpha One. It is going to burn up tomorrow. At least no one else will get the technology."

"What happened?" asked Gannon, "I thought it was in stable orbit."

"The lemurs," said General Z.

They all nodded in understanding.

CHAPTER 18

ALL DOGS GO TO HEAVEN

The bright lights and swirling came to a stop. This time Daniel was not startled. Been there, done that, he thought as he looked around and once again saw a multitude of brilliant white orbs floating around. The scenery, however, had changed - the green hills of Bovine Heaven were replaced by what looked like a farm setting. There were hundreds of big red barns surrounded by trees and brooks. Outside the barns were stacks of bones, feed bowls, and…he looked closer, and yes, those were dog toys. Daniel quickly realized that he was in Canine Heaven. A young girl was at the front of the line. She squatted down and had a big smile on her face as she patted each of the approaching white orbs.

"Hi! Oh, you are so cute! Yes you are! Yes you are! I am so glad to see you!"

Floating video screens were all around and Daniel heard a cacophony of survey questions.

"You have been selected to participate in a survey about your recent life on Earth. The survey results will be used to improve living conditions for your species."

Daniel looked around and saw hundreds of orbs filling out the surveys. He could hear some of the questions being asked to those around him.

"What is your first memory?"

"Did you receive adequate attention from your mother?"

"How was your learning process?"

"Did you have good friends?"

"Did you have adequate sustenance?"

"Were there storms in your life?"

"How did you weather them?"

"Would you have preferred more or less drama in your life?"

"Did you reproduce?"

"How many offspring did you have?"

"On a scale of one to ten, with one being very easy and ten being very difficult, how would you rate your life?"

"How was your end-of-life experience?"

"Was there much suffering?"

"Would you have preferred to live a shorter or longer life?"

"If you had lived longer, what would you have done?"

"What did you learn about life?"

There was no time to lose with the bureaucracy and the forms. He knew his way around Heaven. He brushed past the line of orbs and approached the young girl.

She started to pet him, "Hi! Oh, you are so cute! Yes you are! Yes you…"

Daniel interrupted, "Can you take me to the Cosmic Cannon? I need to get there as soon as possible."

"What?" The young girl had an astonished look.

"I am a seven sevens," explained Daniel, "and got here by mistake. I really need to get to the Cosmic Cannon quickly."

"Sure, I'll take you…Golly gee whiz, I've never met a seven sevens before!"

She took his hand and they disappeared.

CHAPTER 19

PASSENGERS FOR ETERNITY

Daniel reappeared in the First Class lounge outside of the launch chamber of the Cosmic Cannon. Frankenstein was alone at the kiosk looking at a floating blue video screen.

"Daniel?" A startled look appeared on his ghoulish face, "What are you doing here?"

"I've got it!" shouted Daniel excitedly, "I know how to start up the new universe!"

"What? We have been trying for eons and now you think you have the answer?"

"It's the alien. Don't you see? The alien is the key. The alien was sent here for a purpose. Not to wipe out Earth, but to start up the new universe!"

"We have tried other aliens before," sighed Frankenstein, "but I will bring him here." Frankenstein punched buttons on the screen. Instantly a white orb appeared. A few seconds later it materialized into Arminius."

"What is this place?" questioned Arminius as he saw Frankenstein. "I am the greatest and deserve much better treatment." Then he looked over and saw Daniel. "What is this engineering scum doing here? I thought I killed you. Did you do something to kill me?"

"I am glad to see you too." Daniel gave Arminius a reassuring smile. "I was going to kill you, but you killed me first. That is now all in the past. We are assembling an elite team and you are our first choice. We are going to start up a new universe, but first we need to scan you."

"Well of course you want me on your team. I am the best, why have anyone else?"

Frankenstein scanned Arminius. "879 7868 - the nine is for ego."

"No surprise there," noted Daniel. "This is great. Now we need nines that died during the recent battle at San Jacinto. Who had the highest intelligence?"

Frankenstein punched buttons on the video screen and a white orb appeared that materialized into Akoios.

"You have got to be kidding me!" Daniel had a surprised look. "The most intelligent life form that died in the battle was an ant?"

"Don't get me started," threatened Akoios, "I have had a really bad last couple of days!"

"Now we need a good killer. Frankenstein, do you have a killer nine that died in the recent battle?"

Frankenstein punched more buttons and Lantos appeared.

"A lemur?" Daniel was again astonished.

"A bald tailless primate?" Lantos shook his head with disgust.

"What is a lemur doing at the San Jacinto Monument?" questioned Daniel with disbelief.

"I flew there in my spaceship to save your ass!" snapped Lantos angrily.

"It is true," Frankenstein calmly agreed. "He is a space traveling lemur from a different solar system - he is not a lemur from Earth. There used to be a lot of lemurs that took their flying saucers to Earth for Spring Break." He slowly picked Lantos up off the ground, raised him so that he was eye-to-eye, and bellowed with his deep monster voice, "I thought those trips were banned!"

A look of fear swept across Lantos's face as he weakly uttered, "Let me assure you, this last trip was strictly for economic and educational purposes."

"How about logic?" continued Daniel as Frankenstein placed Lantos back on the floor, "Was there a logic nine that died at the San Jacinto Monument?"

A few minutes later, Eudicot, the tomato plant appeared.

"What, what is all of this?" questioned Eudicot.

"We are getting ready to startup a new universe," replied Daniel. "You've been picked."

"Oh, that's just *** great," griped Arminius. "I am going to spend eternity in a new universe with a monkey, an ant and a fruit."

"Hey tough guy," shouted Akoios, "just remember who took you down!"

Arminius was shocked, "It was you? You are so insignificant compared to me!"

"You better believe it was me," hollered the ant, "and I would gladly kill you again!"

"Easy guys," Daniel interrupted. "Frankenstein, do you have a creativity nine from the battle at San Jacinto?"

A few seconds later, Suzie the spider materialized.

"Hello," she greeted the group perkily. "My name is Suzie and I am sooooo glad to be here!" She surveyed the surroundings doing mental calculations for her new home. Instantly a web design incorporating various features of the room popped into her mind. "I really like what you have done with your furnishings."

Arminius was livid, "What the ***? What kind of elite group is this? Now we are going to have little Miss Sunshine around forever?"

"Oh my." Suzie looked sympathetically toward Arminius and spoke with a soothing voice, "I do not believe I caught your name. If there is anything I can do for you, please let me know."

The ant spoke up. "Really? We have to spend eternity with her?"

The tomato plant added, "She made my life hell on Earth, and now I am stuck with her forever?"

Lantos joined in, "Is this some kind of eternal punishment for my Spring Break trips? Do we really need her?"

Daniel sprang to the spider's defense, "Guys, guys aren't you all being a bit harsh on little Miss Suzie?"

Suzie spoke in a cheerful voice as she addressed Daniel. "Oh my, such a thoughtful young gentleman and you are so sweet. Let me assure you that I am used to dealing with a rough crowd. You do know that every day I associate with *shit* eating flies." She stopped and stared everybody down before pleasantly continuing, "and I *eat* them for breakfast!" Suzie's point was well made. Even the Heavenly censors could not stop her profanity. No one was going to mess with her.

"Okay Frankenstein," resumed Daniel, "it is time for a nine with great physical strength. Who was the strongest to die in the battle?" Daniel expected it would be a stocky commando with huge biceps covered with tattoos.

A few seconds later, Skeete the mesquite tree appeared.

The assembled group was shocked and expressed their disbelief. Daniel shook his head.

"Hey guys, I too am surprised, but the more I think about it, there ain't nothing stronger and tougher in Texas than a mesquite tree."

Frankenstein was punching buttons on his video screen. "Are you ready for the most attractive to mate nine from the battle at San Jacinto?"

"Yes!" Daniel was excited, "I have been waiting for this." Visions of gorgeous supermodels flashed through his mind, even though he knew it would never happen since they had not been involved in the battle. As everyone watched, a white orb appeared. It seemed like an eternity passed as the orb slowly materialized revealing a bunny – a real bunny, Missy Lutt, the promiscuous rabbit.

"By the way," mentioned Frankenstein, "your latest batch of bunnies survived the battle."

"Thank God," exclaimed Missy. "When do I get to make some more?"

"What a team!" declared Daniel excitedly. "We were all at the battle at San Jacinto. We have seven nines and a seven sevens catalyst, the perfect formula to startup a new universe. To the Egg everyone, let's launch this baby!"

As they approached the entrance to the Egg, Daniel suddenly stopped. "Wait a minute - we need a bottle of urine for good luck."

Frankenstein interjected, "You do know we are in Heaven. There are no biological processes to produce urine."

Then the ant spoke, "Take this." A urine sample bottle floated to Daniel. "You do know that in Heaven all you have to do is visualize."

Daniel placed the bottle of urine in the doorway of the Egg and looked toward Frankenstein, "Are we ready to launch?"

Frankenstein nodded his giant green head.

"Let's enter the launch chamber," motioned Daniel. "Into the Egg everyone, nines first."

One by one, they stepped down into the capsule that would transport them to another universe. As they entered the Egg they were transformed into white orbs. The orbs mixed to form a homogeneous brew. Daniel was getting ready to enter the mix. Suddenly a bright lightning flash streaked across the room leaving a brilliant white cloud. The cloud subsided and Roger appeared.

"Daniel," Roger demanded calmly, "please stop."

Daniel froze as Roger walked toward him.

"Daniel, I do not want you going. I have other plans for you. I need you back on Earth."

"But, protested Daniel, "it is the perfect mixture – seven nines plus a catalyst. It has got to work!"

Roger shook his head, "It has been tried before."

"Don't you see?" pleaded Daniel. "The formula is now enhanced. We have the alien."

"The alien may help, but we have had other aliens before. From time to time, various aliens have come into our universe and we have launched them."

"Was there a battle with those aliens?"

"No, we just scooped them up and put them in the Egg. Why would it make a difference if there was a battle?"

"Everyone here died in the same battle. They were all part of the same struggle. That is the key – the key to life. You have to have struggles to live! You have to have suffering! This group already does not like each other. They will struggle together, they will suffer together, and they will fight each other. It is from struggles and suffering that life emerges."

"They will kill each other. They are not going to work together."

"By themselves, they won't. But that is where I do my part. I am a seven sevens. I am a catalyst. I bring them together and get them to react. They have to struggle, but not so much that they destroy themselves."

"Yes," agreed Roger, "I can see that it might work. But it needs a stronger catalyst."

"A stronger catalyst?" questioned Daniel. "What could be stronger than a seven sevens?"

Roger paused and slowly said, "Me."

"You?" A look of horror swept across Daniel's face. "You, you, could die…you, you would die to us…there is no way of knowing if there is life on the other side…and even if there is, you won't be returning… there is no coming back…I will never see you again…there will be no one to run Heaven…there will be no one to take care of Earth…what about the Heaven and Earth joint venture?…Above all, I need you!"

"The universe…" Roger paused. His eyes appeared to slowly look around the room, but he may have been seeing every corner of the entire universe one last time. "She will take care of herself. When I am gone, another will take my place – it is the cycle of life. As far as whether I will survive the journey and what is on the other side, it ultimately all comes down to a matter of faith…No matter what happens, I have made provisions for you."

Roger walked to the entrance of the Egg, stopped, and picked up the bottle of urine. "What is this?"

"Pee for the reactor…It's for good luck."

Roger tossed it aside. "We can do better." Two white orbs instantly appeared in the palm of his hands.

"Who, who are they?" asked Daniel.

"FWXY6124 and its Director of Waste Management and Launch Control. Love and Compassion are much better than pee. Button the hatches. Dr. Frankenstein, we are ready to launch."

▲   ▲   ▲

The launch was spectacular. Daniel and Frankenstein watched as the Egg entered the dark portal connecting the two universes. A few seconds later, a dazzling bright light burst out of the portal from the adjacent universe, illuminating the entrance with a warm glow. Shortly thereafter, for the first time ever, a slow stream of cosmic material began flowing from the adjoining universe, through the portal, into their universe.

Emotional confetti poured out from the ceiling in the Egg Launch Bay and congratulatory messages arrived from all across Heaven. It was the largest celebration Frankenstein had ever witnessed. A big smile came across Frankenstein's face. Daniel, however, was sad at the loss of Roger.

Frankenstein put his large monster arm around Daniel consolingly as they walked back into the First Class lounge. Immediately a warm glow spread throughout Daniel's entire body and his skin shined brilliantly. "It is time for you to return to Earth. I gave you something so that you will heal much faster. Promise me that you won't bring back the dinosaurs or construct any hideous creatures." The right eye on his monster face winked. "By the way, you are the best catalyst I have ever seen."

"What?" Daniel was startled by the compliment. "I failed...you heard Roger...I am too weak. I am not strong enough."

"What is the definition of a catalyst?" asked Frankenstein.

"A substance that promotes a reaction without taking part in the reaction."

"Dude," said Frankenstein. "You just promoted the greatest reaction in the universe."

485

CHAPTER 20

THE WORLD OF THE LIVING

Daniel woke when a nurse walked into his private room in the burn unit of John Sealy Hospital in Galveston. He was covered in bandages and attached to monitoring instruments.

"Howdy," he greeted the nurse.

"Welcome back!" exclaimed the nurse with a big smile. "When I came by yesterday you were really out of it – you were delirious. You kept saying that Sam Houston was right…Mo, Larry, and Curly design planets…UFOs are lemurs on Spring Break…and Frankenstein has a really big gun."

She started changing Daniel's bandages and suddenly stopped. "Wow! I can't believe it! I have never seen anyone's burns heal so quickly. I have got to show the doctor. But first, you have visitors in the waiting room that want to see you. Now that you are awake, let me bring them here."

▲ ▲ ▲

A few minutes later, Joshua and Ernesto entered the room.

Joshua had a big grin, "Glad you are back!"

Ernesto beamed, "Man, you are tough. I tried to warn you to not mess with Chupacabras. Those things are really mean." He stopped and stared at Daniel's brilliant white skin. "Dude, you really need to get out in the sun."

"Thanks for coming," Daniel excitedly greeted them. "Has anyone had to pee in the reactor?"

"Nah, but Joshua had to find someone else to talk to about all his crazy stuff. Company hired a new electrical engineer. He is from Texas Tech so he has to be cool."

"The new guy is pretty smart," added Joshua, "and he thinks like us."

"That's all we need," said Daniel as he rolled his eyes, "someone else for *your* kooky conspiracy network."

"I'll get him." Joshua headed toward the door, "He is right outside."

Joshua called and the new engineer entered the room.

"Roger!" shouted Daniel. The new engineer looked exactly like Roger.

The new engineer was startled. "My father's name was Roger, but my name is Devin. Did you know my father?"

Daniel couldn't believe the resemblance, "Our universes may have crossed paths."

Joshua walked over to Daniel's hospital bed, "Oh by the way, Boss Man told me to tell you that even though you are all banged up and in the hospital, your monthly report is still due on the first of the month."

"Death and suffering," smiled Daniel with a twinkle in his eye, "it's the price of life."

EPILOGUE

The three observed the experiment. It appeared to be a success. A new universe was born. If they had emotions, they would have shown excitement.

▲ ▲ ▲

P-rays poured into the Communications Center, millions of bright white orbs filled out surveys at the various entrance gates, seedlings sprouted up through the soil, eggs hatched, life energetically emerged from wombs to face new worlds. Some toiled, others couldn't, some played, others couldn't, all hurt – some more than others, all had joys – some more than others, all suffered, all died. It was the price, the price of life.

The End

or is it?

ABOUT THE AUTHOR

Andrew J. McNabb is a native Texan and grew up in the Dallas area. He and his father were both born on San Jacinto Day – April 21.

After graduating from Texas Tech University with a degree in Chemical Engineering, Andrew moved to Lake Jackson, Texas. During his career in the chemical industry, he designed plants, picked up twelve patents, met many interesting people, and heard lots and lots of entertaining stories.

Andrew and his lovely wife Sharon have raised two beautiful daughters. The family, and now extended family, enjoy seeing the world and have had many travel adventures. When not engineering, writing, or traveling, Andrew plays a variety of sports and is an avid chess player.

Made in the USA
Middletown, DE
09 April 2023